George McCrie

The religion of our literature

Essays upon Thomas Carlyle, Robert Browning, Alfred Tennyson, etc.

George McCrie

The religion of our literature
Essays upon Thomas Carlyle, Robert Browning, Alfred Tennyson, etc.

ISBN/EAN: 9783337174316

Printed in Europe, USA, Canada, Australia, Japan

Cover: Foto ©Andreas Hilbeck / pixelio.de

More available books at **www.hansebooks.com**

THE RELIGION OF OUR LITERATURE.

ESSAYS

UPON

THOMAS CARLYLE, ROBERT BROWNING,
ALFRED TENNYSON,

ETC.

INCLUDING CRITICISMS UPON THE THEOLOGY OF
GEORGE ELIOT, GEORGE MACDONALD, AND
ROBERTSON OF BRIGHTON.

BY

GEORGE M^cCRIE.

London:
HODDER AND STOUGHTON,
27, PATERNOSTER ROW.
MDCCCLXXV.

CONTENTS.

I.

THOMAS CARLYLE ... ... PAGE 1

II.

ROBERT BROWNING 69

III.

ALFRED TENNYSON 110

IV.

HENRY WADSWORTH LONGFELLOW 181

V.

THE SYMBOLIC FORESKETCH OF CHRISTIANITY 223

VI.

THE ÆSTHETICS OF REDEMPTION 255

VII.

A WORD TO GEORGE ELIOT AND GEORGE MACDONALD ... 286

VIII.

ROBERTSON OF BRIGHTON 315

PREFACE.

LITERATURE, in the centuries that went before the Reformation, did an essential service in preparing the way for it. The poet and the littérateur being universally allowed a very great license, even an intolerant priesthood suffered them to speak out the truth, and, despising probably any opposition which came from that quarter, was doomed to find that genius and imagination form the mightiest influence of all.

The same considerations that made literature an admirable herald of the Bible and of the Reformation, render it a dangerous pioneer of doctrine that is likely to overthrow them both. The false in religion, as well as the true, will make appearance first in our literature. When advocated there it makes rapid progress, because it excites no alarm, and because sound theologians are smiling at the flimsiness of the argument, while they forget the fascination by which it is recommended.

Infidelity is making rapid strides in our literature, under the plausible disguise of a new Christianity.

According to the system now adopted by it, miracles are either discarded altogether or are considered of no value as evidence in this remote age of ours. For the same reason it is deemed impossible to establish the historical truth of the Record. The illustrious writers to whom I refer being only men of wit, art, and letters, do not judge it necessary of course to support such positions by profound and learned argument. Meanwhile, having been led in the pride of their understanding to doubt the solid foundations of Christianity, they become, in the first instance, sceptics, and pass through an agonizing ordeal of soul which is considered to be equivalent to a day of religious conviction. This is what constitutes the earnestness of religion in our literary men.

Next, they profess to reach a conviction of the truth of Christianity by a new way of their own; though, as might be expected, it turns out to be a Christianity entirely different from ours. Having looked abroad upon the world in the exercise of their own observation, and consulted with their own inward sentiments, they find that God is a God of love. They say nothing of His justice. No discovery of that attribute seems to have been made by them. But they have found Him out to be a God of love. And now they at once recognise Christ to be the Son of God; not because He is proved to be so by miracle or record, but from His corresponding in character and message with this idea.

What then? Do they receive Him as having come to make an atonement for sin, and turn away the wrath of God from us? Do they recognise the existence of any such wrath? No. Everything in our Bible that seems to teach such things they take leave to discard, as not accordant with the findings of their own observation, and with their inner consciousness or moral sentiments. Would not we ourselves, who are men, they argue, wish all to be saved irrespective of an atonement? Do not we who are men turn away with aversion from the thought of everlasting punishment? Why not consider then that God feels in the same way as we men do? For this very purpose, according to them, was the Son of God made flesh, that God might persuade us how truly human He Himself is. For this, and for no other purpose,

Christ is not so much *God in the flesh* as *the flesh in God*, for that is their favourite phraseology.

In the eighteenth century it was reason that exalted itself above revelation. In the nineteenth it is the moral sense within us that is exalted above it, for modern infidelity holds reason of no account in matters of religion. But every doctrine is to be expunged from our Bible that has not the supposed imprimatur of the natural conscience. Thus, in our day, it is the very vicegerent of God that has rebelled against God.

The object of the present volume is to meet this new Christianity.

First, I have brought the system of Thomas Carlyle for the first time as a whole before the eye of the public, tracing his opinions to their source. For as his style, although eccentric to the last degree, has affected even the English language, so his religious views, however outrageous in themselves, have insensibly coloured the minds of many in the community.

Next I have fully exposed and canvassed the theology taught by Browning and Tennyson. A feeling has universally obtained that these poets have been broaching novel religious tenets, but owing to the obscurity, especially of Browning's style, few seem to know exactly what they are.

Without enlarging at length upon the other contents of this volume, the author has only to observe that he has given an extended criticism of our two most illustrious poets, with a view to settle the question of the comparative merits between them and the poets of a preceding generation.

Finally, in a separate essay, he has ventured to throw down the gauntlet in favour of Henry Wadsworth Longfellow as the truest poet of the age.

THE

RELIGION OF OUR LITERATURE.

I.

THOMAS CARLYLE.

FEW men have occupied so prominent a place in the eye of the community as Thomas Carlyle. No man living has more originality. As a writer he is *per se*, and is allowed by general consent to write as no other man does, violating the rules of English grammar, and even adopting positions in argument which make logicians stare, and men of ordinary sobriety stand aghast. The atonement is of course his genius. Since the English language seems to confine him somewhat, we are willing that he should use certain liberties with it; although it is impossible to say whether his composition be poetry or prose, we are satisfied to have them both at once—why not? and, once in the year, it is felt to be a relief to leave the monotonous champaign of ordinary literature, and, taking up Carlyle, to visit the rude magnificence of its highlands—

> The mountains that like giants stand,
> To sentinel enchanted land ;
> Crags, knolls, and mounds, confusedly hurled,
> The fragments of an earlier world.

Being an author in every respect so eccentric, some might have judged it unlikely that he would produce much impression upon the age. And, no doubt, there are few who might be expected to imitate his style, or endorse his sentiments. But he belongs to a class of writers whose indirect influence

2

is great. The style of our language has been affected by him, whether for the better or the worse we do not stop to inquire. What it has lost in purity, it has gained perhaps in piquancy. Nor can it be denied that, while he is alone in holding many of his wilder opinions, he has inoculated many with his peculiar philosophy.

Whether is the influence he has exerted upon the country to be hailed or deplored? In settling this question, let us first ascertain what is the place he aims at occupying—the mission he has sought to fulfil. We will then be abler to determine whether he has succeeded or failed.

He has appeared amongst us in the character of a Reformer. Again and again has he come forward to address the age and generation—showing no inclination to spare it, and bearing a message which he has inculcated with the fervour of a prophet. He is a religious Reformer. More than a politician, neither is he a mere moralist come to lash the vices of the nation. It is the want of God-recognition he mainly finds fault with. He dates the degeneracy of the land from the Restoration. He bewails the system of government which, ignoring whatever is Divine, steers its course by expediency. With the same feeling does he contemplate the godless science that would reduce the universe to a mechanism. He is the sworn foe of Formalism in religion, and Hearsays, and of all who see no mystery in the system of things around them. "Whither am I going?" "Whence have I come?" The man after his heart is he who has looked beyond the hulls of things—the mere clothes—and, recognising the eternal and irreconcilable distinctions between good and evil, sets himself to obey the sacred call of duty, so help him God, and in defiance of the devil.

They who are acquainted with his writings must be familiar with the mode in which he reiterates these things, setting himself as with Thor's hammer against the Jötuns of secularisms, formalisms, *laissez-de-faires*, dilettantisms, &c. So far well. Earnestness—religious earnestness—is a good thing, and it cannot be denied that his writings have tended to give a stimulus to the energies of the generation. No writer has intenser sympathies with the great men in every department of excellence, or has more powerfully pourtrayed them. Nowhere is the mercenary, the material, the merely intellectual, and the atheistic more mercilessly scourged than in his pages ; and we should be sorry to think that nothing has been effected by all he has said so intensely to exalt humanity, especially as it grapples with the mystery of its own being, and of the universe.

We should say he were an unreasonable soul who doubted the earnestness of Thomas Carlyle ; but our readers may agree with us in holding it to be important to know what is the religion he believes in, for which he is himself earnest, and for which he would wish us all to be earnest. That, again, is exactly the point he considers to be of no consequence. We shall show immediately that, in his judgment, it signifies little what a man's religion may be, if he have one, and (to use an expression of his own) be full of it. Now, here, he differs from other religious reformers whom we have been accustomed to venerate. They have always considered that the kind of religion we adopt is a point as essential as the earnestness with which we pursue it. To put the various religions that are known in the world upon a level, as regards their connection with man's spiritual and eternal interests ; to maintain that men may be saved by any of them as well as by another, and that earnestness in one is as praiseworthy as earnestness in its opposite, is a position which Luther or Knox (whom yet he admires and even worships) would have stared at, as betraying an amount of ignorance they had never encountered, and an excess of boldness scarcely to be credited. Yet this is the position which our author has taken up. Hence the extraordinary medley and jumble of panegyrics which we find in his writings—at one time a life of Cromwell, which would lead simple souls to believe he was himself a Puritan ; next a lecture upon Mahomet, which might have been written by one that was circumcised ; at one time a glowing eulogy upon the Reformation ; next upon the Christianity of the Middle Ages, " a thing for ever memorable and for ever true, as to the essence of it ; " anon, an enthusiastic defence of Odinism.

We merely refer in general terms at the outset to these things, in order to show that if Thomas Carlyle be a religious reformer, he is one of a new and peculiar stamp ; and that, if his earnestness be unquestionable, it would require to be the subject of some investigation.

Let us hear what is his idea of the battle that is to be waged, and of the way in which it is to be set.

" No thought that ever dwelt honestly as true in the heart of man," he writes in one of his *Lectures on Heroes and Hero Worship*, " but was an honest insight into God's truth on man's part, and has an essential truth in it which endures throughout all changes, an everlasting possession for us all. And what a melancholy notion is that which has to represent men in all countries and times except our own as having spent their life in blind condemnable error, mere lost pagans, Scandinavians, Mohammedans, only that we might have the true ultimate knowledge. All generations of men were lost and wrong, only that this present little section of a generation might be saved and right. . . . It is an incredible hypothesis. . . . Are not all true men that ever lived soldiers of the same army, enlisted under heaven's captaincy to do battle against the same enemy—the empire of darkness and wrong? Why should we misknow one another, fight not against the enemy, but ourselves, from mere difference of uniform? All uniforms shall be good—so they hold them true, valiant men. All fashions of arms, the Arab turban, Thor's strong hammer-smiting-down Jötuns shall be welcome. Luther's battle voice ; Dante's march melody, all genuine. Ye are with us, not against us. We are all under one Captain, soldiers of the same——"

Rather than come to the conclusion that so many millions,

pagans and Mohammedans, are perishing, it is best, in order
to avoid melancholy, that we should reckon it to be the
truth, or truth sufficient for salvation, which they hold.
Again, he thinks it enough to prove that religions cannot be
condemnably false if some hundreds of millions have adopted
them. It is impossible that so many people should be
wrong. Would he tell us how many people it is supposable
should go wrong? Does a hundred thousand seem too
many? Or is it when a million have gone wrong that they
must be right? This common warfare which he would have
us to wage alongside of idolaters, Mohammedans, and Papists,
against the empire of darkness, is as pretty a Latitudinarian
fight as a man might wish to see. Against what enemies,
we would ask, are we to fight in this Holy Alliance? We
suppose against all mere Formalists, all who follow Hearsays,
all dilletantists, all who look to mere profit and loss, and are
mercenary men. Ere the expedition commence—are these
enemies few in number, or do they amount to vast multitudes? If few, where the need of such a host to meet them?
If amounting to countless millions, then is it not an incredible hypothesis and too melancholy to judge that all these
should be in "blind condemnable error"? And what is the
common truth we are to contend for? So far as idolaters,
Norsemen, for instance, are concerned, he tells us elsewhere that the "everlasting possession for us all" which
they held was *valour*, and that the great essential truth of
popery, viewed as a Christianism, was *humility*. So, then,
here is an Armageddon struggle for valour and humility at
any rate. He may say, let us contend against all vice,
profligacy, wrong, oppression, covetousness, worldliness.
But why is he so much shocked with those who are wanting
in the duties of the Second Table of the Law, while he is
quite willing to associate with those who are the grossest
violators of the First Table of the Law. He fights shoulder
to shoulder with a man who has robbed God of all the glory
due to His infinite attributes, and given it to a stock ; mean-

while he handles roughly a man who has acted dishonestly and disgracefully to a fellow-creature. He shakes hands with Mahomet, who deceived millions by his fanatical and hysterical delusions, and he fights against those who at the worst are common liars.

The fact that he calls upon us to associate with pagans, papists, and followers of the false prophet, and to recognise them as brother combatants, shows that he considers the points of difference between them and us to be of no vital consequence. According to the terms of this alliance (which, in all conscience, is broad enough) the object of our worship may be idols, or the one true and living God ; our faith may be in Mahomet or Jesus; we may walk by tradition, and decrees of pope and council for our rule, or by the Koran, or by the Bible. All this ranks with the non-essential.

Then as to what he holds to be essential. He holds it to be essential that we have a religion. It may be one Lord, or many gods. It may be a fetish, but we must worship something. He holds it essential that we be earnest in our religion. Whether it be the fetish or Jehovah, signifies nothing, so we be full of either. He holds it essential that there be a message from heaven we believe in. Whether it be that contained in the Koran or in the Bible is a matter of moonshine—whether it be true, even, provided we honestly believe it to be true. He holds it to be essential that we consider right and wrong to be irreconcilably opposed. As to error and truth, Thomas Carlyle is not very particular. Once more, he holds it essential that we believe in future states of separation of the good from the wicked. But whether the heaven we look for be a holy heaven like that of our Bible, or an eternal sensuality like that of the Koran, does not signify : whether we may hold a third state, purgatory, does not signify neither.

These being the essentials according to him, one can see well enough why he can fight alongside of such strange allies as he adopts and would have us to recognise.

Meanwhile the errors of this system of his are palpable enough.

Take his idea, for example, that it does not signify what the object of our worship may be. He overlooks the important bearing which this has upon the honour and glory of God. He must know that we whom he invites to join in this novel order of battle believe that there is only one God, the true and the living God, infinite in all His perfections; and yet he would have us consider it a matter of indifference whether men ascribe this character and glory to Him, or deride Him, and degrade Him in their worship to the vilest things imaginable. He would neither have us to condemn them as inexcusable when they act the latter part, after seeing His works, nor will he allow us to consider them as belonging to the empire of darkness whom we ought to seek to enlighten; for of course it is only in this sense that we think of fighting against them, or of fighting against any. But supposing that Carlyle cannot, for the life of him, see any dishonour that is cast upon God by worshipping Him under the image of a beast, does he not see that the question of the object of our worship materially affects the restraint put upon the conduct of the worshipper? Does he think that the moral restraint exerted upon the worshipper by a multitude of contemptible deities, male and female, and having a licentious history each of them to boot in the legend, is the same with the salutary restraint of one omniscient and righteous Jehovah? And does he not perceive that according to the object we worship will be the estimate we form of our guilt in breaking the law which has issued from it? Will those who have offended gods such as are represented by wooden images of their own making, estimate their guilt at the same figure as those who have offended a Being of infinite majesty, holiness, justice, and goodness?

Then, just think how ridiculous the idea is of its being a matter of no essential importance whether a man be guided by the Bible or by the Koran, which Thomas Carlyle has himself, in his lecture upon Mahomet, declared, after reading it, to contain " a mass of absurdities "!

He seems to think that he has made out all the parties he recommends to our acceptance as brethren in the Lord, or in the gods, to be clean enough when he says that their thoughts about religion, whatever they may be, " dwell honestly in their hearts as true." Honesty is only one of the virtues. If any have been careless in informing themselves of the truth and real nature of the religion they adopt, this is enough to incriminate them. There are steps so important, that carelessness in taking them is criminality enough. A man drinks hellebore, and administers it to his whole family, " honestly believing " that it is a most wholesome beverage. Thomas Carlyle acquits him of all moral blame. Heaven forbid that he should condemn him. The idea dwelt honestly in his heart that the drink was good both for himself and his children ; and " no thought ever dwelt honestly in the heart of a man, but there is an essential truth in it." There must be something that is wholesome in hellebore after all !

One great and cardinal reason why we have always looked upon the various parties which he would have us fraternise with as belonging to the empire of darkness, is that they know nothing of, or deny, or set aside the only atonement for guilt through the blood-shedding of our Lord Jesus Christ. Ignorant of that, we have always considered them to be the children of darkness and not of the day. But this also is a non-essential according to the system of our author.

We have insisted too long upon these very obvious objections to the line of battle proposed by him. We are aware that, as regards many of our readers, the only difficulty must be to see how he could vend such a preposterous doctrine, and they may be anxious to know what are the grounds upon which he endeavours to make good his apologetic views of false religions, and what is the nature of that scheme of Christianity which he has himself adopted.

In the following essay—

I. We shall examine his defences of idolatry, of Islamism, and of popery.

II. We shall set before our readers Carlyle's own scheme of Christianity, and the history of his religious opinions, as this may be gathered from his writings.

III. We shall canvass his theory of hero worship.

HIS DEFENCE OF IDOLATRY.

The view we take of the idolatries of the world will depend upon that which we take of the primeval condition of man. If we are wise and humble enough to follow the account of it given in our Bible, that man was at first made upright, and that God directly made Himself known to him, then we come to view idolatry as a wilful and criminal departure on man's part from the true religion. It was the result, more or less gradual, of that lamentable fall which the Bible also records as having taken place. Once grant that man had fallen and become depraved, and we can easily see how, when abandoned to himself, he should have been unwilling to retain the knowledge of so great and so holy a God as the true God is. His awful attributes of omniscience, infinite holiness, &c., being a restraint, there was an obvious temptation to apostatise to other objects of worship; not to say that we can very well believe how, in the pride of his depraved understanding, beginning to speculate upon a subject too high for him, he became vain in his imagination, and wandered more and more into the wildest superstition. This is the origin of idolatry as we find it fully stated in the opening part of the Epistle of Paul to the Romans. It explains the whole matter of idolatry in a most intelligible form—in a way no doubt that is very humbling to us, and fitted to make us blush for poor fallen humanity, but in a way which justifies God, and bears its own melancholy truth upon the face of it.

Thomas Carlyle belongs to a school which rejects the

scriptural account of man's first condition.   Ignoring the
Fall altogether, and not professing to give any account of
man's first creation, he takes for granted that the primeval
pair began life in a state of savagery.   In his "Chartism, or,
Past and Present," he describes them as "two hairy-naked,
or fig-leaved human figures, who began as uncomfortable
dumbies; but, anxious to be no longer such, endeavoured
with gaspings, gesturings, with unsyllabled cries, with painful
pantomime and interjections, in a very unsuccessful manner
to express themselves."

We can easily see how those who adopt this theory should
profess to find a different origin for idolatry.   It was the first
rude attempt of man to grope his way to that knowledge of
God which, in the progress of society, we now possess ; and,
being prosecuted under every disadvantage, is to be viewed
as a very creditable and even noble commencement. " 'This
is what we made of the world,' may the nations say to us."
We quote him again. " 'This is all the image and notion we
could form to ourselves of this great mystery of a Life and
Universe. Despise it not.' "   Instead of forming a chapter
in the history of the human family, which we must read
with shame-covered face, the story of paganism is one that
records the struggles of early piety.   Instead of being
shocked at the various idolatrous nations of the past, we
recognise them as interesting portions of the Primitive
Church.   He can scarcely find terms sufficiently strong in
which to express his sympathy with these noble first efforts
by which idolatry was achieved. "Look," he exclaims in
triumph, "to what perennial fibre of truth was in that !
. . . . It is thought, the genuine thought of deep, rude,
earnest minds, fairly opened to the things about them ; a
face-to-face and heart-to-heart inspection of the things—the
first characteristic of all good thought at all times."   One
would have thought that the Norse religion would have
staggered him, but here is the effect which it produces.
"There is something very genuine, very great in the ideas

into which the Norse fell as to the creation. That the gods having got the giant Yaner slain, a giant made by 'warm wind' and much confused work, out of the conflict of frost and fire, determined to construct a world with him. His blood made the sea, his flesh was the land, the rocks his bones; of his eyebrows they formed Asgard, their god's dwelling; his skull was the great blue vault of immensity, and the brains of it became the clouds. Untamed thought! Great, giant-like, enormous! Spiritually, as well as bodily, these men are our progenitors!"

Is not this rank nonsense? This theory, if it justify the idolatry of men, does so at the expense of God. Can anything be more odious than the light in which He is here represented as having sent the progenitors of the human family, a couple of hairy savages, into the world; not only leaving them to invent a language in which to converse with one another, but to grope their upward way from idolatry to the knowledge of Him who made them? Meanwhile, this is a question of history. The books of Moses have established the fact that all this is a libel against our Maker; that God directly held converse with man upon his first creation; that He gave him the knowledge of Himself that was necessary; that when man had fallen, and through his lamentable blindness sunk into idolatry, God graciously restored the whole human family once again to the knowledge of the true religion under Noah; and again a third time, through Abraham, separated one nation to Himself, as a testimony against the idolatry into which man still perversely and obstinately sank. If Thomas Carlyle had spent his life in writing a folio volume to controvert the claims of the books of Moses to reception, and had succeeded in making good his point, we would have considered him at liberty to vend theories of the present description. He has neither had the courage, nor has he the learning to do any such thing. We shall therefore take the liberty of considering it as at present historically established that the way in which idolatry came in was exactly the reverse of what he insinuates ; that instead of being a process by which men meritoriously rose from the lamentable state of ignorance in which the Creator first placed them, it was nothing but a gross apostacy from the knowledge of Himself which He gave them more than once. Instead of rising, as Carlyle absurdly supposes, from the images of idolatry to the worship of the true God in the course of ages, " they changed the glory of the incorruptible God " into these images. What he considers to have been an upward was a downward process. And, indeed, if he believes in the historical records of the Jews at all, or in any sense, he must be aware that they had the knowledge of the true religion at the earlier periods of their career, and were constantly sinking down again into idolatry, notwithstanding. the warnings of their teachers. How can he reconcile this with his theory?

He endeavours to establish that the idolatries of the heathen are just a fair and indeed commendable outcome of the wonder which the mystery of the universe excites in their rude minds. The thorough prostrate admiration they had of whatever was great either in things animate or in heroes that had departed, took the form of worship ; and this, instead of being a condemnable sentiment, is judged by him to lie at the foundation of human improvement. " We do not worship," says he, " in that way now, but is it not reckoned still a merit—a proof of what we call a poetic nature—that we recognise how every object has a divine beauty in it ? . . . . They did even what he (the man of genius) does, in their own fashion. That they did it, in what fashion soever, was a merit, better than what the entirely stupid man did— what the horse and camel did—nothing ! Their worship of the hero was just their transcendent admiration of the great man. No nobler feeling than this of admiration for one higher than oneself dwells in the breast of man. Religion, I find, stands upon it—not paganism only, but far higher and truer religion—all religion hitherto known."

He here mistakes the ground upon which any object can be warrantably worshipped. This is not that it be wonderful, or even wonderful to a degree incomprehensible by us, unless we have ascertained it to be the author of its own wonderfulness. If plainly upon the face of it it be something which did not make itself, and could not make itself, then to worship it is an act not only infatuated, but criminal, being an outrage done to the author of it, Unlimited admiration of what is great in the universe will not therefore account for the rise of idolatry; there remains to be explained how, since the objects exciting this admiration were things made, or only creatures, this admiration should have taken the form of worshipping these objects themselves, and not the Maker of them. It is a mistake to say that " all religion hitherto known, even the true religion," rests merely upon the feeling of admiration for one higher than ourselves. This would resolve the distinction there is between our feeling towards God and towards others than God into a mere distinction of degree, whereas it is a distinction in kind. It is not merely that we admire God infinitely more than we do any of His creatures, but that we recognise Him to be the Author of all that is admirable in His creatures. Adoration includes this, or it includes nothing. He may object that the heathen, owing to their ignorance, could not tell whether the great and wonderful phenomena meeting their eye in the universe were self-caused, or caused by another. But it is an insult upon God to say that He has framed man so stupid and irrational as that, in any circumstances, he cannot recognise a thing to be a thing made, the effect of the power of another, when he sees it. If it be a thing material, for example, without life and without intelligence, it were inexcusable for him to worship it, since it is even of less value and dignity than himself, however huge it might be, though it were the sun in the heavens. That sun surely exhibits no signs of life; it surely exhibits no signs of intelligence; it is plainly enough only one part of a great material fabric by which we are surrounded which is senseless, but bearing marks everywhere of intelligent contrivance. In asserting so much we are making allowance for the lowest savagery of condition in which man can be placed, for he is still essentially a rational creature. In fact it requires a much greater exercise of ingenuity for him to disjoin the sun from the rest of the system, and suppose it entitled to worship, than to accept it as just a part of the material system around him, made by one and the same Being; and one may wonder therefore that Carlyle should have failed to recognise some obliquity of man's heart in this matter.

This is what God Himself in His word has called upon us to recognise, but of course our friend was too profound a philosopher to rest in his deliverance—" The invisible things of God from the creation of the world are clearly seen, being understood by the things that are made, even His eternal power and Godhead; so that they are without excuse." He, again, has such exalted views of human nature, that, according to his philosophy, it can never by any possibility be in the wrong. If men worship stocks and stones, we may be sure that those are shallow philosophers who cannot see something good and noble here. Let us recognise that he is at least better than a " horse," which worships nothing. It never occurs to Carlyle that fallen man should do a condemnable thing. This is very much the spirit of his school in other departments of inquiry, and is no doubt very gratifying to poor humanity, which likes to be well spoken of. However, Carlyle has here proceeded, we think, a step rather too far to be successful. As a sycophant overreaches himself when he proceeds to praise a huge wen on the face of his worshipful patron, or some gross bodily deformity, so we fear that Carlyle has gone too far in his praise of our humanity when he has fixed upon our idolatry as the subject of his fulsome panegyric.

There is one passage in which he bethinks himself for a moment of the rather daring position he has taken up in eulogising what the prophets of the Lord have so emphatically condemned. He suggests that the idolatry which they condemned was insincere idolatry—and, making bad worse, and absurdity more ridiculous, he asserts the extraordinary doctrine that the idolatry to be commended is that where the votary is maddest upon his idols. "Condemnable idolatry," he writes, "is insincere idolatry. Doubt has eaten out the heart of it. . . . This is one of the balefullest sights. Souls are no longer filled with their fetish, but only pretend to be filled, and would fain make themselves feel that they are filled." So that the time when the heathen were fervent idolaters was their best time—the day of their espousals, eh? to their "birds and four-footed beasts and creeping things." So long as the Egyptians worshipped their bull with all their heart, believing it to be worthy of divine honours, we are to admire them. When they began to doubt whether after all it was a proper object of worship, then indeed there was no hope of them; till at last a time comes when they begin to worship God only, in which case they recover our admiration, because they are sincere again, but not because they have discarded the bull. The bull was as good as God, so long as they imagined it. Is not this sad stuff? Doesn't he know that superstition and infidelity, as regards badness, are much about six and half a dozen?

The reader may desire to know what is that essential truth in heathen religions which he considers to compensate what is otherwise reprehensible in them, and which entitles the heathen to be considered as fellow-soldiers with us in the same battle against the "empire of darkness." Take the Norse religion then for an illustration. He finds the great lesson Odin taught—the seed-germ of his religion—to be the infinite importance of valour.

"The consecration of valour," says he, "is not a bad thing. . . . . Unconsciously, and combined with higher things, it is in us yet, that old faith withal. To know it consciously brings us into closer and closer relation with the past—with our own possessions in the past. In a different time, in a different place, it is always some other *side* of our common human nature that has been developing itself. The actual true is the SUM of all these; not any one of them by itself constitutes what of human nature is hitherto developed. Better to know them all, than misknow them. 'To which of these three religions do you specially adhere?' inquires Meister of his teacher. 'To all the three,' answers the other, 'for they by their union constitute the true religion.'"

We are here taught that the "actual true" in religion, in other words, the true religion in its perfection, is just the sum of all the developments of human nature in its various sides in the history of the past. The religion of Odin was the struggling into existence, after its own rude form, of that worship of valour lying unconsciously still in the bosom of us all. We may grant that too exclusive a prominence was thus given to a physical quality. But it was only natural that the worship of such-like qualities should make its appearance at the earlier stages of social progress. It was reserved for the religion of Christ to bring forward those other and higher qualities of a strictly moral character, such as humility, charity, patience, and others, where the enemies to be wrestled with are not flesh and blood, but injuries, afflictions, persecutions. Christianity itself, however, is only a development of a higher side of human nature. We are to recognise that there is an underlying worship of such qualities in the bosom of us all as well, only it required the master-skill of that Divine Man, Jesus Christ, who appeared last of all in the list of teachers (if, indeed, He is the last of all), to draw THEM forth.

The defective and mistaken view of Christianity proceeded on in this theory will strike the evangelical reader at once. It is represented not as a thing come for the salvation of humanity, but as the highest development of humanity. We shall have an occasion, however, in another part of this essay, to discuss his low view of Christianity. What we have to do with at present is his extravagantly high view of the paganisms, and here, for instance, of Odinism.

His idea, then, is that it conveyed what he calls " an everlasting possession for us all"—a lesson of infinite importance—by consecrating valour. Was not Odin, whom the Norse worshipped, a hero—a right valiant man? Let us lay aside our prejudice to the mere circumstance of their worshipping the man—it was valour in the abstract to which the homage was paid. Cowards were sent to hell by this religion, and don't they deserve it? Heaven was stocked with gallant captains. Humanity, therefore, was in the right among the Scandinavians, as everywhere else. This idolatry of theirs was a devotion to valour, and surely " the consecration of valour is not a bad thing." He adds, alluding to us who are Christians, " Combined with higher things, it is in us yet, that old faith withal."

There is a good deal of the sly evinced in this last addition of his with its adroit qualification inserted—" *combined with higher things.*" Valour, courage in the field, is no doubt granted by most Christians to be a good thing—but it is considered as holding a very subordinate place, and certainly as holding only one place, if it holds one, in the righteousness whereby a man may see the kingdom of God. Meanwhile our apologist for paganism is bound by his argument to remember that, in the Norse theology, it was valour by itself —martial prowess, and that, perchance, shown in ruthless deeds enough—which was considered as not only entitling men to sit down in the kingdom, but entitling a man to be God in the kingdom. A system of religion fraught with more mischievous and disastrous consequences than this cannot well be conceived of. To assign divine honours to any man for the possession of all the virtues taken together, would have been to forget that these are entirely the production of God, and entitled to no merit whatever. Even had Odin been such a man, to worship him would have been an abominable piece of flattery rendered to human nature, and proved Scandinavian morals to be poisoned at their very source. The case was of course still worse if the possession of one single virtue was deemed sufficient to entitle him to worship, and to entitle men to seats in his Hall; for there is no more dangerous doctrine to broach than that one virtue can be a substitute for the rest. It would appear, however, that the Norse proceeded yet a step farther, and, in good sooth, singled out martial courage as what entitled a creature like themselves to divine honours, while their idea of heaven was that of a band of sturdy warriors with swords in their hands. Valour, in short, was made a god among the Scandinavians, as Reason was made a goddess among the French at the Revolution. The pride which leads fallen humanity to exalt its own qualities, for very obvious reasons, appeared in the worship of valour among savages, and in the worship of reason among civilised infidels. Instead of recognising this perverse monstrosity in the place assigned to valour and reason, Thomas Carlyle, with a simplicity that is fitted to provoke a smile, reminds us that valour and reason are good things! He means, we hope, that they are exalted gifts of God? We hope he grants that God is to be glorified as the Author of them. We hope he does not mean that one way of glorifying Him for them is to worship these qualities themselves, or any fellow-creature who possesses them. Yet, judging from all he writes, we are ashamed to say that the last seems to be his deliberate judgment. Can anything be more palpably absurd? He is himself the author of some thirty volumes, which, on some accounts, merit the very highest reputation. Let us suppose that the nation, acting the same part by him as the Scandinavians did by God, should refuse to acknowledge him as the writer of them, and should bestow the honours due for them upon his publisher, into whose hands the MSS. had been consigned, loading him with every distinction, and praising the writings themselves to the sky for the valour of the sentiments they contained, and the reason everywhere shining through them.

Our friend in these circumstances would perhaps venture to remonstrate against the injustice of such a proceeding. He would insist upon it that he was the real author of the whole thirty volumes, and that, if these qualities of valour and reason characterised them, he alone was entitled to the credit, certainly not the publisher, who was a mere creature of his. But he has unfortunately furnished us with the means of our justification. We would tell him that "the consecration of valour and reason was not a bad thing;" that our infinitely admiring them both as they appeared in his writings was the same thing as acknowledging him; and that there was the less room to complain, as we had given the honours due for the volumes enthusiastically to the publisher. Probably Thomas Carlyle would shake his head at this explanation, and consider that he had been scurvily used. So should we; but, unlike him, we think that so was God by the Norse.

HIS DEFENCE OF MOHAMMEDANISM.

Not satisfied with appearing as the apologist of idolaters (ugly clients enough), he does not hesitate to undertake the cause of the Mohammedans. It may seem strange enough that he should have anything to say in defence of Mahomet. No doubt the prophet showed a determined hatred to idolatry so far as it remained among his tribe, but then Carlyle had just finished an elaborate argument to prove that idolatry was a good thing. His mouth then might seem to have been shut from saying a word in his praise even upon this the only point that was defensible about him. But in imagining that he was foreclosed owing to this circumstance, we would betray the same simplicity as the rustic who thinks it impossible that a counsel at the bar who has pled a certain side of a cause in one court should stand up and plead the opposite side in another. In his lecture upon Mahomet, we have such eulogies upon his destruction of idols as could not have been more eloquent though he had received a retaining fee from the Turks. Having adopted the principle that earnestness in one's religion is everything, and the religion for which one is earnest a matter of moonshine, our author is of course consistent enough in eulogising idolatry, as it goes up, and next sympathising with the zealous man who casts it down. He first cheers on the poor idolater, and bids him be of good heart; then, when he has become somewhat short of wind, less zealous for his fetish, and Mahomet comes and knocks him down, Thomas Carlyle immediately accepts the latter as his champion. This would scarcely do in the ring; but as we have only to do at present with religions, we shall suppose that we must accept it as fair and honourable dealing. So let us proceed to consider his views of the Arabian.

He considers him as a hero. He even accepts him as a prophet. "He is by no means the truest of the prophets," he writes, "but I do esteem him a true one."

We shall have no needless argument with our author. For the sake of narrowing it, we shall give up old Prideaux's opinion, that Mahomet was a downright impostor, and that is conceding a great deal. But we have no need to go farther than Carlyle's own assertions to prove that he was two-thirds a fanatic. A sincere enthusiast, let us say, at the first—a man of heated imagination and epileptick temperament, who mistakes the raptures of his own mind for a communication from spirits (evil spirits at first, good spirits afterwards)— surely this description saves him from the infamy of an impostor at the expense of losing any claim to the title of a hero or a great man. There is not a more despicable condition of a man, were it not that it is pitiable because morbid, than to be unable to distinguish between his own mental exercises and a supernatural communication. Nobody disputes the eloquence of Mahomet, his power of swaying men, and his genius, which shone so wonderfully through the disadvantages of his education; but if the Koran, as Carlyle grants, was merely the outcome after all of his own meditations—what he had taken up of the mystery of the universe with such aids as were around him—then, by sending it forth as a message received by him from heaven, he is proved either to have been an impostor, or to have laboured under some derangement in his upper regions. It is in vain for Carlyle to take up a middle position, and try to save him both from the charge of imposture and fanaticism. He tells us that he has attempted to read the Koran, that "it is an unreadable mass of lumber;" "insupportable stupidity, in short;" and that it is "difficult to see how any mortal ever could consider it as a book written in heaven;" and yet he would have us to accept the man who thoroughly believed that this absurdity of his own brains was a supernatural revelation, as ranking among the great benefactors of the species.

Carlyle has himself loose views of what constitutes a message from heaven, and it is necessary that we examine these if we would see the ground upon which he justifies this visionary.

"Such life had come, as it could, to illuminate the darkness of this wild Arab soul. A confused, dazzling splendour, as of life and heaven, in the great darkness which threatened to be death : he called it revelation and the angel Gabriel—who of us yet can know what to call it? It is 'the inspiration of the Almighty that giveth him understanding.' . . . 'Is not belief the true God-announcing miracle?' says Novalis. That Mahomet's whole soul, set on flame with this grand truth vouchsafed him, should feel as if it were important, and the only important thing, was very natural. That Providence had unspeakably honoured him by revealing it, saving him from death and darkness ; that he was bound therefore to make known the same to all creatures ; this is what is meant by 'Mahomet is the prophet of God.'"

We have here Carlyle's own view of what constitutes a message from God. What any man may have seen more than others of the truth of things in the universe, which may have powerfully impressed itself upon his soul, and so powerfully that he feels impelled to go forth and communicate it to his fellow-creatures, is a message from God, and such a man is a prophet. He grants that this was the only sense in which Mahomet had any revelation, and suggests that it was very natural for him to think that the grand discovery which had burst upon his mind in the Arabian solitudes was from Gabriel.

This is not the place to canvass Carlyle's own theory here thrown out, as to what constitutes a God-message and a prophet. It is enough to say that this is not the definition or understanding of these terms in the common parlance of Christendom. What Mahomet, or any other man, might discover in the exercise of his own faculties, could only be his own message to his fellow-creatures—the result of the investigations of a puny mortal like ourselves, who is subject to the verdict of our own judgment, and who is even liable (as the greatest of men often show in matters of religion) to broach " insupportable stupidity." His heart might be set on flame with some grand truth he professed to have discovered, and he might consider that Providence had unspeakably honoured him by enabling him to discover it ; but we, who are as competent to judge of truth as he is to discover it, are called to ascertain whether it be the truth after all which had inflamed his mind, or whether the devil had not deceived him into a dangerous speculation. Had the Arabians acted this manly and sensible part, instead of being carried away, like Carlyle himself, by weak admiration of a great man, they would have escaped the snare of this erroneous enthusiast of the desert. But, granting a man in the exercise of his natural faculties to have discovered something that is true in the department of religion, and that Providence has thus far unspeakably honoured him, of course he has only by his diligence investigated more thoroughly than others what has already been objectively revealed. He has not made a new revelation to his fellow-creatures. He has only been a more diligent student of the old one already made. But none knows better than Thomas Carlyle that all Christendom has been long agreed, upon testimony that has never been refuted, that God has made from time to time supernatural revelations of Himself to the children of men— revelations of things not contained in the system of the universe before our eyes, and of His own purposes affecting our eternal destinies. Revelations of this kind stand of course upon an entirely different footing than what he is pleased by a confusion of ordinary language to call messages of God. They are clothed with a dreadful authority, being no less than communications from God Himself. He has employed men to convey them to the rest of the human family, but, as might be supposed, He has never employed them without amply evidencing to the men themselves that the message was from Him, and evidencing the divinity of the message to those for whom it was intended. These and these only are prophets.

Mahomet claimed to be a prophet in this sense, and the Arabians received him as a prophet in this sense. It will not do for our author to whitewash Mahomet's guilt in this matter by a rationalistic justification of his own, which he conveniently furnishes him with from the nineteenth century. We dare say Mahomet would have been very much obliged to Carlyle for any such justification at the first stages of his audacious assumption of the prophet's office. His conscience troubled him, as well it might. At first, as we all know, and as his present defender admits, he entertained doubts that his supposed visions might proceed from evil spirits. It was only after a conversation with his notable partner in life, and in this wickedness, Chadidschah, that he was confirmed in his opinion of his Divine mission. What shall we think of a man who proceeded to propagate a new religion in the name of God, having only the judgment of his wife that he was not in communication with the devil ? We would wish to realise all the extenuating circumstances in this extraordinary wild Arab's case. By a violent effort of fancy we carry ourselves

back to the seventh century, and endeavour to conceive of
the state of religion prevalent around him, being a mixture
of idolatry, Judaism, and Christianity. We give him credit
for deep convictions of the evil of idolatry, and can suppose
great and noble ideas to have possessed him of being his
country's reformer; and we can very well suppose how, in
his cave-fastings and meditations, his religious reveries should
have assumed something like the vividness of visions. *There*
was his temptation—a temptation through spiritual pride to
confound what were merely peculiar experiences of his own,
and devout imaginings, with a communication from the
Divine Being. Carlyle sees no great sin there; but this
argues the same obtuseness of moral sense which led him to
see no evil in idolatry. The writer who could not see the
difference between wonder and idolatry cannot be supposed
to see the difference between having an intense apprehension
in his own mind of Divine things, and believing himself to
be the subject of a Divine revelation; between a desire self-
conceived of preaching one's own views, and claiming to be a
prophet, having Heaven's commission. He considers that if
this enthusiast had any truth especially borne in upon his
mind, he was entitled to say that Gabriel had been sent from
heaven to give it to him. He had nothing to authenticate
these visions of his, and yet Carlyle considers that he might
take upon himself the most tremendous responsibility which
any mortal creature can assume, of vending them, not as his
own insight into the truth of religion, but as a positive
revelation he had received from heaven—not making known,
besides, the fact to the world, as an honest man should have
done, that he had doubts from the beginning whether it were
not from the devil, and owed his ultimate clearance upon
that point to the assurances of his own wife. He had no
miracle to certify him or to certify others that it was a Divine
revelation. What of that? "Is not belief," says Novalis,
"the true God-announcing miracle?" It is amusing to see
the profound gravity and reverence with which our author

produces this silly nonsense of a German philosopher, that the earnestness with which Mahomet believed in what he taught, proved his doctrine to be from God, as well as a miracle could have done. If so, then the earnestness with which idolaters in Arabia had previously believed in what they taught, proved idolatry to be from God; and thus we have both idolatry, and Mohammedanism, which denounced it, proved to be from God, for thus saith Novalis.

In proving Mahomet to be a true prophet, he considers it to be enough to show that he had a following of 180 millions of men. Again and again he points to the wide extent of the Mohammedan religion as an argument in favour of its truth. This is one of the illustrations we have in his writings of the fact, that while no man comes down more heavily upon such as are carried away by outside appearances of things, by shams and hulls, there is none who succumbs more than he does before mere externals and adventitious circumstances. He is not one of those who form their estimate of truth by examination of the doctrine itself that is taught, but by the number of those who adopt it. It may be a gross error, but if a thousand men, seduced by the talents and audacity of the man who has vended it, have espoused it, he looks more favourably upon it; if a hundred thousand have swallowed it, it begins to dawn upon his mind to be a truth; but if a million embrace it, he turns pale and includes it among the articles of his faith. It is plain that Thomas Carlyle was never destined to be a reformer. This is not the spirit that has ever regenerated the world or done great things. " There must be some truth," he says, " at the bottom, when 180 millions of men have believed in this religion." Why so? He has told us already that the Koran is " a mass of insupportable stupidity; " and yet after these millions have swallowed all this nonsense, and received it with profound adoration, he would have us think it impossible that they should receive anything but what was true at the bottom of it.

But let us hear what is the essential truth which he has discovered to be at the bottom of this large mass of tom-foolery. We saw that the inculcation of valour was the essential truth of the Norse religion. What is the grand fundamental truth of Mohammedanism, which shall incline us, if not to submit to circumcision, at least to fight along-side of the Crescent against the empire of darkness? He maintains that it comprehends the essentials of all religion, because it includes, first, faith in the greatness of God, *Allah Akbar*, God is great ; and, secondly, submission to the will of God, *Islam.*

" This submission," says he, " is the soul of Islam ; it is properly the soul of Christianity, for ' Islam ' is definable as a confused form of Christianity. Had Christianity not been, neither had it been. . . . ' Though he slay me, yet will I trust him.' Islam means, in its way, denial of self, annihila-tion of self. This is yet the highest wisdom that heaven has revealed to our earth."

Our determination of the question whether " Islam " be the highest wisdom revealed on earth, because it teaches us submission to God's will, must depend entirely upon the view we take of man's present condition. If man be a sinner under the eternal condemnation of the law, and God's will concerning him be that the sentence of the law shall be executed upon his head, surely our author does not mean to affirm that there is any consolation in the doctrine which does no more than inculcate upon him submission to such an awful dispensation of His justice. If this be the soul of " Islam," and its highest wisdom be that it teaches us sub-mission to God's will in the execution of the death-sentence of His law, there is not much comfort to be derived from it in this world, and still less in the next. Most certainly this is not " the soul of Christianity." The glory of the Christian religion is that it meets our forlorn and desperate condition by announcing the great truth that " God so loved the world as to send His only begotten Son into the world, that whosoever believeth in Him should not perish, but have everlasting life." The revelation it has made of the only way of reconciliation with an offended God, through His Son lifted up on the cross for our sins, has generally been considered as the highest wisdom made known to our earth. Having once known how we may be reconciled as guilty sinners to God, we are then, and only then, prepared for submission to His fatherly will. Whether Christian submission thus defined, or " Islam " be the best, we leave it with wise men to determine ; but that they are not the same is plain enough. Of course Carlyle does not accept the above idea of Christianity. But as evangelical Christendom does, he surely cannot expect that we are to subscribe to his fancy of Mohammedanism being essentially Christian, because it teaches submission to the will of God.

Two things connected with Mohammedanism have always attracted attention—its holding out a sensual heaven, and its making proselytes by the sword. One has only to look at them both to find out a much more natural explanation of the number of its followers than that which suggested itself to our author. Unless there had been an essential truth at the bottom of it, he cannot see for the life of him how 180 millions of men should be Mohammedans ; whereas he has only to suppose that half of their ancestors submitted to it with a sword at their throats, and that the others were seduced into a religion which pandered in its eternal sanctions to the flesh. We are sorry to say that he has prostituted his pen by apologising both for Mahomet's heaven and sword.

" That gross sensual paradise of his—that horrible flaming hell—what is all this but a rude shadow, in the rude Bedouin imagination of the grand spiritual fact, and beginning of facts—the infinite nature of Deity. Bodied forth in what way you will, that man's actions are of infinite moment to him, is the first of all truth."

That is, if there was an eternal heaven held out at all by Mahomet, it did not signify though it was represented as consisting in sensual delights, since it held out the infinite importance of man's actions all the same. He forgets that the nature of the heaven we believe in is an essential point, owing to another reason. The heaven which any religion holds out to its votaries is of course understood to represent to them, and impress upon them, what is the highest happiness man should aspire after, and what is the highest point of character they should aim to reach. Its votaries therefore will square their ideas both of happiness and character by the views which their religion gives them of heaven. Our religion holds out a heaven whose enjoyment consists in our being brought nearer to God, and whose occupation consists in serving and worshipping Him. Mahomet's heaven is stocked with ravishing, black-eyed girls, whose society forms the eternal felicity of the faithful. He that has the former hope in him will purify himself; but how the man who has the other should do so, baffles our comprehension. Our philosopher tells us that he is taught even by this heaven of his that "his actions are of infinite importance to him "— by which of course are meant his good and virtuous actions. True; but he is taught that they are infinitely important only as bringing him to a life of eternal sensuality. He is taught to be good and virtuous on earth by the promise of being eternally sensual in heaven. Suppose that Mahomet had promised a heaven where topers would enjoy a never-ending revel, according to Carlyle's doctrine we must have considered his religion as being an admirable one, for it would still have taught that man's actions are infinitely important to them—so important, in fact, that unless they were virtuous on earth they would not be drunkards to all eternity. After this specimen of Carlyle's profound moral philosophy, we are prepared to find him justifying Mahomet's proselytising by the sword. "Even this," says he, "was difficult. You must have those who will become soldiers for your cause, and be strong enough in your cause to conquer the nations to it;" where he forgets that the question is not as to the difficulty of what was done

by Mahomet, but the warrantableness of it. However, he
has a doctrine upon this point, which, if it could be established, would both justify Mohammedanism and highway
robbery and murder. "I care little about the sword; I will
allow a thing to struggle for itself in this world, with any
sword, or tongue, or implement it has, or can lay hold of.
We will let it preach, and pamphleteer, and fight, and to the
uttermost bestir itself, and do, beak and claw, whatsoever is
in it; very sure that it will in the long run conquer nothing
which does not deserve to be conquered."

HIS DEFENCE OF POPERY.

The opinion hitherto held among us is that popery was a
horrible declension from Christianity, brought in by a master-
piece of the devil's subtlety, who contrived gradually to draw
men away from the purity of Christ's doctrine and institutions, and from the Bible itself, where they are revealed;
while the Reformation was caused by the Spirit of God
awakening the attention of men again to the Bible, the only
source of truth, through which they were led out of these
absurdities and monstrous superstitions to the point from
which they had departed. But Thomas Carlyle believes in
no such thing as men going wrong, or any number of them
at least. As he absolutely denied idolatry to have been the
effect of the apostacy of men at first from the true religion,
and boldly advocated it as something good in itself, and upon
the whole a creditable first effort of man in the religious
department, so he refuses to consider popery as an apostacy
from the Christian religion, and maintains it to have been
what he calls a *Christianism.*

By this, as we may gather partly from his lecture upon
" Dante," in his volume of " Hero Worship," and partly from
his lecture upon " Luther," he means a system which, after
Christ had appeared, the mind of man itself developed in the
course of a meditation of ten centuries, expressing the idea
which it took up of the great theorem of the universe. Thus,

speaking of "hell, purgatory, and paradise," as set forth by Dante, he maintains that they were just the reality of the unseen world, expressed in such emblems as suited the state of advancement of the human mind in the middle ages.

" All these make up the true unseen world, as figured in the Christianity of the middle ages; a thing for ever memorable, for ever true—the essence of it to all men. It was a sublime embodiment, or sublimest, of the soul of Christianity. . . . It expresses as in huge, wide, architectural emblems, how the Christian Dante felt good and evil to be the two polar elements of this creation on which it all turns; everlasting justice, yet with penitence, with everlasting pity. All Christianism, as Dante and the middle ages had it, is emblemed here."

Purgatory, indeed, he considers to be the noblest conception of the middle ages. " It is a noble thing that Purgatorio —mountain of purification—an emblem of the noblest conception of that age. If sin is so fatal, and hell is and must be so rigorous and awful, yet in repentance too is man purified—repentance is the grand Christian act. . . . Hope has now dawned, never-dying hope, if in company still with heavy sorrow. The obscure sojourn of demon and reprobate is under foot, a soft breathing of penitence mounts higher and higher to the throne of mercy itself. . . . The joy, too, of all when one has prevailed; the whole mountain shakes with joy. . . . I will call this a noble embodiment of a true, noble thought."

He calls upon us to compare popery with the idolatry of heathen nations, and admiringly to consider what an advancement the human mind had made by this Christianism.

" Paganism emblemed chiefly the operations of nature; the destinies, efforts, combinations, vicissitudes of men and things in this world. Christianity emblemed the law of human duty—the moral law of man. One was from the sensuous nature — a rude, helpless utterance of the *first* thought of man; the chief recognised virtue, courage, superiority to fear. The other was not for the sensuous nature, but for the moral. What a progress is here, if in that respect only."

Having thus represented popery, not as an apostacy from Christianity, but as what he is pleased to call a Christianism, or an advancement made by the human mind, through the help of Christianity, from the idolatry that preceded, he proceeds next in his lecture upon "Luther" to represent the Reformation, not as a return to the Bible, but as the effect of the human mind advancing in its development of the theorem of the universe, and also in the better reading of Christianity.

"A theorem, or spiritual representation, so we may call it, which once took in the whole universe, and was completely satisfactory in all its parts to Dante, had, in the course of a century, become dubitable to common intellects—become deniable, and as to every one of us incredible, obsolete as Odin's theorem. Why could not Dante's Catholicism continue, but Luther's Protestantism must needs follow? Alas! nothing will continue. . . . No man whatever believes or can believe exactly what his grandfather believed; he enlarges somewhat by fresh discovery his view of the universe."

Having given these extracts, I shall now proceed to take up this peculiar view which Carlyle adopts of popery—not as a monstrous apostacy from Christianity, but as itself a Christianism; that is, as the first rude and commendable attempt, after Christianity had been introduced, which man made in the exercise of his own reason, silently meditating for ten centuries to comprehend the theorem of the universe. The name Christianism implies that he views it as a system which was evolved out of Christianity. It was so far a good system—fairly representing Christianity, for he calls it "a sublime embodiment of the soul of Christianity." It was the best which the men of the middle ages could make of it. It was at last felt to be untrue in form at least, and at the Reformation Luther and his compeers came to a juster view of what Christianity really is, and of what the theorem of the universe really is.

It never seems to strike Carlyle that the insuperable difficulty he has to grapple with in this theory of his, is how those who at the start of Christianity had the Bible in their hands, just as truly as Luther had it in the sixteenth century, should have gone into popery, which he acknowledges to be a defective Christianism. If he maintains that it was because the mind of man was not yet able to take up the perfect truth of Christianity as it lay in the Bible; if he maintains that popery was the first rude best which men could make of Christianity, then his position is overthrown by the simple historical fact that the Christianity of the earlier ages was identical with that of Luther and the Reformers. Had popery been the first system of things which prevailed after Christianity appeared, he might with some show of reason represent it as being the only result, rude and imperfect, to be expected at the beginning. But when the historical fact is unquestionable that the Christians of the first ages adopted the same view and practice of Christianity which Protestantism afterwards returned to, it is plain that popery was nothing but an inexcusable, absurd, and perverse departure from better attainments. In the extracts we have given, we are favoured with a most philosophical view of the way in which men in the dark ages marched forward to the farther knowledge of the great theorem of the universe, till at last they advanced to Protestantism. "No man can exactly believe what his grandfather believed—he enlarges somewhat by fresh discovery." In adopting this theory to explain the beginning of Protestantism, he forgets that he thereby renders the beginning of popery inexplicable. The Christians of the first ages being all of the same view which the Protestants of the sixteenth century afterwards returned to, it follows that they should have gone on enlarging their discoveries of things. Instead of this, they went into popery, which by Carlyle's confession was the less perfect system.   Then, with the grossest inconsistency, he tells us in one place that the Reformation was caused (and, indeed, how could he deny it?) by Luther's discovering a Bible and learning out of it the errors of the Popish system.   He calls this a "blessed discovery," although with almost the same breath he had told us that popery "could not have continued, because nothing continues," and that the true theorem of the universe was coming in by the deaths of grandfathers.

He attempts to show that popery, instancing more particularly its three future states of Hell, Purgatory, and Paradise, was "a sublime embodiment of the soul of Christianity."   By the "soul of Christianity" it is evident that he understood the peculiar development which is made under it of the *moral* qualities of our humanity, as distinguished from its *physical*, such as valour and superiority to fear developed in the Paganisms ; and also the discovery it makes of pity as being part of the character of God, and of repentance as being prevalent with Him.   He would have us believe that the Hell, Purgatory, and Paradise which formed the theme of Dante, and which formed the scheme of the spiritual world in the middle ages, was "an embodiment of this soul of Christianity."   First, here were Heaven and Hell representing "good and evil to be the two polar elements of this creation on which it all turns,"—a Heaven and Hell, too, where it is not valour merely that is rewarded, or its opposite that is punished, but where the whole range of moral qualities is recognised; and next, here was Purgatory representing that by repentance man is purified—everlasting justice with everlasting pity.   All this, Carlyle enthusiastically declares, expressed, as in "wide architectural emblems," the truth and reality of the unseen world.   He is especially in raptures with Mount Purgatorio ; "a soft breathing penitence mounts higher and higher to the throne of Mercy itself."

We shall not insist here upon the misapprehension he labours under of what constitutes "the soul of Christianity," for this we have done in a former part of the essay. This lies not in the particular qualities to which it assigns eternal rewards and punishments, nor even in the discovery it makes of God as showing pity upon repentance being forthcoming. It lies in its revealing the atoning blood of Jesus Christ, through whom God is willing, and, consistently with His infinite justice, is able to extend to us the fullest pardon upon earth, without any Purgatory being required. It is plain that Carlyle does not know what Purgatory is. He considers it to have some connection with repentance, and with the pity of God. Any one acquainted with the theology of the Church of Rome knows that Purgatory is a place of penal doom. The Church of Rome considers that upon faith and repentance the eternal punishment of sin is remitted to the believer, but he must still endure the temporal punishment due for certain of his sins by being tormented in Purgatory. Purgatory, therefore, is not a place where there is repentance, but where there is the endurance by torture of that temporal punishment for which no repentance is available. Our author declares it to be "the noblest conception of the middle ages;" but if he had lived in those ages he would probably have found the nobleness of the conception balanced by the tortures which it engendered. If it was an error that caused infinite anguish to myriads of souls for centuries, we profess not to have much admiration for the genius that conceived it. It was the foulest blot upon the pity and compassion of God. It was the absurdest conception, besides, upon the face of it, which ever entered into the hearts of men, because it supposes first that God has remitted the eternal punishment, and then that He refuses to remit the temporal punishment. Your mortal sins shall at once be remitted, but you shall smart for your venial sins. This was the noble conception which our philosopher admires, showing how easily the Church of Rome can entangle the greatest of our thinkers in the worst of her meshes. And then we are called to imagine "the soft breathing penitence mounting higher and higher" from those poor wretches in Purgatory, whose eyes, as Dante himself tells, are sewn with an iron thread, or who expiate their sins under waggon-loads of stones, or in a mass of flames. Purgatory sprang out of base priestcraft; and, if it was a "sublime conception," those who originated it were well paid for it.

It is not wonderful that a writer who has defended pagan rites, and found interesting first efforts in natural religion in Odinism, should have discovered popery to be, not Antichrist, but a Christianism, and should actually in his writings have praised its idolatrous practices. In his "Chartism; or, Past and Present," having first protested against the ungodliness of the Present, he reproves it by presenting to our eye the contrast of the Past. And to what period is he pleased to point us, as exhibiting the palmiest days of religion? To the twelfth century! This is a piece of rationalistic affectation — which we find writers of his stamp indulging in, to show their contempt apparently for Evangelical religion. We find another instance of it in Robert Browning, who, in his " Ring and the Book," puts his best and most liberal theology in the mouth of one of the popes. But to return to Carlyle. We are introduced by him to St. Edmondsbury Shrine, where "regimented companies of men devote themselves to meditate on men's nobleness and awfulness, and celebrate and show forth the same, as they best can, thinking they will do it best here, in the presence of God the Maker, and of so awful and so noble made by Him." Next he holds up to us all as a pattern the honest abbot of this shrine, called Samson, narrating at length how he conducted the offices of the abbey with uprightness and discretion; how he stood up against all and sundry who would trench upon its interests and rights, not excepting Richard Cœur de Lion; and how he put on a hair-shirt at the retaking of Jerusalem by the Pagans. This last act is too much for the feelings of our author, who exclaims: "The great antique heart! . . . . Heaven lies over him wherever he goes or stands on the earth, making all the earth one mystic temple to him, the earth's business all a kind of worship. Wonder, miracle encompasses the man; heaven's splendour over his head; hell's darkness under his feet. A great law of Deity hid in these two infinitudes, dwarfing all else, making royal Richard as small as peasant Samson." It is thus that he rebukes the ungodliness of the Present by holding up to our admira-tion the superstition of the Past. His way of reviving modern Protestantism, which is no doubt cold and dead enough, is by presenting us with popery when it was in its most lively condition. Nobody of course denies that there was individual piety to be found in the middle ages, but Carlyle is here justifying the form it assumed.

He no doubt grants that popery's days are past, but it was good for the time. " In prizing justly," he writes, " the indispensable blessings of the New, let us not be unjust to the Old. The old *was* true, if it no longer is. In Dante's day it needed no sophistry, self-blinding, or other dishonesty to get itself reckoned true. It was good then—nay, there is in the soul of it a deathless good." So Carlyle ; and so, sooth to say, and the more shame, Froude, Macaulay, and others. We may well stand amazed to hear them talk in this way— that popery was a good thing in any circumstances; that it was good for the middle ages and became bad in the sixteenth century; that it was an excellent thing to worship the Virgin in the year of our Lord 1200, and is blasphemy to do it now; that it is a good thing now to keep the saints in their proper place, and was as good long ago to worship their bones; that it is a good thing now to have the Bible in every home and in every hand, but was somehow no worse formerly to burn it, or throw it to the moles and the bats; that it would be a humiliating spectacle to see thousands of young women abjuring marriage now, and taking the veil, and crowds of clerks and well-to-do apprentices assuming the cowl, but

that our progenitors male and female did not make fools of
themselves when they entered the monastery or the nunnery;
that the Abbot of St. Edmondsbury is to be hailed as "a
great antique heart," "heaven's splendour over his head,"
but that we would be entitled to laugh at Thomas Carlyle if
he should now put on a hair-shirt to mourn over the state of
the Holy Sepulchre. It may be all very well for those writers
to hold a position of this kind who do not consider the
practices of popery to be in themselves blasphemous, or idolatrous, or destructive of the souls of men, and branded by
the Word of God; but we must say that it is disgusting to see
them come forth and with the same pen pass glowing panegyrics upon Luther and John Knox. We cannot conceive
of a greater humiliation to these Reformers, were they now
living, than to read eulogistic lectures upon the mighty
work they did in destroying popery, introduced by other
lectures showing that popery was a good thing, and was "in
the soul of it a deathless good "—to have first their indignation roused by imbecile defences of Antichrist, and then be
forced to accept of hero worship from the men who had
made them.

II.—AN INQUIRY INTO CARLYLE'S OWN CREED, AND THE HISTORY OF HIS RELIGIOUS OPINIONS.

Although he recognises idolaters, Mohammedans, and
Papists as brother soldiers, ranged under the same Captain,
he acknowledges himself to be, as to uniform, a Christian.
We shall now show in what sense he is so, as that may be
gathered from his writings.

His earliest contributions to our literature are to be found
in his "Critical and Miscellaneous Essays." Were any man
whom we had first encountered in a splendid oriental costume,
strangely and richly decorated every way, gold-tasseled turban,
and robes dyed with every gaudiest colour, to meet us next
in a plain English suit, we could not be more astonished than
by the contrast between Carlyle's style of composition to

which we have been all accustomed, and that which we meet
with in turning back to these essays. Instead of the strong-
painted, disjointed, grotesque, and supremely imaginative,
we have the simple, classical, and common-place. We do
not mean to inquire into the cause of this, which after all is
a mere question pertaining to the philosophy of clothes. Some
may think it proves that his present style is not natural to
him—rather an awkward circumstance in connection with one
who declaims against all shams. But we think otherwise.
We imagine that it is to be accounted for by a great revolution which his mind underwent—stirring him to the very
depths of his being—a revolution which we shall immediately
bring before the reader, and which, though it took an issue
in our own judgment ever to be deplored, naturally enough
evoked a genius whose consummate power no man will
deny. From the essays it appears that he had plunged
deeply from the first into the study of the German poets and
philosophers. His article upon Goethe, from the enthusiastic
encomiums he passes upon them, shows that he had already
become inoculated with the philosophical views of Christianity
which that poet adopted, and which he propounds in his
"Wilhelm Meister's Wanderjähre." According to that poet
all religion consists in reverence. Men, as to the mass of them,
are wanting in this, though they have enough of that fear
which trembles. A few men only have had this higher sense
of religion, the true saints, or gods of our world, who have
communicated it in various ways to the vulgar. Goethe divided religion thus considered into three stages of historical
progress. *First*, ethnical religion, so called because its
development was connected rather with nations than the
individual. This inculcated reverence *for that which is above
us*. He acknowledges the Jewish nation to have been the
best model of this kind of religion, and their Scriptures to
have been the best, though it is only an equivocal preference of degree he assigns to the Jewish religion. The second
phase which religion assumed was reverence *for that which is*

around us. He styles this a philosophical religion, and he considered Christ to be the great Exemplar of it. It leads us, *first,* to draw down that which is above us to our own level, which Christ did, for He dared to equal Himself with God, nay, to declare that He Himself was God. Christ thus taught us the great lesson of reverence for one's self, which Goethe does not hesitate to call the highest of all the three reverences. By this means man attains to the highest elevation of which he is capable, that of being justified in reckoning himself the best that nature has produced. But, *secondly,* it leads us to exalt that which is below us to our level. Christ sought to make the ignorant wise, to strengthen the weak, &c. This, in its twofold aspect, then, is what Goethe means by Christianity, the philosophical religion which Christ introduced, and which he styles reverence *for what is around us.* Taught by this religion, we learn to rid ourselves of the idea of there being a great distance between God and us, on the one hand ; between ourselves and those below us, on the other. The *third* phase which religion assumed was that of reverence *for what is beneath us ;* viz., afflictions, persecutions, death, &c. Here also Christ is the model, but specially in His sufferings and Passion. So that this also was part of the Christianity which Goethe held. We here enter the Sanctuary of Sorrow. We have been taught by Christ to recognise something Divine in these things, as illustrative and probative of character.

We have been thus particular in detailing the scheme of Goethe's religion, because the sketch which Carlyle gives of it in one of his essays was written at an early period of his life ; and it must be plain to any one who reads his comments upon it, that he lent himself to the adoption of it. It contains the seminal principles of the religion which he afterwards inculcated. The grand and fatal mistake of it lies in ignoring guilt, the curse under which it has brought us, and the entire change which it has produced in our legal relations to God. Goethe starts by dismissing the fear that trembles, because reverence is the form which religion should take. It may be so; but if we have broken God's law, and brought down its penalty upon us, did Goethe mean to say that there is no reason for our trembling? The wretchedness and despair of mankind, since the Fall, arises of course from a sense of guilt. Everybody knows that the glory of the Bible, and the ground upon which the infinitely wise God who wrote it claims to have made foolishness all the wisdom of this world, is its revelation of the only remedy for this guilt. It shows that steps absolutely stupendous were needed to take it away; that the only begotten Son of God needed to be incarnated and crucified, ere the atonement for it could be provided. Upon the ground of it, and only upon the ground of it, are we called upon to dismiss our fears. The poet-theologian of Germany, on the other hand, makes short work of our fears, by telling us that they are not the best form of religion, and that we should cultivate reverence. The view he gives of Christ corresponds with the superficial view he has taken of our condition through the Fall. Christ, instead of being a Saviour for sinners in the way we have described, is a Philosopher, who comes to teach us the proper view we ought to take of what is above us, and of what is around us, and of what is underneath us. He comes to instruct us, not to make expiation for our sins. So far are we indeed from being treated as sinners, that Christ the Philosopher has appeared to teach us self-reverence, and that there is no such gulf between us and God as we imagined. One part of His philosophy is to teach us to bring God down to our own level. Hence the seed of that doctrine of hero worship and creature worship which, as we shall afterwards show, was so largely inculcated by Carlyle, and considered by him to be the grand hope of the world's regeneration. To be sure, another part of Christ's philosophy is to teach us to bring up those who are below to our level, that they may be gods along with us. But the presumption of the first act, whereby we have such prodigious reverence for ourselves, is scarcely compensated by the reverence we thus show to those who are below us. Such was the philosophy of Christ in His life, according to Goethe. Next, that of His sufferings and death consisted in His teaching us to reverence the things that are beneath us, afflictions, persecutions, and every evil, on account of the divine ends they accomplish in connection with our character and God's government. If we have no atonement by Goethe's scheme, we have something that is more poetical—the Sanctuary of Sorrow. Our sins remain, for Christ did not suffer or die to take them away; but we have learned that there is something divine about the consequences which our sins have introduced. Altogether reverence seems to have a potent influence with Goethe. Are we afraid of our sins, and consequently of God? his cure is reverence for Him; are we vile and polluted sinners? he recommends self-reverence; are we afflicted? reverence for our afflictions is the sure antidote. That a German poet should have adopted such an absurd view of Christianity is not wonderful, but that one who had been trained in the scriptural theology of this country should have been misled by it is lamentable enough.

From another of his essays, that upon Voltaire, it appears that Carlyle had come not only to deny the plenary inspiration of the Bible, but to maintain that Christianity, being as to the essence of it written upon man's heart by nature, does not need to be proved either by miracles or by historical documents. It has its foundation in human nature. It is intuitionally discovered by us to be true. On these accounts he meets Voltaire's attacks upon Christianity, not by establishing the truth of miracles, or defending the Scriptures, but by resting its claim for acceptance upon the findings of man's own heart.

" That the Christian religion," he says, " could have any deeper foundation than books, could possibly be written in the purest nature of man, in mysterious, ineffaceable characters, to which books and all revelations and authentic traditions were but a subsidiary matter, were but as the light whereby that Divine *writing* was to be read—nothing of this seems to have, even in the faintest manner, occurred to him. Yet herein, as we believe that the whole world has now begun to discover, lies the real essence of the question—or rather never was divided regarding it—Christianity, the 'Worship of Sorrow,' has been recognised as Divine on far other grounds than miracles. Religion is not of sense, but of faith—not of understanding, but of reason ; and he who has failed to unfold the reason in himself can have no knowledge of the Christian religion."

We are not for a moment to understand that in giving up to Voltaire here the external evidences of Christianity, he takes up his stand upon what we have been accustomed to call the internal evidences of Christianity. Nothing so shallow or superficial as this. What he means is that Christianity has not only its response, but its foundation in this nature of ours—a deeper foundation there than in the Scriptures—that it is there written in mysterious ineffaceable characters, and that the Scriptures are at best only a light whereby the divinely written Christianity within us may be read. The fact is that he had now, as we have shown, expunged from his Christianity all reference to an atonement or to any of the supernatural doctrines of the Bible, and resolved it into those three reverences, all of which lie hidden within our nature, although the Philosopher Christ has appeared to draw them forth by His teaching and by His example. It is easy to see how with such views he should feel indifferent whether Voltaire overthrew miracles or invalidated the written Record, since Christianity was a thing of which we have not only the evidences, but the component elements in our own bosoms.

He even considers the Frenchman, whose works we have been accustomed to look upon as only destructive and pestilential, to have done good service by casting down the confidence men had been disposed to place in miracles, and in the written Record. He and his school are accustomed to speak of Voltaire as the pioneer of a better era, and the French Revolution as introducing what they hope to be a second Reformation. "The better part of our readers," says he in the above essay, "will unite with us in candid tolerance and clear acknowledgment towards French philosophy, towards this Voltaire, and the spiritual period that bears his name." Indeed, we can perfectly understand how our author should have " candid tolerance," and feel himself under " clear acknowledgment " to Voltaire, though it is an ugly symptom of the Christianity he has adopted that it claims to be benefited by the great apostle of infidelity. Carlyle's Christianity being in fact nothing but a spurious Christianity—a mere form of natural religion under the disguise of that name—is felt by him and his disciples to be condemned by the Bible, and they have good reason to bless the man who has undermined the authority of the Bible and its miraculous evidences. Meanwhile here *is* a second reformation in good sooth ! Here is a new Christianity with a vengeance ! Here is Voltaire going before, in the character of John the Baptist laying the axe to the root of every miracle, and casting down the Bible ; and here are Carlyle, Robert Browning, and Tennyson (for they belong, as we shall show, largely to one school), with all the zeal of apostles, preaching a gospel, not such as is a positive revelation from heaven, but such as is " written with ineffaceable characters in the present nature of man."

But it was in 1838 that Thomas Carlyle first formally broached his religious opinions in his volume called " Sartor Resartus." This, in the whole style of it, was an eccentric work, professing to be the lucubrations of a German, *Herr Teuffelsdrök*—this name being a mere blind of course. Herr Teuffelsdrök, in what is called humorously his " Philosophy of Clothes," is represented as looking beyond whatever strikes the senses to the naked truth of things—stripping society in its loud trafficking around us, in its commerce and polity, in its establishments, army, and police, of all the adventitious shows belonging to it ; nay, abstracting his mind from the external system of nature around us, and from this body itself, and asking himself the unanswerable question, Who am I ? the thing that can say I. Whence ?   How ?   Where to ?   But the interesting part of the volume for us is the account given of Herr Teuffelsdrök's conversion and religious experiences. We cannot doubt that they detail those of Thomas Carlyle himself.   To be sure, he is ever and anon, as he details them, calling them "strange utterances," and craving license for his eccentric friend ; but as Herr Teuffelsdrök is a ficti- tious name, he can only have been employed of course to pro- pound Carlyle's own views, who accordingly homologates the " Philosophy of Clothes " at the end of the volume, and, with the enthusiasm of a new apostle, expresses his hope that others might propagate these religious opinions.   Before detailing these, we might just observe that this way of broaching his new gospel, adopted by Thomas Carlyle, does not savour much of the valour which Odinism deified. Luther or John Knox, in propounding their religious views to the nation, would never have skulked behind a fictitious German.

He represents his model man, Herr Teuffelsdrök, as, first of all, passing into a state of scepticism, in which from doubting miracles and the plenary inspiration of the Bible he is led to doubt the very existence of God.   A description is given us of the agony of soul which he endured in this contest with the everlasting No.   It is spoken of as necessary.

" First, must the dead letter of religion own itself dead, and drop piecemeal into dust, if the living spirit of religion, freed from its charnel-house, is to arise on us, new-born of heaven, and with new healing under its wings ? "

It is spoken of as not at all blameworthy.

" Perhaps at no period of his life was Herr Teuffelsdrök more the servant of goodness—the servant of God—than even now when doubting God's existence.   ' Truth,' he cried, ' though

the heavens crush me for following her ! no falsehood, though
a whole celestial lubberland were the price of apostacy ! '
Thus, in spite of all motive-grinders, and mechanical, profit-
and-loss philosophers, with the sick ophthalmia and hallucina-
tion they had brought on, was the infinite nature of duty
still dimly present to me ; living without God in the world,
of God's light I was not utterly bereft; if my sealed eyes
could not see Him, nevertheless in my heart was He present,
and His heaven-written law still stood legible and sacred
there."

We have here the approved system of religious experience
current with our modern disciples of a philosophical or
rationalistic Christianity. In the pride of their intellect, or
infected with vain speculations, they stumble at the supernatural doctrines of the Bible, and at the testimony borne to
the truth of them by miracles ; and, in due time, as might
be expected, they stumble at the evidence we have for the
existence of God Himself. The distress of mind into which
they fall through their scepticism, and the scepticism itself,
they esteem to be an honourable distinction. Instead of
being ashamed of it, they glory in it. Robert Browning, in
his " Ring and the Book," actually maintains in good blank
verse that this scepticism answers the same purpose for
engendering earnestness as the fires of persecution did in the
primitive Church. It never seems to occur to them that
whether this sort of scepticism be a virtue or not depends
upon whether the evidences for the plenary inspiration of the
Bible on the one hand, and the existence of God on the other,
be sufficient. If they are not so, then indeed we may pronounce the doubts justifiable, and sympathise with the distress. But if they are not only sufficient, but overwhelming,
we must come to a different conclusion. We may make
allowance, even in that case, for a man having his doubts for
a time (such is the weakness of the human understanding,
and so apt are some speculative minds to raise difficulties),
but it were ridiculous to praise such doubts. Upon the sup-

position made, they ought not of course to exist. As to scepticism or doubt being desirable, from its leading eventually to a living and earnest faith, we must draw a distinction. If a man has in the first instance been holding any truth ignorantly and without inquiry, an objection brought against it from some quarter outside may stagger him, and the state of doubt into which he is thrown, by leading him to examine the grounds upon which the truth rests, may eventually issue in his having a more intelligent and a more earnest faith. Such doubting did not arise from something sinful discovered in the state of his own mind—from that pride of the fallen understanding, or from that vain speculation which leads some to call the truth in question, but it arose from his being presently unable from want of due knowledge to meet the objection from without. He is only led by it to inquiry ; the temporary doubt is overruled for good ; and he more than ever earnestly believes in the truth he had doubted. Now we should be quite satisfied with Herr Teuffelsdrök's scepticism, that is, with the scepticism of Carlyle and his school, if it were of this description—if, in short, having had some doubts for a time, they were brought after examination to see the groundlessness of them, and embrace Christianity in good or better earnest. But, alas! the earnest and living Christianity with which they end is not the same, as to the matter of it, which they doubted. Their scepticism in the Bible ends, as we shall see, in their denying its plenary inspiration, and coming to have an earnest faith in a spurious Christianity which has its foundation in human nature. Nay (as we shall also show), their scepticism in the existence of God ends by an earnest faith in a very unsatisfactory sort of God indeed.

Herr Teuffelsdrök's state of mind when he doubted of God's existence is represented to us by himself in such commendatory and Thrasonic terms as may well engender the worst suspicions of it in our mind. " ' Truth,' I cried, ' though the heavens crush me for following her ! no falsehood, though a whole celestial lubberland were the price of apostacy!'" &c. That is to say, he was resolved to prosecute this inquiry into God's existence defiantly of those fears by which weaker men are influenced, who are prevented from coming to the negative conclusion by the fear of this being an impiety which will draw down heaven's vengeance, and who allow themselves to come to the positive conclusion (though it might be false), because it is the more pious conclusion, and seems to be the passport to heaven. Such lubberly weaklings, who are influenced in their judgments by the Divine sanctions, he styles "motive-grinders, mechanical profit-and-loss philosophers," &c.

We grant that in such an inquiry as the one now before us a man is called upon to decide by the evidence ; but we are prepared to maintain that it is too proud a position for him to occupy to say that he is not a responsible being in this inquiry, or that he is entitled to deal with the Divine sanctions in this braggadocio style. Here, at the outset of the inquiry, are certain great and glorious objects before him, including the whole fabric of the material universe. The very fact that these *may* be of God, and be the evidences God has been pleased to afford of His existence and of His glorious perfections, lays Him under a responsibility in conducting the inquiry—a responsibility which it is impossible for him to shake off. For if it should be found that the fabric of things around him contains sufficient evidences of God's existence, then for him to fail in recognising God's existence, or to live in the denial of it, would be sin. It is but right and fitting, therefore, that even in such a rudimental investigation, the inquirer should have the whole possible results of it before his contemplation, and should not work it out in the jaunty and vauntingsome style of Carlyle's friend and model, but with a solemn sense of responsibility connected with it, and of the eternal consequences accompanying this responsibility. It seems to be his idea that any sense of this would be fatal to freedom in judging of the evidence — an idea which, if carried out, amounts to this, that all acting under responsibility and under the influence of the eternal sanctions is incompatible with man's freedom and independence. Would he condemn those who patronise such acting as motive-grinders, &c. ? Of course, to be influenced in any inquiry, or in any line of conduct, by no other considerations than the eternal consequences which may follow to ourselves, is mercenary; but God has seen it to be necessary that the most virtuous and noble creatures He has ever made should be encouraged to the good by eternal reward, and deterred from the evil by eternal punishment annexed to it. As to the very question now before us, that of God's existence, although it is a question men should settle by the evidence, is it not well that they should be solemnised by the eternal consequences that must attend the denial of His existence, when duly attested ; all the more, as their evil hearts are only too much inclined to come to the conclusion on this question which would most favour their licentiousness? It was therefore mere pride and presumption on the part of Herr Teuffelsdrök, when prosecuting this inquiry, to trust entirely to his own so sublime regard for truth, and look upon the salutary sanctions by which the settling of the question in favour of God's existence (if the evidence were sufficient) was enforced, as nothing but a blinder to his pure soul. We mention this to show what reason we have to sus-pect that the scepticism itself of the Carlyle school is the scepticism of pride, not that humble doubting which is entitled to respect and commiseration in its distress.

The reader may wish to know how Herr Teuffelsdrök is represented by Carlyle (who of course is describing his own case) as obtaining deliverance from the sore agony and distress to which he was exposed during his scepticism—his conflict with " the everlasting No."

" One day there rose a thought in me—What art thou afraid of, despicable Biped ? Death is the worst. Suppose Tophet, all that the devil or man can do—canst thou not suffer whatever it be, and as a child of freedom trample

Tophet itself under thy feet ? I will meet it and defy it. I was strong, of unknown strength—a spirit—almost a god. Ever from that time the temper of my misery was changed— not fear, not whining sorrow, but indignation and grim-eyed defiance."

This Carlyle calls Herr Teuffelsdrök's " Baphomatic, Fire baptism " (alluding to the famous ordeal for Knights Templar), " the most important transaction in his life, the turning-point in his history ; " and he remarks that " now the old Satanic school had received judicial notice to quit."

First, let us have a clear notion of the nature of his soul's distress—his fear, and the cause of it. He tells us elsewhere that at this time he was supremely miserable, " that he lived in fear, as if the heavens and earth were the boundless jaws of a devouring monster." All this, be it observed, had no relation to his condition as a poor guilty sinner. We do not find that either Thomas Carlyle, or any of his , school, have ever been visited with distress of that descrip- tion. It was not the distress that troubled Luther at all —an infinitely less noble trouble, God knows. What was it then ? Having begun to doubt his Bible, and even the existence of God, his distress we are to suppose arose from the utter darkness and confusion that now filled the future ; nothing but annihilation awaited him ; destruction, and none to save him from it ; nay, as he talks of a possible Tophet, he would seem not to have been altogether certain of there being an everlasting No after all, so that it might fare with him all the worse for his disbelief. -But can there be any- thing more ridiculous than the way in which he effected his escape from this sufficiently wretched state of soul ? Was it by coming to discover his own folly in ever yielding to scepticism, and setting himself in another and a better, because a humbler spirit, to examine into thee vidences both for his Bible and for a God ? Was it by examining evidences at all ? No ; but one day he turns upon all his distress with defiance, and it disappears like a shot. Out of his distress he came like an approved Knight Templar, and having nothing to praise but his own valour. For Carlyle's religion, as represented in Herr Teuffelsdrök, is a piece of vainglory from beginning to end. Thus we find him saying :—

"Capabilities there were in me to give battle in some small degree against the great empire of darkness. Does not the very ditcher and delver with his spade extinguish many a thistle and puddle? How much more one whose capabilities are spiritual, who has learned the grand thaumaturgic art of thought. . . . . Truly a thinking man is the worst enemy the prince of darkness can have."

Without contesting the point with Carlyle whether valour or defiance be the way to escape from the fears of scepticism, we must decisively object to his attempts to show in some parts of his writings that this is also the way to escape from the fears of guilt.

"Shall I be saved? Shall I not be damned? What is this at bottom but a new egoism, stretched out into the infinite? Brother, rise above all that. Thou art like to be damned; consider that as the fact; reconcile thyself even to that, if thou be a man; then first is the devouring universe subdued under thee, and from the black mirk of midnight, and mire of greedy Acheron, dawn of an everlasting morning shall spring. . . . Thy future fate, while thou makest it the chief question, seems to me extremely questionable. Norse-Odin, immemorial centuries ago, did not he, though a poor heathen, in the dawn of time, teach us that for the dastard there was and could be no good fate? . . . A greater than Odin has been here, and has taught us not a greater dastardism, I hope. My brother, thou must pray for a soul; struggle to get back thy soul. Know that religion is no Morrison's pill from without, but a reawakening of thy own self from within."

We had long been very anxious to find out how Carlyle and others of the same views dealt with the question of guilt. They seldom speak of it. But we have the whole question of how it is to be disposed of here brought before us. We have a few remarks to make upon it.

The party whom he here advises is supposed to be anxious about his future state—alarmed in reference to it. He is supposed to be making this the chief question. We shall not dispute with Carlyle whether it ought to be made the *chief* question; as, for example, whether it should occupy a man more than other questions which it is also his duty to consider. If that were all which our author found fault with in the party he advises, less might be said. But plainly the advice given has reference not merely to an undue amount of fear being entertained by a man regarding his eternal state, but to fear being entertained at all. Had the former only or chiefly been in the eye of Carlyle, of course his advice would have been to moderate his fears upon that subject, and to subordinate them to other considerations which were less selfish and more important. His advice would have been moderation, not defiance. His advice plainly has relation to the fears themselves, and the way in which they are to be dealt with. And his counsel is — by defiance. The man is told that his fears are an indication of cowardice. He is not told that they are groundless; nay, he is advised to grant the worst, that his damnation is likely enough, and to brave it out like a gallant Knight Templar.

In speaking thus our adviser was of course aware that the man's alarm in reference to his future state arose from his sins; from his having broken God's law, and having to answer for the violation of it. There are only two suppositions we can make regarding the author when he tenders such advice. The first we are unwilling to make. It is that he himself really believes in the possibility of eternal punishment for sin; in which case he advises the man to take God into his own hands, and outbrave Him as he would do a fellow-creature. We are unwilling to impute to him such an impious, audacious, and monstrous counsel.

5 *

The other is that he does not himself believe that sin is penal, or followed up by eternal punishments, and therefore considers that the fears of which he speaks are groundless, and to be dismissed as cowardly. Now, if they are groundless, they are cowardly. Your *if* is a wonderful peacemaker. Had all the world been of the same happy, superficial turn with our Chelsea philosopher, so as to take it as a thing for granted that no punishment follows the breaking of God's law, there would have been a considerable amount of distress of conscience saved, and a great deal of that valour shown which he admires.

We think the reader will agree with us that the passages quoted exhibit the religion of Carlyle, so far as bears upon the essential point of guilt, as most unsatisfactory and most absurd. The way in which they are expressed, besides, is highly offensive. The blessed atonement of our Lord Jesus Christ must be included when he tells us in contemptuous terms that the remedy is to be found in "no Morrison's pill from without." Again, when seeking to comfort the alarmed sinner, instead of pointing to the cross of Jesus Christ, he points him to his Norse-Odin nonsense of consecrated valour.

Is it not lamentable to think that this is the kind of religion which is now shown by many—consisting in distress and agony of soul sinfully caused by their own scepticism, while on the subject of their personal sin they have never known what it is to be distressed and alarmed? They look upon the distress or fear which their shameless scepticism has caused them as being their Bathomatic Baptism. They actually talk of those as being half-men who have not gone through the distress of infidelity. Their self-conceit prevents them from knowing that the others whom they despise have been suffering meanwhile from that distress of conscience for guilt which the Holy Ghost alone can produce, and which nothing but the glorious atonement of the cross can heal.

But let us now hear what was the nature of that faith which Herr Teuffelsdrök came to when he was delivered, or rather had delivered himself by valour, and "the thaumaturgic art of thought."

First—as to the existence of God. He had doubted of this. He had gone here through the grand ordeal of scepticism. Did he come to faith in it? Yes; so he declares. But, judging by Carlyle's own writings, it is a very unsatisfactory kind of God he groped his way to. Thus in his "Chartism; or, Past and Present," he writes :—

"Is there not a sole reality, and ultimate controlling power of the whole? He who knows this, it will sink silent, awful, unspeakable into his heart. He will say with Faust, 'Who dare name him?' Most rituals or namings he will fall in with at present, are like to be namings which shall be nameless. In silence, in the Eternal Temple, let him worship, if there be no fit word. Such knowledge the crown of his whole spiritual being, the life of his life, let him keep and sacredly walk by. He has a religion. Hourly and daily for himself, and the whole world, a faithful, unspoken, but not ineffectual prayer rises, 'Thy will be done.' He has a religion, this man."

Now we all acknowledge the mystery and incomprehensibleness of God, but the vagueness and blankness of Carlyle's object of worship, as he here and elsewhere refers to it, comes under another category. If we acknowledge something Divine, something that is above all, then, according to him, this is enough, though we cannot tell what it is. We have seen already that according to him we may put Odin, or Jupiter, or God, or the Three-one God into the high place. These are what he calls namings, nothing else; but if a man walk by a Divine something or a Divine anything, which is "the crown of his whole spiritual being, the life of his life," it is all one. Sometimes, with Carlyle, it is the soul of the universe; sometimes the essence of the universe; sometimes "the eternal silences, or stars."

This vagueness is accounted for by the scepticism which led him to reject not only the clear and certain exhibition of the nature of God which is given us in His blessed Word, but even to reject as too inconclusive for his logical mind the evidence which all creation affords upon the subject of God's perfections. We saw already that in his scepticism he fell back in despair upon the moral sentiments of his own nature—the law written upon his own heart, as the only thing evidential to him of something divine. "The infinite nature of Deity was still dimly present to me, if my as yet sealed eyes could not see Him ; nevertheless in my heart He was present, and His heaven-written law still stood legible and sacred there." "At last, that Divine handwriting blazed forth," he says again, " in true sun-splendour." Now it is not denied that our moral nature lays the foundation of an argument for the existence of a God ; it suggests a Divine Being who has impressed this great law upon us. But if we would arrive at any definite knowlege of the nature of God, we must fill up the rudimental idea which our moral constitution suggests of Him by fully availing ourselves of the information to be derived from His works, and especially from His Word. Carlyle, smitten by that evil spirit which is the source of all impotence, and unable to accept of any writing of God as authentic, except that which we bear upon this puny nature of ours—ever " looking into his own navel," to use an expression of his own—seems never to have been able to this day to advance beyond the vaguest knowledge of God ; and while we are all rejoicing in a full and glorious acquaintanceship with His perfections, even with His personalities, he, as if he had been living in some desert island of the ocean unvisited by the gospel, walks on, maundering about " eternal silences, or stars," " the unnameable," " the primeval unspeakable," and such like.

Next we saw that Herr Teuffelsdrök had doubted his Bible, and the miracles by which it is authenticated. Did he ever come back to the faith of Christianity ? He did ;

but let us see to what kind of Christianity. After losing faith in the Bible, he tells us that he went for light to the great men of every age. "For great men I have ever had the warmest predilection, and can perhaps boast that few such in this era have wholly escaped me. Great men are the inspired (speaking and acting) texts of that divine Book of Revelations, whereby a chapter is completed from epoch to epoch, and by some named History."

He mentions Schiller and Goethe.

Having left the guidance of God himself in the Bible, and given himself up to the guidance of great men and "the Divine handwriting" upon his own heart, we need not wonder that he soon imagined himself to have reached what he calls "sunlit slopes."

Now he began to say,—

"O Nature. Ha! why do I not name thee God? Art thou not the living garment of God? O heavens, is it in very deed He then that ever speaks through thee, that lives and loves in me. . . . With other eyes, too, I now look upon my fellow-men—with an infinite love, with an infinite pity. O my brother, my brother, why cannot I shelter thee in my bosom?"

Here he speaks as if he had now arrived at a new feeling and experience with regard to God, and also with regard to his fellow-man. Now, he has not only faith in the existence of God, but finds that he can rejoice in Him—that he loves Him, and is loved by Him: also a new love has sprung up towards his fellow-men, whom he opens his arms to embrace. All this, be it observed, is an experience of natural religion, for he had not yet come to recognise the truth of Christianity, of which afterwards. Upon examination, however, it must appear that all this on the part of Herr Teuffelsdrök was a mere sentimental and fanatical delusion. Being a sinner (it is presumed) like us all, and having broken the law of God, and incurred its penalty, whence did he derive that peace and confidence and joy in God which he expresses?

The school of theologians to which he belongs tell us indeed that they only need to look around them on all creation to see that God is love. But this is sad, loose talk. Tokens meet our eye on every side that man has drawn upon himself judgment for sin, and his own conscience condemns him, and will always condemn him the more he reflects upon his sin. Herr Teuffelsdrök was not entitled to argue to his possessing the love of God because there linger traces in the creation of that goodness which God as Creator showed to man before his fall ; nor was he entitled to conclude that his sins were not to be reckoned for because of the forbearance of his present Providence. He exclaims, " O heavens, is it in very deed He then that ever speaks through thee " (*i.e.*, nature), "*that lives and loves in me.*"

We have underscored the last phrase, for, as those who are acquainted with this school of writers know, it expresses one of their great arguments from nature that God is love, in the sense of being all love, and no judicial wrath in Him against sin. The argument may be stated thus. We are conscious of love going forth from ourselves to others—strong love— love or desire, too, for the everlasting salvation of others. Why should we think that God is less loving than we are ? Is it not God who "*loves in us*" ? What we are ourselves, God is. If we love, then it is God who loves in us. Therefore, God loves and desires the everlasting salvation of all, and to represent Him as subjecting any of His creatures to the curse for sin, or refusing to save them without a Redeemer, who was made a curse for them, is to misapprehend Him. This is one of the famous arguments of this school. It is as flimsy and fallacious as it can well be.

Let us even grant that man's affections, or way of being affected, may be safely taken as a test of God's, what right have they to fix on this one affection, love, and seek to prove thereby that God is all love and benignity? We know that man has other sentiments than love, that he has strong feelings of condemnation of sin when committed by others ;

that he desires to see it punished; that he hates sin, and condemns the sinner. If it be true then that " God loves in me," it must be equally true that "God hates in me," and we shall hereby prove by the same logic that He is a God who is all hatred to sin, and indignation against sinners. Even if God is to be squared and measured by what we are ourselves, we are ourselves the subjects of moral and judicial sentiments, and not of that indiscriminating sentimental love they lay hold of.

But we need scarcely say that we fall into a great mistake when we conclude God to be altogether such a one as ourselves. Suppose that my love or benevolence leads me to desire the everlasting salvation of a fellow-creature, without satisfaction being made in the first place to the violated law, does it follow that because I love in this manner "God loves in me," that is, loves after this manner? Can there be grosser impiety than to palm off upon God all the sentiments and all the sentimentalities of this fallen nature of mine?

But to return to Herr Teuffelsdrök. He had now succeeded, through self-reverence, in raising himself to the level of God; coming to recognise that " God lived and loved in him;" that God, in short, was not different in any respect from himself, so that all fear was cast out. Having thus attained to what I have already shown in a previous part of the essay to be in fact the first part of *Christianity* according to Goethe's philosophical view of it, and having attained to it from the light of nature, nothing remained but that he should have some experience of the higher part of it, viz., reverence for that which was beneath him; that he should recognise something Divine about afflictions, and contumelies, and injuries; that, in short, he should know the worship of sorrow.

This he is represented as doing. And now that he has reached these attainments entirely by the God-written law upon his heart, which he had been driven back upon by the blessed distress of his own scepticism, he comes to be certified of the truth of Christianity. He had, in the first instance, become a sceptic in reference to it because he had lost faith in the Bible, and in the miracles upon which it rests. But now he has found it true by a method independent altogether of the Bible, or of any positive revelation attested by miracles. He has proved it by the light of nature—the feelings of his own heart.

"Is the God present in my own heart a thing which Voltaire will dispute out of me ? In the worship of sorrow, ascribe what origin or genesis thou pleasest, has not that worship originated and been generated ? Is it not here ? Feel it in thine heart, and then say that it is of God. This is belief. All else is opinion, for which latter whoso wills let him worry and be worried. . . . One Bible I know, of whose plenary inspiration doubt is not so much as possible ; nay, with mine own eyes I saw the God's handwriting it ; therefore all other Bibles are but leaves, say in picture-writing, to assist the weaker faculty."

Never was there a grosser delusion than this of the Carlyle school that they can establish the truth of Christianity by this process of theirs. The Christianity in which their scepticism has ended is not the Christianity of the Scriptures at all. The Christianity of the Scriptures is, that we are all under the wrath and curse of God naturally ; that God sent His Son made flesh, made sin, made a curse, to redeem us from the curse of the broken law ; that we are all dead, besides, naturally in pollution, and that the Holy Ghost is sent by Christ to produce a mysterious change upon our moral nature. These are supernatural doctrines, such as it never entered into the heart of man to conceive, and such as Carlyle not only does not profess to find written upon his heart, but repudiates with all his soul. He has no right to palm Goethe's nonsense upon Christ. If he will kiss the toe of a German poet, and fall crouching at the feet of his fellow-creatures, he ought to call the religion he has adopted from them by their name, and not by the name of Christ.

He may say that the Christianity which he and those other great men have adopted is proved to be the true one, as against that which the Scriptures exhibit, or have generally been supposed to exhibit, because it tallies with nature, or what is written upon the heart. But whether any representation of Christianity be the true one or not, is entirely an historical question. Christianity, if it means anything, means the doctrine which Christ taught. It is downright absurdity to say that such and such doctrines must have been taught by Him, because they tally with the God-written law upon our hearts. For aught we know Christ may have taught doctrines subversive of the law of nature; He may have taught anything. What He did teach must be ascertained by examining historical documents, which have recorded and handed down His doctrines.*

Our Scriptures have been shown by testimony which is irrefragable, and which neither Carlyle nor any of his brethren have ventured to contravene, to be the record of Christ's doctrine, and it no more resembles the Christianity of Carlyle (which is a mere development of natural religion) than day resembles night.

We have thus set the religion of Thomas Carlyle before our readers. We are aware that many of them will be shocked at the result of this analysis. As it agrees with his peculiar theory to admire earnestness in every kind of religion, they have in all likelihood formed their idea of this writer from the eulogiums he has passed upon Luther, or Knox, or Cromwell. We ourselves in early life, after reading his " Letters and Speeches of the Protector," formed a very exalted estimate of his evangelical piety, never doubting that he homologated the scriptural principles of his hero. It was only upon taking up that work a second time, after having read and studied his writings as a whole, that we discovered the melancholy and humbling fact that his praise of

---

* This will be proved more at length in the Essay upon Robert Browning.

Cromwell proceeds not from the value he attached to his evangelical views (none of which he holds), but from the value he attaches to what Cromwell held in common with any earnest heathen, Mohammedan, or papist. He admires his recognition of Calvinistic Christianity, not because he himself holds by it, but because Calvinistic Christianity being the right theory in Oliver's judgment, he worships his earnestness. Let the sense of right and wrong fill a man's soul, and it matters not with this writer whether the right he rises up to defend be Calvinism or any other *ism*, God or the gods. Take as a sample his description of the Protector's conversion, and you see that, while it has a very plausible appearance at first sight, it tallies with the representation we have given in this essay of Carlyle's own religion.

" It is therefore in these years that we must place Oliver's clear recognition of Calvinistic Christianity; what he, with unspeakable joy, would name his conversion, his deliverance from the jaws of eternal death. Certainly a grand epoch for a man, properly the one epoch, the turning-point which guides upwards, or guides downwards him and his activity for evermore. Wilt thou join with the dragons? wilt thou join with the gods? Of thee, too, the question is asked ; whether by a man in a Geneva gown, by a man in 'four surplices at Allhallowtide,' with words very imperfect ; or by no man and no words, but only by the silences, by the eternities, by the life everlasting, and the death everlasting. That the ' sense of difference between right and wrong' had filled all time and all space for man, and bodied itself forth into a heaven and hell for him, this constitutes the grand feature of those Puritan, old-Christian ages ; this is the element which stamps them as heroic, and has rendered their events great, manlike, fruitful to all generations."

Such statements, scattered through the work, are not understood by the bulk of readers in this country, nor much attended to as they read it ; but after the exposition we have given of his views, as gathered from his whole ethical and religious productions, they will perceive that they convert the work into a mere heathenish pæan over the Protector.

III.—HIS HERO WORSHIP.

We now come thirdly, and lastly, to speak of his peculiar doctrine on the subject of hero worship.

We would not be insensible to the good influence which his writings have exerted in bringing before the public stirring examples of great men. Never was there a writer who possessed to the same extraordinary extent the power and the sympathies necessary for this. He has filled the land with Titanic images, and has done little more for thirty years than cry aloud as a herald that we should fall down and worship them. He has also done something in teaching us to undervalue such men as common minds are apt to admire—the man of wealth or rank, the man of mere intellect, the man of hearsay, red-tape, and precedent ; setting up none, or comparatively few, upon his pedestal of unhewn stone, but such as have been earnest souls in their way, grappling with the mystery of the universe and the essence of things. And had his object been simply to stimulate us to good or great deeds by the example of good or great men, we should not have added a single word of exception on this head. It must have already suggested itself to our readers, however, that he has had another and a special object in view by his lifelong advocacy of heroism. According to Goethe, whose disciple he became, it is part of religion, and of the Christian religion, for men "to bring themselves up to the level of God," and it is by inculcating this lofty self-reverence that mankind and society are to be regenerated. Thomas Carlyle's zeal in this department cannot be understood unless we remember that it is the zeal of one who has for many years been propagating a new religion. We had been till now under the impression that Christianity had come to convince us of our being vile, worthless, polluted, and undone, and to reveal the remedy in the blood of the Lamb, and the energy of the Holy Ghost who removes our moral inability. The new Christianity which our author adopted, while it wholly ignores guilt, or anything that needs to be rectified in our legal condition, comes to give us an excessively exalted view of humanity, and to regenerate us by impressing our minds with this, and by bringing before us the highest specimens of it which have appeared.

It is no doubt useful to impress upon man the dignity which belongs to him as a rational and immortal creature. But it is just as essential to remind him that he is the mere creature of God—finite in his faculties, and occupying the lowest degree in the scale of rational existence. If we omit to inculcate the one truth, the danger is that he may sink into mean and unworthy pursuits. If we omit the other, we are sure to lift him up with pride and presumption. The Bible is careful to bring both truths before us. It impresses us with the world-value of the soul in its destiny, and dignity, as made originally in the image of God; but it dwells much upon the littleness and insignificance of man, the limited nature of his powers, and the unreliability of his judgment. We shall not find much of the latter unflattering estimate in the writings of the Carlyle fraternity. Man according to them is "the divinest thing in nature, so that we touch heaven when we lay our hand on a human body." So Novalis. "The ultimate attainment of religion," says Goethe, "is reverence for oneself; so that man attains the highest elevation of which he is capable, that of being justified in reckoning himself the best that God and nature have produced." The same writer, as we have shown, tells us that the philosophy of Christ was "to teach us to bring down God, or all that is above us, to our own level." In short, the result of Christ's religion, if we understand Goethe, is very much the result of the religion first inculcated by the serpent upon us all, "Ye shall be as gods." And it must be acknowledged that the whole tendency of

Carlyle's writings is to puff up humanity with the most unlimited conceit of itself. In this respect he has done an essential damage to the age. He has sought to reform men by teaching them to deify their own nature, and by teaching them to worship those of the race who have been more distinguished.

Speaking of the transcendent admiration of great men, he says :—

" Religion I find stands upon it—not paganism only, but far higher and truer religions, all religion hitherto known. Hero worship, heart-felt, prostrate admiration, submission, burning, boundless, for a noblest godlike form of man, is not that the germ of Christianity itself ? The greatest of all heroes is one whom we do not name here. Let sacred silence meditate that matter; you will find it the ultimate perfection of a principle extant throughout man's whole history on earth."

Now we doubt whether he here does justice even to paganism. Its philosophers and teachers never were so superficial as mainly to rest the hope of reforming the species upon this setting up of the lives of distinguished men. They were not so stupidly puffed up with pride of human excellence. The inculcation of morality and the awful sanctions of religion (so far as they apprehended them) was what they stood upon. They would have looked upon it as toadyism to make " a prostrate admiration of great men " the leading motive to virtue. But with regard to Christianity, the very thing which proves it to have come from God, and has always been considered as proving its Divine original, is its having shown that the reformation of fallen man never can be effected either by examples of moral excellence, nor by our own efforts, nor even by the commandments of God enforced with their sanctions. What is born of the flesh it declares to be flesh, and destined so to remain. If Thomas Carlyle expects that in going down to the lanes and closes of our large cities, or going anywhere, he will turn men to righteousness by setting before them the "noblest godlike form of man," he has yet to learn that the depravity of the human heart laughs at all such attempts. Christianity stands not upon this as its mainstay, nor upon anything like it. It comes to us declaring new methods altogether, both for the justification of the guilty and for the regeneration of the polluted. It stands upon the supernatural doctrines of justification through the blood of Christ, and regeneration by the Holy Ghost.

The true hope of the reformation of mankind therefore rests upon the publication of these doctrines; and to say that it rests upon "the transcendent admiration of great men," is to transfer the glory of effecting it from God to man. Does any one believe, for example, that it was admiration of the heroism of Martin Luther or of John Knox that led to the Reformation? On the contrary, it was the doctrines they taught that produced it. What would Luther have said had he heard Carlyle trace the Reformation to himself as a hero, instead of tracing it to the doctrine of justification through the sin-atoning blood of the Lamb, which he was privileged to know and declare? What would he have said to hear that the Reformation stood not upon that doctrine, but "unlimited admiration of his own godlike earnestness"? Nay, Carlyle's system is not consistent with itself. First, he asserts those men to be heroes who have grappled in earnestness of spirit with the great essential truths of existence, God, eternity. Next he represents religion as standing upon a transcendent admiration of, and submission to such men; and he does not see that he thus makes us men-admirers, instead of truth-lovers, which is destructive of all greatness. Instead of calling us to admire great men, it should have been the truths they grappled with he should have insisted upon as important. This is to introduce a vicious element. Thus the writer who has written most against shams, singularly enough, has been imposed upon by the greatest of all shams.

The fact is that, in the writings of Carlyle, truth bulks very little. Those men whom he holds up to our unlimited admiration in the religious department are such as have been distinguished by earnestness, but as this earnestness has been shown in holding the most opposite doctrines, it is plain that he holds the distinction between truth and error as of little or no importance. The earnestness of Luther and of Dante, of Mahomet and of Oliver Cromwell, of Odin and of John Knox, is all one in his eyes. No doubt he endeavours to make it out that there was a something of essential importance in which they all agreed. But this turns out to be little more than that they all held by the eternal distinction between right and wrong. Meanwhile what becomes of the eternal distinction between truth and error? One thing is evident, that the earnestness of the men whom he thus sets up to us as heroes had no relation to the very elementary point of agreement which he mentions, but was entirely directed to those other points which he considers non-essential, but which were the very peculiarities of their system. Thus he would have us fall down in prostrate admiration before men whose whole earnestness and life were directed to the maintenance of what he considers to be of no importance—of no more importance than its opposite. So silly is his admiration of great men! And how ridiculously does he exaggerate the influence which this sentiment has exerted for the regeneration of the world, and is likely to exert for it.

The mightiest of all revolutions for good that ever took place was that which was effected by Christianity upon its first introduction. Were the apostles, I would ask, taking them as a whole, heroes, even in the sense in which Carlyle would understand the term—in the sense of having gone through wonderful experiences in their own minds in grappling with the mystery of the universe? Could he have written lectures upon Peter, or James, or Philip? Everything goes to prove that they were plain, ordinary, average-minded men, and purposely chosen such by God, in order to show that the moral revolution accomplished by them was owing to the truth they proclaimed, and the miracles accompanying it—certainly not to the instruments who were employed. They themselves acknowledged that they could do nothing without the truth. Carlyle's idea is that the truth could do nothing without them. They uniformly repressed with vehement indignation any tendency shown to have "a transcendent admiration of them as great men," or to give them a " prostrate submission ; " and, in doing so, Thomas Carlyle maintains of course that they were repressing the very thing which Christianity stands upon !

Nay, in the extract I have given, he asks triumphantly " whether hero worship, burning, boundless, for a noblest godlike form of man, is not the germ of Christianity itself ? The greatest of all heroes is one whom we do not name here."

He is quite mistaken if he think that he has found the germ of Christianity, or what constitutes its power and glory, in its presenting us with " a noblest godlike form of man." What Christianity truly is we can only learn, as we have shown already, by consulting the historical record we have of it in the universally received canon. There we learn that the grand reason why the Son of God took the form of Man, was that He might thus be capable of suffering and dying for our sins, to deliver us from the wrath to come. So far is the Record from representing God's grand design in the Incarnation as being to swell and exalt our notions of the human nature by setting a " godlike form of man " before us, that it represents God's grand design as being to humble His Son to this vile human nature of ours, in order to an atonement through His humiliation. By the Incarnation no doubt we have a perfect model of humanity ; but to speak of this, or of the effect produced by it, as representing the germ of Christianity, or the grand principle upon which it exerts its powers, shows entire ignorance of this Mystery.

Most certainly its object was not to swell our sense of the greatness of humanity. And while we have the self-denial of the life and death of Christ set before us, which Carlyle may pronounce to be heroism unexampled, it is not of the kind at all which he founds upon, and considers to be so influential. It was not shown by one who was a mere man like ourselves, but by a Divine Person in our nature, and therefore does not go to inflate our sense of human greatness. The very expressions Carlyle uses, " a divine man," " a noblest godlike form of man," instead of God-man, are significant and deceptive; for in the Scriptures it is a Divine Person, and not a Divine Man that is before us. It is God that is glorified, and not the humanity. To make this the more patent, Christ did nothing in His own name even as a Divine Person. He tells us that if He had come in His own name, doing great things as of Himself, the world would have received Him. It would have looked upon him as the greatest of all heroes, and bowed before Him " with transcendent admiration and prostrate submission." Instead of being the servant of the Father, He would then have been the " godlike form of man, " which is the grand affair with the world, and with Thomas Carlyle. But, as it is, Christ is not popular with the world, and it is in vain for Goethe and his disciples to try to make Him so by converting our worship of Him from a God-worship into a man-worship.

But we must close this lecture, which has already swelled beyond just dimensions.

It may be thought by some readers that it was an exercise of unnecessary patience to follow any author step by step through such extravagances of opinion, and to combat with arguments what are the chimeras of the wildest imagination. But his religious notions have been adopted by many men distinguished for genius, if not for solid judgment, and it seemed desirable to refute what has been thought worthy of so much embellishment. When one sees the monstrous

positions that have been held by this writer, he cannot but
. perceive what a gigantic genius he must possess, to have
made his lectures and writings plausible—so plausible that
admiring multitudes read them, and even evangelical men
have cherished, and cherish, the belief that he has contributed to advance the cause of religion.

II.

+ *ROBERT BROWNING.*

BOTH Shakespeare and Milton had the advantage of appearing at a period in the history of our country when the place which they were qualified to fill, the one as a dramatist and the other as an epic poet, had not been as yet preoccupied. The great common passions of humanity form the material for the dramatist, and they are not very many in number. Happy the man who comes first, and transfers to his page the virgin reflection of them! Of course a number of clumsy and ineffectual efforts are made at the outset, but I refer to the man of genius who is able to avail himself of the occasion still standing open. He has possession; and what can they do who come after the king? Shakespeare occupied such a position. Till he appeared, the nation felt that the passions of the heart, and life in its great common aspects, had not yet been perfectly represented, and there was no reason why he should not make them his subject. The English language itself was not yet poetically perfect, and there was no need for his distorting it to make an impression. When a man has thus an opportunity of drawing nature in the beauty of her primitive nakedness, there is no temptation to array her in the dress of civilisation; ornament is unnecessary, and when he has given the world her figure, what remains behind? He has had the pattern upon the Mount, and his are the representations that shall go down the ages. With regard to epic poetry, much the same. The sublime Puritan knew that this region was still his own, if he could occupy it. Nature, in her ordinary aspects, had been taken possession of by the bard of Avon, but Paradise, Heaven, and Hell remained ; he had these great subjects—great to all mankind—entirely within his reach. He made them his own accordingly. Nor was it necessary that he should use unwarrantable liberties with the English language, in order to avoid imitating a predecessor ; he could adopt the one, and perhaps the only, epic style for which the language is naturally adapted.

There still remained one department of nature — the amatory, or that which is expressed in songs. This had not been perfectly taken possession of till Robert Burns appeared. When he wrote, this section also of the natural was foreclosed.

It was to be feared that in this dearth of primitive and virgin subject there would be a divergence into false styles of poetry—less flagrant at the beginning, and becoming more marked as time advanced. So it happened. Unartificial enough in their style of composition, Scott and Byron did not derive their material from the universal model of nature. It was the chivalry of Border life that animated the strains of Scott—life in one peculiar phase of it, seen from the knightly side, resplendent with the romance of one peculiar age. None will say that Childe Harold, Lara, the Giaour, or the Corsair can be accepted as universal types. We grant that both these poets drew largely from nature, having a deep insight into it and an intense sympathy with it ; but the subject from which they drew was not human nature in its essential features, broad and catholic. Neither had either of them, with all their extraordinary talent, that highest mastery of genius which expresses a thing in the perfection of a few words, but needed to make up for it as they best might by lengthened description and splendour of impassioned writing. Both of them were frank in their acknowledgment of this. They confessed that they wanted the divine faculty that distinguishes Shakespeare, Milton, and Burns.

But in the age upon which we have fallen the poets give evidence of being reduced to still more desperate shifts in order to produce an impression, and establish for themselves a reputation. There is no kind of outlandish legend to which they have not had recourse; no liberty they have not used with the English language to produce effect; no formidable species of new metrical or unmetrical lines they have not set upon the wheels. All that is sublime in nature or human life having been already anticipated, they have, as if in revenge, resolved to show what can be done by magnifying the little and the unpromising; so that we are not so much thrilled by the magnificence of nature as by the splendour of art. Instead of natural objects so described as by a master's hand to awaken our emotions, we are treated with a metaphysical analysis of the emotions themselves. It was Wordsworth who may be said to have introduced the plan of kindly informing the reader of the sentiments which flowers and every object in nature ought to suggest. The true poet is not one who affects to find and point out in nature what other people cannot discover, but who gives us nature as she is, leaving her to awaken in our bosom her thousand unutterable impressions.

We have thus " Hiawathas," and " Sagas," and " Red Cotton Nightcap Countries," and " Murder cases at Rome," with the verdict of the judge and the pleadings of the fiscal and advocate for the panel, in inspired verse. Yet the generation is pleased, and considers that Tennyson and Browning are an improvement upon the poets of the past. We say nothing as to this at present. But surely the following exceptions may be taken to modern poetry.

One bad quality too often pervading it is quaintness and eccentricity. We shall maintain it to be a rule, eternal as the course of the sun, that nothing of this kind is destined to live. There must be something essentially defective in any poet who has to draw upon this resource. He wants power when he cannot produce effect without resorting to some violation of ordinary rules. Poetry is in the decline when we meet with the grotesque. The age no doubt admires this sort of thing. Pyrotechnics is popular. A star is nothing thought of; but every sinner turns out to his door to see the comet. Cowley is lauded to the skies; Milton nothing thought of; because he does no violence to the rules of taste, and will not turn his imagination into a harlequin.

Extravagance—the spasmodic—is everywhere abundant. I might instance Browning's celebrated "Abt Vogle." For splendour of artifice it is unrivalled; but it is false in taste. It is the whole affair of music carried out into sublime fustian. The rising of one note and the sinking of another is thus described:—

*　　*　　*　　*　　*　　*　　*

And one would bury his brow with a blind plunge down to hell,
　Burrow a while and build, broad on the roots of things,
Then up again swim into sight, having based me my palace well,
　Founded it fearless of flame, flat on the nether springs.

And another would mount and march, like the excellent minion he was,
　Ay, another, and yet another, one crowd but with many a crest,
Raising my rampired walls of gold as transparent as glass,
　Eager to do and die, yield each his place to the rest:

For higher still and higher (as a runner tips with fire
　When a great illumination surprises a festal night,
Outlining round and round Rome's dome from space to spire),
　Up the pinnacled glory reached, and the pride of my soul was in sight.

It is much more easy to get up this kind of meretricious sublimity than our readers have any conception of. The analogy being once caught hold of, one has only to put on his seven-league boots for this sort of undertaking; and had Browning always got upon a panting Pegasus of this description, he would have befooled himself before the public beyond redemption. Or take his "Saul"—a magnificent poem in some respects. Nothing can be finer than the idea of David having expelled the demon of his melancholy, not simply by the tones of his harp, but by the subjects he brings before

the mind of the heaven-deserted monarch ; nothing finer than
the poet's conception of what might have been the successive subjects he attempted ; nothing more masterly than the
execution of them.   But the beauty is sadly marred by
extravagances.   When young David enters the tent, here
is the spectacle that meets his eye :—

> I discerned
> A something more black than the blackness—the vast, the upright
> Main prop which sustains the pavilion ; and slow into sight
> Grew a figure against it, gigantic and blackest of all ;
> Then a sunbeam that burst through the tent-roof showed Saul.
> He stood as erect as that tent-prop, both arms stretched out wide
> On the great cross support in the centre that goes to each side.
> He relaxed not a muscle, but hung there, as caught in his pangs
> And waiting his change, a king serpent all heavily hangs,
> Far away from his kind, in the pine, till deliverance come
> With the springtime, so agonised Saul, drear and stark, blind and dumb.

The last image is grand enough, though somewhat gro-
tesquely drawn, but the lines are defaced by patches of
spasmodic prose.   Thus—

> He stood as erect as that tent-prop, both arms stretched out wide
> On the great cross support in the centre, &c.,

is wretched ; and this straining after effect in bringing Saul's
postures picturesquely before us, carried out as it is throughout the poem, produces a ludicrous impression.   Thus, when
David has in part roused him from his melancholy, can anything be droller than the following description ?

> And the tent shook, for mighty Saul shuddered, and sparkles 'gan dart
> From the jewels that woke in his turban at once with a start,
> All its lordly male sapphires, and rubies courageous at heart.

Then follows an image which for formidable force and
elaborate additions will be a favourite with certain readers.

> Have ye seen when spring's arrowy summons goes right to the aim,
> And some mountain, the last to withstand her, that held (he alone,
> While the vale laughed in freedom and flowers) on a broad bust of stone
> A year's snow bound about for a breastplate, leaves grasp of the sheet ?
> Fold on fold all at once it crowds thunderous down to his feet,

And there fronts you, stark, black, but alive yet, your mountain of old,
With his rents, the successive bequeathments of ages untold ;
Yea, each harm got in fighting your battles, each furrow and scar
Of his head thrust 'twixt you and the tempest—all hail, there they are !
Now again to be softened with verdure, again hold the nest
Of the dove, tempt the goat with its young to the green on his crest
For their food in the ardours of summer !

A good deal of this sort of writing meets us now-a-days.

Obscurity is another fault. Whatever defects may have characterised the poetry of Great Britain in former times, the manly intellect of the nation preserved it from this. Distinctness of conception, clearness of expression, logical connection were always studied. To derive an appearance of sublimity from mistiness of idea, to gain a reputation for depth of thought by obscurity of style, was reckoned beneath the dignity of a British writer. It was left to the Germans, who, whatever claims they may have to erudition and genius, have by this means gained a reputation for both which is a hundred and ninety-nine times greater than they deserve. A new phenomenon presents itself to us now in our books of poetry. You take them up, and not a word of sense is apparent upon a first perusal. Of course after study you perceive the author's meaning ; your eye having got accus-tomed to the darkness of the cave, you begin to see what is round you—even such splendours of art as the poet has been able to produce. What a despicable artifice is this! In some cases the obscurity is the result of mere affectation ; in others, of an awkward style of composition, which defies the ordinary rules of grammar. We trust that there will be a general rise of the public against what may be called the obscure style, and yet there are circumstances making this unlikely. There is the self-conceit leading young men and young ladies to pride themselves on discovering the sense of these obscure authors. There is the sycophancy that sub-mits to be smitten in the face by false apostles. There is the downright toadyism, for example, of such as Carlyle, who gets down upon his knees before the man who has made

himself incomprehensible.   But if this go on, it is our belief
that the only hope of literature is in the French nation.
Whatever may be the degradation under which they lie for
the moment, through the debasing thraldom of Popery, and
the late humiliating despotism of Napoleon, and whatever
may have been the mediocrity of poetic genius among them
hitherto, there is at least no humbug of obscurity about the
French; such ideas as they have, they distinctly express.
They despise the affectation of violating the rules of grammar.   The Revolution itself left this characteristic of the
French nation untouched ; and if they have given up Alsace
and Lorraine to Germany, they have at least preserved
themselves from the degradation of abandoning to it their
style of thought and of language.

Happily, it is the smaller pieces of Browning that are for
the most part defaced by the vices of style to which we have
referred.   If we would have the best display of his genius,
we must resort to his larger productions, where the extent
of the subject does not afford the same opportunity of indulging in wretched ingenuities.   In this essay we would chiefly
take up " The Ring and the Book."   We shall first consider
its literary merits ; but, secondly, and at much larger length,
animadvert upon the very peculiar theology of our illustrious
poet.

A word as to the subject of this poem.   The author finds
a book upon a stall in Florence, containing a famous trial
for murder in Rome, 22nd February, 1690.   A couple in
ordinary rank of life, Pietro and Violante, have no daughter.
To supply the defect, Violante carries off an infant, Pompilia, from a house of bad fame, and palms her upon Pietro
as being her own child.   Pompilia, grown up to be a girl
of great beauty, is fancied by Guido Franceschino, a noble-
man of reduced circumstances, who had in part taken orders
in the Church of Rome, but never prosecuted that career,
nor been successful in any other.   Her beauty was not the
only attraction for him, but a small fortune which her father

Pietro expected. He comes to a contract with the parents, marries Pompilia, and sets off along with them all to his country-seat in Arezzo, where her parents are subjected to every privation of aristocratic poverty and humiliation. Eventually they make off from this treatment to Rome. Meanwhile Guido acts with the greatest cruelty to Pompilia, who did not at first know, in her girlhood, what the nature of this marriage was, or what it would result in. By and by Violante exasperates him beyond measure, being led, partly from conscience, partly to revenge herself upon him, to make public the fact that Pompilia was not her child at all. Thus he finds that he has no right to the fortune, and that he is married to a prostitute's daughter. He becomes increasingly cruel to his wife. He falls into the diabolic device of trying to entrap her into some amour with Caponsacchi, a young priest. He was a generous young man, had been gay enough in his youth, and was employed by his ecclesiastical superiors in such service among fashion-able lady votaries of religion as he was admirably qualified for. Guido forges letters as from her to him, professing love, and letters much the same as from him to her—the object being to lead her to some reckless step which would entitle him to a divorce. Both the one and the other see through the snare, and are above any such intrigue. At the same time he is greatly impressed with her beauty and touched by the wretchedness of her condition: she, again, has confidence in his virtue. Erelong, feeling that she was soon to be a mother, she resolves, rather for the safety of her infant than herself, to endeavour to effect her escape to Rome. Failing in every other attempt to execute her purpose, whether prudently or not for either party, she gets Caponsacchi to carry her off. Both get near to Rome, but are overtaken by Guido. He has them tried for adultery. The court compromised matters. The young priest was sent to a neighbouring town, where he might live a life of retirement. She was sent to a convent in Rome. Afterwards, however, on the plea of bad health, she was erelong allowed to return to her parents' home, a villa near Rome, where her son is born. The jealousy of Guido being increased under these circumstances, he associated himself with four boors of Arezzo, came in the night, and murdered Pietro and Violante, inflicting such wounds also on Pompilia as proved fatal, though she survives to give her dying declarations. Then came on Guido's trial, in all the stages of it, forming the subject of the present poem. We have the fiscal's charge for the prosecution, the lawyers' speeches on both sides, Caponsacchi's evidence, Pompilia's declarations, Guido's defence, and the Pope's ultimate deliverance upon the cause, when appealed to him.

A poet of the last generation, had he chosen such a subject for poetry as this, would have woven it into a romantic tale, or thrown it into the form of a tragedy. But our author has adopted a plan which would have occurred to none but himself. He has transformed the trial bodily into blank verse, including the whole speeches, defences, declarations, and deliverances aforesaid ; giving us, besides, the judgment of "one half of Rome" when the case broke out ; then the judgment of "the other half of Rome;" and next the judgment of a third, or middle class in Rome! One patent disadvantage resulting from this treatment is the endless repetition into which he is led of the facts. No fewer than a dozen of times does he traverse the details. It shows a matchless hardihood of talent that any writer should venture to occupy four volumes of blank verse in ringing the changes upon this old criminal cause. But such is the variety of characters appearing upon the scene, such the novelty of the situations into which the parties are thrown, that, in the hands of this consummately shrewd observer of life and analyser of the human heart, they seem to suggest inexhaustible materials for meditation. The legal intricacies of the case are handled with the dexterity of the subtlest barrister ; we have a world of moral philosophy applied to the motives of the respective actors; and Dante himself could not have accumulated images more grotesque, sometimes terrific, than meet us in the description. We were not so much impressed with the splendid endowments of Browning on reading the first two volumes of the work, which are somewhat prosy, and somewhat withal in the eccentric and spasmodic strain; defaced too by obscurities, and the detestable jolting abruptness of old Young, of "Night Thoughts" memory. But when he comes to the speeches of the principal actors, his genius at last shines forth, works itself free from its obscurity, and in some measure from its eccentricities, and takes a majestic sweep through regions of the most impassioned eloquence.

The finest of all the poem, in our judgment, is the speech of Caponsacchi. He begins thus, adverting to the very different circumstances in which he was called to address the judges now than on the first occasion, when they had condemned him to retire into the neighbouring city.

> Answer you, sirs?   Do I understand aright?
> Have patience!   In this sudden smoke of hell
> So things disguise themselves, I cannot see
> My own hand held thus broad before my face,
> And know it again.   Answer you?   Then that means
> Tell over twice what I the first time told
> Six months ago ; 'twas here, I do believe,
> Fronting you same three in this very room,
> I stood and told you ; yet now no one laughs
> Who then . . . nay, dear my lords, but laugh you did,
> As good as laugh, what in a judge we style
> Laughter—no levity, nothing indecorous, lords !
> Only—I think I apprehend the mood—
> There was the blameless shrug, permissible smirk,
> The pen's pretence at play with the pursed mouth,
> The titter stifled in the hollow palm
> Which rubbed the eyebrow, and caressed the nose,
> When I first told my tale ; they meant, you know—
> "The sly one, all this we are bound to believe!
> Well, he can say no other than what he says ;
> We have been young, too—come, there's greater guilt !
> Let him but decently disembroil himself,
> Scramble from out the scrape, nor move the mud—

> We solid ones may risk a finger-stretch!"
> And now you sit as grave, stare as aghast
> As if I were a phantom—now 'tis—" Friend,
> Collect yourself"—no laughing matter more—
> " Counsel the court in this extremity.
> Tell us again." . . . For what?
> Pompilia is only dying while I speak!
> Why does the mirth hang fire, and miss the smile?
> My masters, there's an old Book you should con
> For strange adventures, applicable yet,
> 'Tis stuffed with.   Do you know that there was once
> This thing—a multitude of worthy folk
> Took recreation, watched a certain group
> Of soldiery intent upon a game—
> How first they wrangled, but soon fell to play,
> Threw dice—the best diversion in the world;
> A word in your ear—they are now casting lots,
> Ay, with that gesture quaint, and cry uncouth,
> For the coat of One murdered an hour ago!

This is spirited enough. But the marvel is that this strain lasts through 2,105 lines, in one sustained burst of passion, of tenderness, of withering and scathing moral indignation; being, in this respect, unparalleled perhaps in the literature of our country. Caponsacchi's description of Pompilia, the perfect image of sadness and purity, is unrivalled.   Take the lines where he speaks of them sitting together in the carriage by night, as they fled to Rome—the anomalousness, the strangeness, the questionableness of their position.

> For the first hour
> We both were silent in the night I know:
> Sometimes I did not see, nor understand.
> Blackness engulfed me—partial stupor, say—
> Then I would break way, breathe through the surprise,
> And be aware again, and see who sat
> In the dark vest, with the white face and hands.
> I said to myself, " I have caught it, I conceive
> The mind o' the mystery: 'tis the way they wake
> And wait—two martyrs somewhere in a tomb,
> Each by each as their blessing was to die;
> Some signal they are promised to expect,
> When to arise before the trumpet scares:

> So through the whole course of the world they wait
> The last day, but so fearless, and so safe !
> No otherwise in safety and not fear
> I lie, because she lies too by my side."
> You know this is not love, sirs ; it is faith,
> The feeling that there's God—He reigns and rules
> Out of this low world—that is all ; no harm.

It is thus that he resents the foul charge that Pompilia wrote the sinful letters to him:—

> Learned sir,
> I told you there's a picture in our church.
> Well, if a low-browed verger sidled up,
> Bringing me, like a blotch, on his prod's point
> A transfixed scorpion, let the reptile writhe,
> And then said, "See a thing that Raphael made,—
> This venom issued from Madonna's mouth."
> I should reply, " Rather the soul of you
> Has issued from your body, like from like,
> By way of the ordure-corner !"

Then we have Guido's address when his doom was announced to him. This affords Browning an opportunity to express the rage of a low-typed man driven back upon death by the world. This he has done with uncommon power. One had thought that Byron was good at a curse : our modern bard, through an inexhaustible fund of Dante imagery, and a certain vein of defiant satire he has, seems sometimes to outrival him, but he is ever and anon falling into some violation of taste, some wretched jolt in his sentences (for he cannot put them together grammatically), some spasmodic effort, none of which things Byron was ever tempted to commit through the superiority of his genius.

If intensity of passion, allied with imagination, constitute genius, none can question Robert Browning's claim to it. Many good advices have been given him. We believe that his faults are incorrigible. Although he has the poetic element in his constitution, perhaps his proper mission was rather that of a philosopher or moralist—a sort of Jeremy Taylor seven times heated, than that of a poet. It is amazing how some men who have splendid powers of this description — bordering upon the poetic — but who never were intended to be Singers, and want the perfect faculty of musical expression necessary for it, will persist by a prodigious effort against nature in producing works which one knows not well how to denominate. Any imaginative fervour they possess is like the fire in the interior of the earth, which will occasionally force its way with much smoke and noise out of the labouring mountain, amazing us by the streams of burning lava it sends forth ; how unlike, meanwhile, the electric flash of heaven, born of the cloud, flying fast and free through all nature, a spiritual element, and accompanied with voices of definite grandeur—Jove's own !

But it is not with Browning's poetry we have to deal in this essay, but with his theology.

Like many of our other poets and novelists, he is not satisfied with the end of pleasing the generation, but proposes a theology of his own, and aims, as he tells us himself, to "*save the soul.*" Nay, he seeks to carry out a favourite theory of some of our modern thinkers, that religion is to be advanced not so much by the old way of direct dogmatical statement, as by the fine arts.

> Art remains the one way possible
> Of speaking truth to mouths like mine at least.
> How look a brother in the face and say,
> " Thy right is wrong, eyes hast thou, yet are blind,
> Thine ears are stuffed and stopped, despite their length,
> And O the foolishness thou countest faith ! "
> Say this as silverly as tongue can troll,
> The anger of the man may be endured,
> The shrug, the disappointed eyes of him
> Are not so bad to bear—but here's the plague,
> That all this trouble comes of telling truth,
> Which truth, by when it reaches him, looks false,
> Seems to be just the thing it would supplant,
> Nor recognisable by whom it left,
> While falsehood would have done the work of truth.
> But art, wherein man nowise speaks to man,

> Only to mankind, art may tell a truth,
> Obliquely do the thing shall breed the thought,
> Nor wrong the thought, missing the mediate word.
> So may you paint your picture, twice show truth,
> Beyond mere imagery on the wall ;
> So note by note bring music from your mind,
> Deeper than ever the Andante dived ;
> So write a book shall mean beyond the facts,
> Suffice the eye, and save the soul beside.
> And save the soul !   If this intent save mine,
> If the rough ore be rounded to a ring," &c.

These lines contain the secret of that mission, inaugurated by Goethe, which our poets have undertaken to propound religion—a new religion I shall soon show it is—and to regenerate our souls.   It is a crusade upon which they have entered.   It may be advisable for a moment to consider the superior place he here gives to the fine arts as the way of conveying religious truth, and " saving the soul."   As he suggests, there are two ways of dealing with a man if you wish to correct his errors or lead him into saving truth. The one is that of dogmatic teaching or controversial statement.   In plain language you endeavour to show him he is in error, and in so many propositions you set before him the true doctrine.   Our poet doubts the efficacy of this mode, not only because it offends, but because any statement you make doctrinally becomes error in the very attempt to make it.   Now this essential defect in words as a vehicle of thought is a mere fiction of his own brain.   That, in the case supposed, your statement of the true doctrine should look false to the man, is likely enough, but that it should " not be recognisable by yourself who made it," is of course sheer nonsense.   Besides, the reason why it looks false to the man is prejudice on his part.   The fault is in him, not in words as a vehicle of communicating ideas or truths.   There can be no more perfect vehicle in this world of ours of communicating truths. than direct doctrinal state- ment.   Fiction, or art, may be a good way of " obliquely " winning a reception for the truth in unwilling ears, but the idea of its being a more correct medium of communication is one which will not bear to be examined. Indeed, it is ludicrous. Here, let us say, you are anxious to communicate a truth to a man. It seems that out of the whole vocabulary of the English language it is impossible for you to find " a mediate word that shall not wrong the thought," but your plan is to get up a fictitious story,

> And falsehood shall have done the work of truth (! !)

Before this essay is done we hope to show what some of the truths are which Robert Browning has sought to convey " obliquely " into the minds of his readers in fiction of his own. When we shall have stated them in plain words, they will be sufficiently intelligible, and perhaps too much so. They are so subtilely conveyed in his fiction that his readers are apt to imbibe them unconsciously. And this is the true reason why he and others have resorted to fictitious writing as the means of vending their theological crudities; the very opposite reason to that which the lines quoted above profess. Were they in plain words, and in perspicuous prose to state the doctrines which they propose, these are so untenable and so unsound that they would not obtain reception. As it is, they resort to the system of bringing them in obliquely by fictions which " breed " the heretical thought, and hide it at the same time.

"*And save the soul!*" There is a great deal more necessary to save a soul than most poets are aware of. Let us inquire what is Robert Browning's scheme of theology.

We shall first summarily state in our own words what we consider this scheme of his to be, after studying his writings. That God is love, is the grand truth with him; not in the sense, however, understood in the old theology still current among us, and embodied in the Scriptures; not in the sense that in His great love he provided His Son to be a redemption for us from the curse of the law by being made a curse for us, and delivering us from the wrath of God due for our

sins.   According to Browning, God is love in the very opposite sense—that there is no such thing as wrath in Him.
The idea that there is so is an entire mistake, and arises
from our considering that God has less love than ourselves.
We would not hesitate a moment to step forward and save
any man with an everlasting salvation, but unfortunately we
consider that God is unwilling to do so.   Hence the necessity of the truth being discovered to us that God is not
different from ourselves in this respect.   To discover this
was the great end of the incarnation of the Son of God.   He
was not sent for expiatory purposes at all, but to show that,
so far from entertaining any wrath, God sympathises with us
under our sufferings.   Christ is just the humanity that was
originally in the Godhead discovered to us; that is to say,
He has been incarnated to show us that God is no other than
man, or one like unto ourselves, in His mode of thinking
and feeling; that, to use a phrase of Browning's own, " He
is human at the red-ripe of the heart."

We shall now proceed to show, by reference to and quotations from Mr. Browning's poems, that these are his sentiments, and consider the positions and arguments by which
he seeks to establish them.

We might take up his lyric upon " Saul," already referred
to.   He represents David, when comforting the king, as
beginning last of all to have longings after his everlasting
salvation, but he feels as if he had no warrant to entertain
such a loving desire.

> I would give thee new life altogether, as good ages hence
> As this moment, had love but the warrant love's heart to dispense.

Then he corrects himself for thinking that God did not love
as much as he did; and, in taking a survey of the whole
round of creation, finds that " all's love."

> Yet with all this abounding experience, this Deity known,
> I shall dare to discover some province, some gift of my own !

*   *   *   *   *   *

> Behold! I could love if I durst,
> But I sink the pretension in fearing a man may o'ertake
> God's own speed in the one way of love!
> Do I find love so full in my nature, God's ultimate gift,
> That I doubt His own love can compete with it? here the parts shift?
> Here the creature surpass the Creator? the end what began?

Here David, being dressed up as a modern rationalist, is represented as coming from his own experience of love and desire to save Saul eternally, to conclude that God must have a like desire. In the same way, as the poem advances, he is led from the principles of reason, or from the feelings of his own humanity, to anticipate that God's Son will be sent into the world to save Saul and the rest of us by suffering and dying—suffering and dying, of course, merely to show His sympathy with us.

> It is by no breath,
> Turn of the eye, wave of the hand, that salvation joins issue with death.
> As Thy love is discovered almighty, almighty be proved
> Thy power that exists with and for it of being beloved.
> He who did most shall bear most, the strongest stand the most weak;
> 'Tis the weakness in strength that I cry for, my flesh that I seek
> In the Godhead! I seek and I find it. O Saul, it shall be
> A face like my face that receives thee—a man like to me.
> Thou shalt love and be loved for ever. A hand like this hand
> Shall throw open the gates of new life to thee! See the Christ stand!

We all know that David had express promises in the Bible that Christ was to come into the world in the fulness of times; but here, dressed up in the ridiculous garb of a modern rationalist, he is described as working out the conclusion by a natural syllogism that Christ must make His appearance. We all know, too, that the Christ whom David looked forward to with satisfaction was one who, being made a burnt-offering for his guilt, would atone for those innumerable sins which pressed him down to the ground. But the Christ whom Robert Browning here represents him as looking forward to is one who, by suffering and dying, should prove that God, whose " love is discovered to be almighty " in the natural world, has the power, in almighty measures, of making Himself beloved.

> 'Tis the weakness in strength that I cry for, my flesh that I seek
> In the Godhead !

According to the theology of the Scriptures hitherto current among us, it is "the Godhead in the flesh" appearing to make atonement for our sins that we seek and find comfort from ; but here it is "the flesh in the Godhead" which is represented as the comfortable and desired discovery. In other words, finding that, after all, God, essentially considered, is nowise different from humanity in His mode of loving and feeling. The humanity, even my flesh (according to this new theology), was in the Godhead before the incarnation of the Son of God took place ; indeed, the great end of that incarnation was just to discover to us that it was there. In the lines I have quoted, the great end of the coming of Christ is set forth to be this—to discover to us that God's love is almighty, and that He would be beloved. What we needed was evidence upon that point. The whole of salvation, according to Robert Browning, as could be proved from his writings *passim*, is merely a scheme to rectify our mistake regarding the character of God; a discovery to us of the fact, which we had lost sight of, that God loves us and sympathises with us.

The same doctrine is brought out in his memorable and much - admired Invocation to Lyrical Love in the " Ring and the Book," where I understand him to refer to the incarnation and humiliation of the Son of God in the lines which I have taken the liberty to underscore.

> O Lyric Love, half angel, and half bird,
> And all a wonder and a wild desire,
> Boldest of hearts that ever braved the sun,
> Took sanctuary within the holier blue,
> *And sang a kindred soul out to his face,*
> *Yet human at the red-ripe of the heart,*
> *When the first summons from the darkling earth*
> *Reached thee amid thy chambers, blanched their blue,*
> *And bared them of their glory—to drop down*
> *To toil for man—to suffer and to die.*

> This is the same voice ; can thy soul know change?
> Hail then, and hearken from the realms of help.
> Never may I commence my song, my due
> To God who best taught song by gift of thee,
> Except with bent head and beseeching hand—
> That still, despite the distance and the dark,
> What was again may be ; some interchange
> Of grace, some splendour once thy very thought,
> Some benediction anciently thy smile ;
> Never conclude but raising hand and head
> Thither where eyes that cannot reach still yearn
> For all hope, all sustainment, all reward,
> Their utmost up and on, so blessing back
> In those thy realms of help, that heaven thy home,
> Some whiteness which, I judge, thy face makes proud,
> Some wanness, where, I think, thy feet may fall.

Though Lyric Love is here a quality personified, it seems to be so interchangeably with Christ. After addressing it as Lyric Love, and describing it as the boldest of all spirits or inspirations, he represents it as taking " sanctuary within the holier blue " — the third heavens ; and as " singing a kindred soul out to His (God's) face, yet human at the red-ripe of the heart "—that is, evoking " a kindred soul," even our flesh—our humanity—from the depths of the Godhead, which, though Divine, is yet human at the core—evoking or singing it out " to His face," *i.e.*, into manifestation—at the time when, the Fall having taken place, it felt itself, in the Person of the Son of God, summoned amidst its chambers " to drop down to toil for man, to suffer and to die."

This is the interpretation we attach to the lines, though we have heard that some interpreters have actually considered them to be addressed to his wife ! If anything could serve to show how preposterous is the obscurity in which he involves himself occasionally, it is to find that intelligent readers should have supposed that these lines addressed to the Saviour (as we understand them) were an Invocation to Mrs. Browning ! If we are right, the lines bring out the idea elsewhere broached *passim* by our poet that the incarnation of the Son of God was simply the humanity that is essentially in the Godhead, " the soul kindred " with ourselves, sung out or evoked ; that is to say, it was meant to discover to us God's identity with us in His feelings and views. Some simple-minded evangelicals may be disposed to think that Robert Browning in all this is orthodox enough—that when he speaks of Christ, or the gospel, as having brought out the humanity that is in the Godhead, he merely refers to some one phase of redemption-work which has not been sufficiently dwelt upon. But this theory of his plucks up by the roots the whole scheme of redemption commonly received among us. We do not hesitate to say that the Christ whom he advocates is one of the Antichrists which are now in the world. Instead of being the Son of God made flesh in order to be a sin-offering to deliver us from the wrath to come, He is the Son of God made flesh to discover to us the humanity which was essentially in the Godhead from the beginning—or to show us that God "is human at the red-ripe of the heart." And if Mr. Browning were pressed to tell us what rendered it so necessary that this discovery should be made to us, he would no doubt confess what he is scarcely bold enough to speak out often openly, that it was our mistaken idea of there being such a thing with God as wrath at all, our delusion regarding everlasting punishments, and the necessity of an expiation.

Since, according to the imaginative theologians of our day, the great end of the Incarnation was such as we have described —to discover to us the humanity that is in the Godhead (that God, in short, is one like unto ourselves)—it is only to be thought that they should hold at the same time that humanity, in its natural sentiments, independently of revelation, is the standard or test to go by. If God has incarnated His Son for no other reason than to show that He is " human at the red-ripe of the heart "—that the sentiments of humanity are not different from His own—then, upon the whole, we are not likely to go very far wrong in following the sentiments of humanity. One object with which the " Ring and the Book " is written is to show that these are a surer standard than the Bible itself. There are three illustrious examples set before us in the poem, Pompilia, Caponsacchi, and the Pope, as he decided the present case ; and it will be found that the main thing in them all entitling them to our admiration is their following the dictates of nature and humanity in preference to any written rule, God's Word not excepted.

That Pompilia, being the wife of Guido, should fly to Rome with a young priest, was, in one respect, to break the ordinance of God ; but she is to be commended for following the dictates of nature. The poet makes a good deal more of this, to serve his purpose, than needs be. Alluding to the circumstances in which she was then placed, as about to be a mother, he says :—

> How the fine ear felt full the first low word,
> Value life, and preserve life for my sake !
> Thou didst . . . how shall I say? receive so long
> The standing ordinance of God on earth.
> What wonder if the novel claim that clashed
> With old requirement, seemed to supersede
> Too much the customary law ? But, brave,
> Thou at the first prompting of what I call God,
> And fools call Nature, didst hear, comprehend,
> Accept the obligation laid on thee,
> Mother elect, to save the unborn child.

That Caponsacchi, being a priest, should have accompanied the young wife of another man to Rome, was contrary to conventional and ecclesiastical rules, and he too is bold enough to follow the sentiments or impulse of his own heart. Nothing is said of his following the rule of God's Word, although Mr. Browning must have known well enough that the Word of God would have suggested his doing the lady this good turn ; but it is not his way or object to praise God's Word, but rather to exalt another standard. He thus enthusiastically describes the peerless pair as they met at the window to plan their Rome-going,

influenced by what he calls " a new attribute," and Christ
Himself.

> Thus stood the wife and priest—a spectacle
> I doubt not to unseen assemblage there.
> No lamp will mark that window for a shrine,
> No tablet signalise the terrace, teach
> New generations, which succeed the old,
> The pavement of the street as holy ground ;
> No bard describe in verse how Christ prevailed,
> And Satan fell like lightning.
>
> *   *   *   *
>
> Here the blot is blanched
> By God's gift of a purity of soul
> That will not take pollution, ermine-like,
> Armed from dishonour by its own soft snow.
> Such was the gift of God, who showed for once
> How he would have the world go white ; it seems
> As a new attribute were born of each,
> Champion of truth, the priest and wife I praise.

Next, that the Pope should sanction these doings of
Pompilia, who disobeyed the advice of his clerical subor-
dinates, and of Caponsacchi, who had acted the gallant
rather than the priest ; and that he should condemn Guido
himself, an ecclesiastic who had appealed to his sacred
tribunal, was scarcely to have been expected. But he, too,
is represented as holding by the dictates of his inner humanity, as superior not only to tradition, but the Bible.

It is here that Browning's new theology becomes apparent
enough. The Pope thinks he finds that in deciding this case
he has to walk not only without the guidance, but against
the deliverances of the Divine Record; and our bard, dressing
him up in the garb of the rationalist, describes him as
rejecting the written revelation and following the higher
standard.

> What if thyself adventure ? Leave pavement, and mount roof,
> Look round thee for the light of the upper sky,
> The fire which lit thy fire which finds default
> In Guido Franceschini to his cost.

What if above in the domain of light,
Thou miss the accustomed signs, remark eclipse?
Shalt thou still gaze on ground, nor lift a lid
Steady in thy superb prerogative,
Thy inch of inkling, nor once face the doubt,
I' the sphere above thee, darkness to be felt.

*   *   *   *

Yet my poor spark had for its source the sun,
Thither I send the great looks which compel
Light from its fount.

*   *   *   *

As I know,
I speak ;—what should I know, then, and how speak,
Were there a wild mistake of eye or brain
In the recorded governance above?
If my own breath, only, blow coal alight,
I called celestial, and the morning star,
.   .   .   .   .   .   Shall I lack courage ?

*   *   *   *

There is besides the works, a Tale of thee
In the world's mouth, which I find credible,
I love it with my heart ; unsatisfied,
I try it with my reason, nor discept
From any point I probe, and pronounce sound.

Indeed, if man's own mind be what he proceeds to decribe, "a convex mirror, wherein are gathered all the scattered points picked out of the immensity of the sky, to reunite there," he could not be very far wrong in holding it to be the place of final appeal. Man, in short, he describes as representing God on earth.

This is the theology current with our rationalistic poets and moralists of the day. While they hold on the one hand that there is humanity in the Godhead (that God is " human at the red-ripe of the heart "), they hold on the other hand that there is what may be called the Godhead in humanity ; they find, in other words, that the sentiments and mind of the Godhead are sufficiently represented in man's own heart. This two-sided theory of theirs is amazingly convenient.

By their doctrine of the humanity in the Godhead, they hope to convince us that there is nothing like penal wrath with God—nothing of that inflexible justice which requires an atonement for our sins—nothing of those mysterious and unhumanly sentiments which evangelical divines have ascribed to Him. When, in answer to this, we refer them to the Bible as affirming these tenets, they bring forward their other doctrine of the Godhead in humanity, that man's own heart or mind is the highest declaration of God. As for the Bible, it is a " Tale in the world's mouth," which they condescend to believe to be credible, but which they receive only so far as their own reason pronounces it to be sound. As to the human mind, it is a " convex mirror," &c.

To such a pitch does Robert Browning carry his faith in the findings of nature, that he bases his acceptance of Christianity altogether upon its ascertained harmony with these findings. He grants that Christianity was at first attested by miracles and apostolic testimony, but he maintains that these have no place as proofs of the truth of Christianity to us now. We shall proceed to substantiate this charge against him, that it may be seen what kind of theology it is which is being now propagated throughout the land by our illustrious poets.

His peculiar sentiments upon this point are brought out fully in his poem entitled " A Death in the Desert." In this poem, John the Evangelist is supposed to be dying in a cave, with Pamphylax the Antiochene, Xanthus, &c., as his attendants. He describes in his last words to his disciples how, in the first instance, he produced converts by historic testimony, witnessing what he saw and heard of Christ both by word and writing, also by miracles. But suddenly beginning, under Robert Browning's management, to speak as a rationalist, he intimates a time coming when this process of making converts would become obsolete, for men would say, " Was John at all ? Assure us of this, ere we ask what he might see."

> I cried once, " That ye may believe in Christ,
> Behold the blind man shall receive his sight."
>
> *   *   *   *
>
> Urgest thou, for I am shrewd,
> And smile at stories how John's word would cure—
> Repeat the miracle, and take my faith ?

The dying Evangelist (that is, Browning's rationalist) goes on to canvass the question how then Christianity would obtain credence in the latter days, since neither miracles nor apostolic testimony would be available as proofs ? The answer is found in this, that we moderns in the progress of the human mind have become able to know that God is love, love infinite as well as power infinite, and therefore there is no difficulty in apprehending Christ, whom the gospel reveals, to be the true Son and manifestation of God. All life—the whole world as it lies patent to our observation—is full of examples of love or goodness exposed to suffering, crucified in short (witness Pompilia and Caponsacchi), and rising out from the conflict by a species of resurrection, triumphant ? What is this but Christ's life and resurrection illustrated ? As we grow more acquainted with it therefore (which is the case as society advances), we are no more as the little children of the Primitive Church, who needed miracles and historic testimony to prove to them that Christ was the Son of God, but are able to apprehend the truth of Christianity without anything of this kind.

John himself, that is, Robert Browning's John, gives us the following account of his extraordinary experiences as he grew older, and, we must suppose, wiser :—

> To me that story, ay, that life and death
> Of which I wrote "it was "— to me, it is—
> Is here and now : I apprehend nought else.
> Is not his love at issue still with sin,
> Closed with and cast and conquered, crucified,
> Visibly, when a wrong is done on earth ?
> Love, wrong, and pain, what see I else around ?
> Yea, and the resurrection and uprise

> To the right hand of the throne—what is it beside,
> When such truth, breaking bounds, o'erflows my soul,
> And, as I saw the sin and death, even so,
> See I the need yet transiency of both,
> The good and glory consummated thence.

He tells Pamphylax and Xanthus, however, that *they* cannot yet prove the truth of Christianity in this advanced way, but must be content to receive it upon the baby ground of miracles and historic testimony.

> But ye, the children, his beloved ones too,
>
>   *   *   *   *
>
> Ye needs must apprehend what truth
> I see, reduced to plain historic fact ;
> Then stand before that fact, that life and death,
> Stay there at gaze, till it dispart, dispread,
> As though a star should open out on all sides,
> And grow the world on you, as it is my world.

That is, the time would come when, living longer, they would come to see, as he had done, Christ to be only what is more widely illustrated in the way already mentioned throughout all the world we live in, which is just a broader display of Christ in His death and resurrection.

The reader may thus learn somewhat more of Robert Browning's theology.

It consists of three positions.

1. He grants the truth of the miracles that were wrought to attest Christianity, and of the apostolic testimony that was borne to it. His judgment is that these were essentially necessary in the first century.

2. He maintains that a miracle is only a proof when actually wrought before one's eye, so that the miracles cannot be a proof of the truth of Christianity to us now. Neither can historic testimony prove Christianity, for " we are shrewd, and ask, ' Was John at all ? '"

3. He holds that we can now establish the truths of Christianity without either miracles or historic testimony. In the progress of the world's history we have had ampler

opportunity of discovering that the God who governs it is love, at issue with sin, suffering opposition from it, and triumphing eventually over it. The consequence is that the story of the cross is intuitively recognised by us to be true, because it tallies with our findings in the world around us. The manifestation which the gospel makes to us of God tallies with the manifestation of Him which we have in the world around us, and must therefore be true.

We shall proceed to consider these positions.

We are glad to find that our poet grants the truth of the miracles and historic testimony in favour of Christianity. But one would wish to know how, consistently with his second position, he arrived at this conclusion. He there maintains that in the nineteenth century miracles can never be accepted as true, since a miracle to be satisfactory must be actually wrought before our eye; also he denies that we can ascertain the truth of the historic testimony alleged in behalf of Christianity, or even know whether such men as the apostles ever existed. How then did Mr. Browning, who happens to live in the nineteenth century, find out that miracles were really wrought at the beginning of the Christian era? and that sufficient historic testimony was afforded to men then of the truth of the gospel? His two first positions upon the face of them are not consistent. He may hold either the one or the other of them, but it is impossible that he should hold them both. If he holds that Christianity was attested at the beginning by miracles from heaven and by apostolic testimony, and even enlarges, as he does in many parts of his poem, upon the necessity there was for this, then of course he overthrows his second position, which is that we now-a-days cannot tell whether the miracles were true or the historic testimony good. In order to escape the horns of this dilemma, it will not do for him to say that he first establishes the claims of Christianity to reception in the rationalistic way he proposes, and then reaches the belief that the miracles alleged in its favour were actually wrought, and that the historic testimony alleged for it was good and sufficient. For, supposing him for a moment to have proved the truth of Christianity in the way he mentions, this would be so far from leading us to believe that miracles were ever wrought at first in support of it, that it would lead us to believe the very reverse. The very fact of our having reached the proof of the truth of Christianity without needing signs or wonders to assist us, would lead us rather to infer that so might others who went before us. Mr. Browning foresaw well enough the pressure of this difficulty in his argument, and tries to make out the point that, though we in these days can prove the truth of Christianity by the rationalistic method, or simply by observational knowledge of the world around us, the men of the first century could not, and needed miracles and historic testimony. According to him, we have the advantage of them here.

How—in what sense?

> Whether a change were wrought i' the shows of the world,
> Whether the change came from our minds, which see
> Of the shows of the world so much as, and no more,
> Than God wills for His purpose. I know not,
> Such was the effect.
> So faith grew, making void more miracles,
> Because too much : they would compel, not help ;
> I say the acknowledgment of God in Christ,
> Accepted by thy reason, solves for thee
> All questions in the earth and out of it,
> And has so far advanced thee to be wise.

Here two reasons are given why a revelation professing to come from heaven can be proved true or false by us now, though it could not by men formerly, without miracles needed, and simply by our judgment accepting Christ as being the true manifestation of God. The first is that in these latter days "a change has been wrought in the shows of the world," that is, in the phenomena it presents to our view. What does he allude to? He cannot logically refer to any change Christianity has itself impressed upon the world, proving its truth by its fruits; for to adopt this line of argument were to depart from his famous position, which is to prove Christianity not from the supernatural effects wrought by it or by anything supernatural at all, but by reason. Besides, as any extraordinary effects produced by Christianity in the world have been produced hitherto by those who have held by the whole of the Scriptures, such a line of argument would prove too much for our friend, who " discepts " from a large part of the doctrines contained in our Bible, which have produced these fruits. But indeed every reader of Browning knows that he undertakes to prove the truth of Christianity solely and entirely by the manifestations of God's being love, which we find so abundantly in the world around us, and which are enough to convince us that the manifestation of God which we have in Christ is true. What new, and peculiar, and changed " shows of the world " they are which he refers to, as now seen by us moderns, affording more satisfactory manifestations of the truth that God is love, who can say, and the likelihood is Mr. Browning could not tell. He only ventures to speak of them in the way of conjecture. The second advantage which we moderns may possess in ascertaining the truth of Christianity, is, according to him, that a change has been wrought in our minds, which see the phenomena of the world around us better than our predecessors did; for, he adds, " men see so much of the shows of the world and no more than God wills for His purpose." In short, he conjectures that God in these latter days may have willed to give us a faculty of more clearly discerning the phenomena of the world around us. This of course is a supernatural faculty. We are glad to see a rationalist granting the supernatural at all in these days. One would say that, if it comes to the supernatural being necessary, the best way would have been for God "to have willed that we should see" the truth of Christianity at once and directly; but Mr.

8

Browning prefers the roundabout way, that God should first "will us to see more of the shows of the world around us," and then by means of this supernatural illumination as to the phenomena around us, enable us to prove the truth of Christianity without anything supernatural being required.

It must ever remain a secret, then, how Mr. Browning, holding as he did his second position, should have come to believe in his first. And we now go on to observe that it is difficult to see how, holding the first, he should have adopted his second. If the miracles wrought by Christ and His apostles were sufficient to establish the truth of Christianity at first, why not to establish the truth of it to us? If the historic testimony in favour of Christianity was conclusive for the men to whom it was first proposed, why not with us? Does he really attach any force to the idea that a miracle, in order to its being satisfactory, must be wrought before our eyes? Is he not aware that, were miracles repeated to every generation, they would cease to be miracles, and no longer serve the purpose for which they were intended? The time for doctrines to be established as doctrines from heaven is surely when they are first promulgated; and if supernatural fire burned up to heaven from Mount Sinai, for example, when the Law was given to the Jews, was it not enough that a whole nation who witnessed the spectacle should hand down the record of it, or must the mountain be kept blazing down throughout the ages, becoming nothing more than another Vesuvius? Does Robert Browning think that no amount of historic testimony to the truth of the facts and miracles of Christianity, handed down to us, could be satisfactory proof to the end of the world of their having taken place? Even David Hume took up no position so preposterous as this. He maintained that no amount of testimony could prove a miracle, and this because we must rather disbelieve any amount of human testimony than credit such an extraordinary event. But Robert Browning grants the miracle. He believes that all the signs and wonders took place at the commencement of Christianity ; he swallows the miracle without difficulty, but he cannot see how any amount of testimony should satisfactorily hand it down when it has taken place! Hume considered no amount of testimony sufficient to prove that a miracle could take place; Browning considers no amount of testimony sufficient satisfactorily to hand down the record of a miracle which has really taken place. The former position has some show of reason in it, the latter is preposterous. If he once grant, as he does, that miracles took place at the beginning of the Christian era, common sense dictates that the very stupendousness of such events must have created a sensation producing such a body of evidence and such an abundant record as would constitute a foundation for the belief of all future ages. The same remarks apply to the historic evidence in favour of Christianity. In his second position he maintains that it must go for nothing as a proof with us now, and accordingly considers himself forced to have recourse to his novel rationalistic mode of proof. Is it his opinion that nothing which happened 1800 years ago can be proved to us by historic evidence? Or is it his opinion that when a miracle has taken place it is impossible to record it ? and, again, that if a man be an apostle, it is impossible ever to establish by historic evidence that he had an existence? He ought to know by this time of day that the historic evidence we have for the miracles and facts of Christianity is a hundredfold stronger than we have for the truth of anything else. But what may well amaze us in Mr. Browning is, not so much his rejecting what is sufficient and satisfactory, as the shallowness of the credulity with which he accepts the insufficient and unsatisfactory. We saw already that he demurred to words as a sufficient vehicle of thought, preferring fiction upon the whole ; and now he demurs to receiving historic testimony as a proof of Christianity, and must prove it by his famous third position, which is a curiosity in its way. Let us proceed to consider it.

He thinks then, that, at this advanced stage of time, by observing the phenomena and events of the world around us, we can obtain such discoveries of God being love, and of His love being at issue with sin and suffering, and finally triumphing over them, as enable us (without any miracles or historic testimony being needed) to recognise the God of the gospel to be none other than the God working all round us, and thus to prove the truth of Christianity.

Now, at the very outset, we defy Mr. Browning to prove the historic truth of Christianity, or of any such person as the Lord Jesus Christ having actually appeared in our world, by these mere analogical findings of his in the world around us.

Let it be remembered that in his second position he has scouted the idea of the facts of Christianity being proved by historic testimony at this distant date; and he is, therefore, bound to establish them by this new analogical argument of his. It will not do for him merely to show that the Christ of the Gospels is just such a manifestation of God's love as tallies with what the world's phenomena exhibit. May not Christ have been a mere fiction or portraiture of some devout imagination? May not some speculative writers, availing themselves of those very findings regarding God in the natural world which Mr. Browning speaks of, have drawn this Christ from the fancy? Mr. Browning himself has felt this weak point in his argument, and the indignation with which he speaks of any man who would be sceptic enough to make the supposition we have now made, shows how much he feels the force of it. He maintains that this is nothing less than the unpardonable sin—the sin that is unto death.

> When, beholding that love everywhere,
> He reasons, "Since such love is everywhere,
> And since ourselves make the love, and would be loved,
> We ourselves make the love, and Christ was not,"
> How shall ye help this man who knows himself
> That he must love, and would be loved again,

> Yet owning his own love that proveth Christ,
> Rejecteth Christ through very need of Him?
> The lamp o'erswims with oil—that man dies!"

Good; but it is impossible, nevertheless, for our author to meet or rebut the supposition which we have already stated, and which he so much reprobates. It is vain for him to think that he has proved the historical existence of Christ by merely finding that the Christ described in the Gospels answers to certain manifestations of God he thinks he finds in the world around him. There is no way of proving the historical existence of any one except by historic testimony. If you have first proved, by sufficient historical testimony, that Christ appeared in our earth and did the things we read of, it may be competent enough, perhaps, as a side confirmation of our faith, to show that the manifestation of God, made by and in Him, tallies with that which we have of God in the world around us; but when Mr. Browning would endeavour to prove a historical Christ exclusively from these analogical findings, he makes an attempt both hopeless and absurd. He is led to make the attempt from a desire to humour the infidelity of the age, which will not submit to the ordinary probations of Christianity. But God frowns upon all this, and he must just be humble enough to accept the testimony of the Almighty.

What is the argument of Mr. Browning, we ask again? It is of this sort, if we understand it. He finds in the Gospel story that God is said to have sent His Son into the world in our nature, that He wrought works of beneficence and mercy, that He combated with sin, suffered, died, and rose again. His position is—I have no need of the truth of all this being proved to me by historic testimony or miracles. To me it bears intuitive evidence of being true; or, rather, is proved true by my observations of the world on every side of me, which is full of evidences that God is love, and that He is at issue with sin in the very way this Gospel represents Him. Now to this it is enough to reply that such a line of argument can never prove that the things represented in the Gospel actually took place. Just to give an illustration in point. We shall say that the fact to be proved is that A came forward in behalf of a man who was beset by some twenty or thirty assailants at once, and saved his life at the risk of his own. The fact is called in question. Some propose to produce the testimony of eye-witnesses. But here comes forward one who says, "There is no necessity for testimony on the matter; I can prove the fact without testimony of any description, and this from having had reason to know so much of A otherwise—his muscular strength, and generosity of character, always at issue with wrong wherever it exists, so that this is the very thing he would have done." What would be said to this wiseacre? Would he not be told that what was wanted was not to know whether A *would* have done it, but whether he did it?

Thus Mr. Browning can never by this new and boasted test of his prove the historical truth of Christianity.

Besides, the Christianity which he professes to be able to prove true, is not that Christianity which we profess in evangelical Christendom, and which is contained in our Scriptures.

He starts by finding "a tale of Christ in the world's mouth," that is, by finding Christianity professed in the world, and proceeds to prove whether it be true or not by his test. But the question is, what is "this tale of Christ in the world's mouth," this professed Christianity, which he is about to proceed to test? Is it that which is contained in our Scriptures, received in their entirety? Is it the story that proclaims Jesus Christ sent to be a redemption for us from the eternal wrath to come by being made a curse for us? Not so. He goes to the Scriptures indeed, but (as he has told us already) he claims a right to "discept" from what his reason disapproves in them. In other words he concocts out of the Scriptures his own scheme of Christianity, which is that the Son of God was sent into the world simply to discover to us the humanity that is essentially in the Godhead—that God is " human at the red-ripe of the heart "—and that all such unhuman sentiments as judicial wrath, inflexible justice, and vindicating of the broken law by satisfaction or atonement rendered for sin, are quite alien from him. And then he proceeds to put this Christianity of his own to the test of his third position. No wonder that he seems to find the truth of it in what he observes of God by his own reason in the world around him, for the Christianity he is testing has first been moulded by his own reason, guided by these very observations. He first starts by accepting nothing as Christianity but what tallies with his own rationalistic observation of things in the world, and then exclaims in triumph that he needs no miracles nor historic testimony to prove the truth of Christianity, seeing that it tallies perfectly with his observation of things in the world ! We dare swear it does.

It thus turns out that Mr. Browning takes his own findings in the department of natural religion — what he has observed of God from reason exercised upon the phenomena without—as the standard by which to judge whether any revelation professing to come from God is to be received, or how much of it is to be received.

How unsafe and absurd a method is this !

Limited in our faculties at best, most of all unable to judge of God, His perfections and administration, and blinded by sin, what trust is to be placed in our findings regarding Him from a survey of the world we live in ? We see what these findings have amounted to in any land where the Bible has not come. They are grossly erroneous, and if the various lands, our own among the rest, when Christianity was first subjected to their faith, had proceeded to adopt our sentimental friend's rule, and rejected whatever was contrary to their own findings and conclusions drawn from the world around them, they would all have been idolaters to this day. It would be a very extraordinary thing if human reason, after having made such a blundering commencement, and having been thus found to be indebted to the Bible for its deliverance from the most hideous mistakes, should presume to set up its judgment above the Bible in other and far higher and profounder points. If it erred in its findings even with regard to the nature of God altogether, His unity, His majesty, His immateriality (the Bible requiring to set it right there), can there be an absurder arrogation than that it should set itself up in opposition to the teachings of the same Book upon the very highest points of the Divine administration? Of course Mr. Browning would protest against the idea of opposing his conclusions to the deliverances of what was proved to be a Divine revelation, and will remind us that the very question to be settled at present is—what is to be considered as proved really to be a Divine revelation. Exactly; but if he make his reason the test of what is to be received as a Divine revelation—refusing to receive that as a Divine revelation which his own reason "discepts" from, or denying certain parts of our Bible, for example, simply because his own reason discepts—then he has set up his reason as higher than God Himself.

He probably thinks that he cannot be wrong in going to God's own world in order to find what God is, and that he can thus ascertain what is to be received or rejected in the revelation contained in our Scriptures. Now, no doubt the scheme of redemption, which he would thus proceed to sit in judgment upon, proceeds from the same God whose works are before our eyes; but the work of redemption must, of course, be entirely different in its nature from God's other works. Let us suppose that Mr. Browning has, by a series of the most profound investigations, discovered what is that manifestation of God which the world round us makes. This will not necessarily enable him to pronounce judgment upon another manifestation which God has made of Himself to man now that he is a sinner; nor will the manifestation God has made of Himself to fallen men in His common providence (which is a mere dispensation of forbearance and preparation) enable him to sit in judgment upon a revelation which sets forth God's final dealings with fallen men. In the world around us we have a display of His infinite power, but we have not a display of the infinity of His justice, because His justice has not yet received its full manifestation. What if, in the scheme of redemption set forth in the Scriptures we find that it, like all God's other perfections, is infinite, and demands that an awful satisfaction should be forthcoming to the violated law in the extension of mercy—are we to reject the Scriptures which declare this because we find nothing like this manifestation of God in the world around us? These remarks may show that Mr. Browning has vastly over-estimated not only the capacity of human reason, but the materials for forming a judgment which the theatre of this world presents.

Last of all, when we come to examine what are the findings and conclusions he has reached with regard to the display God has made of Himself in the world before our eyes, they turn out to be most superficial and shallow. He seems to have found nothing, in fact, but that God is love. This is much too simple a finding upon the face of it to be true. The world is full also of very awful proofs of God's wrath against sin. Take the universal prevalence of death—its prevalence even over such as Pompilia, who, although she had never fallen by the hands of Guido, must have been subjected to this awful visitation in which God setteth our secret sins in the light of His countenance. When we think that the whole human family in its successive generations has been swept into the tomb, this is surely a finding that should lead us to say, " Who knoweth the power of thine anger?" Had Mr. Browning, instead of following his one-sided and shallow philosophy, kept this finding in view, he would have applied his test somewhat differently. If, again, perceiving from his observation of this world's phenomena that all God's other perfections which met his eye were infinite, he had come to the analogical finding that God's justice also

must be infinite, he might have been so far on his way
to qualify him for judging of the revelation he was about to
test.   Bearing as this revelation must needs do upon the
mode in which the Judge of the universe has proposed to
save and redeem sinners, plainly one attribute of God concerned there was His justice ; and had he been led by the
analogy already referred to to conclude that the mode of
procedure would be consistent with infinite justice, and
therefore abundantly formidable, he would have been nearer
the mark in this presumptuous and hazardous line of testing
Divine revelation.   But it is a remarkable fact that while our
sentimental theologians and rationalists are always talking
of infinite power, and infinite love, and infinite wisdom, they
never breathe a syllable of infinite justice, in the sense of
God's determination not to clear the guilty but vindicate
His broken law being inflexible ; nor do they once speak of
His infinite holiness, in the sense of His detestation of sin
being such as to lead Him to visit it with marks of His
indignation inconceivable by us.   By these remarks we must
not be understood to blame Mr. Browning for his erroneous
findings from the works of God.   The truth is that it is a
matter too high either for him or any other to think to test
Christianity by findings from that quarter.   If the argument
had been one affecting the administrations of a creature like
ourselves, the case would have been different ; but to endeavour to judge beforehand as to what will be or ought to be
the administrations of God, or even to endeavour from one
of His administrations given us to judge what may or ought
to be His administration in another department, is too high
a thing for us.   " Who can by searching find out God ? "

We   have   thus   terminated   our   examination   of   Mr.
Browning's theology.   One object we have had in view is
to convince those of our readers who are themselves of
evangelical sentiments that it is most dangerous, and wholly
subversive of the Scriptures.   There is so much of the
insidious in it, that they are apt to be carried away by the

charitable belief that after all there is nothing essentially bad in it, and no need to sound the trumpet of alarm against this theology which is now poured forth in the land, in prose and verse, by laymen and clergymen.

First, when he talks of proving the truth of Christianity exclusively by the grand manifestation it makes of God's being love, they smile at this as being no more than an exaggerated importance attached to one of the internal evidences of the truth of the gospel — such an amiable exaggeration, in short, as may be forgiven a poet. But have they understood what Mr. Browning means by the manifestation which the gospel makes of God's being love ? He does not refer at all to the manifestation He made of it in sending His only begotten Son to be an atonement for our sins, and deliver us from eternal wrath by being made a curse for us. He understands the reverse. He refers to the discovery which the gospel has made to us of God's being only love, with no such thing in Him as a judicial wrath which requires propitiation. His scheme, as we have shown and demonstrated, is that God's Son was sent into the world solely to discover to us what we are ignorant of, and our ignorance of which leads us to speak of atonement or satisfaction for sin ; that God is love—that He is " human at the red-ripe of the heart "—having no such unhumanly sentiments as we Evangelicals or Calvinists have supposed. The Son of God was made flesh, and became one like unto ourselves, simply to discover to us this humanity which from the beginning and essentially was in the Godhead. Accordingly, while we are accustomed to speak of "*God in the flesh*," this school speak of "*the flesh in God*." For their theology is that the Son of God was made flesh to discover to us this flesh or humanity which was in the Godhead—in other words, to discover to us that God is one like unto ourselves in His sentiments and judgments of things. This is one of the Antichrists abroad in the land, and Mr. Browning is its poetical apostle.

Secondly, when he maintains that Christianity cannot be proved to us now by miracles or historic testimony, our evangelical friends grant that this is outrageous enough, but remind us that after all he considers Christianity may be proved true in another way of his own ; and, if it be proved at all, what great matter is it ? Besides, they say, is it not well that he grants Christianity to have been proved true at the first by miracles and apostolic testimony ? But do they understand what Christianity it is which Mr. Browning grants to be proved true ? It is not that which is contained in our Scriptures. We have shown that he first claims the right to cut out from the Scriptures what his own reason discepts from, the result of which is to leave that peculiar Christianity of his own, already described, and it is this he professes to establish. But, indeed, though all this had not been true, is it any apology for his attempting to throw down the main pillars of the Christian evidences, miracles and historic testimony, that he should profess to mount to a conclusion in favour of the truth of Christianity by a few rotten planks of his own ?

We believe Mr. Browning to be one of our most illustrious poets, and one of our shallowest theologians. His qualifications as a poet are undeniable. He excels in passionate dialogue. In grim humour, in a certain hyena laugh of withering scorn, he has no rival; his imagery is original, sometimes terrible ; but no sooner does he begin to sing his rationalistic sermons, than he is weak beyond belief.

When he enters upon the regions of theology he loses himself immediately, as might be expected of one who has abandoned the absolute guidance of God's Word. He becomes confused and feeble, as always happens with those who have assumed a calling that does not belong to them. But, besides this, he leads us to wonder at what university he has learned the science of logic. He has written his poems, as he tells us, with the intention of " saving the soul." But if we have carried the convictions of our readers

along with us, they will be of the opinion that he has taken
the most effectual way of defeating his purpose by withdraw-
ing it from the blessed rock of revealed truth to the quick-
sands of speculation.   One thing we have reason to be
thankful for.   Such is the obscurity of his style, that we
do not believe half of his admirers have understood the
errors he vends.   There are some men, such as David
Hume, who have unfortunately made even their Atheism
attractive by an admirable perspicuity.   Fortunately Mr.
Browning has made his Christianity unpopular by a composition which needs hard study to be intelligible.

III.

ALFRED TENNYSON.

IN a previous essay we have touched upon the new religion current amongst us, characterised by the earnestness of scepticism, and resulting in the adoption of a Christianity not very much better than natural religion. Without inquiring at present into its mischievous effects, it must be granted that it has proved in one sense a godsend to the poets of this generation. Anything that begets earnestness is of the nature of a stock-in-trade to poets. The help in this way was the more seasonable, as other generators of steam had been used up. Several poets in the beginning of the century had exemplified all that can be done in creating poetry out of the passions of the human heart, idolatrously going forth with the imagination upon nature and the world. The due demand had been made upon the chivalry of the middle ages. The classical mythology and model had been made amply available. But the new turn of religious thought has engendered an earnestness of quite a novel description. Our men of imagination, having lifted the landmarks of revelation, and refused to accept the dogmas of the Bible, find themselves in contact with the mysteries of the universe, and burdened with the high and sacred mission of solving the riddle of life which of course perplexes them on every side. Samuel Johnson doubted whether the holy themes of religion were suitable for poetry. He considered that there was a restraint laid upon the imagination by the very sacredness of the subjects. But of course the great lexicographer, whose own character was marked by an incorruptible integrity, took for granted that the poet would start with a firm belief in the dogmas of revelation, and a firm determination to be circumscribed by them. This was a very groundless supposition as regards our new school of poets. Religion has become with them a region of clouds, and sublime mystery, and interesting uncertainty. His remark might apply to such as Cowper, who strung his harp to the acknowledged verities of the gospel; but our foolhardy bards who "ring in the Christ that is to come," are animated with the fervour of new apostles, bring with them the burden of another revelation which they have found within themselves, and are inspired by the agonies of an intense scepticism.

The remarks now made apply to Robert Browning and to Tennyson, though in a somewhat different degree. The former being a man of more robust understanding, comes forward to advocate the new Christianity with all the ardour of a poetical polemic. He casts his coat, and fights for it in good earnest. The latter, though his whole works are pervaded by its spirit, only occasionally introduces it in a direct form. He has said of himself :—

> And my Melpomene replies,
>   A touch of shame upon her cheek,
>   "I am not worthy even to speak
> Of thy prevailing mysteries ;
> For I am but an earthly muse,
>   And owning but a little art,
>   To lull with song an aching heart,
> And render human love his dues."

Still it cannot be denied that his poems are written under the afflatus of the new religion, and that much of the charm they have for the present generation lies in the singular mixture they present of love and sentimentality on the one hand, with mystic philosophisings upon life and man's eternal destiny.

> He murmurs, as he comes along,
>   Of comfort clasped in truth revealed,
>   And loiters in the master's field,
> And darkens sanctities with song.

We might refer to another circumstance which has given an advantage to our modern poets, and this, not like the former, an illegitimate one. The great discoveries made in science have given a stimulus to the public mind, and could not fail to impart it to our poets. It was almost impossible that in such an age of intellectual excitement they could surrender themselves to any tame type of excellence. Indeed it is wonderful that, in one department of science at least, they have not found an available and altogether new theme. I refer to geology. Subjects for the muse having been exhausted in this hackneyed world of ours, why have they not taken flight to the pre-Adamic? The awful and sublime part of the earth's history for the first time revealed to our view, might be thought to have been an inviting region. There may be something ominously prosaic in the old red, the carboniferous, and the oolitic; but when we convey ourselves in imagination to this primeval, and unhistorical, and even preternatural world, as it stood in solitary grandeur, a spectacle to angels and not to man, its strange vegetations, and its unrestrained wars of bestial dynasties, there is surely scope for a Shiggianoth strain. The absence of man and of human associations might seem to make it a subject unfit for poetic treatment, and it is this which has probably deterred any from adopting it. Indeed the author of such a poem would land himself in a miserable failure, should he content himself with transferring to verse the mere botany or zoology of the periods. He would need to clothe the whole with some spiritual interest of his own creation. The magnificently wild visions of Hiawatha have shown that no difficulty is too great for genius to overcome, and its author is perhaps the only man living who was able to be the poet of these creation cycles. Craving pardon of the reader for this passing suggestion, it will be granted, at any rate, that the scientific discoveries of our age have been favourable to the development of the imagination. Our increased acquaintance, too, with the literature of Germany, while it has done an essential damage to the theology of our poets, has been of advantage in other respects. The English mind is apt to go in tracks. We want plasticity and boldness of originality. In the department of theology, where God Himself has made the track, following is all that is necessary. It is impossible to improve upon Deity. What can the man do who cometh after the King? Religion being a matter of eternal importance, where to err is to perish, Infinite Wisdom has itself marked out the line. But we have an absurd tendency in England to walk in beaten places, where no responsibility lies upon us. Conversance with Germany has thrown us loose from some self-imposed restraints. Again, it cannot be denied that so far as mere style of language or composition is concerned, our modern poets start with a great advantage. Owing to various causes, our language has come to partake of a richness and variety and freedom formerly unknown. The full powers of it seem only now to have been discovered. In times like these, when every editor and even sub-editor of a Daily wields a style of no common brilliancy, and there is scarcely a private circle in society without its writer of creditable verses, it may be expected that the author who claims to rank as one of the poets of the age will possess no ordinary merit.

In this essay upon Alfred Tennyson we would, First, make some general observations upon him as a poet; Secondly, as mere general criticism is unsatisfactory, take up his larger works *seriatim;* and, Thirdly, consider the new religion which he preaches to the age.

A GENERAL CRITICISM.

Is Alfred Tennyson an original poet? Before this can be answered in the affirmative, more is necessary than merely

9

to show that he has founded a new school, and has had his many imitators. So much will be granted, and seems to be referred to by himself in the " Flower."

> Once in a golden hour
>   I cast to earth a seed,
> Up there came a flower,
>   The people said, a weed.
>
> To and fro they went
>   Through my garden bower,
> And muttering discontent,
>   Cursed me and my flower.
>
> Then it grew so tall
>   It wore a crown of light,
> But thieves from o'er the wall
>   Stole the seed by night.
>
> Sowed it far and wide,
>   By every town and tower,
> Till all the people cried,
>   Splendid is the flower !

One may establish for himself a reputation quite distinct from any other poet, while this is owing merely to a certain style he has adopted, and which may be followed by a host of imitators. This does not prove him to have originality of genius. He may have adopted a false style. He may have violated the rules of taste—the general rules that ought to be observed by all—classic, let us call them. In failing to keep these, he is like the competitor who has leapt the course, and is justly considered as out of the race. You may call such a rider original. He has brought his horse to the goal by a peculiar route, certainly, and so have all that followed him, but every one knows that it is owing to a certain weakness which incapacitated him from reaching it in the ordinary way. A poet may make himself original, again, by elaborate artifice. He may resolve never to express anything as others have expressed it — never to word a sentence in the same way as others would word it

—to search out in the remote distance for his images—so that we shall recognise not only an originality, but a strangeness in his poetry; experiencing a kind of distress on this very account, as if we would be thankful, in this superabundance of dainties, to get common bread to eat, or in this gorgeousness of stained windows to see the light coming through plain glass again; feeling, in a word, as if we would be thankful provided the author would only contemplate nature with eyes of the same construction as our own. For some such peculiarities was Cowley, for example, universally considered in his day to be the most original poet alive— much more so than John Milton. Indeed the modest Puritan seems to have been bewitched and befooled into the same belief, and declared that "the three greatest English poets were Spenser, Shakespeare, and Cowley." He himself had only described Satan's flight from hell to earth, and drawn in plain, unvarnished language sundry other scenes in Paradise and heaven, but had no pretensions to rival the poet who thus describes the dress of Gabriel: —

> He took for a skin a cloud most soft and bright,
> That e'er the midday sun pierced through with light;
> Upon his cheeks a lively blush he spread,
> Washed from the morning beauties' deepest red;
> A harmless fluttering meteor shone for hair,
> And fell adown his shoulders with loose care;
> He cuts out a silk mantle from the skies,
> Where the most sprightly azure pleased the eyes;
> This he with starry vapours sprinkles all,
> Took in their prime, ere they grow ripe and fall;
> Of a new rainbow, ere it fret or fade,
> The choicest piece cut out, a scarf is made.

Time, I need not say, has reversed this judgment. The originality of the man who trafficked in this kind of celestial millinery is seen now to have been a thing itself made and manufactured. That of the Puritan is seen to have been made without hands, belonging to the essential constitution of the man's genius. He is original without violating any

law of taste, or adopting any elaboration of artifice.   Having
appeared, he is recognised to be a new creature in the poetical kingdom—not merely different from Horace or from
Pindar, but different from Homer, and Virgil, and Tasso,
different from them without having followed different rules,
or outraged any proprieties.   It is not the same wine spiced,
but another vintage.   In the same sense was Robert Burns
original.   It was not by uttering things so strange, as to
seem something which we had never heard before ; rather
by uttering things so simple, as to make us wonder that they
had not been said before.   It was not by departing from
nature, but from his peculiar power of touching her chords.
Other writers who preceded him having been simple and
natural in their style, he did not affect the opposite qualities,
but he uttered something that had escaped them.   The instrument was the same, but when they laid it down, he
brought music out of it which was not forthcoming from their
hands.   Lord Byron was original.   It was in a legitimate
way.   He did not adopt rhythms and measures unheard of.
It was not an imposition upon the eye by using more brilliant
colours, nor was it an imposition upon the ear by using
artificial melodies.   The peculiarity for which he stood, and
stands aloft, was a peculiarity not of dress, but of the man ;
not in the application of faculties, but in the kind of faculties
he possessed.   And so with Scott.   If he was different from
all other poets, ancient and modern, it was by the inheritance
of essential qualities, entirely original, entirely natural.   It
was no mere word spell, but a new power over all nature, to
conjure her up before our eyes, to all our senses, to the very
smell of the ground we tread upon.

Is Tennyson, then, entitled to rank among those great men
who have borne the stamp of a genius essentially original.?

It is a question somewhat difficult to decide.

We are not prepared to agree with those who would
deny his title in a very absolute way, and hold rather a
disparaging view of his high claims.   They are disposed

to grant him nothing more than artistic skill and power of embellishment. According to them he is only possessed of a second-rate poetical faculty, but endued with immense powers of application and self-control, enabling him patiently to call up all that is necessary to complete and perfect his picture, excluding whatever is common-place, or expressing whatever is common in a new and striking form. Even his "In Memoriam" they reckon to be merely an extraordinary Chinese expenditure of manual skill, and a triumph of exquisite taste and polish. They would have us believe that this of itself is high praise. That any man in so imaginative and cultivated an age should reach the pre-eminence he has gained, is a high achievement. But while they grant him to be the fit representative of the taste and poetic feeling of the nineteenth century, they would repudiate his claim to be considered as one of the great typical poets of this country.

We are not prepared to endorse the steps by which they reach this verdict.

They must surely grant, for one thing, that Tennyson is not an imitator. He elaborates and ornaments, let us say ; but what is it that he elaborates and adorns ? Is he a mere reproduction of some preceding poet bedizened with jewel-lery ? If so, of whom ? We know no poet to whom he bears the slightest resemblance. If they have any sus-.picions, let them observe him narrowly at any time when he has laid aside his ornaments. Does he walk like any preceding poet ? We are not asking if he walks in other men's clothes, but when, in his easy moments, he throws open what is alleged to be his laced waistcoat, and we get a view of his nude muscular build and conformation, is it the same with any of his illustrious fraternity ? We know no poet more free from the challenge of imitation. This is surely a good sign.

Again, do these parties mean to assert that he wants the *fervidum ingenium* ? Do they mean to say that he perpetrates a cold-blooded system of building up his poems by square and rule, that he carries on a trade as carver and gilder of materials for the public market, and prosecutes a sort of poetical upholstery business? I think they would come nearer the truth were they to consider that his genius is generally at a white heat. For ourselves, after reading through his works to write an essay upon them, we feel that we shall have enough to do in the way of condemning his extravagances, but the idea of his being a mere artistic elaborator will not stand examination for a moment. No; these exquisite vases they speak of must have come out of some fires.

Once more—do they deny him the possession of ideality? This is the faculty of a true poet. It consists in the power not only of giving

> to airy nothings
> A local habitation and a name,

but of converting what has a local habitation and a name into something ethereal and imaginative—not only of making the ideal a reality, but a reality ideal. From the want of this magic power many a subject, handled skilfully enough otherwise by a poet, is seen too much, as it were, under daylight, or as belonging to this every-day world. But take some of Tennyson's smaller pieces, such as the "Lotos Eaters," the "Lady of Shalott," "Marianne; or, the Moated Grange," &c., into what gorgeous shadows of an ideal background are they thrown! In the "Lotos Eaters" the cardinal difficulty was to get the island where these "mild-eyed melancholy" dreamers dwelt so transferred into the realm of the imagination as to be distinct from any of the thousand and one islands which are to be found actually in our seas. This is done in the very first lines:—

> "Courage!" he said, and pointed t'ward the land,
>   "This mounting wave will roll us shoreward soon."
> In the afternoon they came unto a land
>   In which it seemèd always afternoon.

The lines which follow are surely in a fine vein of poetry.

> Hateful is the dark blue sky,
>   Vaulted o'er the dark blue sea.
> Death is the end of life ; ah ! why
>   Should life all labour be ?
> Let us alone. Time driveth onward fast,
>   And in a little while our lips are dumb.
> Let us alone. What is it that will last ?
>   All things are taken from us, and become
> Portions and parcels of the dreadful Past.
>   Let us alone. What pleasure can we have
> To war with evil ? Is there any peace
>   In ever climbing up the climbing wave ?
> All things have rest, and ripen t'ward the grave
>   In silence ; ripen, fall, and cease ;
> Give us long rest or death, dark death or dreamless ease.

Hearken next how ingeniously these slumber-lovers dispose of the suggestion that they should trouble themselves to return home :—

> We should but come like ghosts to trouble joy,
>   Or else the island princes over-bold
> Have eat our substance, and the minstrel sings
>   Before them of the ten years' war in Troy,
> And our great deeds as half-forgotten things.
>   Is there confusion in the little isle ?
> Let what is broken so remain.
>   The gods are hard to reconcile :
> 'Tis hard to settle order once again.
>   There is confusion worse than death,
> Trouble on trouble, pain on pain,
>   Long labour unto aged breath,
> Sore task to hearts worn out with many wars,
> And eyes grow dim with gazing on the pilot stars.

Hearken once again (for there is surely grandeur in the lines) how they justify slumber by the gods themselves :—

> Let us swear an oath and keep it with an equal mind,
> In the hollow Lotos-land to live and lie reclined
> On the hills like gods together, careless of mankind.

For they lie beside their nectar, and the bolts are hurled
Far below them in the valley, and the clouds are lightly curled
Round their golden tresses, girdled with the gleaming world,
Where they smile in secret, looking over wasted lands ;
Blight and famine, plague and earthquake, roaring deeps and fiery sands,
Clanging fights, and flaming towns, and sinking ships, and praying hands.
But they smile, they find a music centred in a doleful song
Steaming up, a lamentation and an ancient tale of wrong,
Like a tale of little meaning, though the words are strong ;
Chanted from an ill-used race of men that cleave the soil,
Storing yearly little dues of wheat, and wine, and oil ;
Till they perish and they suffer—some, 'tis whispered, down in hell—
Suffer endless anguish ; others in Elysian valleys dwell,
Resting weary limbs at last on beds of asphodel.
Surely, surely, slumber is more sweet than toil, the shore
Than labour in the deep mid-ocean, wind and wave and oar,
Oh, rest ye, brother mariners, we will not wander more.

The " Lady of Shalott " illustrates the same remark. The
whole proves the powerful ideality of its author, thrown, as
the subject is, into the deep rich shadows of the purely
imaginative. We are left with the dreamiest conception
possible of the many - towered Camelot, and the island of
Shalott as well.

On either side the river lie
Long fields of barley and of rye,
That clothe the wold, and meet the sky,
And through the fields the road runs by
    To many-towered Camelot ;
And up and down the people go,
Gazing where the lilies blow,
Round an island there below,
    The island of Shalott.

Willows whiten, aspens quiver,
Little breezes dusk and shiver
Through the wave that runs for ever
By the island in the river
    Flowing down to Camelot.
Four gray walls and four gray towers
Overlook a space of flowers,
And the silent isle embowers
    The Lady of Shalott.

This is a good specimen of the difference between a poet's
description of places and a common guide-book. Are any of
our readers the wiser after reading it with regard to the
topography of Camelot or Shalott? We hope not. Nay,
when the Lady, in her unchained boat, after winding "the
willowy hills and fields among," effects her landing at Camelot, the same blessed and delightful obscurity hangs over her
entrance.

> Under tower and balcony,
> By garden wall and gallery,
> A gleaming shape she floated by,
> Dead-pale between the houses high,
>   Silent into Camelot.
> Out upon the wharfs they came,
> Knight and burgher, lord and dame,
> And round the prow they read her name,
>   *The Lady of Shalott.*

The parties from whose flat and absolute undervaluation
of the Laureate we are now dissenting, may call upon us to
note the circumstance that he seldom rises easily and
naturally to the lofty in thought or conception, and that, on
the other hand, he never can say anything that is common in
a common way. From this they would argue that any excellence he has is achieved by mechanical means and effort;
that the soil is thin, only cultivated with amazing pains, and
covered with splendid buildings. Now, it is granted that
Tennyson is not characterised by sublimity. This is no
reason why we should deprive him of his claim to beauty.
The question is whether such luxuriant vegetation as meets
us upon those lower grounds of his, could come from any but
the richest soil and the warmest climate. The question is,
moreover, whether the palaces that cover them could be
reared without much wealth of mental endowment? In fact
the mode of argument they employ would condemn not only
Tennyson, but the southern part of the island to which he
belongs, because it does not present us, like Scotland, with
the Grampians and other mountain ranges, interspersed

with wild heathery muirland. No doubt the traveller to our highlands is delighted with the spectacle of nature in her rude magnificence and mountain altitudes, which it would be profanity to adorn, and her ravines as savagely steep again; and he may feel that all this is only set off to greater advantage by the turf-shiels that send up their smoke, as of an humble sacrifice to the great Creator. But may he not experience another charm of its own kind when he wanders south the Tweed, where the lowlands are covered with the glory of a soft vegetation, where the streams, if they do not leap impetuous over the linn, are embosomed in overhanging woods, and are not the less romantic because they wind by aristocratic mansions standing on their smooth-shaven terraces; while farther down their course they trail through flowers so abundant as to be rotting in their prodigality, or anon silently glide past rose-crowned gateways of orchards, on the top of which

Now droops the milk-white peacock like a ghost?

What then? We have defended Tennyson from these Vandals. We have especially scouted the idea that a poet whose every page bears the impress of passion is only a master in ornamentation. At the same time we have to crave the indulgence of some of our readers when we venture to show cause why he can scarcely rank with the highest order of genius.

In the highest order of genius, as we understand it, passion is allied with a certain intuition which enables its possessor to make such a selection of the essential features of a landscape, and of human character, as produces an indelible impression, and weds itself to immortality. Such a poet having at once struck the chord that is required, does not need to give us any lengthened, confused, and tumultuous symphony as a substitute, and it will be generally found that his style of poetry is quiet and subdued. The intensity of the passion has expressed itself in the master-stroke which has overwhelmed us, and there is no need why it should show itself in any illegitimate way. The poet again who has passion, but wants this higher intuition, while he fails to produce the immortal result, puts forth displays of power which may be much more demonstrative and imposing to superficial judgments. The steam when doing its proper work, and most exerting its formidable momentum, is silent; meanwhile the tremendous sound it issues when escaping by the valve affects the crowd most. To change the figure, you go abroad some night when there is wild fire illumining the whole heavens, and there is something imposing no doubt in those broad, loose, far-spreading lightnings; but the triumph of electricity is when the splendid long summer heats have accumulated, and it concentrates itself into the few heart-shaped flashes which overawe whatever they illuminate, and consume whatever they strike. This illustrates the difference, as we venture to think, between our modern poets, like Tennyson and Browning, and those greater masters in the art who have gone before them. We have certainly more imposing displays of power in their productions than in those of their predecessors. The passion, concentrated in the latter, spreads in more formidable and diffused demonstrations in the other.

Let us give one or two specific instances of what we mean. We might refer to Tennyson's " Charge of the Light Brigade." It runs in such strains as the following :—

> Half a league, half a league,
> Half a league onward,
> All in the valley of death,
> Rode the six hundred.
> " Forward, the Light Brigade !
> Charge for the guns !" he said ;
> Into the valley of death
> Rode the six hundred.
>
> *   *   *   *
>
> Cannon to right of them,
> Cannon to left of them,
> Cannon in front of them,
> Volleyed and thundered.

> Stormed at with shot and shell,
> Boldly they rode, and well,
> Into the jaws of death,
> Into the mouth of hell,
>   Rode the six hundred.
>
> Flashed all their sabres bare,
> Flashed as they turned in air,
> Sabring the gunners there,
> Charging an army, while
>   All the world wondered.
> Plunged in the battery-smoke,
> Right through the line they broke,
> Cossack and Russian
> Reeled from the sabre-stroke
>   Shattered and sundered ;
> Then they rode back ; but
>   Not the six hundred.

I say nothing of the feebler lines. The failure lies in the strongest. What have we here but the high-pitched tone of martial words, such as we find *ad libitum* in Macaulay's "Lays of Rome." The author enters, of course, into the spirit of the hopeless charge, but his description evaporates in strong opposition of words : " Cannon to right of them ;" "Cannon to left of them;" " Flashed all their sabres bare," &c.; also in declamatory appeals to admiration : " All the world wondered ;" " Oh, the wild charge they made !" &c. How different Thomas Campbell, in his " Battle of the Baltic " ! No noise of words.

> Like leviathans afloat
> Lay their bulwarks on the brine ;

this is all that is said to convey to us the order of the battle, and it is enough. One stroke of the imagination has conjured up the spectacle. Another follows, and leaves nothing necessary behind it to convey the horror of the battle down to all posterity :—

> Each gun
> From its adamantine lips
> Shed a death shade round the ships,
> Like the hurricane eclipse
> Of the sun.

The "feeble cheer of the Dane," sent back to ours, is another touch of the higher and intuitive genius, as distinguished from mere passion venting itself in words, however spirited and forcible. Such was Campbell! When his first juvenile performance appeared, there was nothing in the mere mode of it to affect originality: it was in the old measure, it was in the old style. But the chords of nature were struck once more. That was it. We all felt that whether he described woman's first appearance in Paradise, or Warsaw's last champion, or Hope lighting her torch at Nature's funeral pile, we had amongst us another inspired man.

What we desiderate in our modern poets is the power of representing nature by selecting a few catholic features of the landscape. Wanting the eye for this, they seek to make amends by introducing ever so many particulars to give definiteness to the picture. Unable to conjure up the one or two points that would suggest the whole beauty of the landscape, they feel themselves under the obligation to ornament the details which should have been left to the imagination. If they would speak the creative word, we would paint the details for ourselves. The scene where Burns had his last meeting with his Highland Mary will stand green and fragrant in his song so long as summer unfolds her robes ; and yet it would defy us all to tell by what intuition he transferred it there, for he says very little.

> Ye banks and braes, and streams around
>   The castle o' Montgomery—

that is all. That is the foundation of the whole landscape in two lines. Having created it, he blesses it.

> Green be your woods, and fair your flowers,
>   Your waters never drumly !
> There simmer first unfauld her robes,
>   And there the langest tarry ;
> For there I took the last fareweel
>   O' my sweet Highland Mary.

So with "Afton Water," by the margin of which his other Mary slept, and will sleep for ever, for who will awaken her after that tender adjuration of the poet ? The scenery is a perfect thing, according to the grand secret of poetical creation—"the glen resounding with the echo of the stock-dove," "the thorny den with its wild whistling blackbirds," and the

> neighbouring hills
> Far marked with the courses of clear winding rills.

It may be said that by admitting none to the order of the highest poetical genius but those who can thus represent nature by a few creative touches, and who can intuitively strike the chords of the human heart, we seem to exclude some who by general consent belong to it. What, for example, it may be objected, of Shelley or Byron ? In Shelley do we not see everything rather under an etherealised and unearthly aspect, as through a stellar mist or lunar radiance ? In the pages of Byron do not humanity and nature seem to be irradiated only by lightnings out of the cloud ? Granting this, it does not follow that both of them had not the highest poetical insight into nature. It only proves that they were led, the one by his singular disembodied fancy, the other by his passionate and scorpion-stung genius, to dwell upon those phases of humanity and those aspects of nature that are removed from the eye of common contemplation. In reading them we may say, " This is uncommon," and yet we feel and acknowledge it to be natural ; just as we are still in the natural world, although at one time we may stand among the weird phenomena and aurora-borealises of an arctic latitude, or at another climb in awe-struck wonder among the Alpine solitudes, where the chamois leaps graceful on the precipices, and there are it may be so many voices of thunder that speak to the ear of the Almighty.

One thing is certain, that we never find Byron or Shelley diverging into the unnatural. But the same cannot be said of Tennyson. For I now go on to notice that there are many extravagances which it must be confessed disgrace his productions. Amongst these we would specify an excessive sentimentality. This appears in various forms, especially in connection with the amatory, which occupies a large place in his writings. He has without controversy introduced a new description of lovers to our notice, whose wailings and ravings under love-disappointment are sufficiently sickening. We have reason to be thankful that he has seldom if ever prostituted his muse to licentiousness. But the love he describes exhibits itself often in that ultra-sentimental form which degenerates into silliness. The lovers of Alfred Tennyson are the victims of a fiery frenzy. It is—

> O Love, Love, Love! O withering might !
> O sun, that from thy noonday height
> Shudderest when I strain my sight,
> Throbbing through all thy heat and light ;
> Lo, falling from my constant mind,
> Lo, parched and withered, deaf and blind,
> I whirl like leaves in roaring wind.
>
> Last night, when some one spoke his name,
> From my swift blood that went and came,
> A thousand little shafts of flame
> Were shivered in my narrow frame.
> O love, O fire, once he drew
> With one long kiss my whole soul through
> My lips, as sunlight drinketh dew.

One would not wonder that they should express themselves in this way, but they actually die off in the issue, and their dead bodies, clothed in white, are carried by boat down rivers, with their last letter in their dead hands, for the inspection of the knight who has murdered them with his grace and valour. Let any one look at the figures with which the artist has illustrated certain editions of our poet's works, and he will find a just representation in woodcut of his *inamoratos.* Such swooning and hideously-sentimental shapes of humanity were never beheld. This sort of thing has done an essential damage to the generation. The worst is that his male lovers make as egregious fools of themselves. Was there ever such a rejected lover as he of " Locksley Hall"? Even had he perpetrated no other crime than telling us that in the days of his love he

> Many a night saw the Pleiads rising through their mellow shade,
> Glitter like a swarm of fire-flies tangled in a silver braid,

he ought to have been hanged by the neck with a rope of stars.   But he actually begins to detail to us the philosophic and cosmopolitan visions he had in his younger days, and which were all blasted by Amy's infidelity.   Next he entertains the project of setting off—where? Not to some cold country or scene of Lapland desolation suited to his hopeless state, but to some happy clime where " hangs the heavy-fruited tree;" and this not to remain a sighing hermit all the days of his life, but to marry a black woman, who

> Shall rear his dusky race,
> Iron-jointed, supple-sinewed, they shall dive, and they shall run,
> Catch the wild goat by the hair, and hurl their lances in the sun, &c.

Upon second thoughts he rejects this project, and resolves to remain in Europe.

> Better fifty years of Europe than a cycle of Cathay.
> Mother-age (for mine I know not) help me as when life began;
> Rift the hills, and roll the waters, flash the lightnings, weigh the sun.
> Oh, I see the crescent promise of my spirit hath not set,
> Ancient founts of inspiration well through all my fancy yet.

This is assuredly bad enough; but these blemishes, which will meet us when we come to consider his larger productions, must not blind us to the exalted gifts of our Laureate. Before drawing our general criticism to a close, a word might be said upon the somewhat invidious theme of the comparative rank he holds among the poets of our own country.   The only other name which is naturally suggested to us in rival connection with Tennyson is Robert Browning. They are both possessed of pre-eminent endowments, and have both split upon the rock of extravagance. In many respects the last is the more powerful genius. His images have an originality and terrible force, reminding us of the author of the " Inferno." He can remain much longer upon the wing. For reasons that are obvious enough he is not fully appreciated by the general public. He lies under a . triple curse of obscurity. He constructs sentences that admit of a great many more meanings than the one he would convey. He burrows into the moral philosophy of human nature, and he propagates a new theology not under-stood by three-fourths of his poetical constituency, and it is in the interior of all this labyrinth that the Rosamond of his royal genius is concealed. There is the formidable length, too, of his poetical productions. Many who would gladly take a pleasure trip to France or Germany, have no inclina-tion to relax themselves by a voyage to Valparaiso, especially if many parts of it are to be described under fogs and deep-sea mists. On the other hand, it is little to say that Tennyson is popular. Even where he has shown himself untrue, if we may presume so far, to his proper mission, he has secured popularity. If he had followed out the more serious and reflective strain in which he began when he wrote his " In Memoriam," we may question whether he would have surrounded himself with the constituency he now possesses. Rising from the solemn orisons of friendship, he suddenly diverged into the regions of love-sentimentalism, and " multiplied the nation " of his readers, if he did not " increase the joy " of first admirers. If his productions are slighter than those of Browning, they have the perfect polish and melody necessary to possess the fastidious ear of the times. There is abundance of sentimentalism in his poetry to attract the one sex, and just as much of the spirit of modern science as is fitted to captivate the other. He would not have been the seer or poet for this generation if he had had any dogmatic faith—and he has none. Tennyson, then, is unquestionably the most popular poet of the age.

A CRITICISM OF HIS LARGER POEMS.

Let us begin with the " Idylls of the King."

Arthur of the Round Table is a great subject. John Milton hesitated between it and Paradise Lost. If he had not chosen the Fall of Man he would have fixed upon the Wars with the Saxons. The scene instead of being Eden would have been Wales, and for Adam and Eve we should have had Arthur and Guinevere. We are called in the name of all humanity to rejoice that the heavenly muse, whether she came from the secret top of Sinai or from Sion hill,

> And Siloah's brook that flowed
> Fast by the oracle of God,

guided him to select the first of these topics, for next to the loss of Paradise would have been the loss of " Paradise Lost." And yet the very greatness of that production must convince us what an epic poem " Arthur " would have proved in his hands. Who that reads the few verses in Genesis recording the Fall could have supposed any man able to compose an epic out of them as diversified in its scenes and incidents, and introducing as many actors as the Iliad itself? Let none of us doubt that out of the scanty historical records of Arthur, assisted by monkish legends and ancient song, Milton would have constructed a poem worthy of the ages. The twelve wars of Arthur would have outrivalled those of Greece and Troy; his sixty knights would have been invested with distinctive characters, and their names would have been made more familiar to our ears and more renowned than Hector, Ajax, or Achilles. Guinevere would have had some tragic interest thrown around her in connection with these wars, and been illustrious as ever was Helen of Troy. What warlike broils and rude merriment would have immortalised the feasts of the Round Table, to say nothing of national songs of the past from the harp of Thaliessen ; and if he had carried the king to the fairy island to be cured of his wounds, we should have seen what a poet, of all others the most ideal and creative, could accomplish in an episode scene of Elfdom.

With Alfred Tennyson the subject takes a slenderer form. One has no reason to complain of this. He did not propose an epic. He has at the same time taken unwarrantable liberties when he represents the Round Table as having been an order of chivalry, and Arthur as having gathered round him a band of knights-errant, sworn to fight for their lady-loves, and spending in gay jousts the time that was spared from redressing the wrongs of captive maidens. Is not this a gross anachronism? The age of chivalry was surely a great many centuries later than the times of the Ancient Britons. We say nothing at present of the absurd attempt which our poet has made to impart to Arthur the character of a modern rationalistic Christian, and the opportunity he has taken in the " Holy Grail " to vend his peculiar theology. This will be duly exposed when we come to animadvert upon Tennyson's religious sentiments. Meanwhile it is surely to be regretted that, under his treatment, the Round Table degenerates into a mere partnership of gallantries. Instead of the twelve wars we have five love intrigues. No lances are broken, but hearts enough. Arthur's heroic struggles to save the land from Saxon invasion we read nothing of: it is his struggles with the infidelity of his spouse.

Well, let us take the matter as we find it, and judge by the rules to which the lighter theme is subject. He has well called these poems Idylls, for they come not exactly under any category of productions with which we are acquainted. This, as we have stated already, is one thing we like about the Laureate. He never imitates: what he does is done in his own style. They are for the most part narrative poems, where the interest depends upon the incidents introduced. Invention was, therefore, indispensable, and although our author has not the faculty of forming a connected plot or a thrilling drama, he does not want a power of introducing by-incidents and circumstances suf-ficiently piquante to enliven the story. Yet here, if we mistake not, lies the essential defect of the Idylls. Since he does not possess in any high degree the power of invent-ing a plot or conducting a story, he would require to have made up for the want of this by exerting that faculty of descriptive painting known to be possessed by him to an extraordinary extent. His is a mind which requires to dwell with concentration upon its theme, and his most successful attempts have been those where the limited nature of the subject admits of this. Instead of attending to this rule he runs on with an unfortunate facility in his narrative, never dwelling upon any part so as to become great or splendid: the result is a mere series of sketchy paintings. Sir Walter Scott had not the splendid bursts of passion which abound in Byron, but won his laurels by the transcendent beauty of his plot and story. Byron, again, had not his rival's faculty of invention, but established his reputation in the other way. In the Idylls we have neither what charms us in the story of "The Lady of the Lake," nor what astonishes and appals us in the powerful passages of "The Giaour." They go forward in a sort of epic prattle, which neither degenerates to common-place nor rises to the extraordinary.

While we consider this to be a well-founded general criticism upon them, there are some exceptions that must be made to it. There are some passages, as may well be supposed, of great beauty, and there are others betraying a deplorable want of taste.

Among the former might be mentioned Arthur's dream before his last battle, in which he sees the ghost of Gawain, one of the lightest and vainest of all his knights.

> Before that last weird battle in the west
> There came on Arthur sleeping Gawain killed
> In Lancelot's war, the ghost of Gawain blown
> Along a wandering wind, and past his ear
> Went shrilling, " Hollow, hollow, all delight !
> Hail, king ! to-morrow thou shalt pass away.

> Farewell ! there is an isle of rest for thee,
> And I am blown along a wandering wind,
> And hollow, hollow, hollow all delight."
> And fainter onwards, like wild birds that change
> Their season in the night and wail their way
> From could to cloud down the long wind, the dream
> Shrilled ; but in going mingled with dim cries
> Far in the moonlight haze among the hills,
> As of some lonely city sacked by night,
> When all is lost, and wife and child with wail
> Pass to new lords ; and Arthur woke and called,
> " Who spake ?   A dream.   O light upon the wind
> Thine, Gawain, was the voice—are those dim cries
> Thine ? or doth all that haunts the waste and wild
> Mourn, knowing it will go along with me ?"

We think it right to give the only description we have of any of Arthur's battles.

> On the waste sand by the waste sea they closed,
> Nor ever yet had Arthur fought in fight
> Like this last, dim, weird battle of the west.
> A deathlike mist slept over sand and sea ;
> Whereof the chill, to him that breathed it, drew
> Down with his blood, till all his heart was cold
> With formless fear ; and even on Arthur fell
> Confusion, since he saw not where he fought,
> For friend and foe were shadows in the mist,
> And friend slew friend, not knowing whom he slew.
> And some had visions out of golden youth,
> And some beheld the faces of old ghosts
> Look in upon the battle, and in the mist
> Was many a noble deed, many a base,
> And chance and craft and strength in single fights,
> And ever and anon with host to host
> Shocks, and the splintering spear, the hard mail hewn,
> Shield breaking, and the clash of brands, the crash
> Of battle-axes on shattered helms, and shrieks
> After the Christ, and those who falling down
> Looked up for heaven, and only saw the mist ;
> And shouts of heathen, and the traitor knights,
> Oaths, insult, filth, and monstrous blasphemies,
> Sweat, writhings, anguish, labouring of the lungs
> In that close mist, and cryings for the light,
> Moans of the dying, and voices of the dead.

> Last, as by some one death-bed, after wail
> Of suffering, silence follows, or thro' death
> Or deathlike swoon, thus over all that shore,
> Save for some whisper of the seething seas,
> A dead hush fell ; but when the dolorous day
> Grew drearier toward twilight falling, came
> A bitter wind, clear from the north, and blew
> The mist aside, and with that wind the tide
> Rose, and the pale king glanced across the field
> Of battle, but no man was moving there ;
> Nor any cry of Christian heard therein,
> Nor yet of heathen ; only the wan wave
> Brake in among dead faces, to and fro
> Swaying the hollow helmets of the fallen,
> And shivered brands that once had fought with Rome,
> And rolling far along the gloomy shores
> The voice of days of old and days to be.

The very excellence of this description leads us to regret that, instead of regaling us with so many idle gallantries, the Laureate had not girt himself to sing Arthur's battles. After reading it, we feel disposed to say to him, like Mercutio, " Why is not this better now than groaning for love ?" and to remind him of his own words elsewhere :—

> But great is song,
> Used to great ends : ourself have often tried
> Valkyrian hymns, or into rhythm have dashed
> The passion of the prophetess ; for song
> Is duer unto freedom, force, and growth
> Of spirit, than to junketing and love.

In his " Guinevere," the flight of the unhappy queen to the holy house at Almesbury, after her disgrace, and the interview between her and Arthur, afforded him a high theme for poetry. The conqueror of the Saxon hordes, agonizing under this wound in the only part where he was vulnerable, and come on his way to his last battle to upbraid the wife of his bosom for her infidelity ; she again called to see the frown that was the terror of armies on the brow of an injured husband ; this was a subject which, to be perfectly painted, would have required much time and study ; and if he has failed altogether to reach the mark, it is owing to the hurry and precipitation too visible here and elsewhere in the Idylls.

The worst of them, in point of taste, is "Geraint and Enid." A more grotesque and ridiculous story was never made the subject of poetical description. This Geraint had been led by sensitive jealousy of his wife to withdraw from the Round Table, where scandals had become notorious, to his possessions in the country. She, on the other hand, is grieved that his arms should rust in inglorious ease. One night, as fate would have it, in the restlessness of his bed he had

> cast the coverlet aside,
> And bared the knotted column of his throat,
> The massive square of his heroic breast,
> And arms on which the standing muscle sloped
> As slopes a wild brook o'er a little stone.

The inspection of her husband's bust leads her to soliloquise aloud and upbraid herself with being the cause of so sturdy a warrior remaining at home inactive. The soliloquy unfortunately ended—

> O me, I fear that I am no true wife.

This was quite enough for the jealous knight, who, awaking at the moment, considers that all his worst suspicions of her fidelity have been justified. She is ordered to prepare herself for riding forth with him straightway to the wilderness. Off they set accordingly on this strange expedition, she having peremptory orders to ride before on her palfrey. Various encounters take place with knights-errant upon the journey, and when these are overthrown, it is poor Enid's office to tie the reins of their horses together, and drive them with their suits of armour before her. After a deal of this adventure carried forward without a word of explanation from this madcap husband, he gets at last a sharp cut which lays him low, and affords her an opportunity of showing him her affection. They are found upon the road in this condition " at the point of noon," that is, twelve of the clock, by one Earl Doorm,

> Broad faced, with under-fringe of russet beard,
> Bound on a foray, rolling eyes of prey.

This formidable peer, having conveyed them both to his hall, begins during the carousals in his mansion to wax merry, and use some familiarities with her, when Geraint, recovering from his swoon, delivers him of his head, and is delivered himself eventually from his jealousy.

No skill in the execution could make a story like this tolerable. But the execution in many parts is as bad as the plan. What do our readers think of the following description of Geraint's first love for Enid, as she waited upon him at table in her father's hall ?

> Geraint had longing in him evermore
> To stoop and kiss her tender little thumb,
> That crossed the trencher as she laid it down.

Nay, his glances of affection are compared to those of a robin redbreast :—

> Never man rejoiced
> More than Geraint to greet her thus attired,
> And glancing all at once as keenly at her
> As careful robin's eye the delver's toil,
> Made her cheek burn and either eyelid fall ; &c.

But that we may not be thought to show things to a disadvantage, here, then, is about the best of the verses. They describe her when she was first told by a friend, before retiring to rest, of the fact that Geraint loved her.

> But never light and shade
> Coursed one another more on open ground
> Beneath a troubled heaven, than red and pale
> Across the face of Enid, hearing her ;
> While slowly falling as a scale that falls,
> When weight is added only grain by grain,
> Sank her sweet head upon her gentle breast ;
> Nor did she lift an eye, nor speak a word,
> Rapt in the fear and in the wonder of it—

> So, moving without answer to her rest,
> She found no rest, and ever failed to draw
> The quiet night into her blood, but lay
> Contemplating her own unworthiness.

The gradual falling of her head to her breast, as grain by grain goes into the scale (he does not say whether troy or avoirdupois), is of the worst taste surely in the art ; and the same may be said of "her failing to draw the quiet night into her blood."

"Merlin and Vivien" lies open to objection from another quarter. As if it were not enough to stain the fame of the Round Table by such an example of an insane knight as we have just contemplated, he conveys us to the "wild woods of Brocelland," to witness a wanton intrigue between the sage of Arthur's camp and this flirt of the sixth century. Whether he thought to confer a benefit upon our drawing-rooms by bringing such an unseemly picture before us, we cannot tell : it is in every respect unworthy of the author of "In Memoriam," and the less needs be said of it, as it is nearly the one instance in all his writings where he has violated the rules of propriety. He probably imagined that this generation of ours stood less in need of being stirred up to high deeds by the attempts of the Ancient Britons to drive back Saxony from their shores, than to be instructed by the attempts of a light girl upon the virtue of old age. Instead of bringing a warrior from that old epoch to arouse our effeminate and enervated souls, he takes a young lady, who might be the subject of a modern sensational novel, and gives her the advantage of the background of an ancient British forest to practise her flirtations before our eyes.

One turns with pleasure from this idyll to that of "Lancelot and Elaine ;"

> Elaine the fair, Elaine the lovable,
> Elaine the lily maid of Astolat !

There is an indescribable charm of purity and world ignorance, and thorough devotion of heart, in this heroine. The very forwardness and impatience of her love for Lancelot, leading her to take the initiative always in its advances, although, as described by the poet, it might seem to be untrue to the nature of woman, is felt to answer to the enthusiasm of this untaught girl. She casts her soul at once upon the venture of her first and last speculation. And this simple demonstrative love is more beautiful by contrast as felt for one who was himself familiar with the arts and even the seductions of a court. This child-love accuses him by its innocence; and when, on recovering from his wound, he finds her watching over his sick-bed with the eyes that betrayed what he never could return, he strives in all good conscience to quench the fire which he had kindled by short and cold answers.

> She knew right well
> What the rough sickness meant, but what this meant
> She knew not, and the sorrow dimmed her sight,
> And drave her ere her time across the fields
> Far into the rich city, where alone
> She murmured, " Vain, in vain : it cannot be :
> He cannot love me : how then, must I die ?"
> Then as a little helpless innocent bird,
> That has but one plain passage of few notes,
> Will sing the simple passage o'er and o'er
> For all an April morning, till the ear
> Wearies to hear it, so the simple maid
> Went half the night repeating, " Must I die ?"
> And now to right she turned, and now to left,
> And found no ease in turning or in rest ;
> And, " Him or death," she muttered, " Death or him,"
> Again, and like a burthen, " Him or death."

Here is the dénouement—upon Lancelot's announcing his departure : —

> " Going ? and we shall never see you more.
> And I must die for want of one bold word."
> " Speak : that I live to hear," he said, " is yours."
> Then suddenly and passionately she spoke :
> " I have gone mad. I love you : let me die."
> " Ah, sister," answered Lancelot, " what is this ?"
> And innocently extending her white arms,
> " Your love," she said, " your love—to be your wife."

Who will ever forget these, or the lines that follow, in which he offered every consolation for not giving her what he never could bestow?

> While he spoke
> She neither blushed nor shook, but deadly pale
> Stood grasping what was nearest, then replied :
> "Of all this will I nothing !" and so fell.

There can be but one opinion of the beauty of these passages. But it is the fate of our modern school of poets not to know the boundary line of good taste. The story ends by this young lady not only dying of love, and singing a song in which death is declared to be sweeter than love, but giving directions for a sentimental burial.

Upon the whole, the reputation of Tennyson has not been greatly advanced by the Idylls.

"The Princess," on the contrary, is a magnificent poem. Its theme being woman's rights, or rather her claim to university privileges and intellectual equality with man, it might have been judged one far less promising than the Round Table. But the Laureate's genius has shone inversely to the greatness of his subjects. While Arthur degenerates into a few rapidly-sketched pictures of knightly amours, this poem swells into the dimensions of a great painting, every part of which testifies to the fullest application and the happiest exertion of his faculties. It shows the most exuberant fancy, and is full of the most beautiful passages. In the Idylls we have as it were extended but thinly-planted lines of trees—these besides rather poles after all, or only leaves atop; in "The Princess" we have the luxuriant forest, close-embowering shades, the warmth of every variety of fairy vegetation, and the songs of life and music from the warblers in the midst of it.

Another poet, without studying the advantage of an ideal perspective, would at once have proceeded to describe the wonders or the monstrosities of a female university; but our poet, while he makes his heroine a princess, plants his university in the border of her kingdom, where its environs are made attractive by all the embellishments of fancy. Here she has retired with her attendant train of young ladies, having brought them under a solemn vow not to go beyond these liberties for three years, nor hold any communication with the inferior sex of mankind, who, by the inscription upon the gate, are forbidden to enter upon pain of death. The young prince of an adjacent territory having been betrothed to her from childhood, and entertaining the most devoted attachment for her, can only obtain access for himself and two of his young companions by being disguised in woman's garments. Once introduced, we have them in the interior of this mystic college,

> With prudes for proctors, dowagers for deans,
> And sweet girl-graduates in their golden hair.

The prince, in his disguise, has abundant opportunities in conversation of drawing from the lips of his mistress the peculiar doctrines of which she was the patroness, and her high-minded contempt especially for the passion of which he was himself the fond votary and slave. Can anything be better than the following withering ridicule which he entailed upon his head by singing in her presence a love-madrigal ?

> "Not for thee," she said,
> O Bulbul, any rose of Gulistan
> Shall burst her veil : marsh-divers, rather, maid,
> Shall croak thee sister, or the meadow-crake
> Grate her harsh kindred in the grass ; and this
> A mere love-poem ! O for such, my friend,
> We hold them slight ; they mind us of the time
> When we made bricks in Egypt. Knaves are men,
> That lute and flute fantastic tenderness,
> And dress the victim to the offering up,
> And paint the gates of Hell with Paradise,
> And play the slave to gain the tyranny.
> Poor soul ! I had a maid of honour once,
> She wept her true eyes blind for such a one,
> A rogue of canzonets and serenades.

> I loved her. Peace be with her. She is dead,
> So they blaspheme the more ! But great is song,
> Used to great ends : ourself have often tried
> Valkyrian hymns, or into rhythm have dashed
> The passion of the prophetess ; for song
> Is duer unto freedom, force, and growth
> Of spirit, than to junketing and love."

The prince and his companions having been eventually discovered to be of the wrong sex, he has now to resort to entreaties with a view to melt the heart of the princess, but is doomed to find that a prince at her feet is no temptation with her to abandon the grand sentiment which has taken possession of her soul.

> I wed with thee ! I bound by precontract,
> Your bride, your bondslave ! not though all the gold
> That veins the world were packed to make your crown,
> And every spoken tongue should lord you. Sir,
> Your falsehood and yourself are hateful to us.
> I trample on your offers and on you :
> Begone ! we will not look upon you more.
> Here, push them out at gates.

The reader will notice that our poet has been fortunate enough, owing to his subject, which is modern, to fall upon an entirely original heroine, for no poet had ever described a young lady animated by the pride of female intellectualism, and appearing as the advocate of woman's superiority to love. Neither had any lover except this prince ever encountered such a strange obstacle to his suit. Tennyson has admirably availed himself of this advantage. As the plot advances, another rare opportunity for poetical description is afforded. The prince's father, imagining his son to be in danger in the other kingdom, comes with an army for his rescue, while an army appears in her father's kingdom to oppose it. A mêlée takes place, in which the princess's troops are successful, and the prince is wounded. The triumph of her arms proves the overthrow of her heart. She now compassionates him when wounded, and, waiting upon him on his sick couch, gives him eventually her hand.

The prince at the same time gallantly meets the claims of
the other sex half way, nor could there be anything finer in
poetry, nor more perfect as a settlement of the great woman-
question, than the following lines with which the poem concludes, spoken by the prince.

> The woman's cause is man's, they rise or sink
> Together, dwarfed or godlike, bond or free.
>
> *   *   *   *
>
> Let her make herself her own,
> To give or keep, to live and learn, and be
> All that not harms distinctive womanhood.
> For woman is not undeveloped man,
> But diverse : could we make her as the man,
> Sweet love were slain ; his dearest bond is this,
> Not like to like, but like in difference.
> Yet in the long years liker must they grow ;
> The man be more of woman, she of man ;
> He gain in sweetness and in moral height,
> Nor lose the wrestling thews that throw the world ;
> She mental breadth, nor fail in childhood care,
> Nor lose the childlike in the larger mind ;
> Till at the last she set herself to man,
> Like perfect music set to noble words ;
> And so these twain upon the skirts of time
> Sit side by side, full summed in all their powers,
> Dispensing harvest, serving the To-be.
> Self-reverent each, and reverencing each,
> Distinct in individualities.

" The Princess " is in various respects a counterpart to
" Love's Labour Lost."   There King Ferdinand and his
three companions in their zeal for study enter into the
same seclusion of themselves as men which the princess
and her companions did as women.   In the one case all
intercourse with ladies, in the other all intercourse with
gentlemen, was forbidden, and the interval the same,
for three years.   In both cases love proved mightier than
philosophy.   We have only to read Shakespeare's play
(and it is by no means his best), to see the difference between the highest order of genius and poets such as

Tennyson, however they may abound in beautiful description
and talent and sentimentality. The object of both being
to show that love will triumph over all attempts after
such a pursuit of philosophy as would ignore its power, how
simply does the intuitive genius of Shakespeare accomplish
his end! Ere the resolution of Ferdinand is well formed,
the Princess of France with her three beauties chance to
come on an embassy to his court. No sooner do the sovereign and his three lords see them, than their intellectual
determinations melt away. The four are hopelessly in love.
Byron, having gone to a retired place in the royal park to
bemoan his fate, recognises the king approaching, climbs a
tree, and overhears his confession—who again steps aside on
the approach of Longueville, to obtain ear-witness of his condition. In short, they discover to their confusion that they
are all already perjured men. Upon which Byron truly
observes :—

> Have at you then, affection's men-at-arms ;
> Consider what you first did swear unto,
> To fast, to study, and to see no woman—
> Flat treason 'gainst the kingly state of youth.
> Say, can you fast? your stomachs are too young,
> And abstinence engenders maladies.
> And where that you have vowed to study, lords,
> In that each of you hath forsworn his book,
> Can you still dream, and pore, and thereon look?
> For when would you, my lord, or you, or you
> Have found the ground of study, excellence,
> Without the beauty of a woman's face ; &c.

So the immortal dramatist ; and how true is all this to
nature! Now let us see how our Laureate manages it. He
represents the princess, who with her followers had made
her rash vow, as having been precontracted with a foreign
prince. This prince, in order to gain access to her, has to
form the expedient of dressing himself and attendants in
women's clothes. By-the-bye, it is noticeable that though
Shakespeare often makes his heroines don man's attire, he

does not adopt the other expedient, because it makes the parties ridiculous. But, passing that, as a discovery takes place, the princess is reasonably enough offended with this direct infringement upon the rules of her institution, and therefore it is not to be expected that love would triumph. So our author has to hunt about for another way of it. He brings two armies into the field, and gets the prince wounded; his wound excites compassion, and love, being akin to pity, is at last produced. What a deal of clumsy machinery is here!

"Enoch Arden" has found many admirers. A certain simple beauty characterises it, and none will deny the pathos of its close. It lies exposed, at the same time, to many exceptions. These are partly connected with the treatment of the subject, and partly with the subject itself. Our author has fallen into the common snare of supposing that the description of a scene in humble life is not subject to the same rules as the description of incidents connected with the upper ranks of society. He imagines that in this case there is no necessity of putting forth the whole power of the imagination, and that a plain bald narrative of events is enough. The result is prosiness, which is supposed to be naturalness. This is a mistake into which poets who have been born in the upper ranks are apt to fall. You will never find the Ayrshire ploughman guilty of such an error. First, he knew that it is only what is poetical in humble life that admits of poetical treatment; and he was divinely gifted in his selection of such incidents and scenes. Next, he knew that, human nature being the same great thing in one rank of life as in another, he must employ the same exalted expression and perfect style in dealing with both.

The subject itself was an unfortunate one. The case of a young wife marrying a second time, under the impression that her husband is dead—when, in point of fact, he makes his appearance again — is in one sense terrible, but in another allied with a feeling least of all akin to the serious.

No doubt we have a pathetic description of poor Annie's vague fear, after she had formed the new alliance, of something that might occur; but this wicked heart of ours will somehow experience another feeling than the tragical in the apprehension of a husband turning up, who, if he was not dead, ought to have been so. How long a woman whose husband has disappeared from the field of vision, whether by land or sea, but whose death cannot exactly be proved, is bound to wait before she marry again, is a nice piece of casuistry; but to marry at all is a very questionable step. But what shall we say of Enoch's return? There can be nothing more distressing than for a man to find, when coming home from a distant voyage, that another has filled the situation he left vacant, even supposing this to have been nothing other than a business situation; how much more to find that some cuckoo has taken possession of his marital nest—that some idiot lover, not knowing the difference between a wife whose husband is still within the possibilities of existence, and a widow, has quietly taken possession of a doubtful territory. Enoch, we should say, on discovering the awful fact, if he did not immediately institute an action for damages, ought to have absconded from the neighbourhood and from the country, if not from the continent. But nothing would satisfy him except to have one look, at any rate, into the interior of the house, and to mount a tree for the better inspection of his family. We are told, too, by our Laureate, that it was a yew-tree (which shows how careful he is in authenticating his facts), and it was in the middle of March that the ascent was made; and we are further informed that Philip's house was the last house in the street!

In "Maud" we find Tennyson for once adopting something like the spirit and strain of Lord Byron. We have the gloomy and passionate and egotistical ravings of one who in the beginning of his career had been stung by the world, and contemned it; and who, being equally unfortunate in his after-love, from having slain in a duel the brother of his mistress, is haunted by her spectre. The misanthropy of Lord Byron's heroes was always rendered interesting by the transcendent qualities they personally possessed, and not a little by the belief we all had that they reflected the gloom of his lordship's own spirit. That of Maud's lover cannot be said to possess such claims upon our romantic consideration, being only known to us as the son of one who had been led on to ruin by a designing money speculator, and who had committed suicide in a neighbouring quarry. This is an ugly subject to begin with. The speculator whose villainy had thus darkened his youthful soul was none other than Maud's father; and yet, since they had played together in their childhood, he yields himself up to a fatal attachment, which is reciprocated. The first part of the poem, which describes the rise and progress of this singular courtship, is remarkable chiefly from the absolute nothingness of the incidents around which so many highly melodious but rather namby-pamby measures are strung. He meets her at the head of the village, when "the sunset burned on the blossomed gable-ends," and this forms the subject of one distich. He meets her in the village church, and his heart beat so loud that he "could not hear the snowy-handed, dilettante, delicate-handed priest intone." She waves her hand one day to him on horseback, when he was a mile, and, as he avers, more than a mile, from the shore :—

> I was walking a mile,
>   More than a mile from the shore ;
> The sun looked out with a smile
>   Betwixt the cloud and the moor ;
> And riding at set of day
>   Over the dark moorland,
> Rapidly riding far away,
>   She waved to me her hand.

Most of this part of the poem is written in the very worst taste. Take even the best of it :—

I.

Maud has a garden of roses
And lilies fair on a lawn ;
There she walks in her state,
And tends upon bed and bower ;
And thither I climbed at dawn,
And stood by her garden gate.
A lion ramps at the top ;
He is claspt by a passion-flower.

II.

Maud's own little oak room
  (Which Maud, like a precious stone
Set in the heart of the carven gloom,
  Lights with herself, when alone
She sits with her music and books,
  And her brother lingers late
With a roystering company) looks
  Upon Maud's own garden gate ;
And I thought, as I stood, if a hand as white
  As ocean foam in the moon were laid
On the hasp of the window, and my Delight
  Had a sudden desire, like a glorious ghost, to glide
  Like a beam of the seventh heaven down to my side,
  There were but a step to be made.

Some may think that it showed no small measure of coolness on the part of the lover to notice that there was a lion perched upon the top of the gate, but they will please observe that it was claspt by a passion-flower. He has taken special note too that Maud's room is oak-panelled, and the idea suggested to him is a pretty one, that she is the gem, and that the four carved walls are the frame. He was of course right in his conjecture that the window, being a low one, there was but a step to be made in order to her being at his side ; though, with very proper caution, he adds that this was upon the supposition that her hand were laid on the hasp. The whole is as sorry verse as can well be conceived.

The poetry in the second part is in a higher strain. Some readers may think that it is as high as Byron's—others may think still higher. But the question is what judgment those

may arrive at who have read the pages three times over.
We are afraid such will find that in those wailings, tender
and passionate as they are, there is little but tragical sound
and pretty sentimentalities. Here, for example, is an average
specimen : he is referring to the spectre that haunted him
in the crowded city.

> A shadow flits before me,
> Not thou, but like to thee ;
> Ah, Christ, that it were possible
> For one short hour to see
> The souls we loved, that they might tell us
> What and where they be.
>
> It leads me forth at evening,
> It lightly winds and steals
> In a cold white robe before me,
> When all my spirit reels
> At the shouts, the leagues of lights,
> And the roaring of the wheels.
>
> *   *   *   *
>
> Do I hear her sing as of old,
> My bird with the shining head,
> My own dove with the tender eye ?
> But there rings on a sudden a passionate cry,
> There is some one dying or dead,
> And a sullen thunder is rolled ;
> For a tumult shakes the city
> And I wake, my dream is fled.
> In the shuddering dawn, behold,
> Without knowledge, without pity,
> By the curtains of my bed,
> That abiding phantom cold.
>
> *   *   *   *
>
> Would the happy spirit descend
> From the realms of light and song,
> In the chamber or the street,
> As she looks among the blest,
> Should I fear to greet my friend,
> Or to say, " Forgive the wrong,"
> Or to ask her, " Take me, sweet,
> To the regions of thy rest " ?

> But the broad light glares and beats,
> And the shadow flits and fleets,
> And will not let me be ;
> And I loathe the squares and streets,
> And the faces that one meets,
> Hearts with no love·for me ;
> Alway I long to creep
> Into some still cavern deep,
> There to weep, and weep, and weep
> My whole soul out to thee.

The whole poem is full of extravagances. Oddity seems one of the characteristics of our present bards. Maud's lover is eventually advised by her in a dream to enlist for the Crimean war; and the poem ends by telling us all what we had been unable for the life of us to discover, the good effected by that war, which it seems was that it delivered us from the evils of peace.

It is refreshing to leave a poem of this description, and come to "In Memoriam," justly looked upon as the chief work of Tennyson, the most condensed in thought, and as to its execution, perfect.

As a tribute to the dead it stands unrivalled. That was a sublime and eternal crag of a monument which Milton reared above the sea to him who sank in

> That fatal and perfidious bark,
> Built in the eclipse, and rigged with curses dark ;

but never surely did art and genius together rear anything so exquisitely ornamental as the thousand-mansioned mausoleum of Hallam. The very length of the elegy overwhelms us, for it seems as if this procession of draped chariots of the Muses, and flaming torches, and innumerable pall-bearers from the realms of fancy, and thousands upon thousands of embodied forms of the imagination conjured up as accompanying representatives from every quarter of the world and of nature herself, would never pass by in conveying the remains of this youth to a distant posterity. It is the intensity of

,passion evinced by this fixed and long gaze after his departed friend that indicates the extraordinary character of the author's mind: The only parallel that suggests itself to us is Dante, who in his endless Canzonière persists in kindling the flame again and again on the altar of the inexorable Beatrice, as if he were bound never to let it die there. Her charms had awakened an hour's admiration in many a heart, or caused a month's unrest to others; but it was in the great Florentine that they awoke the passion which poured itself forth in these inexhaustible songs.

> The circling year's cold point I have attained
> When the horizon gives the sun repose,
> And in the east brings forth the heavenly twins.
> The star of love remains removed from view,
> Hid by the lucid ray across it thrown,
> So widely as to form for it a veil;
> The planet also which gives strength to frost
> Moves full disclosed through the capacious arch,
> In which each of the seven cast little shade :
> And yet no thought of love,
> With which I am loaded, ever quits my mind,
> That harder is than agate to retain
> The image of a lady formed of stone !
>
> In Ethiopia's sands the pilgrim wind
> Arises and the lurid air disturbs,
> That burns beneath the scorching solar ray ;
> Then, the sea passing, draws from it a mist
> So thick, that if no other wind disturb,
> It covers and shuts up this hemisphere,
> And then dissolves, and falls in whitened flakes
> Of chilling snow, or showers of noisome rain,
> Whence saddened is the air, and nature mourns.
> Yet Love, who all his nets
> Withdraws to heaven as the tempest swells,
> Never abandons me, beauty so great
> Adorns this cruel lady whom I serve.

The marvel in the case before us is that friendship, commonly reckoned the weaker sentiment, should have burned with a flame intenser than love itself. Nothing can reflect more honour upon the heart of Tennyson, than that Hallam should have inspired as deep a passion as Beatrice.

> In star and flower
> He feels him some diffusive power ;

he has no joy more in " the herald melodies of spring ; " and, gazing on the old yew that " nets his dreamless head " in the grave, and thinking of its thousand years of gloom, he seems " to fail from out his blood and grow incorporate " into its stem. This is his blessing upon the ship that brought " the dark freight—his veiled life."

> Henceforth, wherever thou may'st roam,
>   My blessing, like a line of light,
>   Is on the waters day and night,
> And like a beacon guards thee home.
>
> So may whatever tempest mars
>   Mid ocean, spare thee, sacred bark;
>   And balmy drops in summer dark
> Slide from the bosom of the stars.
>
> So kind an office hath been done,
>   Such precious relics brought by thee,
>   The dust of him I shall not see
> Till all my widowed race be run.

And this is his description of the hideous dreams which now haunted his soul, mingled with the appearance of his friend.

> I cannot see the features right
>   When on the gloom I strive to paint
>   The face I know ; the hues are faint,
> And mix with hollow masks of night.
>
> Cloud-towers by ghostly masons wrought,
>   A gulf that ever shuts and gapes,
>   A hand that points, and pallid shapes
> In shadowy thoroughfares of thought ;
>
> And crowds that stream from yawning doors,
>   And shoals of puckered faces drive,
>   Dark bulks that tumble half alive,
> And lazy lengths on boundless shores ;

> Till all at once beyond the will
> I hear a wizard music roll,
> And thro' a lattice of the soul
> Looks thy fair face and makes it still.

If Dante possessed an advantage over Tennyson in having female beauty to apostrophize, and not merely an accomplished fellow-student, so also had he the benefit of an infinitely melodious language. He lived in a country where, as if by way of some small compensation for the incubus of popery, God has driven every cloud from the sky and all dissonance from the language. Our poet in writing his "In Memoriam" not only laboured under the disadvantage of our rugged English, but unfortunately adopted the most wretched measure known in this country. Even had he chosen the metre of the psalms of David, he would at least have pleased the ear by a constant musical descent. As it is, we are deprived of this gratification, and there is nothing but an eternal revolution of these monotonous muffled cylinders. It must ever be considered as a miracle that he escaped ruining the poem by subjecting himself to this gratuitous source of annoyance.

All the disadvantages have not yet been mentioned which he has triumphed over in this singular production. Bereavement may be granted to be a good theme for poetry, but might have been judged to be thoroughly exhausted in a world where death has reigned so long. Besides, it is in some respects a narrow theme, suggesting to ordinary minds only a few materials for verse, and these as obvious as they are transcendently solemn and important. These have been so infinitely diversified, however, in the poetical description, that the "In Memoriam" may be compared to the wonderful instrument of Sir David Brewster. Just as the few bits of glass turned round undergo every metamorphosis that can entrance the wondering eye of childhood, so were it impossible to tell the different forms of beauty which strike the eye as the subject revolves in the endless parts of this immortal kaleidoscope. At one time, in thinking of his exalted friend, he compares himself to some village maiden, victim of a hopeless love for one in high station.

> He past ; a soul of nobler tone :
>   My spirit loved and loves him yet,
>   Like some poor girl whose love is set
> On one whose rank exceeds her own.
>
> He mixing with his proper sphere,
>   She finds the baseness of her lot,
>   Half jealous of she knows not what,
> And envying all that meet him there.
>
> The little village looks forlorn ;
>   She sighs amid her narrow days,
>   Moving about in household ways,
> In that dark house where she was born.
>
> The foolish neighbours come and go,
>   And tease her till the day draws by :
>   At night she weeps, " How vain am I !
> How should he love a thing so low ? "

The poet turns the subject round in his hands, and now his friend looks down upon this world, as one who has risen from humble birth to be prime minister of his country may think of the fields where he played in childhood, and where some school companion of his may even now be following the plough.

> Dost thou look back on what hath been,
>   As some divinely gifted man,
>   Whose life in low estate began,
> And on a simple village green ;
>
> Who breaks his birth's invidious bar,
>   And grasps the skirts of happy chance,
>   And breasts the blows of circumstance,
> And grapples with his evil star ;
>
> Who makes by force his merit known,
>   And lives to clutch the golden keys,
>   To mould a mighty state's decrees,
> And shape the whisper of the throne ;

> And moving up from high to higher,
>   Becomes on fortune's crowning slope
>   The pillar of a people's hope,
> The centre of a world's desire.
>
> Yet feels, as in a pensive dream,
>   When all his active powers are still,
>   A distant dearness in the hill,
> A secret sweetness in the stream,
>
> The limit of his narrower fate,
>   While yet beside its vocal springs,
>   He played at counsellors and kings,
> With one that was his earliest mate,
>
> Who ploughs with pain his native lea,
>   And reaps the labour of his hands,
>   Or in the furrow musing stands ;
> Does my old friend remember me ?

Once again the magical instrument revolves, and the hopeless elevation of the glorified one changes into the possibility of his being advantaged even in heaven by remembrance of his early friend.

> Sweet soul, do with me as thou wilt,
>   I lull a fancy trouble-tost
>   With, " Love's too precious to be lost,
> A little grain shall not be spilt."
>
> And in that solace I can sing,
>   Till out of painful phases wrought,
>   There flutters up a happy thought,
> Self-balanced on a lightsome wing :
>
> Since we deserved the name of friends,
>   And thine effect so lives in me,
>   A part of mine may live in thee,
> And move thee on to noble ends.

As the elegiac strain flows on we find him in one place exulting in the blessed fellowship he shall have with the loved one in heaven ; when, again, suddenly he is struck dumb with the reflection that his friend having had the start of him by a lifetime, he may never overtake him throughout eternity.

What wealth of fancy meets us in this poem! what prodigality of thought! what felicities of expression! We are conducted through innumerable chambers of imagery; we walk through a thousand and one dim-lighted corridors; we step out into ever so many gardens of flowers; we are in the night always, more or less, but it is through all kinds of darkness we pass, of the wood, of the sky, now starless, now full-mooned; but when all nature has been ransacked, not even then does the poet seem able to discover considerations enough to heal the great wound that death had made in his soul. The following verses, in which he is fain to discover one consolation in its being better to have lost his friend than never to have known and loved him, have been always admired for the exquisiteness of their expression.

> I envy not in any moods
>   The captive void of noble rage,
>   The linnet born within the cage,
> That never knew the summer woods.
>
> I envy not the beast that takes
>   His license in the field of time,
>   Unfettered by the sense of crime,
> To whom a conscience never wakes;
>
> Nor what may count itself as blest,
>   The heart that never plighted troth,
>   But stagnates in the weeds of sloth,
> Nor any want-begotten rest.
>
> I hold it true, whate'er befall,
>   I feel it when I sorrow most,
>   'Tis better to have loved and lost
> Than never to have loved at all.

We venture to suggest that the second verse mars the rest. We are not sure if the illustration it contains logically applies; it is an ugly one at any rate, and perhaps the least fitted to carry our assent of any he could have produced.

In so long a poem many mediocre and poor passages may be
expected to occur.   Referring to the consolation that might
be suggested to him of bereavement being something common to all, he considers it necessary to insist upon the wide
prevalence of that calamity in such verses as the following,
some of which are doggrel enough.

> O father, wheresoe'er thou be,
>   Who pledgest now thy gallant son,
>   A shot, ere half thy draught be done,
> Hath stilled the life that beat from thee.
>
> O mother, praying God will save
>   Thy sailor, while thy head is bowed,
>   His heavy-shotted hammock-shroud
> Drops in his vast and wandering grave.
>
> *   *   *   *
>
> O somewhere, meek, unconscious dove,
>   Thou sittest ranging golden hair;
>   And glad to find thyself so fair,
> Poor child, that waitest for thy love !
>
> For now her father's chimney glows
>   In expectation of a guest,
>   And, thinking this will please him best,
> She takes a ribbon or a rose ;
>
> For he will see them on to-night,
>   And with the thought her colour burns ;
>   And, having left the glass, she turns
> Once more to set a ringlet right.
>
> And, even when she turned, the curse
>   Had fallen, and her future lord
>   Was drowned in passing through the ford,
> Or killed in falling from his horse.

Our readers will agree with us that what Tennyson says
of this argument itself for consolation, is applicable to his
own verses upon it.

> And common is the common-place,
> And vacant chaff well meant for grain.

Sometimes we have an elaborate attempt to ornament nothing. Instead of saying "that if ever he was sinful enough to become indifferent to his friend, he hoped God, who saw such a thing likely to happen, might kill him," he writes :—

> And if that Eye which watches guilt
>   And goodness, and hath power to see
>   Within the green, the mouldered tree,
> And towers fall'n as soon as built ;
>
> Oh ! if indeed that eye foresee,
>   Or see (in Him is no before)
>   In more of life true life no more,
> And love the indifference to be ;
>
> Then might I find, ere yet the morn
>   Breaks hither over Indian seas,
>   That shadow waiting for the keys,
> To shroud me from my proper scorn.

Nay, there are whole hundreds of lines together not very much above mediocrity. But these blemishes, what are they but as the dull spots on the face of the shining Orb that rules and will never cease to rule the night ; and when they have been pointed out, it remains true that seldom has there been written a more marvellous work than the " In Memoriam ;" elaboration and passion both combined in it ; not an elegy, but one hundred and thirty-one elegies, sustaining the interest of the reader throughout without plot or connection ; any one of them enough to have done credit to a poet, but when taken together well entitling him to the Laureate crown.

THE RELIGION OF TENNYSON.

If we proceed now to close a criticism which has been largely laudatory with unmingled censure, it is because Tennyson, not satisfied with being a poet, has considered it necessary to broach those dangerous religious sentiments of which he is a neophyte.

The views he holds upon religion are largely those of Browning and of Carlyle, and we must refer our readers therefore to the essays upon these writers in the preceding part of this volume. We have shown there what is their theory of the history of all true, vital religion in the soul of any man.

First, there is a season of distress, almost despair, arising from scepticism not merely with regard to the truth of Christianity, but the very existence and personality of God Himself. This is so far, according to them, from being a wrong, and a dangerous and a criminal experience, that it is represented as a desirable and salutary process to begin with. It is with them the first sign of life, and in many respects the best regenerator. The way in which they emerge from this salutary despair into the faith both of God and of Christianity is equally novel. They come to faith in God's existence again, but it is not by the old way of coming to be satisfied by evidences of Divine power and wisdom in His works around them. They maintain that all such intellectual arguments are unsatisfactory, and they rest exclusively upon that apprehension they have of His existence partly intuitive and partly gathered from the law written within our hearts. So with Christianity. They come back to the faith of it. But it is not in the old way, not in the way of being convinced by evidence of the truth of the historical Record, or of the miracles. They judge all such evidence to be unsatisfactory ; and, besides, they reckon it to be unnecessary. They profess to reach faith in Christianity by the law within, and the light of nature. Looking there, they have found God to be a God of love, and therefore Christ, who is the incarnation of love, is commended to them to be really and truly the Son of God, without any other evidences being required.

If Tennyson hold this theory, then, we may expect to find him in his poetry showing and commending that noble agony of soul which consists in doubting ; for another thing, we may expect to find him ignoring the Bible, and striving to solve the mysteries of life in the same melancholy way in which a heathen philosopher would do, who had nothing but the light of human reason to work by; once again, we may expect to find that when he comes to speak of Christ it will be with a vague uncertainty of belief. How far our readers can testify from their own experience to his poetry as being thus characterized we cannot tell. But we shall proceed to state our proof from his writings that he holds by the strange and pernicious theory to which reference has been made.

In proof of his maintaining the doctrine that a sceptical distress or despair is what forms the effective turning point for a man in religion, let us refer to his poem entitled

" THE PALACE OF ART."

Evidently the object of this poem is to show that the tendency of man is to seek his satisfaction, in the first instance, in a proud, selfish, isolated cultivation of his intellect, and enjoyment of all that is beautiful in art and in nature. This the poet sets forth figuratively when he represents himself as having built this lordly palace for his soul, which contained emblematically within it whatever was great in art, nature, and philosophy. At this stage of his experience he had no sympathy with, and took no interest in, suffering humanity around him, and the painful riddle which it exhibits, though sometimes glanced at superficially, did not disturb his happiness at all.

> My soul would live alone unto herself
> In her high palace there.
>   *   *   *   *
> Full oft the riddle of the painful earth
> Flashed through her as she sat alone,
> Yet not the less held she her solemn mirth
> And intellectual throne.

He was able, under the influence of such teachings and tastes as he had in this isolated palace, to look down upon the low profligacies of the sensual, but it was with a certain pride and complacency.

> O godlike isolation which art mine,
> I can but count thee perfect gain,
> What time I watch the darkening drove of swine
> That range on yonder plain ;

> In filthy sloughs they roll a prurient skin,
>   They graze and wallow, breed and sleep,
> And oft some brainless devil enters in
>   And drives them to the deep.

He had, moreover, a proud self-sufficient belief of a future state, and that all would be well with him hereafter; and, stored as he was with the knowledge of all that was great in mental acquirement, and all that was great in human achievement, he had no regard to one religious creed more than another.

> Then of the moral instinct would she prate,
>   And of the rising from the dead,
> As hers by right of full-accomplished fate;
>   And at the last she said —
>
> "I take possession of man's mind and deed,
>   I care not what the sects may brawl;
> I sit as God, holding no form of creed,
>   But contemplating all."

Let us stop here for a moment. Such then is the representation Tennyson gives us, so far as we have gone, of his first—shall we call it his unconverted state? For if he means anything by the description he presents us with in this poem, it is to set forth a great change which he experienced, and which we must all experience. The poem contains, if it contains anything, the view of our friends of the new school of theology (since our poets are standing forth now as theological teachers) with regard to the great change which our souls must undergo—shall we call it a saving change?

Let us notice that the description he gives us of the first state of his soul exactly answers to the doctrine of Carlyle, who grants that the mere cultivation of the intellect and of the arts is not enough; also that there is a certain selfishness which is natural to us, and a proud self-sufficiency, which must be knocked out of us.

Well—to go on with the poem—next comes the great change which took place, Tennyson's account of his own conversion in short, for if it does not mean that, what other great change is it that he refers to—it being of sin and purgation from it that he speaks so explicitly at the close. Here it is; speaking of his soul :—

> And so she throve and prospered ; so three years
>   She prospered ; on the fourth she fell,
> Like Herod, when the shout was in his ears,
>   Struck thro' with pangs of hell.
>
> Lest she should fail and perish utterly,
>   God, before whom ever lie bare
> The abysmal deeps of personality,
>   Plagued her with sore despair.
>
> When she would think, where'er she turned her sight,
>   The airy hand confusion wrought,
> Wrote " Mene, mene," and divided quite
>   The kingdom of her thought.

Further on he still describes the state of his soul.

> A spot of dull stagnation, without light
>   Or power of movement, seemed my soul,
> Mid onward-sloping movements infinite,
>   Making for one sure goal.
>
> A star that with the choral starry dance
>   Joined not, but stood, and standing saw
> The hollow orb of moving circumstance
>   Rolled round by one fixed law.
>
>   *   *   *   *
>
> " No voice," she shrieked, in that lone hall ;
> " No voice breaks through the stillness of this world :
>   One deep, deep silence all ! "

Thus his soul certainly went through an experience of distress, and almost of despair, which he describes as having been necessary, and without which it would have " failed and perished." When Tennyson and his companions Carlyle and Browning come before the nation to detail the processes of conviction and sore agony by which they reached salvation at last, they are entitled to expect that we shall seriously and reverentially consider them. How was this distress or despair then produced ?   We may in part gather this from the title he gives to God, who produced it :—

> God, before whom ever lie bare
> The abysmal deeps of personality.

It seems to have been then " *the abysmal deeps of personality* " into which he was plunged. The language is obscure, and may refer either to the author's own personality—that, in short, he was plunged into such deep questions as Carlyle represents to suggest themselves to one who has begun to think seriously—connected all with the *Ego*, " Whence did I come ? whither am I going ?" &c.; or it may refer to God's personality—the deep perplexing question whether there be a personal God.   But whether it mean the one thing or the other, it comes out distinctly enough in the verses I have quoted that this distress by which he was seized was not caused by a sense of guilt brought home to his conscience by the Word of God.   This is what has generally been understood by all Christendom to be the distress out of which any good eventually comes.   But that which Tennyson here speaks of, so far from arising out of any such quarter, arose from his being plunged into the " abysmal deeps " of speculation with regard to whether there be a God at all.   It is not that he hears God's voice thundering against him for sins he has done, but it is that there is no voice breaking through the stillness of this world :—

> " No voice," she shrieked, in that lone hall,
> " No voice breaks through the silence of this world :
> One deep, deep silence all; "

or, as he expresses it in a previous verse, that there is nothing to be seen but

> The hollow orb of moving circumstance
> Rolled round by one fixed law.

Again, the distress and despair arises from this, that in looking round him upon the natural world he sees an infinite

number of things all accomplishing surely their ends, while
he cannot understand for what end he himself was made.

> A spot of dull stagnation, without light
>   Or power of movement, seemed my soul;
> Mid onward-sloping movements infinite,
>   Making for one sure goal.

All this distress and despair of his, in one word, is nothing
but an experience of doubt and perplexity connected with the
existence of a personal God, and with regard to his own
place physically in this mysterious system of the universe.
This is quite of a piece with Carlyle's teaching, which would
have us consider that there is no hope of a man till he
comes into a state of agonizing doubt with regard to such
subjects. A wonderful virtue is attached by it to this distress. So in this poem. The author describes his soul,
when thus led down into " the abysmal deeps of personality,"
as being thereby led into the knowledge of her sins. The
sense of solitude into which she is brought in part produces
this.

> Deep dread and loathing of her solitude
> Fell on her, from which mood was born
> Scorn of herself.

In his soul he now feels he is a sinner.

> She howled aloud, " I am on fire within,
>   There comes no murmur of reply.
> What is it that will take away my sin,
>   And save me lest I die?"

In other words, Tennyson was led to see that he was a
sinner, and to cry out, " What shall I do to be saved?"
But how? Not by the Word of God at all—but by this
doubt and darkness process, which by the very torment and
despair it caused made him seriously to think. Nay, it is
described, in the end of the poem, as being the means of
humbling him, and commencing a new life of penitence and
prayer.

> So when four years were wholly finished,
>   She threw her royal robes away.
> " Make me a cottage in the vale," she said,
>   " Where I may mourn and pray.
>
> " Yet pull not down my palace towers, that are
>   So lightly, beautifully built ;
> Perchance I may return with others there
>   When I have purged my guilt."

After this humiliation, undergone through scepticism, and the blessed despairs connected with it have had their full work, in short, he will speedily be all right, and mount his Rock again.

Now there cannot be a more erroneous or a more dangerous doctrine than this, that all true religion in the soul begins with scepticism and speculative perplexity, and that the distresses connected with these are of the nature of a wholesome humiliation, ending in salvation. It is the more necessary to speak decisively upon this point, as the effect of this deplorable teaching has been to produce in our country, judging by the countless doggrel verses that infest our higher periodicals, a host of young men who confound the wailings of scepticism with earnestness in religion. What is begotten of pride never can produce true humility. Nothing but what is evil can come out of scepticism. Its distresses are the just punishment for the rejection of evidence. The only good that can come out of them is that the party who suffers under them be led thereby to see the error of his having ever yielded to scepticism, and to reverse his exercise and retrace his steps. When, on the contrary, such men as Tennyson and Carlyle and Browning glory in this sceptical distress of theirs, and count it to have been, in fact, their baptism of fire, it will be found that they have come out of it having parted with truths far more valuable than can ever be compensated by the spurious humility and earnestness with which they think that they now hold the miserably few truths which they retain.

In proof that Tennyson dishonours the Bible by ignoring

it in the most elemental points of religion that require to
be settled, take

"THE TWO VOICES."

In this poem he describes a contest he has with a desperate temptation to commit suicide, and at once rid himself
of a miserable existence—a temptation which he meets by
a variety of arguments shown why he should still live on.
The one of the two Voices is that which tempts him to despair.   The other, with which the author identifies himself,
argues upon the side of hope, and of continuing to war on
in the battle of existence.   Let it be noticed that this better
Voice, as appears from all the arguments adduced by it,
is the author's own reason.   Never once does he refer to
a third Voice, that of God Himself speaking in His Word,
and which settles (as one would surely say) this whole
question.   Tennyson might have found the decisive settlement of the question there—and for him to seek the solution
of it from this croaking voice of his own reason, suggesting
some thirty and four arguments why he should not cut his
carotid, is abundantly ridiculous.   If from the poem it appeared that he was merely endeavouring as a holiday exercise
to show how the question could be settled by human reason,
condemned him for that.   But he is evidently in earnest.
without referring to positive revelation, we would not have
Nay, he absolutely cries and weeps.   Thus, reasoning with
the ugly voice that would lead him to commit suicide—

> I would have said, "Thou canst not know;"
> But my full heart, that worked below,
> Rained thro' my sight its overflow.
>
>   *   *   *   *
>
> I wept, "Tho' I should die, I know
> That;" &c.

He thus evidently writes as one who felt that the only satisfactory settlement of this question was to be found in such
ridiculous argumentation as this of his own reason, and that
if it failed his hope and comfort were gone!   "The Two

Voices " is a production showing that its author belongs to a school of writers who have surrendered their faith in the Bible as in itself satisfactory even for determining whether suicide be a virtue, or man have any higher and better destiny. He sighs and groans under agonies of soul upon these points, all the same as if he lived in a heathen land, where he had to solve the mysteries of existence; and he expects besides that we are to sympathise with the maudling distress of such an experience as he describes.

Let it not be said that we have exaggerated the constructive dishonour put upon the Bible by this poem. He no doubt in one passage of it refers the foul tempting Voice to Stephen the martyr :—

> I cannot hide that some have striven,
> Achieving calm, to whom was given
> The joy that mixes man with heaven.
>
> Who, rowing hard against the stream,
> Saw distant gates of Eden gleam,
> And did not dream it was a dream;
>
> But heard, by secret transport led,
> E'en in the charnels of the dead,
> The murmur of the fountain-head—
>
> Which did accomplish their desire,
> Bore and forbore, and did not tire,
> Like Stephen, an unquenchèd fire.
>
> He heeded not reviling tones,
> Nor sold his heart to idle moans,
> Though cursed and scorn'd and bruised with stones.

But (1) the foul Voice having objected to this, that Stephen had no fixed grounds for that hope of his, but was merely a man of a kindlier nature than the commonalty of men—

> Not that the grounds of hope were fix'd,
> The elements were kindlier mix'd—

does Tennyson immediately resent the insinuation by averring that the grounds of his hope were God's infallible Word? Not he: he goes on maundering with his philosophical arguments. The very way, then, in which this reference

to Stephen is disposed of is an additional dishonour cast
upon the Bible.   (2) The way in which the reference to
Stephen is introduced, shows that in mentioning him Tennyson does not mean to fortify himself by the authority of the
Bible, or of the Christian creed or faith, but only by the
example of good men in general; for he introduces it by a
contemptuous slight cast upon all creeds :—

> I know that age to age succeeds,
> Blowing a noise of tongues and deeds,
> A dust of systems and of creeds.

Then comes in the passage I have quoted above :—

> I cannot hide that some have striven,
> Achieving calm, &c.;

among whom he mentions Stephen, but only as one of the
great men of any creed as well as another, upon whom we
know that Carlyle builds his confidence more than the Bible
or any written record.

Next, we may be reminded, in his defence, of the way by
which at the close of the poem he represents himself as being
relieved from his temptation. Well, what is that ? He chances,
it being Sabbath morning, to hear the church bells ringing,
and to see the country people with their families walking to
the sanctuary.   This is represented as restoring his drooping
hope regarding man's destinies. And how ? By suggesting
a sentimental, intuitive conviction of there being something
in religion, as indefinite, however, as may be.   He calls it

> A little hint to solace woe,
> A hint, a whisper breathing low,
> "I may not speak of what I know."

> Like an Æolian harp that wakes
> No certain air, but overtakes
> Far thought with music that it makes ;

> Such seem'd the whisper at my side ;
> "What is it thou knowest, sweet voice ?" I cried.
> "A hidden hope," the voice replied.

It is enough to make one smile to see how willingly this

writer renounces the infallible certainty of the Bible for this sweet little hope of his, begotten of church bells and the sight of people going to church, though he does not go to the church himself; for the best of the joke is that, instead of joining this goodly company, he adds :—

> And forth into the fields I went,
> And nature's living motion lent
> The pulse of hope to discontent! &c.

We have only to add that the whole of this production, judged by the rules of art, is not of the highest; a half-way halt between prose and poetry, so that any man having Tennyson's abilities might drive three lines in hand of this quality to the end of time, without deserving much praise after all.

I have shown at length in the essays upon Carlyle and Browning, that, according to them, the essential design of Christianity was to show us that God is love—in the sense that there is no such thing as wrath in Him. They consider that the Son of God became Flesh, not to make an atonement for our sins by His blood-shedding, but, on the contrary, to show that there is no necessity for any such atonement being made—that there is nothing in God of this peculiarity of wrath or inflexibility of justice — to show, in short, that God is one like unto ourselves, or (to use their own language) to show " the flesh that is in God." Hence they renounce the phraseology we have been accustomed to, and instead of talking of " God in the flesh," are fond of using the other expression, " the flesh in God." Having thus changed Christianity altogether, and represented the object of Christ's mission and incarnation as having been simply to convince or inform us that God is love—they are prepared, secondly, to maintain that miracles and the written Record are quite unnecessary to prove the truth of Christianity, since the law within our own hearts, and observations of the natural world around us, tell us that God is love. They begin in the pride of their understanding with the rejection of miracles and all that is supernatural and distasteful in the contents of the Bible. Having presumptuously changed Christianity into the system I have mentioned above, they judge this to be one great recommendation of it, that it is a Christianity which can be proved by the indigenous sentiments of our own heart, and from the light of nature herself.

Alfred Tennyson has adopted these views. His faith, too, as he expresses it in his "Enoch Arden," is

> In that mystery
> Where God-in-man is one with man-in-God.

In proof that he looks upon Christianity as being nothing more after all than what is written naturally upon our hearts, let us look to his

"IN MEMORIAM."

In sections xxxi. and xxxii. Christmas Eve suggests the subject of his friend's resurrection and continued existence in another world, and starts the question as to whether friends there may recognise one another. Notice is taken of Lazarus's resurrection, and that nothing is said in Scripture of Mary having interrogated her risen brother regarding his experiences after death. Both subtile questions and " curious fears " are represented in her case as swallowed up in joy and love.

> All subtile thought, all curious fears,
> Borne down by gladness so complete,
> She bows, she bathes the Saviour's feet
> With costly spikenard and with tears.
>
> Thrice blest whose lives are faithful prayers,
> Whose loves in higher love endure;
> What souls possess themselves so pure,
> Or is there blessedness like theirs?

What does Tennyson mean by her "curious fears" being borne down? He can only mean such fears as curiosity might have suggested to another, as to whether a death and resurrection had really taken place at all. Let it be noticed, then, that our poet has passed from the trifling subject of her not having asked her brother of his experiences

after death to the very different and much graver point of
her not having entertained "curious fears" about the whole
subject of this miracle of a resurrection. He would have us
believe that these were banished from her mind, not by the
indisputable evidence of her own eyes, which saw him rise
from the grave after four days' interment, but by gladness
and love. And he considers her as being blest in this simplicity of hers.

That this is his view of the matter comes out by his proceeding, in the section (xxxiii.) which follows, to counsel those
who may "seem to have reached a purer air" by taking the
law within as the rule of their faith, not to vex their sisters
—poor things!—who, in their simplicity, accept without
doubting all that is miraculous in the Record.

> O thou, that after toil and storm,
>   May'st seem to have reached a purer air,
>   Whose faith has centre everywhere,
> Nor cares to fix itself in form.
>
> Leave thou thy sister when she prays,
>   Her early heaven, her happy views ;
>   Nor thou with shadowed hint confuse
> A life that lends melodious days.
>
> Her faith, thro' form, is pure as thine,
>   Her hands are quicker unto good ;
>   Oh, sacred be the flesh and blood
> To which she links a truth divine.
>
> See thou, that countest reason ripe
>   In holding by the law within,
>   Thou fail not in a world of sin,
> And e'en for want of such a type.

Let us examine this. The party he counsels is he who
"counts reason ripe in holding by the law within ;" that is,
who thinks the most advanced stage of enlightenment is
reached when, instead of making a positive revelation like
that of the Bible the ultimate rule of faith, we prefer the law
written indelibly and universally upon our hearts. This is
the idea of our more thorough and radical modern rationalists.
They consider that Voltaire and others at the period of the

French Revolution did no essential damage when they over-threw all faith in the Christian Record or in Christ Himself; for they profess to discover that God is a God of love, and willing to save us all, from the natural world around them, and the sentiments originally engraven upon humanity. They are well described in this section as they

> Whose faith is centred everywhere,
> Nor cares to fix itself to form ;

—that is, to any one formulated and embodied system, such as Christianity is.

Now of these out-and-out, or more radical rationalists, Tennyson affirms their faith to be " pure." Indeed, with regard to the sister, all he claims for her is—

> Her faith, thro' form, is pure as thine.

These rationalists, according to him, possess the " truth divine ; " the only difference is that she links the truth divine to " flesh and blood ; "

> Oh, sacred be the flesh and blood
> To which she links a truth divine.

No doubt he warns them lest, in holding by " the law within," they should fail in such a world as this, " even for want of such a type "—meaning such a type or embodied manifestation as Christ or Christianity affords of the Divine truth (*that God is love*) engraven upon the heart.

But in going thus far, Tennyson goes no farther than Carlyle and Robert Browning, who are Christian rationalists. With him Christianity is only a " type " or " form " of that Divine truth which is written upon the hearts of us all by nature. We learn by " the law within," and observation of the world around us, that God is love, or willing to pardon and save us all, and that there is a blessed future before us ; only it was necessary that this Divine truth should be taught us in a " typal," " flesh and blood " way, which it is in what they are pleased to call " the tale that is abroad in the world " of Christ, or the Son of God incarnate. He accord-ingly proceeds to show in sections xxxiv. and xxxv. that all the essential truth regarding man's eternal well-being in a future world can be discovered and reasoned out by Nature's light. Then in section xxxvi. he shows that the service done by Christianity is merely in having made the truth more patent, especially to humbler and meaner capacities.

> Though truths in manhood darkly join,
>   Deep seated in our mystic frame,
>   We yield all blessing to the name
> Of Him who made them current coin ;
>
> For wisdom dealt with mortal powers,
>   Where truth in closer words shall fail,
>   When truth embodied in a tale
> Shall enter in at lowly doors.
>
> And so the Word had breath, and wrought
>   With human hands the creed of creeds,
>   In loveliness of perfect deeds,
> More strong than all poetic thought ;
>
> Which he may read that binds the sheaf,
>   Or builds the house, or digs the grave,
>   And those wild eyes that watch the wave
> In roarings round the coral reef.

Thus the only truth that is necessary unto salvation—the truth that God is love, and willing to save us all—is one which can be known by human reason and the light of nature ; and all that Christianity has done is to make it patent to field-labourers, masons, and grave-diggers.

We have not space nor leisure to show the utter fallacy of this view of Christianity, which resolves it into nothing more than what natural religion, after all, can teach. Our end has been gained when we have established what it is that Tennyson means by Christianity—what an entirely new religion it is which he and other singing apostles of our day are propagating in the land, and what it is they mean when they say—

> Ring in the Christ that is to come.

Not only is Christianity, as understood by Tennyson and his school, something entirely different from what all evan-

gelical Christians understand by the term; but having rejected the evidence of miracles and of the historical Record,
they have no proof even of the existence of Christ. All they
can say is that nature testifies that God is love, and Christ,
as manifested in the gospel, is such a manifestation of love
as we might expect. Our readers will observe that in the
above quotation Tennyson calls the gospel a "tale." So
does Browning—"a tale that is abroad." Accordingly, was
there ever such a miserable exhibition of scepticism as
Tennyson exhibits in the very exordium of his "In
Memoriam"?—

> Strong Son of God, immortal Love,
>   Whom we that have not seen Thy face,
>   By faith and faith alone embrace,
> Believing where we cannot prove.
>
>   *   *   *   *
>
> Thou seemest human and divine,
>   The highest, holiest manhood, Thou;
>   Our wills are ours we know not how,
> Our wills are ours, to make them Thine.

In the first of these verses, while he professes to embrace
Christ by faith, he acknowledges that he cannot prove His
existence. He is perfectly right there. I have shown to
demonstration, in the essay upon Browning, that none of
their school who have rejected miracles and the Record can
prove the historical existence of Christ. But I had not
thought that Tennyson would have had the simplicity to
confess so much before the face of his fellow-countrymen.
"Thou seemest human and divine" is the very bathos of
religious confession—the very getting down upon his knees
in the humiliation of rationalistic helplessness. He cannot
tell for his part whether Christ be both human and divine,
but he rather thinks so! See to what a wretched pass of
uncertainty those are reduced who have left the sure and
divinely-attested Record, and who have adopted a Christianity which has to be groped after through the light of
nature!

To give another illustration of it farther on in this poem.

Instead of grounding his hope in an everlasting salvation upon the sure ground of the Bible, he persists in arguing for it from the light of nature. He thinks that he finds a conviction in his own heart that all men will be saved—that not one will perish—

> That not one life shall be destroyed,
> Or cast as rubbish to the void,
> When God hath made the pile complete.
>   *   *   *   *
> The wish that of the living whole
> No life may fail beyond the grave,
> Derives it not from what we have
> The likest God within the soul."

But, alas ! looking abroad, he shortly finds that God in the natural world seems careless of *individual* life at least. This staggers him.

> But I, considering everywhere
> Her secret meaning in her deeds,
> And finding that of fifty seeds
> She often brings but one to bear ;
>
> I falter where I firmly trod, &c.

Down he falls accordingly

> Upon the great world's altar-stairs
> That slope through darkness up to God.
>
> I stretch lame hands of faith, and grope,
> And gather dust and chaff, and call
> To what I feel is Lord of all,
> And faintly trust the larger hope.

When he has thus got a faint hope again, however, it is doomed to a speedy extinction. He suddenly bethinks himself next of geological discoveries, and finds that God is careless not merely of individual life—*types* and *genera* of the animal creation have disappeared. This throws him into new convulsions.

> " So careful of the type ! " but no,
> From scarpèd cliff and quarried stone,
> She cries, " A thousand types are gone ;
> I care for nothing, all shall go.

" Thou makest thine appeal to me ;
  I bring to life, I bring to death ;
  The spirit does but mean the breath :
I know no more." And he, shall he,—

Man, her last work, who seemed so fair,
  Such splendid purpose in his eyes,
  Who rolled the psalm to wintry skies,
Who built him fanes of fruitless prayer ;

Who trusted God was love indeed,
  And love creation's final law ;
  Though nature, red in tooth and claw
With ravine, shrieked against his creed ;

Who loved, who suffered countless ills,
  Who battled for the true, the just,
  Be blown about the desert dust,
Or sealed within the iron hills ?

No more ? A monster then, a dream,
  A discord. Dragons of the prime,
  That tear each other in their slime,
Were mellow music matched with him.

O life as futile, then, as frail,
  O for thy voice to soothe and bless ;
  What hope of answer or redress ?
Behind the veil, behind the veil.

The above verses are magnificent poetry. As I have said at the beginning of the present essay, we are indebted for the most splendid passages of modern poetry to the fearful struggles which these infant Herculeses " crying in the night " of noonday revelation have imposed upon themselves by choosing to disbelieve their Bible. But the question is whether this be a legitimate and praiseworthy source of the sublime ? The highest bursts of genius to be found in Byron were inspired by the agonies he drew down upon himself through his erratic career, and the collision into which this brought him with the world. The irregularity of his passions was not the less to be condemned because it added to his verses, and we decidedly object to the gratuitous agonies to which some of our modern poets are indebted for their inspiration. In this respect we place this last quotation from Tennyson alongside of Byron's famous forgiveness-curse in the last canto of his " Childe Harold."

The limits of this essay warn us that it is high time to close our remarks upon the peculiar religious sentiments of Tennyson ; but we cannot do this without adverting to the opportunity he has embraced of introducing them into his Arthur and

" THE HOLY GRAIL."

The opinion has sometimes been expressed that our author in the " Idylls of the King " intended to convey some religious instruction — nobody exactly knows what. We are surprised at this. Those who are acquainted with the theological school to which he belongs must be familiar with the plan adopted by its poets and literary men in order to spread its doctrines. They fix upon some marked character in past history, whom for the nonce they adopt for their hero, representing him as having been above the religious prejudices of the times when he lived—influenced in his conduct, not by the dogmas of the Church or of the Bible, but by the law within his own heart — and arriving at their kind of Christianity by the way they speak of, not by being satisfied with miracles or the truth of the Record, but by the intuition of reason. Thus Robert Browning in his " Ring and the Book " finds the Pope who gave decision in his famous murder case at Rome to have been one of these lights of the world—a man whose Christianity was entirely after his taste, being derived not from councils or decrees of the Church, nay, not from the Bible itself, but from " the law within "—the only Christianity which he accepted being that which this " law within him " approved. The more eccentric Carlyle selects one Sampson, an abbot of the twelfth century, as his model, one whose " *Catholicism was something like the* ISM *of all true men in all centuries, I fancy.*" Now Tennyson with the same object in view has selected Arthur of the Round Table. Nothing, to be sure, can be more ridiculous than to have chosen the formidable warrior and enemy of the Saxons as an example of the rationalistic Christianity of the nineteenth century. But we know how men of this school worship heroes of all sorts, and consider that they were as truly God-raised and inspired as the prophet-kings of the Bible.

That he looked upon Arthur as having established, in " The Round Table," a most important Order in the world, bearing upon the interests of religion as well as of society in general, must have struck every reader of the Idylls. Thus at the close he represents the king, when he dies, as comforting one of his followers under the breaking up of this establishment ;

> The old order changeth, yielding place to new,
> And God fulfils Himself in many ways,
> Lest one good custom should corrupt the world.

And when the king, in his phantom bark, becomes a speck in the distance on his way to the Fairy Isle, the whole poem ends with the enigmatical line,—

> And the new sun rose, bringing the new year.

What does this " new sun " and " new year " mean ? Those only who are acquainted with the peculiar views of the school will know this. It evidently refers to the new development which religion in its onward progress was now about to take in the peculiar phase of what we condemn as popery, but what they consider to have been, and call, the "*Christianism*" of the Middle Ages. I have shown at length, in the essay upon Carlyle, that they consider this " Christianism " to have been one grand stage in the onward development of the human reason after Christ's coming ; the Reformation being the second stage, and the French Revolution being the third. Popery with its visions (such as " The Holy Grail," which indicated its approach), its miracles, its transubstantiation, its purgatory, &c., they hol 1 of course to be a thing now exploded, but they consider it to have been good at the time; to have been the best which the human reason, after the teaching of that "divine man" Christ, could make of religion during these centuries. Carlyle does not hesitate to call it "a sublime embodiment of Christianity." Then came the Reformation, when that blessed thing, the human reason, in its onward march, exploded what was false in the forms of religion during popery; but it was still too weak to shake off credence in apostolic miracles, in the plenary inspiration of the Bible, and in such odious doctrines as the inflexible justice of God and the necessity of an atonement. Next came the French Revolution with its apostle Voltaire, whom they commend and consider to have done good service in his attempts to invalidate miracles and the Record, since the true evidence for Christianity and test of what it is (according to them) is to be found not in these, but in "the law within."

Let these remarks be considered, and our readers will not only see what Tennyson meant by "the new sun" and "new year" coming in upon Arthur's death, but a flood of light will be cast upon that mysterious episode in the Idylls, "The Holy Grail."

Arthur is represented throughout as one of those tall men of the past who were ahead of their age, and anticipated the boasted rationalistic Christianity of the nineteenth century. His poor knights again are more behind in their theology. Belonging to the common mass of men, they must come under the influence of that popery of the Middle Ages which was drawing near, and which, though it dealt in visions and superstitions, was one stage in the advancing development. Influenced by a holy nun, sister to one of the knights, they show a determination accordingly to set out in pursuit of "The Holy Grail," under the firm belief that if they get a vision of this famous sacramental cup used by our Lord Himself at the first communion, and which had been brought by Joseph of Arimathea to Glastonbury, they will be saved. Tennyson hereby represents the new era that was coming in.

Meanwhile all this is described as distressing Arthur. He considers this vision of " The Holy Grail "

> A sign to maim the Order which I made.

He considers that the knights would have been better employed had they kept to their own vocation, as—

> Men
> With strength and will to right the wronged—of power
> To lay the sudden heads of violence flat ;
> Knights that in twelve great battles splashed and dyed
> The strong White Horse in his own heathen blood.

He was of the same opinion in short as Carlyle advocates in his " Sartor Resartus," that action is the main thing, and to set ourselves to duty is all. Not that Arthur disapproves of this expedition in quest of the " Grail." He is represented as being quite as enlightened as Carlyle or Tennyson, who hold that the visions and superstitions of the Middle Ages were all good and profitable to those that believed in them. Speaking of his knights, accordingly, who thought they had seen this same cup, he says,—

> Blessed are Bors, Lancelot, and Percival,
> For these have seen according to their sight ;
> *   *   *   *
> And as they saw it, they have spoken truth.

What then ? Is Arthur ready to go in pursuit of the " Grail " himself—is he led away by these visions of the popish sort? No. He is represented as ahead of all this. So far from being weak enough to see supernatural visions, he is described, in true Goethe style, as recognising nature and all material things round him to be only a vision, while the glorious *Ego* (of which our rationalistic school speak so much) is the only reality, and God, and Christ, of whom he is represented as having an intuitional discovery. It is as follows that this rationalistic divine of the sixth century, made for the occasion, expresses himself : —

> And some among you held, that if the king
> Had seen the sight, he would have sworn the vow :
> Not easily, seeing that the king must guard
> That which he rules, and is but as the hind
> To whom a space of land is given to plough,
> Who may not wander from the allotted field
> Before his work be done ; but, being done,
> Let visions of the night, or of the day
> Come, as they will ; and many a time they come,
> Until this earth he walks on seems not earth,
> This light that strikes his eyeball is not light,
> This air that smites his forehead is not air
> But vision—yea his very hand and foot—
> In moments when he feels he cannot die,
> And knows himself no vision to himself,
> Nor the high God a vision, nor that One
> Who rose again : ye have seen what ye have seen.

No wonder if Sir Percival, after hearing this, utters the line with which " The Holy Grail " concludes :—

> So spake the king : I knew not all he meant.

I dare believe he did not, nor any of the dear society of stalwart knights who surrounded him. But if they had read Carlyle they would, who says, in his " Sartor Resartus "— " So that this world after all is but an air-image—our *Me* the only reality, and nature with its thousand-fold production and destruction but the reflex of our own inward force, the phantasy of our dream, or what the Earth-spirit in Faust names it, 'the living visible garment of God.'"

I feel, however, that it is high time to close these remarks upon the religious tenets of Tennyson. From the last instance adduced, it must appear that he cannot even write Idylls upon a British warrior but he must propagate them. And if our modern writers of this school did the thing openly, a man would not blame them. It is this hiding of their views behind historical personages that disgusts frank and true men ; and that the nation should submit to be befooled by such obscure drivel of poetical theology is a lamentable proof that if men smite us on the face, we will suffer them.

IV.

HENRY WADSWORTH LONGFELLOW.

THAT this poet occupies a very high place in the admiration of our country will not be denied. If we succeed in accomplishing the object of our present essay, we hope to convince our readers that he ought to occupy a place still higher; that, in fact, he is the truest, and, in that sense, the greatest poet of our age.

The reputation he enjoys as yet amongst us is rather founded upon his smaller poems. These are widely read, universally known, and universally appreciated. They have even taken deeper hold of the community than the minor poems of our national bards, being both more easily understood, and coming more home to the heart. They have certainly exercised at least a more healthy influence. The "Psalm of Life," and kindred verses of his, have made themselves heard with a clarion sound in the conscience. "Excelsior" has been written upon all our souls. There is not a haberdasher's apprentice but walks now with a deeper and prouder sense of the importance of human life, as one who would wish to leave behind him "footprints on the sands of time." This is surely a better state of things than prevailed under the old dogstar of Passion, when a young man was trained to be a corsair by Byron, or too apt to become a child of reckless whim with Burns.

So far, then, as usefulness is concerned, there may be less reason to lament that his reputation should hitherto have rested largely in this country upon his smaller poems. But as we have come, under a later study of his larger productions, to the conclusion that they entitle him to rank highest, perhaps, of all in our literature, we shall make it our chief object in this essay to establish that position.

One reason why he has not hitherto been accepted according to his full worth is his having dispensed with rhyme. He has employed blank verse not only of the heroic measures, but of all measures from five to fifteen feet. This proceeds from no want on his part of the rhyming faculty, which is developed in him as largely as in any other poet. He can command music of this description to any amount. We need not say that in refusing to avail himself of it in most of his larger works, he did a very adventurous and hazardous thing. One who may have the humblest genius can hope, so long as he uses rhyme, that what he writes will be accepted as poetry. If, on the other hand, there is to be no rhyme, what is to distinguish his composition from prose, unless he possess a poetical genius of the very highest order? First of all, his conceptions and descriptions must be so essentially imaginative as of themselves to entitle him to claim being inspired. Again, there must be that rhythmical music in the lines, as a whole, which will console the ear for the want of a terminating chime. The highest poetic faculty is demanded, and this is not enough unless he be endowed with an extraordinary facility and flexibility of language. In short, no poet can dispense with the adventitious helps of art unless he have great resources of nature to fall back upon. A small man must put on high-heeled shoes; the girl who was not born under the star of beauty must multiply the rings upon her fingers, and have tinkling ornaments on her ankles. If any poet have the higher qualifications we have referred to, we do not see for our part why he should not dispense with rhyme. We are not competent to deal with the historical origin of the practice—when it began to be introduced, and why it was ever thought of. It was not practised in Israel. The inimitable poems of the Bible do not come to us " making a tinkling with their feet." The great poets of Greece and Rome would have thought themselves encumbered and disgraced by the custom. Why then has rhyme claimed dominion over us in modern times? Is it that the ear has become fastidious in the latter days? or is it something in the construction of our modern languages? or is it simply a prejudice? Can it be possible that our poets have all this time been vexing themselves in vain? not only contorting the last foot of every other line by an application of artificial Chinese bandages, but subjecting their own genius to a torture worse than that of the Inquisition, by forcing it in successive lines to invent chimes innumerable? We believe that it has been left to Longfellow to burst for ever these fetters, and that in doing so he has conferred what is equivalent to an emancipation upon the whole singing fraternity. Meanwhile, like all men who have made discoveries, he has been for a time a martyr to his own invention.

Another thing has stood considerably in his way. His productions want the perfect finish and exquisite polish necessary to please the ear of this nation. The whole condition and situation of our friends on the other side of the Atlantic tends to make them regard *things* rather than *words*. They don't like the sham of artifice of any kind; in contact with the new, they have no patience to polish up the old. The genius of their writers is affected by and reflects the state of their continent. Where there is such extent of territory, there is no need of excessive cultivation; the city goes up with more respect to hasty grandeur than exact rule. It is not for those who walk by great rivers artificially to terrace the banks of them, or carefully to adorn the dwelling that hangs over the fall. But not to speak of his country, look at Wadsworth Longfellow's countenance, as we have it in the frontispiece of his works. Patience is not the characteristic of it. If you wish to see that grace, contemplate the profile of our own Laureate, where the pain and even the exhaustion of deep thought are apparent enough.

Haste, the impetuosity of inspiration, are marked upon the visage of the other. It is fire that has consumed him, and not labour. Such a temperament is favourable in one sense, but against a man's way to reputation in another; and so with Longfellow. He rushes up a precipice to get some wild flower that has caught his fancy. His more scientific brother gathers up some rare plants which grow below, and had escaped him in his haste, patiently putting them into his herbarium. He himself, meanwhile, seated upon the high cliff, is dreaming over the sweet thought of God he finds in the apparently wild and worthless thing he holds in his hands. One who has acquired a fortune by hard application spends it to great advantage; another, born to an estate, is apt to have a spendthrift disposition. It must be owned that there are marks of a prodigal negligence in the works of Longfellow. What meets the eye is extensive and enchanting forests of natural self-sown birch, small-leafed, beautiful, silver-rinded; glades innumerable, which the deer loves to haunt; and the very fantastic sport nature has made with the branches that have never seen the axe is worth admiring. At the same time there is not the strength of stem and the luxuriousness of vegetation which is represented in the woods where there has been something of man's hand as well as of God's operation.

The reader will discern the scope of these remarks. We grant that he falls short in perfectness of style; and the observation applies not only to his poetry in detail, but to his larger poems viewed as a whole. They may not be able to compete with the more elaborate and finished productions of our two greatest national poets. All we assert, and hope to prove is, that there are possibly more of the elements of true poetry in them.

There is in them more of nature, we venture to think. In reading the others we still have a feeling somehow that we are not brought into direct contact with her; it is her gloved hand, and not her naked hand, that we shake; she is there, but there is a veil over her face ; if her fields are spread out before us, the grass is unnaturally coloured, and the flowers with which they are gorgeously enamelled have no smell. It may be a mere idea of our own. It strikes us as if our bards were self-conscious that other poets going before have won her affections ; that it is hopeless for them therefore to think to win her heart. Still, from admiration of her beauty, they hang on, but always too proud to make proposals, lest they should be rejected ; hence they are never wedded to her (for Nature will marry none who do not place full confidence in her), although it cannot be denied that they are upon a footing of intimacy. Of Longfellow, again, we may say, as he says himself of Walter of the Vogelweide :—

> His song was of the summer time,
> The very birds sang in his rhyme,
> The sunshine, the delicious air,
> The fragrance of the flowers was there.

Should you ask him where he found these songs of his ? Listen to his own answer in the quaint rhythms of his " Indian Carol :"—

> I should answer, I should tell you,
> In the birds'-nests of the forests,
> In the lodges of the beaver,
> In the hoof-prints of the bison,
> In the eyrie of the eagle !
>   All the wild-fowl sang them to me,
> In the moorlands and the fenlands,
> In the melancholy marshes ;
> Chetowaik, the plover, sang them,
> Mahng, the loon, the wild goose, Wawa,
> The blue heron, the Shu-shu-guh,
> And the grouse, the Mushkodasa.

Not only is his manner of treating his subjects always natural, but his subjects themselves are generally such as carry us back to the primitive simplicity of the world. Here he had an advantage in being an American. Where were such subjects to be found by a British poet ? All the mountains and streams of his native land had been sung and immortalized already. Not so the rivers and forests of the American continent, which, being entirely new, stood ready to be possessed not only by the first hand of business adventure, but by the imagination of the first poet who should plant the flag-staff of his genius upon the region. This Longfellow did in his " Evangeline." You may say that our poets had it in their power to go back to the hoary antiquity of this our country, and find a subject in its primitive inhabitants, customs, and legends. Unfortunately there was nothing poetical in the horrible superstitions of the Druids. Meanwhile, as Longfellow discovered, there was something romantic and picturesque in the Indian legends, and he availed himself of them in his " Hiawatha." Thus, while our poets have been forced to go for their subjects to the Middle Ages, or where they best might, the American bard found themes at home, less artificial, appealing more to the universal humanity that is in us.

The poets of our own nation have fallen into the perverse habit of seeking to produce effect by embellishment, by mere sentimentality, or by grotesqueness ; while sometimes (which is always a sign of the worst) they hide themselves in an impenetrable obscurity. Tastes of this kind are alien both to the country and the constitution of our poet. An American hates obscurity.

> Thorough, yet simple and clear, for sublimity always is simple,
> Both in sermon and song, a child can seize on his meaning.

While Longfellow is always intelligible, he produces impressions, not by word - paint, but by intuitive selection of the features in objects, and the circumstances in scenes, which at once give us a life representation of them. How much of the spasmodic is there in Browning ; how much in Tennyson of the false taste that seeks to give vividness to the description by telling us the exact hour of the clock when an event happened, or the exact place in the street where the house stood, or the precise distance in space.

> I was walking a mile,
>   *More than a mile* from the shore,
> The sun looked out with a smile
>   Betwixt the cloud and the moor ;
> And riding at close of day,
>   Over the dark moorland,
> Rapidly riding far away,
>   She waved to me her hand.

No doubt these vices of style are exceptional with both Browning and Tennyson. We merely notice the fact that Longfellow is by constitution simply not capable of such things.

The greatness of his genius is seen in the infinite ease with which he describes all things. It is not only what he accomplishes, but the unexampled facility by which the feat is done. In a moment, without an effort, he is in the third heaven of sublimity ; in another, he is upon the ground again. It is a grotesque suggestion, but we are reminded of his own great Indian dancer.

> First he danced a solemn measure,
> Very slow in step and gesture,
> In and out among the pine trees,
> Through the shadows and the sunshine,
> Treading softly, like a panther ;
> Then more swiftly, and still swifter,
> Whirling, spinning round in circles,
> Leaping o'er the guests assembled,
> Eddying round and round the wigwam,
> Till the leaves went whirling with him,
> Till the dust and wind together
> Swept in eddies round about him.
> Then along the sandy margin
> Of the lake, the Big-Sea-Water,
> On he sped with frenzied gestures,
> Stamped upon the sand, and tossed it
> Wildly in the air around him:
> Till the wind became a whirlwind,
> Till the sand was blown and sifted
> Like great snow-drifts o'er the landscape,
> Heaping all the shores with sand dunes,
> Sand-hills of the Nagow Wudjoo.

Take his "Building of the Ship." Here are first the orders to build it simply given.

> Build me straight, O worthy master,
> Staunch and strong, a goodly vessel,
> That shall laugh at all disaster,
> And with wave and whirlwind wrestle.

Before we have well got started with these few lines, which surely do not promise much, we have such a description of the master proceeding to form his model as could only have been written (one might say) by a man who was in body and soul a ship carpenter. The ship is to be called the *Union.* And now at his side we see a youth; and the bargain is that this youth is to have his daughter for bride on the day he shall worthily finish the building of the ship according to the inimitable model of the father-in-law.

> The master's word
> Enraptured the young man heard ;
> And as he turned his face aside,
> With a look of joy, and a thrill of pride,
> Standing before
> Her father's door
> He saw the form of his promised bride.
> The sun shone on her golden hair,
> And her cheek was glowing fresh and fair,
> With the breath of morn and the soft sea-air.
> Like a beauteous barge was she,
> Still at rest on the sandy beach,
> Just beyond the billow's reach ;
> But he
> Was the restless, seething, stormy sea.

Then the work begins under love's auspices, and now the author becomes the veritable spirit of a dockyard; for it is needless to conceal the fact that the very implements, one and all, are in his imagination, and that we smell pitch. Another poet might have told us of the various kinds of wood composing the ship, and conveyed us in fancy to the forests whence they came; but our readers will notice in the following lines the difference between embellished painting and the master-strokes of nature.

> Long ago,
> In the deer-haunted forests of Maine,
> When upon mountain and plain
> Lay the snow,
> They fell—those lordly pines !
> Those grand, majestic pines !
> 'Mid shouts and cheers,
> The jaded steers,
> Panting beneath the goad,
> Dragged down the weary, winding road,
> Those captive kings so straight and tall,
> To be shorn of their streaming hair,
> And, naked and bare,
> To feel the stress and the strain
> Of the wind and the rushing main,
> Whose roar
> Would remind them for evermore
> Of their native forests they should not see again.

Whether the bridal of old ocean with the ship, or that of the young builder with the maiden, be most beautifully described, we leave it with others to determine ; but who does not admire the perfect ease with which both descriptions are given, succeeded immediately, as if nothing had been done, by the well-known magnificent lines upon his native country.

> Thou too, sail on, O ship of state,
> Sail on, O Union, strong and great !
> Humanity with all its fears,
> With all the hopes of future years,
> Is hanging breathless on thy fate !
> We know what master laid thy keel,
> What workmen wrought thy ribs of steel,
> Who made each mast, and sail, and rope,
> What anvils rang, what hammers beat,
> In what a forge and what a heat
> Were shaped the anchors of thy hope !
> Fear not each sudden sound and shock,
> 'Tis of the wave and not the rock ;
> 'Tis but the flapping of the sail,
> And not a rent made by the gale !
> In spite of rock and tempest's roar,
> In spite of false lights on the shore,

> Sail on, nor fear to breast the sea !
> Our hearts, our hopes, our prayers, our tears,
> Our faith triumphant o'er our fears,
> Are all with thee—are all with thee !

Look at his " Rain in Summer." Many poets could give us a grand picture of this phenomenon, we have not a doubt of it. But in the present case, if our poet had pulled some string connected with the great bath of the universe, he could not have more effectually drenched us all ; for we who dwell in the city hear it gushing and struggling out from the throat of the house-spouts with a vengeance ; meanwhile the boys are down the street, to sail their mimic fleets in the gutters ; in the fields, again, the oxen which have been toiling at the plough, " lifting their yoke-encumbered heads," with dilated nostrils inhale the clover-scented breeze ; the honest farmer, as he eyes the whole affair, hopes that since it is for the general good he may conscientiously bless God for it, though it makes for his own particular benefit. The poet is engrossed with the rainbow, and follows the rain in his imagination down the earth to the regions of the dead, and its everlasting fountain-heads. How much better is nature than art !

It seems to be a maxim with the poets of our own country now that common things ought to be said in an uncommon way. Now even common things ought to be said by the poet in a poetical way. If his mind be poetically constituted, he will have his own imaginative way of viewing the least as well as the highest things. His genius will be as the moon, which throws its rich dreamy radiance upon the turnpike, as well as upon the forest and cataract. What we object to is not their maxim, but the way in which they understand it, which seems this—that they are to set themselves laboriously to ornament the common-place. Thus they are always upon stilts. There are no pleasant inequalities in their productions. They cannot trust themselves to be easy, natural, and simple. Longfellow is superior to all this.

When he comes to speak of common things, he speaks simply, and yet poetically. It is a bird's run along the ground; and, ere we are aware, his muse is in the air again, and describing those eagle gyrations in the sky which establish his claim to be one of the first poets of the age. There is a rhythmical grace in the following lines, even when describing Prince Henry and Elsie travelling along the highway to Hirschell.

Elsie : Onward and onward the highway runs to the distant city, impatiently bearing
Tidings of human joy and disaster, of love and hate, of doing and daring !

Henry : This life of ours is a wild Æolian harp of many a joyous strain,
But under them all there runs a loud perpetual wail as of souls in pain.

Elsie : Faith alone can interpret life, and the heart that aches and bleeds with the stigma
Of pain alone bears the likeness of Christ, and can comprehend its dark enigma.

Henry : Now, they stop at the wayside inn, and the waggoner laughs with the landlord's daughter,
While out of the dripping trough the horses distend their leathern sides with water.

Elsie : All through life there are wayside inns, where man may refresh his soul with love ;
Even the lowest may quench his thirst at rivulets fed by the springs above ; &c.

But, that we may have done with generalities, let us now direct our criticism to some of his well-known productions.

" HIAWATHA " is the most perfect piece of music that was ever sung to the astonished ears of those whose faith in the necessity of rhyme had previously amounted to a superstition. Adopting a trochaic instead of an iambic measure, he has struck upon the melodies best fitted,

> With their frequent repetitions,
> And their wild reverberations,

to recount the wonders of his Indian Edda.

The subject of the poem is happily chosen. The story relates to the earlier stages of society, when nature has not yet been invaded by civilisation ; when the timber that is to form our boasted architecture is yet waving in the forest, and the stone that is to rear the city is hanging in savage cliffs above rivers not yet navigated ; when, instead of teeming populations and smoking manufactories, there are only the magnificent solitudes, the flower-clad meadows, the silent mountains and valleys. The people introduced to our notice are of the tribes newly emerging from barbarism, simple with the simplicity of our own childhood, which never returns, and is an eternal regret ; ignorant of our conventionalities, but having the compensation of the primitive virtues ; naked, as it were, but walking unashamed in the wilderness gardens of their first estate. Even had this been all, Longfellow, by the choice of his subject, has a great advantage over our poets, who, stopping at what we call the Middle Ages, strive to interest us with the gallantries of knights and ladies. But availing himself, moreover, of the legends of the people, he has been able to add sublimity to beauty, by interweaving with his narrative the wonders of preternatural agency. We have not only the primitive wildernesses of America to attract our eye, but we have Gitche Manito, the Mighty, the Master of Life, descending upon them. We have more than a mere description of the first rise of the arts of peace among India's warlike tribes ; we have a wild narrative of the legendary and marvellous way in which their prophet Hiawatha, whose grandmother fell from the moon, introduced the Indian corn, and the canoe, and the rod-fishing, and the draining of fen and marsh. If along with all this it be considered that Hiawatha, though descended from the moon, is represented as a veritable youth of flesh and blood, capable of love and marriage with Minehaha, the girl born by the side of the Laughing Water, or Falls of St. Anthony, it is plain that here was a subject which for splendour was wholly unrivalled.

But what signifies the best subject in the hands of a common man? Is there any who could have handled it in the manner Longfellow has done? A thousand to one it would have been felt by us all to be at best a gifted and highly-embellished painting of Indian times by a man of the nineteenth century. The production before us is essentially different.

The author seems, such is the native force of his genius, to have undergone a metempsychosis; he is possessed throughout by the soul and spirit of the wild Indian. The very melody of the verses has a veritable sound of the first ages of humanity. The delusion is perfected by his introduction of a whole vocabulary of Indian names for birds, beasts, things, and persons—most euphonious names withal, which have a strange charm in them. As for the legends, nothing is so unearthly and strange that he cannot describe it. The apparently impracticable is played with by him; what other poets never would have ventured to touch upon is sported with by this man of infinite humour and inexhaustible fancy.

What a Homeric simplicity in the convention of the warriors of all the tribes by Gitche Manito, the Great Spirit! This must be done, according to Indian fashion, by smoking the peace-pipe, and here is one worthy of the gods:—

> From the red stone of the quarry
> With his hand he broke a fragment,
> Moulded it into a pipe-head,
> Shaped and fashioned it with figures;
> From the margin of the river
> Took a long reed for a pipe-stem,
> With its dark green leaves upon it;
> Filled the pipe with bark of willow,
> With the bark of the red willow:
> Breathed upon the neighbouring forest,
> Made its great boughs chafe together,
> Till in flames they burst and kindled;
> And erect upon the mountains,
> Gitche Manito, the mighty,
> Smoked the calumet, the peace-pipe,
> As a signal to the nations.

> And the smoke rose, slowly, slowly,
> Through the tranquil air of morning ;
> First a single line of darkness,
> Then a denser, bluer vapour,
> Then a snow-white cloud unfolding,
> Like the tree-tops of the forest,
> Ever rising, rising, rising,
> Till it touched the top of heaven,
> Till it brake against the heaven,
> And rolled eastward all around it.
>   From the Vale of Tæwasentha,
> From the Valley of Wyoming,
> From the groves of Tuscaloosa,
> From the far-off Rocky Mountains,
> From the northern lakes and rivers,
> All the tribes beheld the signal,
> Saw the distant smoke ascending,
> The Puckwana of the peace-pipe.
>   Down the rivers, o'er the prairies,
> Came the warriors of the nations,
> Came the Delawars and Mohawks,
> Came the Choctaws and Camanches,
> Came the Shoshomis and Blackfeet,
> Came the Pawnees and Omawhaws,
> Came the Manduas and Dacotahs,
> Came the Hurons and Ojibways,
> All the warriors drawn together
> By the signal of the peace-pipe,
> To the mountains of the prairie,
> To the great red pipe-stone quarry.
>   And they stood there in the meadow,
> With their weapons and their war-gear
> Painted like the leaves of autumn,
> Painted like the sky of morning,
> Wildly glaring at each other ;
> In their faces stern defiance,
> In their hearts the feuds of ages,
> The hereditary hatred,
> The ancestral thirst of vengeance.

Hiawatha's marriage with Minehaha differs altogether from the innumerable descriptions we have of such sort of things. With the pomp of nature's great forests and rivers for its background, solemnized before the stars for witnesses;

the silence of rapture only interrupted by the sound of
Laughing Water; Minehaha given away by her old father,
the arrow-maker of Dacotah, in days when there was no
distinction of crowned heads; the bridegroom entering the
wigwam with the deer upon his shoulders, for his wedding
gift, while the bride rises from the rush-mat she had been
plaiting, to give him nothing but her heart—such is the
marriage that forms the centre-piece of tenderness in this
narrative of wonders.   He thus describes the home-going :—

> All the travelling winds went with them,
> O'er the meadow, thro' the forest ;
> All the stars of night looked at them,
> Watched with sleepless eyes their slumber ;
> From his ambush in the oak-tree
> Peeped the squirrel, Adjidamo,
> Watched with eager eyes the lovers ;
> And the rabbit, the Wabasso,
> Scampered from the path before them,
> Peering, peeping from his burrow,
> Sat erect upon his haunches,
> Watched with envious eyes the lovers.
>   Pleasant was the journey homeward,
> All the birds sang loud, and sweetly,
> Songs of happiness and heart's ease ;
> Sang the blue-bird, the Owassa,
> " Happy are you, Hiawatha,
> Having such a wife to love you.'
> Sang the Opechu, the robin,
> " Happy are you, Laughing Water,
> Having such a noble husband."
>   From the sky the sun benignant
> Looked upon them thro' the branches,
> Saying to them, " O my children,
> Love is sunshine, hate is shadow,
> Life is checkered shade and sunshine ;
> Rule by love, O Hiawatha."
>   From the sky the moon looked at them,
> Filled the lodge with mystic splendour,
> Whispered to them, " O my children,
> Day is restless, night is quiet,
> Man imperious, woman feeble ;
> Half is mine, although I follow,
> Rule by patience, Laughing Water."

Such is the variety characterising this poem, that it would
not be difficult to select passages rivalling all our most celebrated poets in each of the different styles in which they are
supposed to be masters. We are familiar, all of us, with the
bold life-strokes with which Burns describes the tenants
whether of air, or stream, or loch ; whether water-fowl that—

> Peaceful keep their dimpling wave,
> Busy feed, or wanton lave ;
> Or, beneath the sheltering rock,
> Bide the surging billow's shock ;

Or " saumont " that—

> Stately sail,
> And trouts bedropped wi' crimson hail,
> And eels weel kenn'd for souple tail,
> An' geds for greed.

The same eye for nature appears in the account we have
of Hiawatha's fishing in the Gitche Gumee, the Big-Sea-
Water.

> On the white sand of the bottom
> Lay the monster Mishe-Nahmer,
> Lay the sturgeon, king of fishes.
> Through his gills he breathed the water,
> With his fins he fanned and winnowed,
> With his tail he swept the sand floor.
>   There he lay, in all his armour ;
> On each side a shield to guard him,
> Plates of bone upon his forehead,
> Down his sides and back and shoulders
> Plaits of bone with spines projecting !
> Painted was he with his war paint,
> Stripes of yellow and of azure,
> Spots of brown and spots of sable ;
> And he lay there on the bottom,
> Fanning with his fins of purple,
> As above him, Hiawatha
> In his birch canoe came sailing,
> With his fishing line of cedar.

> *   *   *   *

> Slowly upward, wavering, gleaming
> Like a white moon in the water,

> Rose the Ugudwash, the sun-fish,
> Seized the line of Hiawatha,
> Swung with all his weight upon it,
> Made a whirlpool in the water,
> Whirled the birch canoe in circles,
> Round and round in gurgling eddies,
> Till the circles in the water
> Reached the far-off sandy beaches,
> Till the water-flags and rushes
> Nodded on the distant margins.
> But when Hiawatha saw him
> Slowly rising thro' the water,
> Lifting his great disc of whiteness,
> Loud he shouted in derision,
> " Esa ! esa ! shame upon you,
> You are Ugudwash, the sun-fish,
> You are not the fish I wanted,
> You are not the king of fishes."
> Wavering downward, white and ghastly,
> Sank the Ugudwash, the sun-fish ;
> And again the sturgeon Nahmer
> Heard the shout of Hiawatha,
> Heard his challenge of defiance,
> The unnecessary tumult,
> Ringing far above the water.
> From the white sand of the bottom
> Up he rose with angry gesture,
> Quivering in each nerve and fibre,
> Clashing all his plates of armour,
> Gleaming bright with all his war-paint ;
> In his wrath he darted upward,
> Flashing leapt into the sunshine; &c.

For startling imagery and invention of circumstances in the department of the terrible, the following passage may compare with the " gruesome " in " Tam O'Shanter." It narrates the calling up of the ghost of the departed friend of Hiawatha by the magician, the Wabeener.

> From the sand he rose and listened,
> Heard the music and the singing,
> Came, obedient to the summons,
> To the doorway of the wigwam,
> But to enter, they forbade him.
> Through a chink a coal they gave him,

Through the door a burning firebrand ;
Ruler in the land of spirits,
Ruler o'er the dead they made him ;
Telling him a fire to kindle
For all those that died thereafter,
Camp-fires for their night encampments
On their solitary journey
To the kingdom of Ponemah,
To the land of the Hereafter.
   From the village of his childhood,
From the homes of those who knew him,
Passing silent thro' the forest,
Like a smoke-wreath wafted sideways,
Slowly vanished Chibiates.
Where he passed the branches moved not.
And the fallen leaves of last year
Made no sound beneath his footsteps.
   Four whole days he journeyed onwards
Down the pathway of the dead men ;
On the dead man's strawberry feasted,
Crossed the melancholy river,
On the swinging log he crossed it ;
Came unto the Lake of Silver,
In the stone canoe was carried
To the Islands of the Blessed,
To the lands of ghosts and shadows.
   On that journey, moving slowly,
Many weary spirits saw he,
Panting under heavy burdens,
Laden with war-clubs, bows and arrows,
Robes of fur, and pots and kettles,
And with food that friends had given
For that solitary journey.
   " Ah ! why do the living," said they,
" Lay such heavy burdens on us ?
Better were it to go naked,
Better were it to go fasting,
Than to bear such heavy burdens
On our long and weary journey."

To refer to another passage—have we anything in Coleridge
more weird, more fitted to make the blood chill in our veins,
and the hair to stand up, than the visit of the ghosts to the
wigwam of Hiawatha ? Not that we have the same exquisite-

ness of imagery or perfect polish of expression which we find in the "Ancient Mariner." The genius of Longfellow is Homeric. He polishes nothing. He never paints. So far as the scene to be described is concerned, it is brought before us by a record of circumstances, but how poetical! how sublimely simple! And what the actors, produced upon the scene, say is never embellished; it is what they *do* say that melts, or thrills, or terrifies us. This is the highest poetry, consisting in things, not words. In the present case, for example, here is young Hiawatha come home from his hunting, full of lusty life and health, the red deer on his shoulders, his heart exulting at the prospect of seeing his Laughing Water, and the moon-descended Nekomis, her grandmother. On entering the wigwam he sees the two strangers, ghosts of the departed, cowering and crouching in the shadows. The hospitality of the tribe forbids that he should ask any questions. From whatever world they come they are welcome to the Indian's tent; and not even the insolence of these bloodless spectres is resented, as they sprang from the recess among the shadows of the wigwam, and for supper seized the choicest portions of the day's hunt. In the awful nights of their stay they steal out to the forest to bring pine-cones to burn, for fire seems their only consolation. On one of the nights Hiawatha, as he sleeps on his hides of bison, is startled by a sob—a sighing. He rises— he turns aside the deer curtains. He beholds both the pallid guests. He asks them whether there had been any violation of the rules of hospitality—whether Minehaha or Nekomis had offended them. Such are the circumstances which this poet—this great master of poetry—calls up, and we will all be agreed that the man who can summon them may dispense with painting and embellishment, whether he means to awaken love or excite horror. Listen, too, to the cause of their sighing, for it is enough to awaken tears so far as it touches this common humanity of ours, and simple terror, so far as it spoke the Indian superstition.

> Then the shadows ceased from weeping,
> Ceased from sobbing and lamenting,
> And they said, with gentle voices,
> "We are ghosts of the departed,
> Souls of those who once were with you.
> Cries of grief and lamentation
> Reach us in the Blessed Islands ;
> Cries of anguish from the living,
> Calling back their friends departed,
> Sadden us with useless sorrow.
> Think of this, O Hiawatha !
> Speak of it to all the people,
> That henceforward, and for ever,
> They no more with lamentations
> Sadden the souls of the departed
> In the Islands of the Blessed.
> Do not lay such heavy burdens
> In the graves of those you bury,
> Not such weight of furs and wampum,
> Not such weight of pots and kettles,
> For the spirits faint beneath them.
> Only give them food to carry,
> Only give them fire to light them.
> Four days is the spirit's journey
> To the land of ghosts and shadows,
> Four its lonely night encampments ;
> Four times must their fires be lighted.
> Therefore when the dead are buried,
> Let a fire, as night approaches,
> Four times on the grave be kindled,
> That the soul upon its journey
> May not lack the cheerful firelight,
> May not grope about in darkness.

It so happens that the poem of " Hiawatha " terminates very much in the same way, as to subject, with the " Idylls of the King."   Just as Arthur passed away, when his mission was done, to the Fairy Isle, so Hiawatha, having discharged his prophet trust, departed mysteriously by ship for another world.   Our readers may be interested to compare the two descriptions together.   Here is the passing of Arthur :—

> And slowly answered Arthur from the barge :
> "The old order changeth, yielding place to new,

And God fulfils Himself in many ways,
Lest one good custom should corrupt the world.
Comfort thyself; what comfort is in me?
I have lived my life, and that which I have done
May he within himself make pure; but then,
If thou shouldst never see my face again,
Pray for my soul.   More things are wrought by prayer
Than this world dreams of.   Wherefore let thy voice
Rise like a fountain for me night and day.
For what are men better than sheep or goats,
That nourish a blood life within the brain,
If knowing God, they lift not hands in prayer,
Both for themselves, and those who call them friend?
For so the whole round earth is every way
Bound by gold chains about the feet of God.
But now farewell.   I am going a long way
With these thou seest—if indeed I go
(For all my mind is clouded with a doubt)
To the island-valley of Avilion;
Where falls not hail, or rain, or any snow,
Nor ever wind blows loudly, but it lies
Deep-meadowed, happy, fair with orchard lawns,
And bowery hollows crowned with summer sea,
Where I will heal me of my grievous wound."
  So said he, and the barge with oar and sail
Moved from the brink, like some full-breasted swan
That, fluting a wild carol ere her death,
Ruffles her pure cold plume and takes the flood
With swarthy webs.   Long stood Sir Bedivere
Revolving many memories, till the hull
Look'd one black dot against the verge of dawn,
And on the mere the wailing died away.

*   *   *   *

Thereat once more he moved about, and clomb
E'en to the highest he could climb, and saw,
Straining his eyes beneath an arch of hand,
Or thought he saw the speck that bare the king,
Down that long water opening on the deep,
Somewhere far off, pass on and on, and go
From less to less, and vanish into light.
And the new sun rose, bringing the new year.

The following is the departure of Hiawatha, after commending the Christian missionaries who had arrived to the
care of his fellow-countrymen :—

"I am going, O Nekomis,
On a long and distant journey,
To the portals of the sunset,
To the regions of the home-wind,
Of the north-west wind, Keewardin.
But these guests I leave behind me,
In your watch and ward I leave them,
See that never harm comes near them,
See that never fear molests them,
Never danger, nor suspicion,
Never want of food or shelter,
In the lodge of Hiawatha!"
    Forth into the village went he,
Bade farewell to all the warriors,
Bade farewell to all the young men,
Spake persuading, spake in this wise :
"I am going, O my people,
On a long and distant journey ;
Many moons and many winters
Will have come and will have vanished
Ere I come again to see you.
But my guests I leave behind me ;
Listen to their words of wisdom,
Listen to the truth they tell you.
For the Master of Life has sent them
From the land of light and morning!"
    On the shore stood Hiawatha,
Turned and waved his hand at parting,
On the clear and luminous water
Launched his birch canoe for sailing,
From the pebbles on the margin
Shoved it forth into the water.
Whispered to it, "Westward! Westward!"
And with speed it darted forward.
    And the evening sun descending,
Set the clouds on fire with redness,
Burned the broad sky, like a prairie,
Left upon the level water
One long track and trail of splendour;
Down whose stream, as down a river,
Westward, westward, Hiawatha
Sailed into the fiery sunset,
Sailed into the purple vapours,
Sailed into the dusk of evening.
    And the people from the margin

> Watched him floating, rising, sinking,
> Till the birch canoe seemed lifted
> High into that sea of splendour,
> Till it sank into the vapours,
> Like the new moon slowly, slowly
> Sinking in the purple distance.
>   And they said, " Farewell for ever ! "
> Said, " Farewell, O Hiawatha ! "
> And the forests, dark and lonely,
> Moved through all their depths of darkness,
> Sighed, " Farewell, O Hiawatha."
>
>   *   *   *   *
>
> Thus departed Hiawatha,
> Hiawatha the belovèd,
> In the glory of the sunset,
> In the purple mists of evening.
> To the regions of the home wind
> Of the north-west wind, Keewardin.
> To the Islands of the Blessed,
> To the kingdom of Ponemah,
> To the land of the Hereafter.

Such is this splendid production of Longfellow. Reasons could easily be assigned why many do not appreciate it. We have spoken already of the rhyme being wanting. They no more account any composition to be a poem without rhymes, than certain other folks would count it to be Sabbath-day if there were no ringing of the church bells. No man, besides, can relish this poem unless he has become body and soul, for the time being, an aboriginal Indian ; and how few are capable of such a transmigration, needs not be told. So wild and strange is the whole composition—such an intermixture of the natural with the legendary—that none except one whose ideality is of the largest will appreciate this great " Midsummer Dream " of the prairie. They would be well content to join Pope or any of his compeers in their old-fashioned chariot, and even to accompany Browning or Tennyson on the rail ; but it is with no small trepidation that they get into the car of Longfellow's balloon, which goes careering in the skies, over Gitche

Gumee, the Big-Sea-Water ; and the likelihood is that, after a scud before the west wind, even Mudjekeewis, they are glad to get alighted over the wigwam of Laughing Water, and refuse to ascend again with this daring poet, leaving him to pursue alone his sublime flight to the kingdom of Pone-mah, the land of his own deserved and immortal hereafter.

In any criticism upon "Miles Standish," notice would need to be taken of his poetic skill in choosing his subject. He does not, as another might have done, take up the landing of the *Mayflower*. When the poem commences, the first sad winter of the Pilgrims is already over. Spring has dawned, and the ship is lying in the harbour, ready to start home again for England on the morrow. The last link between them and the old country was not broken so long as that vessel remained ; but now it was about to sail back to the blessed shore they would never see again. Had the poet fixed upon the landing of the *Mayflower* he might better have awakened, it may be, philosophical reflections connected with that world-pregnant disembarkation ; but, by the plan he adopted, the great sacrifice made by the Pilgrims, and which was necessary to begin the Republic as with their outpoured hearts' blood, is brought more home to us all.

Long in silence they watched the receding sail of the vessel,
Much endeared to them all, as something living and human.
Then, as if filled with the Spirit, and rapt in a vision prophetic,
Baring his hoary head, the excellent Elder of Plymouth
Said, "Let us pray," and they prayed, and thanked the Lord and took
    courage.
Mournfully sobbed the waves at the base of the rock, and above them
Bowed and whispered the wheat on the hill of death, and their kindred
Seemed to awake in their graves and to join in the prayer that they
    uttered.
Sun-illumined and white on the eastern verge of the ocean,
Gleamed the departing sail, *like a marble slab in a graveyard,*
Buried beneath it lay for ever all hope of departing.

We have underscored the image which the poet employs, because we look upon it, for poetical conception, as the finest thing we have ever read. In any case, the comparison between a distant sail at sea, "sun - illumined," and a sepulchral slab, would have been both true to nature and original; but when one considers the circumstances in which the Pilgrim Fathers were placed, the *Mayflower's* sail being now made suddenly to assume even the palpable form of the gravestone of their hope of return, is unspeakably beautiful.

But we anticipate matters when we speak of the vessel as having departed. During most of the time embraced in this poem the *Mayflower* is still in the harbour, thus giving grandeur to the whole scenes in the narrative. It lies at anchor before us, close by the Plymouth Rock,—

> That had been to their feet as a doorstep
> Into a world unknown—the corner-stone of a nation !

The conception of Miles Standish and John Alden and Priscilla as the groundwork of the piece, shows also great genius. No general description of the infant colony, however elegantly given, would have so strikingly illustrated its history as the selection of this single group. The interest of a domestic incident is thrown round this nation-commencing crisis. The love incident again, which, apart from any such juxtaposition, would have been an interesting one, is intensified by its Plymouth connections, like some humble homestead that has its picturesque background on the Appenines.

In the present state of poetical literature, when extravagance of style prevails to such an extent, it is refreshing to see that Longfellow, in the characters in this piece, seeks to produce effect only by conforming to the truth of nature. We could not have a more lifelike portrait than that of Miles Standish, a genuine soldier-graft of a Puritan, professionally having more faith in gunpowder when dealing with Indians than in the Bible, and constitutionally less fit to court a woman than to win a fortress. Having lost his first wife, he is not the man in any department to lose heart, and moves forward so suddenly for the acquisition of a second, as

wholly to disconcert his young secretary, John Alden, who
finds to his astonishment that his friend has singled out the
very object of his own affections, and commissioned him
moreover to be his agent in this, to himself, uncongenial
species of assault and battery. John Alden is drawn also to
the life; so soft and amiable, that he consents to sacrifice his
own interests to the stronger-willed little man ; so religiously
conscientious, that he looks upon this trial as the Lord's controversy with his own soul. We have thus the sterner and
the softer side of Puritanism represented, and strikingly
separated. We have no such nice discrimination of character in any of our other living poets. Nothing meanwhile
can be better than the description of the way in which
both these men proceeded to fulfil their work.

First, Miles certainly executed with a vengeance the mission nature had assigned him, as a belligerent against the
Indians.

After a three days' march he came to an Indian encampment
Pitched on the head of a meadow, between the sea and the forest ;
Women at work by the tents, and the warriors, horrid with war-paint,
Seated about a fire, and smoking and talking together ;
Who when they saw from afar the sudden approach of the white men,
Saw the flash of the sun on breastplate, and sabre, and musket,
Straightway leapt to their feet, and two from among them advancing,
Came to parley with Standish, and offer him furs as a present;
Friendship was in their looks, but in their hearts there was hatred.

    *   *   *   *   *

Then Wattemot advanced with a stride in front of the other,
And with a lofty demeanour thus vauntingly spake to the captain :
"Now Wattemot can see, by the fiery eyes of the captain,
Angry is he in his heart ; but the heart of the brave Wattawamet
Is not afraid at the sight. He was not born of a woman,
But on a mountain at night, from an oak-tree riven by lightning,
Forth he sprang at a bound, with all his weapons about him,
Shouting, "Who is here to fight with the brave Wattawamet?"
Then he unsheathed his knife, and whetting the blade on his left hand,
Held it aloft, and displayed a woman's face on the handle,
Saying, with bitter expression and look of sinister meaning,
"I have another at home, with the face of a man on the handle :
By-and-by they shall marry, and there will be plenty of children !"

Then stood Pecksurt forth, insulting Miles Standish,
While with his fingers he patted the knife that hung at his bosom,
Drawing it half from its sheath, and plunging it back as he muttered :
" By-and-by it shall see ; it shall eat ; ha ! ha ! but shall speak not !
This is the mighty captain the white men have sent to destroy us,
He is a little man ; let him go and fight with the women !"

  *   *   *   *   *

All the best blood of his race, of Sir Hugh, and of Thurston de Standish,
Boil'd and beat in his heart, and swell'd in the veins of his temples.
Headlong he leapt on the boaster, and snatching his knife from its
  scabbard,
Plunged it into his heart, and, reeling backwards, the savage
Fell with his face to the sky, and a fiendlike fierceness upon it.
Straight there arose from the forest the awful sound of the war-whoop,
And, like a flurry of snow on the whistling wind of December,
Swift and sudden and keen came a flight of feathery arrows.
Then came a cloud of smoke, and out of the cloud came the lightning,
Out of the lightning, thunder ; and death, unseen, ran before it.
Frightened, the savages fled for shelter in swamp and in thicket,
Hotly pursued and beset ; but their sachem, the brave Wattawamet,
Fled not, he was dead.   Unswerving and swift had a bullet
Passed through his brain, and he fell with both hands clutching the
  green sward,
Seeming in death to hold back from his foe the land of his fathers.

These are lines which for strength and spirit equal any that
can be quoted from the pages of our modern poets.   The
terrific sarcasm of these Indians, and their grim humour may
be matched no doubt by some of the descriptions in Robert
Browning, who excels in this kind of writing ; but in him it
is often to be regretted that such passages in his works are
deformed by something unnatural in the subject itself, or in
his method of treating it.   With the passage we have just
quoted, no such objection can be taken.   It is sublime, and
yet the proprieties are observed.   It affords subject for a
magnificent painting.

Neither can anything be better than the description of the
manner in which John Alden executed the mission laid upon
him by the captain.   Priscilla, the Puritan maiden !   How
much more artistically conceived than either the Pompilia
of Browning or the Elaine of Tennyson.   No interest

thrown by them around these ladies, by placing them in sensational situations, and by high - wrought sentiment, comes up to that which Longfellow produces by his mastery in availing himself of natural and legitimate circumstances. As she appears in his poem, Priscilla is regarded by us as the first destined bride, so to speak, of the States; she stands before us in the uncorrupted simplicity of the Plymouth time—the Eve of the Republic ; the representative of the primitive innocence of the United States. As she sits at her wheel, an orphan in that new land, with the snow-white carded wool upon her knee, and her white hands feeding the "ravenous spindle," the poet has already invested her with a national and world interest. And what a truly drawn womanhood. How intuitively she discerns the love which Alden bears to her, under all the dissimulations of the com-missary office he had undertaken.

But as he warmed and glowed in his simple and eloquent language,
Quite forgetful of self, and full of the praise of his rival,
Archly the maiden smiled, and with eyes overrunning with laughter,
Said, in a tremulous voice, " Why don't you speak for yourself, John ? "

With regard to the measure in which the poem is written, when we first begin to read, we are disposed to shake our head and ask ourselves how possibly the author can ever wield these long uncouth lines of fifteen feet. Nor do we mean to justify them. There are many of them which read like unmistakable prose. And yet, as he proceeds, such is the power of his genius, that even these long trailing measures become electrified with life and rhythmical with beauty, and ere long, in his sublimer moods, forked light-nings in his hands, by which he strikes dismay into our hearts.

What shall we say of "Evangeline"? It holds a place entirely by itself in our literature, in so far as immortal praise is due to its author not only, and not so much for his manner of treating the subject, as for his discovery and conception of the subject itself. The idea of a girl who has been torn from her lover by enemies who have invaded their home settlement, and embarked them in ships to two different ports in America; her search after him through the provinces of that continent, down its great rivers, and through its interminable forests—again and again finding traces of him, only to end in disappointment; catching a vain hope from the smoke that ascends above every encampment in the wilderness; refusing to part with life's earliest dream, and still believing that God will direct her steps through those labyrinths of nature to the object of her love; the unutterable longings; the sickness of hope deferred, till youth at last passed away, and her tresses became grey in this mysterious love journey—-this is a form of calamity that was never conceived of in the imagination of any other bard, and the bare presentation of which to the reader is so suggestive of the highest poetry, of all that is trying in situation and tragical in sentiment, as to amount in the simple conception of it to a triumph of genius. True, Longfellow was an American. But that cannot account for such an idea having entered his mind as forms the groundwork of this story. There are millions in the States to whom the boundlessness of their continent suggests thoughts of ambition and of enterprise: there is only one to whom it would have suggested the despair of an Evangeline in search of her lover. The idea could only have entered into the soul of such a poet as he is, for sublimity is an essential element in him. Sublime poets delight in vastness and infinite space. Look to Milton. What fills his mind is the conception of the immeasurable gulf-distance between hell and our earth, up which Satan steers his ascending flight.

A dark

> Illimitable ocean, without line,
> Without dimension, where length, breadth, and height,
> And time and place are lost.

In the poem before us the vastnesses of the American continent are with us and before us throughout, while the interest of tenderness is awakened by the utter inability of this lover in her maiden helplessness to contend with them ; for it is the very magnificence of nature in its forests and prairies and rolling rivers that is against her—it is the wideness of space that overwhelms her.

The conception having once entered into Longfellow's mind, how masterly is his way of managing it. Supposing the idea to have been hit upon by any poet of the hopelessness of this love-search, there were various ways of developing it. When Byron would impress us with the loneliness of the Chillon imprisonment, he makes the prisoner himself describe it, which he does, no doubt, in sentimental and exquisitely musical lines. When Tennyson would affect us with the tragical sorrows of Maud's lover, he too makes him his own narrator, striving to create and sustain interest (as is the way with our modern poets) by throwing the poem into a series of sensational ballads. With more trust in nature, and with more command over the ways by which the human heart can be reached, Longfellow has adopted another method. He commences the poem with a simple narrative of the days when Evangeline and Gabriel were happy youthful lovers at Grand Prè in their own beloved Nova Scotia. We are apt to consider the description needlessly detailed, even common-place and prosy. Ignorant souls that we are ! Unconsciously, insensibly are we prepared with infinite skill for the coming catastrophe. There must be first a picture of the perfect peace of that home settlement—quiet but humble—the nest as God made it, moss-fashioned, softly lined with the loves that are in it. We must first have visited and looked into it, then we shall feel the tragedy of the hour when this sanctuary was ravished and violated by ruthless hands. In the very common-placeness of Evangeline's first prospects, well-to-do on her father's farm, no bar of poverty, no obstacle to her heart's affection, everything holding out the likelihood of a life monotonous, but perfectly level with her desires, there is a dreadful preparation planned by contrast for the extraordinary fate that awaited her.   The tame and unattractive landscape, too, of Nova Scotia, so dear to her heart by the loves of Gabriel and her old father—how does it contrast with the gorgeous scenery through which she is afterwards led —the pomp and prodigality of nature which was to mock her heart.   How well does the poet sustain the picture of perfect peace and love happiness that reigned at Grand Prè up to the very last moment before the thunder-storm burst upon it; up to the last night when, the humble preparations for her marriage being all made, Evangeline retired to her bedroom.

Simple that chamber was, with its curtains of white, and its clothes-press
Ample and high, on whose spacious shelves were carefully folded
Linen and woollen stuffs, by the hands of Evangeline woven.
This was the precious dower she would bring to her husband in marriage,
Better than flocks and herds, being proofs of her skill as a housewife.
Ah ! she was fair, exceeding fair to behold, as she stood with
Naked snow-white feet on the gleaming floor of her chamber ;
Little she dreamed that below, among the trees of the orchard,
Waited her lover, and watched for the gleam of her lamp and her shadow.
Yet were her thoughts of him, and at times a feeling of sadness
Passed o'er her soul, as the sailing shade of clouds in the moonlight
Flitted across the floor, and darkened the room for a moment.
And as she gazed from the window, she saw serenely the moon pass
Forth from the folds of a cloud, and one star followed her footsteps,
As out of Abraham's tent young Ishmael wandered with Hagar !

Any other poet than Longfellow might have shrunk from an attempt to describe the varied regions through which his heroine passed.   It was, in fact, to undertake to give a panoramic view of whatever is wonderful on the American continent.   But difficulties of this kind vanish before his rich and prodigal fancy.   Whether he lead us past the Ohio shore and the mouth of the Wabash, down the swift Mississippi or by the lakes of the Atchafalaya, or westward where the Oregon flows and the Walloway and the Owyhee, we have the characteristic scenery conjured up, every variety of vegetation, every species of bird, every strange and picturesque freak of nature. Wherever the despair of Evangeline's love carries her, his transcendent genius accompanies her, depicting each region of her wanderings, so that we see it gleaming under the tenderness of her moonlights, or reddened by the sunsets that closed her unavailing journeys. Seldom has there been a greater master-stroke in the pathetic than his bringing the two lovers on one of the nights to the very point of meeting. The exhaustion of nature leads her to retire for the night to slumber on the banks of the river, and he passes by ! The mockery of a moment's proximity added to the misery of a lifetime separation. Hapless Evangeline !

Thus did the long sad years glide on, and in seasons and places
Divers and distant far was seen the wandering maiden ;
Now in the tents of grace of the meek Moravian Mission,
Now in the noisy camps and the battle-fields of the army,
Now in secluded hamlets, in towns, and populous cities ;
Like a phantom she came, and passed away unremembered.
Fair was she and young, when in hope began the long journey ;
Faded was she and old, when in disappointment it ended.
Each succeeding year stole something away from her beauty,
Leaving behind it, broader and deeper, the gloom and the shadow.
Then there appeared and spread faint streaks of grey o'er her forehead,
Dawn of another life, that broke o'er her earthly horizon,
As in the eastern sky the first faint streaks of the morning.

The close of the story is well conceived. We feel it to be a relief when this child of suffering comes up with him at length; and when we connect this her last embrace of him in the hospital of Pennsylvania with the preparations for marriage in Grand Prè, it seems to us as if here were the beginning and the end of a love, all the intermediate stages of which are wanting—the mere foundation stone and cope stone of a building which God had made frustrate!

Let us now look at the "Golden Legend."

We cannot agree with the author in admiring the legend upon which this poem is founded. He is quite in raptures with it. "It seems to me to surpass all other legends in beauty and significance." What is it? A prince, the Prince of Hohonek, labours under a deep melancholy. Certain doctors of Salerne give it as their opinion that his malady is not curable unless a young maiden be found willing to die for him. A young girl, Elsie, the daughter of one of his tenants, is willing to undergo this fate. She communicates her intentions to her old father and mother, both of whom, after some very small demurrance, consider that this must be nothing less than a suggestion from above. The prince hesitates in the first instance. He goes to consult the priest in confessional. The priest would have stood out against the proposal, but having left the church before Hohonek arrives, Lucifer in disguise gets into the confessional and sanctions it. Upon this, the prince proceeds along with Elsie on the journey from his castle on the Rhine to Salerne, where the death was to take place. Upon reaching it he changes his purpose. He now decisively refuses to allow her to die. Whether through the benefit of a popish miracle, or of the fresh air on the journey, he recovers from his melancholy. He resolves to marry her, and she returns to his castle his wedded wife.

We wonder that our author should admire a story like this, founded upon a proposal of death wanting in morality and probability, and certain therefore to fail in æsthetics. He looks upon Elsie's act as one of wonderful devotedness.

> God sent His messenger of faith,
> And whispered in the maiden's heart,
> "Rise up, and look from where thou art,
> And scatter with unselfish hands
> The freshness on the barren sands
> And solitudes of death."
> O beauty of holiness,
> Of self-forgetfulness, of lowliness !
> O power of meekness,
> Whose very gentleness and weakness
> Are like the yielding but irresistible air !

> Upon the pages
> Of the sealed volume that I bear
> The deed divine
> Is written in characters of gold,
> That never shall grow old,
> But through all ages
> Burn and shine
> With soft effulgence !
> O God ! it is Thy indulgence
> That fills the world with the bliss
> Of a good deed like this.

There can be no question of the beauty of these lines, but as to the deed they commend—well, what shall we say? If a man were in danger by exposure to enemies, or from fire or water, that a young woman should interpose to save his life at the sacrifice of her own, would entitle her to be considered as a heroine. But if he be labouring, like Prince Hohonek, under some malady in the providence of God, that she should subject herself to a violent death in order to effect his recovery, is a monstrosity in two senses. She is fool enough to think that any death of the kind could have such an effect. Next, she does an unauthorised thing, for no one is warranted to give away life for the cure of another's melancholy. The doctors at Salerne had no doubt given out their opinion that a young woman's blood was the only remedy for hypochondria ; but it is plain from the narrative itself that the prince did not consider their authority as sufficient, that he considered it necessary to consult the priest, and that the priest himself repudiated in his heart the proposal. It was only Lucifer that sanctioned it, by our author's own showing. How then can he approve it? Nor will it do to say that the girl believed the thing to be right, and considered the whole to be a suggestion of heaven. This removes the case into the fanatical, which is condemnable, and never æsthetical. A girl acting under such influence can never fully sustain our admiration. The act is too high-flown and improbable to be accepted in morals or in art. The same may be said of her father and mother, who, after a single conversation with her at their bedside, consent to her self-immolation. This lowers them at once in our eyes. But what shall we say of Hohonek himself— of the man who consented to the proposal of being cured of his melancholy by this child's blood ? He no doubt changes his purpose at last, but who can admire such irresolution ? Thus, there is a fault in all the characters, which is the more to be lamented, because the scenes of the poem are magnificently described.

The " Golden Legend " is full of genius, and written with infinite talent. Even the parts of Hohonek and Elsie, if we exclude the unnatural design of their journey, are finely conceived. The legends which they recite to each other in the garden are rendered, like all his other legends, with singular grace, airyness, and loveliness; and the prince's address to her on the terrace of the castle at the close, reminds one of the musical and impassioned tenderness of Lord Byron.

But the chief charm of the poem, and that which stamps it as entirely original, is the description given us of the whole services, offices, and officials of the Church of Rome, as they came under the observation of the two lovers on their journey to Salerne. When they came to Strasbourg Cathedral, besides a splendid description of the structure itself, we have a sermon from Friar Cuthbert to the crowd round the pulpit on Easter Sunday, followed by a miracle play. At the Convent of Herschau we have Friar Claus's exultations in the wine-cellar, and Friar Pacificus's complacencies over his illuminated Gospels. At the school of Salerne we have scholastics and doctors disputing their theses. No doubt there is a certain oddness of style, which approximates too much to the viciousness of our false modern school of poetry, and we prefer the other larger poems of Longfellow, as written by a purer standard. But the description is splendid, and shows a power of entering into the very persons he describes superior to that of any other of our poets, and amounting to a metempsychosis. No friar in the Middle Ages could have preached with more characteristic mixture of humour and profanity than Friar Cuthbert does when describing the resurrection of Christ, accompanied by the cracking of his whip and the cheers of the mob. So also have we had many pictures of wine-loving friars, but this probably excels them all. Claus thus soliloquises in the cellar over a cask of Bacharach :—

> Now, here is a cask that stands alone,
> And has stood a hundred years or more,
> Its beard of cobwebs long and hoar,
> Trailing and sweeping along the floor,
> Like Barbarossa, who sits in his cave,
> Taciturn, sober, sedate, and grave,
> Till his beard has grown thro' the table of stone !
> It is of the quick and not of the dead,
> In its veins the blood is hot and red,
> And a heart still beats in these ribs of oak,
> That time may have tamed but has not broke !
>
>   *   *   *   *
>
> Behold where he stands all sound and good,
> Brown and old in his oaken hood ;
> Silent he seems externally
> As any Carthusian monk can be ;
> But within, what a spirit of deep unrest !
> What a seething and simmering in his breast !
> As if the heaving of his great heart
> Would burst his belt of oak apart !
> Let me unloose this button of wood,
> And quiet a little his turbulent mood.
> See how its currents gleam and shine,
> As if they had caught the purple hues
> Of autumn sunsets on the Rhine,
> Descending and mingling with the dews ;
> Or as if the grapes were stained with blood
> Of the innocent boy who some years back
> Was taken and crucified by the Jews,
> In that ancient town of Bacharach.

He next transmigrates into Friar Pacificus, the transcriber
and illuminator, as follows :—

> There, now, is an initial letter,
> King Réne himself never made a better !
> Finished down to the leaf and the snail,
> Down to the eyes on the peacock's tail !
> And now, as I turn the volume over,
> And see what lies between cover and cover,
> What treasures of art these pages hold,
> All ablaze with crimson and gold,
> God forgive me ! I seem to feel
> A certain satisfaction steal
> Into my heart and into my brain,
> As if my talent had not lain
> Wrapped in a napkin, and all in vain.
> Yes, I might almost say to the Lord,
> " Here is a copy of Thy Word,
> Written out with much toil and pain ;
> Take it, O Lord, and let it be
> As something I have done for Thee."

(He looks from the window.)

> How sweet the air is ! How fair the scene !
> I wish I had as lovely a green
> To paint my landscapes and my leaves !
> How the swallows twitter under the eaves !
> There, now, there is one in her nest,
> I can just catch a glimpse of her head and breast,
> And will sketch her thus, in her quiet nook,
> For the margin of my Gospel book.

Meanwhile the abbot moralises outside the cloisters :—

> Slowly, slowly, up the wall
>   Steals the sunshine, steals the shade ;
> Evening damps begin to fall,
>   Evening shadows are displayed.
> Round me, o'er me, everywhere,
>   All the sky is grand with clouds,
> And athwart the evening air
>   Wheel the swallows home in crowds.
> Shafts of sunshine from the west
>   Paint the dusky windows red ;
> Darker shadows, deeper rest,
>   Underneath and overhead.

> Darker, darker, and more wan
> 　In my breast the shadows fall ;
> Upward steals the life of man,
> 　As the sunshine from the wall ;
> From the wall unto the sky,
> 　From the roof along the spire ;
> Ah ! the souls of those who die
> 　Are but sunbeams lifted higher.

We cannot dwell upon the " Saga of Olaf." The warlike encounters of the Norse had long been familiar to our literature, but the first introduction of Christianity by force into their regions was a new and fine subject for poetry. Under the bold exorcism of Longfellow's imagination this burlesque mission rises up in living form and startling embodiments. Thor, defiant, meets us on the threshold ; and, as a closing contrast, we have the voice of the Evangelist John heard in a vision of the night, advising love, not force. The body of the poem records, in sea-fights and graphic scenes, the exploits of King Olaf, who confounded the sword with Christianity, and of Thaugbrand, his priest, who confounded wholesale baptism with conversion. But as the Saga takes the ballad form, accompanied by some of the extravagances often connected with it, we scarcely look upon them as illustrating the truer style of poetry which our author has exhibited to our age.

We may be expected, perhaps, following the rule adopted in preceding essays, to say something of the religious sentiments of Longfellow, as those appear in his writings. But we would not be considered as in this volume presuming to be censor general of the religion of our bards. The cases of Browning and Tennyson were peculiar. They have made their poetry a vehicle for introducing a new species or form of Christianity. This cannot be said of the poet who forms the subject of this essay. Writing on the other side of the Atlantic, he is not affected by the spirit pervading this school of religionists. He does not write under the agonies or earnestness that have originated in scepticism.

At the same time, Longfellow, in religion, seems to be of the Broad school.　We have no intention of animadverting upon the kind of religion advocated by the Theologian forming one of his party in the " Wayside Inn," and which represents his own views.

> A Theologian, from the school
> Of Cambridge on the Charles, was there ;
> Skilful alike with tongue and pen,
> He preached to all men everywhere
> The gospel of the Golden Rule,
> The new commandment given to men,
> Thinking the deed and not the creed
> Would help us in our utmost need.
> With reverent feet the earth he trod,
> Nor banished nature from his plan ;
> But studied still with deep research,
> To build the universal Church,
> Lofty as is the love of God,
> And ample as the wants of man.

He thus explains himself :—

> I stand without here in the porch,
> I hear the bells' melodious din,
> I hear the organ peal within,
> I hear the prayer, with words that scorch
> Like sparks from an inverted torch.
> I hear a sermon upon sin,
> With threatenings of the last account.
> And all, translated in the air,
> Reach me, but as our dear Lord's prayer,
> And as the Sermon on the Mount.
> Must it be Calvin, and not Christ?
> Must it be Athanasian creeds,
> Or holy water, books, and beads ?
>   *   *   *   *
> Not to one Church alone, but seven ,
> The voice prophetic spake from heaven ;
> And unto each the promise came,
> Diversified, but still the same.
> For him that overcometh are
> The new name written on the stone,
> The raiment white, the crown, the throne,
> And I will give him the Morning Star.

In short, the religion here taught to be important is that which appears in the life, irrespective of creed; and, if we understand him aright, he means to say that the Bible inculcates the same view, contemplating all Churches as good enough, and their peculiar creeds as very much a matter of indifference, compared with matters of life and practice. True religion, according to him as he "stands in the porch," or as "translated in the air," *i.e.*, as separated from the dust thrown around it by ministers and churchmen, is comprehended, in the summary spirit of it, in the " Lord's Prayer and the Sermon on the Mount." How deep the Charles may be at the point where the Cambridge school stands, we cannot tell; but the theology of the school itself must be very shallow if this be the amount of its teaching. What right has any man to cull out one part of the Bible, especially the Sermon on the Mount, where our Lord is simply inculcating the practical rules of the Christian religion, and to cashier all the rest of the Record? If the Bible, when "translated in the air," appears reduced to these three chapters, most of us will prefer our own English version, which gives us the whole of the original. We can easily see why he singles out these chapters. Containing as they do nothing but what is common to Christianity with other religions, they afford him a foundation broad enough upon which to build up his "universal Church." Meanwhile what does he make of the rest of the Record which declares at great length what is peculiar to Christianity; as, for example, that the eternal Son of God was made flesh in order that he might be made sin, and atonement for it; that we are all born into this world guilty and polluted, needing to be washed in the sin-atoning blood of the Saviour, and to be born again by the Holy Spirit before we can keep the rules laid down in the Sermon on the Mount? All this is what the Cambridge scholar would call creed. Of course it is; but, whatever it be, he is bound to receive it; and any man with half an eye can perceive that our life and practice must be essentially affected according as we receive or reject it. This creed, if it be true, is infinitely more momentous than life or practice, for it concerns the whole matter of our everlasting salvation, with the life and practice besides.

As already stated, we have no intention of animadverting upon Longfellow's religious sentiments. But we have made these statements to show that he cannot be considered as an Evangelical, in the sense of a Calvinistic poet.

A Calvinistic poet! Some may sneer at the term. But we hold this to be the great *desideratum* of the age. Let us for a moment consider what constitution of a man we need at present in this department of our literature.

First, then, he would need to be in sympathy with the Creator in that world of beauty by which we are surrounded, in its magnificence, its beauty, and its tenderness; having, in short, as one half of his qualification, that which forms very nearly all the qualification which our modern poets of the higher order possess.

Next, he must be in sympathy with the same glorious Being in the great work of Redemption, acquiescing in His views of the awful demerit of sin, accepting man's eternal condemnation upon account of it, and responding to His infinite love in sending His Son to be our surety-expiation upon the cross. This is the other half of the qualification needed. If he has not seen the glory of the Maker of all worlds in this department of his operation, he lacks just so much of the inspiration which makes up the perfect poet.

Milton treated the Fall Calvinistically. He threw the Bible truth of that event into the region of the imagination, where it will ever remain. He represented sin, according to the truth of it in the Bible, as that which, even in one act of it, deserves hell. The poem stands out therefore in the sublimity to be expected from a Divine idea.

In his " Paradise Regained " he failed utterly, because he swerved from Calvinism, that is, from the Bible view of Redemption, fully and faithfully and at once accepted. He deserved to fail.   Following his own reason, which I suppose had led him into Arianism, or something like it, he placed the battle-ground of Redemption in the wilderness, instead of placing it on Calvary.   He made it an affair of obedience, and not of expiation.   There is no sublimity in Redemption unless you take the Calvinistic view of it.   Even the enemies of this view object to it upon the ground of the stupendous steps which it supposes God to take; and, from the very reason why they reject it, we must infer that, if well founded, it furnishes the greatest subject for the human imagination.

What we need, then, is an epic poet to do for the Cross what Milton did for the Fall; that is, to treat it Calvinistically, and at the same time throw it into the realm of the ideal.   How this is to be done must be left to the coming poet to determine.   Meanwhile, let none imagine that the Crucifixion has become so much a plain, established verity of fact, along with all the circumstances of it, as that it never can be made the subject of such a poem.   What took place on Calvary was only the transaction as it appeared to the human eye.   Meanwhile the whole grandeur of the transaction lies invisible behind, something which faith glories in realising, and something which genius could render irresistibly attractive.   The Socinian's cross is nothing at all. The cross of Browning, Carlyle, and Tennyson is merely the sanctuary of sorrow; but the Cross, Calvinistically viewed, where the surety-Saviour hangs to deliver us from the wrath to come, is a sublime cliff, whence the eagle imagination will some day or other take its flight, which is destined to soar to the highest heaven of song.

V.

THE SYMBOLIC FORESKETCH OF CHRISTIANITY.

IMMEDIATELY after the Fall we read of animal sacrifice. I shall take for granted that we admit this to have been a Divine institution, intended to prefigure the atoning death of our Lord. Meanwhile, have we considered what follows from such an institution, or rather from the principle of symbolism it proceeds upon? Has it occurred to us that if God has thus resolved to represent one thing belonging to Christianity under a figure, it is the first step taken to symbolise the whole of it? For, if the plan be good in reference to one particular, why not make it of universal application? Does not the congruity of things demand it?

If the atonement is to be represented by animal blood, plainly God Himself is not the congruous object to be approached by such blood, but a Shekinah or luminous appearance grossly setting Him forth. For the same reason, in this symbolical system let the throne on which the Eternal sits propitiated be represented by a small wooden chest, overlaid with gold, and a lid of pure gold above it, to be called the Mercy Seat. Let heaven be represented by an apartment so many cubits long and broad. It must be so. If the atonement is lowered down to bullock's blood, the heaven which is thus purified must be brought down in the same proportion. Then, as the cardinal truth of Christianity was to be the Incarnation, it was necessary that all the things we have mentioned, the Shekinah, the Mercy Seat, the Most Holy, should be inclosed within a tabernacle, this being a figure of " the more perfect tabernacle " of Christ's human nature—a poor figure no doubt, but the whole mystery is dwindled down into a proportional insignificance.

In such a symbolical system it is plain that the Lord Jesus Christ could never Himself be the priest. The priesthood also must be lowered in the same proportion. A mere man clothed in garments of glory and beauty, with a linen mitre, will do ; and, so far as holiness is concerned, the word itself graven upon a plate of gold on his mitre will suffice. Thus when we advance from the Fall to the period of Moses, we discover that the symbol of animal sacrifice was only the first step taken in a singular plan which had entered into the mind of Jehovah to foresketch in outward symbol the whole objective of Christianity.

But what as to the subjective ? The people who were to be set down before this symbolic system must correspond to it. They must be a people the subjects of a proportionally insignificant redemption. Here again the everlasting salvation sinks down into connection with deliverance from slavery in Egypt, and from the Red Sea. Satan is Pharaoh, and heaven is Canaan. When God had resolved to perfect the symbolic system at Sinai, it was in connection with a people, the Jews, who in their outward history and political separation held out the true redeemed of God upon the same small proportional scale.

Thus it entered into the mind of God to foresketch all Christianity objectively and subjectively. Now this, when we think of it, was a very strange scheme. Has it been sufficiently considered, and the reasons for it in the wisdom of God ? We shall afterwards show how it was designed by God to constitute one of the evidences of Christianity when it appeared. But we shall presently inquire into the Divine purposes served by it under the former Testament.

We shall first inquire why God saw fit to begin by employing the symbolic method of dealing with the Church, giving the shadow of heavenly things before He brought in he heavenly things themselves.

We are accustomed to say that it was more suitable to the infancy of the Church, just as pictures are employed in the nursery. What do we mean by the infancy of the Church ? We are not to confound it with an infancy of society or of the human race in general. The idea which suggests itself to some is the want of intellectual development in mankind in the earlier ages. We would protest against this being considered as the reason why symbol was more suitable at the beginning in matters of religion. We would demur to the doctrine that there was a natural infancy of human society requiring that Divine things should be exhibited in this way, and then a natural development in human society under which it became susceptible of the full doctrinal revelation. There is nothing in such an idea but mysticism, and even a dangerous error. The natural faculty of man stood at zero after the Fall, as to religion, and made no advancement in it by a natural process. Progress in religion was supernatural. It is the Church and not the world Paul speaks of in his famous illustration of an infancy, a minority, and a manhood; and the Church is to be considered as having been in the one or the other of these stages entirely because of the measure of Divine revelation granted to her, less or more. What made the infancy of the Church was the small quantity of Divine revelation granted at first; that, and that only. Does any believe that Adam and Eve and their first descendants could not have understood the full gospel afterwards revealed, without first having gone through some process of development ; and that they would not have been fit enough for its institutions, if God had been pleased to set them up? The whole depended upon God's sovereignty. And just as He has purposed that man himself should pass through the various stages of growth, and no other reason can be given for it but His purpose, so it was His sovereign will that revelation should dawn gradually upon the world, and reach its noonday above the cross.

Even when the apostle suggests an infancy, minority, and

manhood of the Church itself, he is rather describing the successive modes which God was pleased to adopt in dispensing the covenant, than describing any successive development that went forward in the Church. We are not to conceive as if under the patriarchal dispensation it was growing and preparing for the Sinaitic, and under the Sinaitic growing and preparing for the Evangelic. For what do we mean by the Church growing? Why, of course, those members of the Church that underwent the training of the patriarchal dispensation were swept away by death and never entered upon the Sinaitic; and such as were schooled in the Sinaitic did not survive to pass into the light of the Christian economy. Could you suppose an individual born in patriarchal times to have lived some two thousand years, then might you conceive of him as being the subject of such a dispensational experiment. All we can say, then, is that God was pleased to adopt these successive economies, and that the Church under them is fitly viewed either as the infant, or the minor under tutors, or the grown heir.

When the Church, owing to the small measure of supernatural revelation yet granted, was thus in its infancy, and the heavenly things afterwards to come were as yet defectively made known in doctrine, it pleased God to give a symbolical representation to them of those things, over and above the doctrinal. Those symbols were intended more for impression than for instruction—not so much to add to their information, as to impress upon their senses the things revealed, and thus make up to them, as it were, in one way, what was wanting in another. This meets a difficulty that must have staggered our minds had they been intended for instruction, since information is in fact much more hard to apprehend by symbols than by plain words. Take the other view, and their adoption in the Church in these earlier ages is justified. How essential that, when the heavenly things were as yet but imperfectly revealed in doctrine, they should be all the more vividly represented to their faith, or rather to their senses! The atonement commends itself sufficiently to us now when it is exhibited in all the satisfactoriness of a completed event, so that there is no necessity for an animal sacrifice and sprinkling of blood to impress it upon us. The Priesthood of Christ is a doctrine so fully revealed to us as to be fraught with comfort enough, without having a figure of Him in the Aaronic priest before our eye. So with other parts of the theological system. We can all see how necessary the figures were to those who lived under the former Testament. Nor does it affect the point now insisted upon that they must have been unable to know the theological significance of those figures. This is in part true; in part not. It is not pretended that they exactly apprehended the philosophy of the symbolic scheme—the full mystery of the temple symbolism, for example, as it is unfolded in the Epistle to the Hebrews, but the great truths of—God present—and God dwelling in the midst of them—of the atonement, &c.— were clearly enough known to them, and were comfortably applied to their faith by the symbolic arrangement. Without supposing them to be able to unravel the whole evangelical mystery of "the worldly sanctuary," it might yet be the fittest medium for impressing all the well-known truths of religion upon their consciences and hearts. All the Jews might not be aware that the tabernacle which stood before them was a figure of the Son of God incarnate, as we know it to have been from Paul, who tells us that it meant "the more perfect tabernacle" of His human nature. But here at least was God associated with an outward structure, and thus brought very near to them, and, indeed, dwelling in the midst of them.

We very much doubt whether many of us sufficiently realise the advantage of the Jews in this symbolic manifestation by which God was with them. It was such as to strike the senses with awe; it was a local approximation of the Deity. What would be the sensation produced amongst us if God should establish His residence in the metropolis of this kingdom in any architectural structure? So near an approach was this—so dreadful was this place—that instead of wondering at the veneration in which it was held by the Jews, the marvel is that society in that land represented its usual levities, while the mystery is that idolatry and every moral abomination found way in the community. Here was God dwelling in their very midst in a tent or house. Here, again, was a man, the high priest, who with the mitre upon his head, and the Urim and Thummim upon his breast, was the visible representation of Christ in His priestly office ; while the whole work of the atonement was so sensibly before their eye in the sacrifice he offered up, and the absolution so comfortably realised by the blood sprinkled upon their persons, that we are apt to envy the Jews their dispensational privilege. The whole, however, was a wise and condescending advantage which God gave them under that defective economy. Now that we have the truth of God's nearness and reconciliation fully made known to us ; now that we have the atonement fully revealed in the redemption actually brought in by Jesus Christ ; there is not only no necessity for such sensible confirmation of our faith, but any attempt made by the Church of Rome, or Romanizing Churches, to produce such impressions upon the senses have been fraught with unspeakable mischief. Symbols added on by God's appointment to a defective revelation helped faith, but when associated by men with the gospel, they only foster superstition. What was useful as a crutch, becomes deadly when it is no longer necessary, and yet is retained. A vicar of Christ, after Christ has Himself been manifested in the flesh ; a sacrificing priesthood, after the one sacrifice has already been offered ; an altar, after Christ, who was the antitype of it, has appeared ; lighted candles, when the Sun of righteousness has ascended the meridian ; teaching by church architecture, when Christianity has itself come in— we might laugh at it all as an absurd graft of the Old Testament into the New, were it not as pestilential as it is ridiculous !

Let us attend to the progressive history of symbols—the way in which God was pleased to introduce them. Only a very few symbolical ordinances and arrangements were brought in during the patriarchal age—sacrifice indeed being the principal one. There was neither a priesthood then symbolising Christ's Priesthood, nor was there a tabernacle. Priests indeed are spoken of before Aaron's appointment to his office, but these were only men who for conveniency's sake, or from regard to order, offered up the sacrifices for a community: meanwhile the right of sacrificing remained with the heads of all families. But when Aaron was appointed priest, all right of sacrificing was taken from heads of families and heads of smaller communities in Israel, and Aaron became sole high priest—a symbol for the first time of the Lord Jesus Christ. Such priests as were before Aaron were only common or ministerial, not symbolical: we except of course Melchizedec, whose priesthood was entirely peculiar, and intended to prefigure what was extraordinary about Christ's Priesthood and superior to the Aaronic. During the patriarchal age, then, there was no symbolic priesthood, and neither was there a symbolic or "worldly sanctuary." God was not worshipped in any one place; He was worshipped as dwelling in heaven, not as dwelling in any particular structure upon earth. On this account we might be apt to fall into the mistake that the patriarch's privilege was superior to that of the Jew. He had the right of sacrificing in his own family, while by the law of Moses this was lost, and the right of ten thousand sacrificers was taken away, to be supplanted by one man, who alone was allowed to offer the sacrifice, and considered as making atonement for them all. Was not this a limitation of their religious privilege? But here it is to be considered that whatever brought Christ's one sole and effectual priesthood before their view, and served impressively to seal it to their faith, went much farther for their comfort than any dignity implied in being personal sacrificers. Till Aaron appeared, they had no symbol of Christ's priesthood. They had only a symbol of His sacrifice. The privilege of the Church thus made a perceptible advance as the symbolic picture was being carried to its perfection. When they offered their own sacrifices, nothing was sealed and symbolised to them but the death of Christ. When one high priest was consecrated with the mysterious oil, this held out to them another feature in redemptive work—Christ's glorious priesthood. The same remark applies to the tabernacle. One might object that the patriarch's worship, which contemplated God as dwelling in the skies, was a sublimer worship than that of the Jew, who was called to contemplate God as dwelling in a material structure, and who, besides, was restricted to one place in the worship of God. But not to say that the Jew was never taught to view God as confined to the tabernacle, and still regarded Him as the God of heaven and earth; not to say that it was the sacrificial worship of God only that was limited to one place; we are to remember that our comfort as sinners depends much less upon the majesty of God than upon the knowledge and assurance of His nearness to us. God dwelling in the sky communicates small comfort. God dwelling in the midst of us is the inestimable blessing. When He pitched His tent in Israel, this was the very figure of Immanuel—God with us. This privilege the patriarchs wanted.

At last the time drew near when the symbolic privilege of the Church was to be perfected by the whole system of heavenly things being represented sensibly and materially to the eye. And the first thing necessary to this was that a people should be separated from the rest of the world, who should themselves be a symbol of the redeemed, for a symbolical people were of course to stand before the symbolical or worldly sanctuary. Such was Israel, whose separation was political; whose calling was to a land belonging to this world; whose redemption was from bodily slavery; whose exodus was a procession from Egypt; whose way was through a literal wilderness; whose journey was one geograpically described, and beset with difficulties of a corresponding character. We cannot but feel the fitness there was between such a symbolical people and the symbolical system that was about to be set up, and we cannot sufficiently admire the symmetrical beauty of the whole arrangement, which, in the very nature of things, could only have entered into the mind of God, and only been executed by Him.

The next thing necessary was that the symbolic ordinances should be given forth and promulgated to the Jews at first, in such a manner, and with such a manifestation of God as, being itself symbolical, would correspond with them.

It was not enough that they should come with Divine authority as a revelation from heaven (this the gospel did), but they must come from "a mount that might be touched." The Jews were brought to the foot of Sinai, which, for the time, became the throne of God, and represented with an impressive materialism whatever is awful or solemn about His immediate presence. Upon this mountain was exhibited in symbol all that is terrible and all that is comfortable in our religion.

First, what is it that constitutes the truly terrible or formidable in religion? Unquestionably it is the majesty and wrath of an offended God. This was displayed only in external phenomena — blackness, fire, tempest, earthquake. This method of representing His rectoral majesty and His offended justice was well fitted to strike the senses and the imagination. It was an advance upon any manifestation God had hitherto given of Himself in the Church; it was something much more impressive than Abraham or any of his immediate descendants had witnessed; and it was in character as a sanction to the system of symbolical ordinances now to be brought forward. At a period when the doctrinal revelation regarding the infinite justice and majesty of God, and regarding everlasting punishments, was yet defective, such a symbolical representation was fitted to help their faith and fill their minds with salutary awe. As for us, we are come to the things themselves; for it is a great mistake to think that, when the apostle says (Heb. xii. 18), " Ye are not come unto the mount that might be touched, and that burned with fire, nor unto blackness and darkness and tempest," he means to say merely that we are come to something that is more comfortable. Whoever reads the passage throughout will see he intends to say that we are come to something much more formidable and terrible, even to the things which were symbolised by these phenomena on the mount which he specifies. We are come not merely to the symbols of God's judicial majesty, but " to God himself, the Judge of all." " Our God is the consuming fire." In the full revelation we now have of His infinite holiness and inflexible justice and incurred wrath, we have something much more awful than the Sinaitic phenomena. Hell is brought so near that we see the smoke of its ascending torments. The end of all things is brought so near that we see the world wrapt in the flames of her final conflagration. In the Cross we have a manifestation of the wrath of God which dwindles down the Sinaitic manifestation into insignificance, for *there* there fell down a darkness greater than the absence of light, and the fire that consumed the sacrifice of the world's expiation. At the same time we need not say how well adapted the symbols of Sinai were to the people gathered around the mount. We see how they served to impress them with their true position as perishing sinners, and constrained them to appropriate the comfortable part of our religion, which was also, as I have observed, symbolised upon the mount.

For what is it that constitutes the comfortable in our religion ? It is the mediatorship of our Lord Jesus Christ. And this was symbolized in that of Moses. Now for the first time was the mediatory office of Christ symbolised to the Church, and a lively figure afforded of the nature, necessity, and comfort of it. When upon this point I might take occasion to illustrate the position which Moses occupied in comparison with Christ, for it is a point which is not often insisted upon satisfactorily.

There was a species of unprecedented boldness and faith shown by Moses in the exercise of his mediatorship. He was called to ascend the mount alone. Of the people there was none with him. They dared not face the terrors that compassed the mountain, nor answer the summons of that fearful trumpet. He advanced forward and upward before the eyes of an awe-stricken people, who must have watched him as he prosecuted his perilous ascent, until ere long he vanished from their view amidst the tempestuous elements into which he entered. After all, however, we have seen that it was only the faint symbols of the wrath of God which he confronted, and in respect of which he mediated—the electric flash, the meteoric fires, the earthquake which shook the mount that might be touched. We on the other hand are come to the true Mediator, the man Christ Jesus. The approach he made to God, how inconceivably more awful! Summoned by no trump of archangel, but by God the Father, in the name of His people, and with the liability of our accumulated sins upon His head, He went forward into the blackness and darkness of Divine desertion, to face the terrors of majesty incensed, and justice demanding its satisfaction. It was into heaven itself that He ascended through the intervening cloud and tempest of His sufferings, and having purged away our sins by the blood of an awful expiation, He sat down for ever upon the right hand of the throne of the Majesty on high. And what was the result of these respective mediatorships? Moses brought down from the mount a dispensation or system containing only the figures of good things to come, a result forming all that could be expected from him who had only combated with the figures of the wrath that needed to be turned away. Christ imparts to us from heaven the benefits themselves. Through Him we are come to the heavenly Jerusalem, to the innumerable company of angels, to the general assembly of the first-born which are written in heaven, and to the spirits of just men made perfect."

The majesty of God having been symbolically represented, and also Christ's mediatorship, the laws were given forth from Mount Sinai.

I am not called at present to speak of these laws in general, but only of the symbolical ordinances.

It was now that God completed the picture of that symbolic representation of all heavenly things, of which the rite of animal sacrifice had been the pledge, although we may safely say that no man on earth or angel in heaven could have conjectured it to be the first material fragment intended to be afterwards fitted in to a complete symbolical foresketch of Christianity. It was now that, as the atonement had been dwindled down into an animal sacrifice, suddenly, as if by enchantment, all heavenly things went down into a similar insignificance; the Godhead into a luminous cloud called the Shekinah; the throne of God into a box so many cubits long and broad; the heavens into an apartment of certain dimensions; the human nature of Christ into a tent, and His priesthood into a man standing before it, whose qualifications were that his bodily members were complete, and that he had " Holiness to the Lord " engraved upon a golden plate above his head, and had been anointed with oil of a particular composition; while, in the court of the worshippers, the ransomed from everlasting destruction stood diminished into a nation of emancipated slaves.

It must immediately strike us that when this peculiar system of the representation of heavenly things was adopted, it followed that the subordinate parts must run upon the same principle. We must expect that a symbolical character more or less will be made to attach to the whole frame of the worship and institutions and arrangements of the Jewish Church. Sin and holiness, even, let us be sure of it, will be thus shadowed off and diminished into material type. It

shall be a very special sin to touch a dead body, and to eat
of the eagle or the ossifrage the same, for beasts and birds
alike have become clean or unclean, and the Jew is one or
the other according as he has observed the regulation. God
forbid that we should say it was all one whether he were
morally pure or impure; but over and above the moral in-
junction there is the ceremonial regulation to impress the
lesson. And now it is a matter of conscience with him
whether the animal he eats divides the hoof. The atonement being represented by animal blood, reverence for it is
impressed upon him by abstinence from blood as an article
of ordinary diet; and if they abstain from eating things
strangled they shall be a holy nation to the Lord. The
influences of the Holy Ghost being symbolised by water and
oil, the worshippers are holy (so far as the worldly sanctuary
is concerned) if their bodies are washed with pure water;
and they are devoted to the Lord if they are anointed. Now
it is *taste not, touch not, handle not,* and religion is associated
with things and actions that are material.

If the objection be urged that all this had a tendency to
lower religion and to introduce a carnal element into it,
which had not attached to the patriarchal form, the best
answer that can be given is, that if a principle be good, it is
best to carry it out. If it was a good thing to symbolise the
death of Christ by an animal sacrifice, because, with their
defective doctrinal revelation, the symbolism impressed that
death and its atoning nature in a more lively way upon their
imagination, then it must be still better that all other things
of a like nature should be symbolised as well—that the de-
filing nature of sin, for example, should be impressed upon
them by regulations connected with the dead body, and that
the necessity of holiness unto the Lord should be taught
them by a number of interdictions laid upon their food, &c.
If the fragmentary symbol that first made its appearance
was good, the economy of course goes forward to perfection
when the symbolic picture is perfected. The question is

whether, under an economy where the doctrines of our holy religion were yet insufficiently made known, a nation like that of the Jews did not require to be brought under a system of this sort ? To decide that question in the negative, it is not enough to insist that the Jews under such a system fell into the error often of substituting the ceremonial for the moral. We know they did. But the prophets were able to check this error. Every system has a side upon which it lies open to be perverted by the corruption of those who are under it. Meanwhile the symbolism might do a vast deal more to reinforce faith and help holiness than it had a tendency to become a substitute with the Jews for the things signified. It was a Jew's mistake to think that the ceremonial might be a substitute for the moral, but the mistake which we Christians are apt to fall into, is, thinking that the moral would have stood for a single century with that nation without the ceremonial being added on. The Jews, in the sense I have so often referred to, were as children, and we know the rudimental way in which we teach children; illustrating their books with pictures; enforcing authority by its visible emblems; and setting up a system of disciplinary regulations, compliance with which is, as it were, an infantile code of morality that becomes conscience with them. All this might be considered by very intellectual educators as having a tendency to distort both their mental and moral perceptions, but the system is the best for its purpose, and so was the Mosaic.

Such being the system which God intended to pursue, it is noticeable that the symbolical among the Jews took precedence of the moral worship of Jehovah. They had their meetings throughout the land for prayer and reading of the word of God, but the temple was above the synagogue. There was no public ministry set apart to preach the word, but there was the priesthood and the Levites for conducting the sacrifices of the temple. These taught the law, but the prominent part of their office was to carry on the ceremonial service. Indeed, this followed from the radical principle of the economy, in which God manifested Himself by the She-kinah, and Christ Himself was represented by the high priest who stood before the temple. The heavenly things being represented in symbol, of course the service went forward according to the symbolical principle; and the people, even when they engaged in religious services of a moral descrip-tion, did so in the way of looking to the temple, where God had recorded His name.

Finally, the sanctions of the Jewish economy assumed a symbolical aspect. Life and immortality not being fully brought to light, nor the doctrine of everlasting punishments, it was all the more necessary that there should be at least impressive symbols of them present. Hence the awful death-penalties that were attached to the law of Moses; not merely to some of the ceremonial regulations, but to the violation of some of the moral precepts; not merely to violations of commandments belonging to the first table of the law (for then they might have been said to have had their origin merely in Israel's being a theocracy), but to others belonging to the second table. The adulterer was punished with death; the stubborn son was put to death. Hence the land of Canaan given to them, and promises of outward prosperity in the land. Now that heaven and hell have been clearly revealed, religion can maintain itself in the world without a system of temporal sanctions of an extra-ordinary kind; but we may doubt whether it could have done so in Israel. There never was a wilder theory broached than that which has been held by some, that the doctrine of man's eternal destinies was unknown among the Jews; but it were to betray ignorance of facts to deny that under the Old Testament the prominent thing brought forward is the temporal doom of nations, or their prosperity; that the wrath of God is still coming forth in outward calamities, and His goodness evaporating in terrestrial blessings. We see constantly before our eyes that Jewish nation, which being the type in her history of all spiritual things, we must be content to see them through the dim speculum of her deliverance from Egypt, or of other passages of her history down to her captivity in Babylon; and prophets are continually passing before us, carrying with them the doom of nations, and only indirectly pointing to the eternal destinies of humanity. Meanwhile we cannot endure this veil by which whatever is momentous in man's eternal fate is hidden under the insignificance of the destruction or restoration of kingdoms; and whatever is great in heaven is dwarfed into tabernacle dimensions, and whatever is vast in the atonement is reduced to animal sacrifice. Upon entering the New Testament we are at once relieved of all this. Every nation is now swept away from the theatre of observation, and man is before us in his catholic individuality. Not only (God be praised) is the temple thrown to the ground, but the Jewish nation itself, which was a huge symbolism, is scattered to the four winds of heaven, and the whole system of representing the mysteries of our holy religion by symbols is at an end.

But what a singular system was this altogether! I have only given a rough sketch of it. Extended, the subject might occupy a volume, and opens up a distinct department of theological science. But the above remarks have been only introductory to the main point of illustrating the end which God had in view by this symbolic foresketch, so far as we who live in the latter days are concerned—this being to constitute an extraordinary evidence of the truth of Christianity.

I have now, then, to call the attention of my readers to what may be considered as a somewhat new branch of the evidences of Christianity.

Infidelity is making rapid advancement amongst us. Into the causes of this I shall not at present inquire. We know from the holy Scriptures themselves that the doctrine contained in them is distasteful to fallen humanity, and, indeed, cannot be discerned without the holy Spirit. We may only expect, therefore, that this antipathy will periodically accumulate, till it break forth into daring attempts to subvert the authority of the Bible. As the clergy are officially brought more into contact with the doctrine, and are called to preach it continually, the antipathy will naturally make its appearance first of all in the house of God. If there be something offensive to the nostrils in any article of consumption, they will naturally feel its offensiveness most who have professionally to do with it, whether by retailing it or in the processes of its composition and manufacture. I do not say this to excuse the infidelity that has made its appearance lately in the ranks of the clergy; but one may charitably thus find its source in the depravity of heart common to us all, and distinguish this sin of theirs from the other of retaining their church offices and emoluments notwithstanding their infidelity, which degrades them below the meanest man who breaks stones upon the public road.

A determined effort must be made to meet the flood of prevailing scepticism. When the foundations are threatened with destruction, attention should be withdrawn from doctrines of subordinate importance. In Scotland, for example, we have had years of conflict (necessary ones) for adjusting the relations between Church and State. The establishment of religion has no doubt deserved our consideration. But the thing that comes up now is, whether we have any religion to establish. The controversy has passed over from points merely of Church government or worship to something more vital. Christianity, or what alone deserves that name, is itself being undermined. In these circumstances, when an attack is made from within upon the citadel, it becomes a sin for any man to be defending the walls.

But how are we to meet the progress of infidelity? There seems no other way of it than to fight hand in hand with the enemy upon the various objections they have brought forward against the authority of Divine revelation, and to bring forward in all their strength before the community the evidences for the truth of Christianity. It will not do to sit down upon the statement with which we started, that the infidelity prevailing has its foundation in the depravity of the human heart, and that the only way of meeting it is to pray for the revival of vital godliness. We know that the cause of war is the lusts that are in our flesh, but what should we think of the policy that recommended us on that account not to do battle with the enemies which will presently invade us, and this with sword and bayonet at their several points of attack. The soundness of our philosophy upon the cause of war in general would be but a poor consolation for territories burnt up through our negligence in defending them. Are we asked what good resulted from the series of learned defences which came out last century against its deistical writers? Are we reminded that it was the revival of practical religion, and the formation of Bible and missionary societies at the close of last century and the beginning of our own, that effectually accomplished the desirable end? The answer is abundantly obvious. To say that the noble champions who refuted these deistical publications did nothing effectual, because they achieved not the same sort of service as the revival of vital godliness accomplished, were as unjust as to undervalue the services of Wellington or of Nelson, or of others who conquered the enemies of our country, and to ask what good they did after all, and whether the revival of a better international policy has not done more, by tending to render war unnecessary.

I propose in this essay to state and enforce the argument for the truth of Christianity (in some respects peculiar) to be derived from the symbolical foresketch of it under the Old Testament.

It is, in so far of course, the same argument which we have usually derived from the predictions of Christianity contained in the Jewish Scriptures—this foresketch being essentially a symbolical prediction. On this account it may be pardonable just to remind the reader for a single moment of the nature of this general argument.

Plain it is, that if God had seen fit He could have incarnated His Son, and brought in the great redemption, at the beginning of the world's history, instead of the middle of it. It has been thought, from the names the patriarchs gave to their sons occasionally, that they entertained such an expectation, and God might have fulfilled it. He might also have given the whole Scriptures that were to be the record of life, and the guide of the Church, in one perfect and instantaneous revelation. I do not insist upon all the disadvantages and dangers at present that must have attended such an immediate introduction of Christ and Christianity. Lord Brougham, whose lightning eye penetrated the depths of all the miscellaneous subjects he handled, and this among the rest, notices the risk that must have been run by placing the evidences of our holy religion so far back. They lose nothing by the comparatively moderate distance at which they stand from us at present, but they would have been sensibly placed under disadvantage had we only seen them through the mist of such a primitive antiquity. But not to dwell upon this and other obvious objections to the mode of dispensation which God did not adopt, we cannot but admire the manifold wisdom of the device which assigned the crucifixion of Christ and the full announcement of Christianity its place at the central period of the world's history, that there might be a prediction of its facts and a successive series of gradually developing revelations. This, in the very nature of things, was a plan which God only could execute, since He only foreknows the future, and can work upon a plan that takes in the ages. The evidences of our holy religion thus connected themselves as by huge clamping irons with whole centuries of time. There was thus furnished an evidence for the truth of Christianity which is unassailable by those who controvert miracles and ridicule the supernatural. For it has just two sides. Here are certain writings of the Old Testament, which were unquestionably in the hands of the Jews long before Christ appeared, and here, on the other hand, are Christ and Christianity, which manifestly are a fulfilment of what these Scriptures contain. It will not do to say that these Old Testament writings were the gradual development of man's own religious ideas or consciousness—his conceptions of God becoming clearer as the centuries advanced, and his own experience driving him more and more into the conviction of a strong Son of God coming to deliver us.   In the first place, the authors of these writings do not propound their doctrines as the result of their own excogitation, but distinctly claim to have received them by immediate revelation from the Most High—a succession of liars, if they wrote from themselves and claimed for prophets—at once the worst and the best of men if we accept this monstrous supposition of our opponents.   In the second place, this attempt to explain a forerunning announcement of Christianity can only apply to its doctrines, and not to its facts.   They who urge it will surely not pretend to maintain that any amount of elevated piety could have enabled the authors of the Jewish Scriptures to tell which of the tribes, or which of the families in Israel the Messiah would spring from, and the exact period of time at which He would appear, and the exact kind of works He should do with His hands, and His rejection by the Jews, and the hundred other circumstances down to the minutest details of His death and His resurrection—circumstances depending not upon Himself only, but upon the conduct of others.   Even granting it were an anticipation of doctrines and not of facts which our opponents are called upon to explain, this theory of theirs will not suffice.   Man's ideas develop from the erroneous to the true.   But the doctrine of the Old Testament Scriptures throughout is from the beginning perfect, although in miniature compass—it is as the germ to the oak, the infant to the man.   Finally, it is so far from being a doctrine which either naturally occurs to man or is relished by him, that it never could have entered into his heart to conceive of it, and, when revealed, it is considered by him to be foolishness.

We have to apologise to the reader for this reference to the usual line of proof for the truth of Christianity from prediction.

I shall now show that the proof becomes entirely novel and more convincing when we look at the symbolical foresketch of Christianity.

See, for example, how it meets and confronts the suggestion of modern infidelity just referred to. I can understand one to allege that the human mind might have anticipated Christianity as a system. But will any venture to say that the symbolising of all the mysteries of Christianity which meets us in the Old Testament can be accounted for by any process of man's own internal consciousness or development? Does it consist with any known law of mental physiology, or with observation, that a system of truth should make its appearance, first in an array of symbols and material figures, and then, in an after age, doctrinally? Infidelity cannot evade this appeal by reminding us that these symbols were just the human mind, in the infancy of the earlier ages, working out, in a grosser and ruder type, the more spiritual form of Christianity that was afterwards developed. For it is an utter fallacy to suppose that the human mind can arrive at the knowledge of the symbol of a thing before it has got the knowledge of the thing itself. It might be very profitable for the Church, when it had yet an imperfect knowledge of heavenly things, and was, so to speak, in its infancy, that God should adopt symbols as pictures are employed in the nursery, to help the understanding and please the imagination of childhood. But what infidelity suggests is the preposterous idea that symbol is the way in which the human mind would naturally first of all grope its way to the discovery of the truths contained in the system of Christianity! This is to mistake the nature of the symbols altogether, which suppose the truth clearly apprehended, and are an arbitrary sign of it materially represented. For example, the Ark with a lid over it, called the Mercy Seat, sprinkled with blood, and having the tables of the law under it, represented God as being just to forgive us our sins through the atonement of our Lord Jesus Christ. But who can suppose that the human mind began to work out this doctrine by the conception of a chest besprinkled with blood, and having the Decalogue inside of it? It is true that the things which were symbolically represented were things already known among the Jews doctrinally. They knew that God was just, and that He was at the same time merciful, and that the coming death of Christ was what reconciled these two procedures together. But they knew it, according to our view, only by immediate revelation from God, and, the revelation being defective, God added on the symbol to seal it and make it more impressive. That is the position we maintain. What is their theory? What is the absurdity to which they are reduced? It is that of imagining that the human mind was both working out itself the knowledge of this strange and mysterious doctrinal truth, and (for some reason unknown) was symbolising it in arbitrary material forms at the same time. *Credat Judæus!* But their theory breaks down altogether when we reflect upon a fact which, I think, can be established, that the symbols went ahead of the doctrinal revelation—a thing which can never be accounted for except by supposing that they were given forth from God, who perfectly foreknew all that was afterwards to be doctrinally revealed. Does any man believe that the wisest theologian among the Jews could have drawn up such a perfect system of theology as the tabernacle, with its accompanying priesthood, symbolically contained?

The infidel, therefore, must account for the appearance of this Tabernacle, or Worldly Sanctuary.

This brings me to what may be considered as one of the distinct evidences of the truth of Christianity.

Paley, by a watch found on the heath, defies atheism. By this perfect representation of Christianity found in the tabernacle, ages before Christ appeared, we might easily confound infidelity. It is Christianity systematised; it is Christianity in architecture. "The stone shall cry out of the wall, and the beam out of the timber shall answer it."

It may be objected, Do you mean to say that the tabernacle was really such a composite of figures as you represent? What if the whole of this conception originate in the fancy? Ingenious men have found an allegorical meaning in almost every part of the Bible. Are we to find an evangelic mystery in everything about the tabernacle, even to its snuffer-dishes? Infidelity may attempt by allegations and sneers of this kind to get out of the net in which it is here caught, but we will not allow it to escape in this way.

(1) Can it be denied that the Ark was a figure to the Jews of God's throne? This is impossible, for He is everywhere represented to the Jews as dwelling enthroned between the cherubim.

(2) Can it be denied that the lid above the Ark symbolised the truth that God is in the Church merciful and forgiving our sins? For it was in so many words called the Mercy Seat.

(3) Is it denied that the animal blood, sprinkled upon the Mercy Seat, symbolised the truth that, without shedding of the blood of Christ, there is no remission? This is surely as plain as that two and two make four.

(4) Can it be denied that there was something symbolised by placing the two tables of the law in the Ark and below the Mercy Seat? Without pretending to infer anything very particular, is not the general inference plain enough that it meant that the law is maintained and vindicated in God's procedure, even as He is gracious and merciful — that "justice and judgment are the habitation of his throne, while mercy and truth go before his face"?

(5) Will it be denied that the high priest, with the mitre

upon his head, and the names of the twelve tribes upon his breast, was a symbol of the better High Priest to come? He could not be understood to be qualified himself to make atonement for the sins of the people, for he was made to offer a sacrifice first of all for himself. He must, therefore, have been a symbol of a better High Priest to come, who was to make atonement for Himself and for all.

(6) Can it be denied that when the high priest went up to the Ark, which, as already seen, symbolised God's throne, and sprinkled it with blood, and offered up incense before it, he was an exact figure of Jesus, under the New Testament, when He entered heaven, having purged away our sins by His own blood, and intercedes for us. I am not asking the infidel to grant that the Lord Jesus Christ does any such things as I now allege. But the New Testament Scriptures, he must acknowledge, set Him forth as doing these things, and infidelity is forced to grant, looking at the Jewish Scriptures, that the Aaronic priest, ordained fifteen centuries before, went through in sacred pantomime the very same steps. He did in the symbolic sanctuary what Christ is represented in the New Testament as doing in the real sanctuary, in heaven. Even the infidel must grant that these two things historically coincide. We allow him to laugh at the idea that the eternal Son of God did by His death make atonement for sin; but will he continue to laugh when he observes that this spectral figure appears upon the Jewish stage, dressed up in priestly robes, to enact the thing he ridicules?

(7) Will the infidel deny that the inner apartment was designed to represent heaven, where the throne of God is— " a figure of the heavenly places," as the apostle calls it?

(8) The sanctuary of the Jews, viewed as an entire thing, took the shape of a tabernacle, and was a symbol as plainly of the human nature of Christ, in which the Godhead dwelt and dwells with us. It will not do to say that it was merely a necessary covering of the sacred utensils from the weather,

or a mere structure such as the heathens erected for their gods, in order to give them a decent shrine; for the reason of its tent-form was given by God—"Let them make me a sanctuary that I may dwell in the midst of them." His dwelling in the heavens conveys no comfort to us, but His dwelling in the midst of us, His being God with us, by an act of sovereign condescension, is a different thing. All the nations of the earth could say that God dwelt in heaven; the Jews only could say that God dwelt with them; the symbol or pledge being that here was His tent, or house, as truly in the midst of them as that of any man. Having found that the other parts of this mysterious structure had their evangelic counterpart in the things of the New Testament, we cannot doubt that this tabernacle-form of the structure finds its antitype in that human nature of Christ in which God tabernacled with man, and which is the foundation of His inhabitation with His Church. This the apostle declares (Heb. ix. 11): "But Christ being come an high priest of good things to come, *by a greater and more perfect tabernacle*, not made with hands, that is to say, not of this building; neither by the blood of goats and calves, but by his own blood he entered in once into the holy place." Now by the holy place into which He entered is meant heaven; and what can be intended by the "greater and more perfect tabernacle" by which He entered into heaven, if not His human nature? He entered it, in short, as man, and with His own blood. The tabernacle, then, was a symbol of Christ's human nature. As He said, speaking of His body, "Destroy this temple, and in three days will I raise it up again."

(9) Here was a people, the Jews gathered round the tabernacle, who were, as I have shown, an exact symbol in their outward history of the redeemed of God.

Taking all these things together, who can deny that here we have a symbolical representation of the whole peculiar mysteries of our holy religion, a foresketch in symbol of all the heavenly things that were afterwards revealed?

Having brought forward the *data*, I now proceed to show that this was something so indisputably from the hand of God, and supernatural, as to confound infidelity.

1. Take the essential idea of this symbolic representation, and it is something which could never have entered into the imagination of man to conceive of. Look at it for a single moment. It was a plan for rendering heavenly things into a complete system of material figures. God being first represented by a luminous cloud, the Shekinah, His throne assumed the corresponding puerility of a wooden chest; and heaven the form of an apartment; and the atonement is represented by an animal sacrifice; and the high priesthood of Christ meets us in the like diminution of one who, in his mitre and dress, is a mere shadow of it; and the Jews, in a like diminished figure of the redeemed, take their place as the worshippers. Once grant that this was of God, and we can assign a reason for it. I have shown, in the foregoing essay, that this system was admirably adapted as a mode of impressing the things signified upon the minds of those who had only an indistinct revelation of them. What was wanting in revelation was made up in sensuous impressions. But infidelity is bound to show how this thing could have originated with man. I have shown that it never could have been the shape which the human mind took in the conception of divine things. But, indeed, such a thing is disproved by considering that this symbolical system came forth from Sinai at once, and as a whole—not being the result of the excogitation of ages, but given forth instantaneously. Such being the case, there are two suppositions to which infidelity is driven, both wild, and one of them ridiculous. The one is to suppose that any man then living, Moses included, possessed such knowledge of theology, in its systematic connection, as is symbolically contained in the tabernacle and its priesthood. In this worldly sanctuary, or symbolical structure, by the light of the New Testament we find the whole mystery of evangelical worship, with the

interposed mediation of Jesus Christ, symbolically represented; but we know that there was no such systematic
acquaintance with it existing in Israel at that time, and no
knowledge of Christ's exclusive priesthood (worthy of the
name) — His sacrifice or atoning death being the only
point of truth concerning Him which could be said in any
measure to have been revealed. This is the first difficulty.
There was no man in Israel who had theological knowledge
enough to erect this sanctuary. But granting there was,
the second supposition to which infidelity must resort is,
that it entered into his head to reduce this theological
scheme into material figures! For what purpose? With
what end? What *we* say is that the infinitely wise God
adopted this symbolical system as a sensible and lively help
to the faith of those who yet had a defective revelation. But
surely the infidel will not suppose that there was any man
who, by virtue of an immense intellectual or religious
superiority, adopted the system for any such purpose as this,
being able to deal with all his contemporaries and his suc-
cessors for fifteen centuries as a parcel of children? If not,
what assignable impulse could have led any man to adopt
the singular device of a symbolic structure such as this?

2. If this unheard-of plan had made its appearance for
the first time at Sinai, we might have indulged the wild
conjecture that it originated with some distinguished individual such as Moses. But we find animal sacrifice
existing long before, indeed, from the beginning; and it was
one fragment of this great symbolic system, afterwards to be
duly fitted in. Whoever appointed animal sacrifice must
have had the essential idea with him of the whole system
introduced two thousand years and more afterwards. This
method of procedure perfectly consists with our conceptions
of God. The whole design being before His infinite mind
from the beginning, He yet does not introduce it at once in
its entirety, but only that fragment of it which was seen to
be absolutely necessary already for the comfort of the

Church. But man never knows of a magnificent plan without revealing it to his fellow-creatures; he is too proud of his discovery to give them the benefit of it in one particular, and carry the generalization undivulged with him to the grave. He would have said that if the symbol was good for the Church in one point—viz., the atonement—then it was good for it in reference to all heavenly things, and let the symbolic pattern be completed at once. I believe, for my part, that God introduced the fragmentary symbol first, and the whole pattern two thousand years after, that He might establish the divinity of the whole plan. The reader will notice, on the other hand, that if the symbolic system had been introduced gradually — first, sacrifice, and then another, and yet another part of it in slow gradation, till the symbolic picture was completed, it might have been inferred that this was the human mind itself working out by degrees the whole system of religion in a development of rude type. The symbolic pattern was suddenly and simultaneously produced at Sinai, which forbids that supposition.

3. If there be any truth in what I have stated, there was not only the objective of our religion symbolised in the tabernacle and priesthood, but the subjective of it was symbolised also in the people who stood before it. That is, the Jews in their whole history were a symbol of the redeemed, having been the subjects of a PASS-OVER by the Destroying Angel in Egypt, which was a figure of our escape from everlasting destruction through the blood-sprinkling of Jesus Christ; and having been outwardly and politically separated from all other nations, which was a figure of the spiritual sense in which we are a peculiar people. I only mention a tithe of the points in which the Jews were plainly a figure of the redeemed. Who does not perceive that they were the fit people on this account to place in front of the sanctuary, which was the mere figure of heavenly things? But who does not see also the corollary from this, which is that God alone could have been at the bottom of all this

arrangement ? For surely the Jews could not of themselves have fallen into the exact historical circumstances, and brought themselves (indeed it was their worst enemies who brought them) into the emergencies and escapes which were necessary to fit them for such a symbolic part ? This was plainly the doing of the Lord ; and since the subjective part of the symbol was of Him, we have another proof that the objective part, which was concurrent, must have been from Him also.

I think that these few considerations taken together prove that no other explanation can be given of this mysterious foresketch of Christianity in Israel, than that it was a Divine and supernatural device, intended, no doubt, as I have shown already, to benefit the Old Testament Church by an impressive ceremonial, but intended by God also to constitute in the latter days one of the most irrefragable proofs of the truth of our holy religion. What will infidelity say to it ?

The arguments it has taken up against miracles as an attestation of our religion will not apply here. These are said to be incredible in the very nature of them. But here is something preternatural, and demonstratively not of man, and which yet obtains place and makes appearance in the Church without any such subversion of natural laws as they choose to reject. In opposition to infidelity, we maintain that the symbolic institutions of Moses were established to be of Divine origin by the miracles with which they were introduced. But our present argument is drawn from the symbolic institutions themselves. The infidel cannot deny that these were observed among the Jews during the long centuries of their national existence, and that they were erected at the commencement of their national career. He is bound to explain how this astonishing scheme arose whereby all Christianity was foresketched. If he will burst God's bands asunder, there is a double adamantine chain he must break. It is not only that he must dispose of verbal prophecies by the hundred which were made in the Old Testament Scriptures and fulfilled in the New, but he must show us how it could enter into man's mind to reduce the whole system of the Christian religion into a complete symbolic picture ages before it appeared. To have set up an impressive ceremonial system so complete as that of Moses, would have been feat enough for any man; but when we find that besides its adaptation for the wants of the Jews for fifteen centuries, it contained a prefiguration of things that were afterwards to be brought in under another economy, to last till time's end, this carries us beyond the range of human attainments altogether. The infidel is bound to prove how by any device of man such a gigantic scheme should have been enacted upon the platform of a nation—which nation, upon the appearance of Christianity, as if its symbolic mission was at an end, vanishes and is dissolved into its original elements. He is bound to account for the alarming fact (alarming to him) that Christianity, ere it came up, projected its own shadow, perfect in every part, and palpable as if its body had come between the Old Testament Church and the sun. In a word, he is bound to show us where Moses got the pattern after which, upon the mount, he drew the similitude in sharp outline of all that is now before us in the shape of a doctrine and a worship.

If what I have established in this essay be true, equally vain is it for modern infidelity to try to get quit of the supernatural by suggesting that the Scriptures may after all be only a record of such piety and wisdom as were of nature's growth—a record of the religious consciousness of the past, to be supplemented by the religious consciousness of the future, why not of the present? Granting that it could thus rid itself of the inspiration of the Scriptures, here are these symbolic institutions which stand outside the Scriptures altogether, and were the observed ceremonial of a nation for ages. How is it to find any but a supernatural origin for them? I have shown that it is not possible, and this, therefore, is a distinct field in the evidences upon which infidelity is met and confounded.

In closing this essay, let me observe that what took place upon the introduction of Christianity proves that the hand of God was as distinctly interposed for the taking away of the symbolic institutions as for the first erection of them.

Infidelity has to explain not only how they came into existence, but how they ceased, when Christianity appeared.

We, on our side, maintain that Christianity was an extraordinary revelation from heaven, and that, the symbolic institutions being no longer necessary, God inspired the apostles, and especially the Apostle Paul, to show the Christian converts that they were so, and to comprehend the whole original design of them. We maintain, moreover, that God, in His providence, put a speedy and decisive termination to them by sweeping away the symbolic nation. Thus we account for the whole matter by the supernatural —by God, and not by man.

But infidelity has a hard task always. Here it is bound to show how Christianity was introduced by a development of man's own religious ideas and consciousness, and how man of himself came to throw off the symbolical, and advance into Christianity. A miserable attempt has been made to show that there were various causes of a secondary kind in the history of the Jews after the captivity tending to produce a change of religious thought and conception. Nothing, meanwhile, is more undeniable than that the whole tendency of the Jews, when Christ made His appearance, was to cherish the ceremony and the symbol more than ever, and to look upon the Mosaic system as a permanent instead of a transitory thing. Christianity was entirely antagonistic to the views of the nation, and the question is how it should have risen in the mind of the man Christ Jesus, supposing Him to have been a mere man, and in the minds of His apostles, supposing them to have been uninspired. The difficulty is immensely increased to infidelity by the sudden-

ness with which the entire and perfect system of Christianity
started up, which answers to a revelation from heaven, but
disagrees with the laws of natural development. If the
Jewish religion, with all its carnal ordinances, was the
result of the religious consciousness or thought of man
taking a symbolic direction in the earlier ages, how did it
happen to take the new and more spiritual form of Christianity all at once, and in the mass ; so that, as the symbol
system went up simultaneously at Sinai, it went down
simultaneously at this one period of time? Add to this,
infidelity has to explain how, when the perfect symbolic
picture of Christianity was to go up, the Jews, who were the
subjective fit for it, immediately make their first appearance
as a nation, and when again the symbolic picture is to go
down, the Jewish nation, in God's providence, immediately
disappears.

Finally, it was Paul who, in his Epistle to the Hebrews,
shows that he had most perfectly apprehended the design
of the whole symbolical system ; but does he appear to us
in that epistle as one working his own way out of the
symbolical into the spiritual, and not rather plainly as one
who professes, being inspired, to tell us what the Holy
Spirit signified by every part of the symbol—declaring that
it was all a pattern of heavenly things given by God originally to Moses on the mount. So far was Paul from being
a man whose own religious consciousness or thought enabled
him to advance from the symbol to Christianity, that he was
in the earlier part of his life a determined opponent to
Christianity, so that either he received all his knowledge of
it from heaven, or he was the most profane impostor, or he
was the most deluded fanatic, that ever walked the earth.

VI.

THE ÆSTHETICS OF REDEMPTION.

THE remark has often been made that there is a certain style characterising the works of every artist or literary writer—the distinctive impress of his genius. His productions may exhibit variety of subject, and develop, as they come before the public eye, new powers which the author was not supposed to possess, but careful investigation will discover the traces of his manner. The name does not need to be written under the canvas that we may know this to be the painting of Titian and that the painting of Raphael. The immortal figures of the great statuary do not more faithfully represent their subject than they reflect their author; they are all made, in a sense, after the image of him who created them. Should any writer, well known in the republic of letters, issue some publication from the press, of which a sense of shame, or say of personal safety, made him wish to hide the authorship, he would require not only to withhold his name from the title-page, but artificially to violate the whole texture of the composition; and when this were done, it would be found after all to have been a most ineffectual attempt at concealment, for very few would fail to detect the source whence the anonymous licentiousness or Atheism had emanated.

We might observe that this sameness of style marking the successive works of the same author is by no means a proof of infirmity. So far from it, we will exclusively or chiefly encounter it in men of the most commanding genius. Men of an inferior order of mind have nothing characteristic about

their productions. As these succeed one another, we could
not tell from internal evidence that they had proceeded from
the same hand ; or, if we could, it would be because through
poverty of parts the author had repeated himself, in which
case we have the same *performance* before us, rather than
evidence of the same *performer*. The writer who only
reaches mediocrity may thus be detected to be the author of
his own successive publications ; not, however, because of
any distinctive style he has in the moulding of his materials,
but because the materials themselves are constantly repro-
duced. It is the prerogative of genius alone to stamp upon
its own varied productions the identity of an original image
that cannot be imitated, and that is instantly recognised.

More than all, then, might we infer that a certain characteristic style would distinguish the works of God. If the
higher orders of intelligent creatures possess a power of impressing an unmistakable character upon their productions,
sufficient to identify them, much more must we suppose that
the Creator is able so to authenticate His works that we
shall be constrained to say, "This is the doing of the Lord."
While it is reasonable to conclude that His works will be
marked out with infinite distinctness from the works of the
creature, it is not presumption to expect that they will
exhibit a certain trace in themselves of having proceeded
from the same hand. Such are the resources of the Godhead, indeed, that we may look for an endless diversity of
operation, but it is the one selfsame Spirit that worketh
in all, and He will leave His specific impress upon every
department.

The circumstance we refer to is not one to be noticed for
the mere gratification of curiosity. It suggests one criterion
by which, supposing us to have ascertained one work to be
of God, we may certify ourselves as to the Divine origin of
another. Has it the characteristic style of the first ? The
analogies that may be traced in the three great works of
Creation, Providence, and Redemption, are in this way

highly confirmatory to our faith. While each of them is capable of being shown to be a Divine work by a direct process of probation, the other two derive benefit from this probation, for they bear indubitable traces of having proceeded from the same hand. Good service has been done to the argument in favour of the Divine origin of the scheme of Redemption by all who have discovered new analogies between it and the other two great works of God. In the following observations we propose to establish one that has not perhaps attracted the amount of attention to which it is entitled. I refer to the illustration which the work of Redemption affords of a regard to the *tasteful* or the *beautiful*. We shall first advert to this as a characteristic of God's other works, and shall then proceed to inquire whether this is proved to be a characteristic of what may be called His last, as it is indeed His greatest work.

I.—CREATION.

Beauty, as well as power, characterises the work of creation. We cannot look abroad upon it without perceiving the traces of an infinite power. There is the mere ponderosity of our globe. What a vast accumulation of material! Upon what a magnificent scale is every department of our globe constructed! Let us think of its solid continents, stretching far and wide, affording ample bounds for the various kingdoms and empires of the human family, and comprehending unknown tracts that may yet tempt the restless foot of human enterprise and discovery. Let us think of the oceans that separate these continents, rolling over channels still more extensive, which no human eye may ever see—the great congregation of tumultuating waves, white-crested, ever heaving that swell so far off that imagination endeavours in vain to travel over them, and gladly returns to the ark of its own limited and dimly-lighted conception. Let us walk by their ironbound coasts, and see the stupendous masses of overhanging rock, such as no machinery of man could elevate, and which yet are disposed in every variety of the most fantastic forms. These are only some of the views we may take of the globe we inhabit, calculated to impress us with the idea of power.

If, lifting our eyes upward, we contemplate the starry firmament, there we seem, indeed, to see nothing that is ponderous, for the apparent heavens above our heads wear a light and etherial aspect. Science, however, acquaints us with the fact that all the magnitudes of creation are in this airy vault—countless worlds, as really material as our own, with diameters greatly larger, and circumferences unspeakably more formidable, so that our planet is proved to be but an inconsiderable unit in the sum of worlds that variegate the immensity of space.

Were these worlds of matter simply upheld at all in space, we would feel amazed at the strength of the arm that sustained them in their position of rest. But when we think of their being in a state of motion, that they career through the amplitudes of heaven with the speed of lightning, describing in perfect safety without collision the magnificent circles that Infinite Wisdom assigned them—when we come to know that the universe comprehends systems of mutually dependent worlds, hung forth in the ethereal void, then indeed we are seized with a sensible impression of Omnipotence.

Such are the illustrations we have of power in the universe. Let us now trace the presence of a certain regard paid throughout every department of it to the tasteful or the beautiful.

Here let it be observed that it is quite conceivable that the ends aimed at in the various parts of creation might have been compassed, while at the same time there might have been nothing to please the eye or the ear; nay, there might have been much to offend the taste. A work may be executed, and yet not æsthetically. So far as man is concerned, when any work of essential importance and of vast magnitude and difficulty is entered upon, we do not expect that our sense of beauty is to be gratified. We are content that many things positively offensive should be encountered. We are not so unreasonable, for example, as to look that the means by which the end is accomplished can be altogether hidden from view, although this may mar the effect upon the eye, as when some huge weight is to be suspended at a great altitude, and we detect plainly the props and artificial contrivances by which it is upheld. In such a case we lavish admiration upon the elevated structure, and readily wink at the elaborate apparatus essential to its support, but partially destructive to its elegance. If powers in like manner have been discovered by man producing great and momentous effects, we do not quarrel with the minor circumstance of there being something that offends the eye or the ear in their application. We reconcile ourselves to the din of his machinery in the factory, the deafening and discordant roar of the steam - engine, and its trail of smoke, that betokens advanced civilisation, though it darkens the scenery of nature.

But in creation the mightiest feats of power are accomplished without any sacrifice of beauty. The great is achieved, and the æsthetical is observed. There stands the immensity of nature's fabric in the perfect simplicity of a work made without hands and without machinery, a firmament supported without pillars, worlds suspended without the formality of foundations. Look up to the nightly heavens. You may either gaze upon them with the eye of a philosopher, and then every star that shines, being viewed as a distant world, there is before you a spectacle of omnipotence ; or you may gaze upon them with the eye of a poet, and then every star being viewed only as a decorating light, and every constellation as a mere garnishing of the heavens by God's Spirit, you have before you a spectacle of infinite loveliness. Now, how passing strange is it that these intractable, huge worlds, whose regulation within any boundaries might have seemed an impossibility, should have been so perfectly under God's control, that He has scattered them according to the minor considerations of elegance and tastefulness along the sky,—that He has made use of them in their formidable courses to beautify our midnight,—that He has studied their æsthetical appearance to the human eye? But this regard to the law of beauty may be traced in the most stupendous works of God, where, more than in His other works, we might have looked that it would be neglected. We have another example in the tides of the ocean. An amply wonderful achievement it might have seemed to us that so vast an element as the ocean should have been carried backwards and forwards within fixed limits in whatever manner that had been done, for in any way it would have been a superhuman feat, but by the Almighty the work is done so as to please as well as to astonish. Standing by the shore, we see the tide advancing by no power that is grossly mechanical, or even visible—advancing in such a manner, wave after wave, that all is music to the ear, and harmony to the eye, and rapture to the imagination. Each successive wave, as it breaks along its whole line into whitening foam, is a spectacle of beauty—it not only exhibits an effect of power, but it inspires a dream.

The whole of nature shows the regard to tastefulness and beauty that characterises the Creator. There is not a horizon of our globe but comprehends some landscape worthy of the artist's pencil, varied by the graceful undulation of hills, or the wooded and picturesque declivity; while even the clouds and vapours of the sky follow the æsthetical proprieties, so that if they did not fertilize the earth we might say they were only designed to ornament the heavens—for either they sail in fragmentary sublimity above us, white and pure as the very investiture of the Deity, or they lie spread out motionless like an archangel's wing, with soft downy feathers along the sapphire firmament. There is not a river that hastens to the ocean by a straight, monotonous, canal-like course, but, taking its impulse from the beauty-loving Creator, it is away in the curvatures that are the most true to tastefulness, carrying with it indeed the necessary life to vegetation, but at the same time charming the eye of humanity ; rolling over channels that are more variegated with stones of every colour than the best mosaic, discharging itself over the natural cascade, losing itself in the overhanging woods, and then after all these windings, evanishings, and picturesque extrications of itself, pouring its flood, now ennobled with the accessions of many a tributary, into the great receptacle of waters. There is not a flower that unfolds itself upon the mountain steep or in the garish meadow but affords demonstration of the fact that there is no such lover of beauty as this great Maker of worlds ; and it is a theme for an unparallelled meditation to think of Him who " looseth the bands of Orion," and " bringeth forth Mazzaroth in his season," decorating the fragile leaf with hues that baffle imitation. But such is the characteristic of His operation, and if we descend into the abysses of the sea we shall find the very weeds that lie upon its unseen channels embroidered by the fastidious fingers of Omnipotence. There is not a creature of any species that has not, besides the essential organisms of life, some suited elegance of shape or embellishment of colour. Indeed, we cannot have a more marvellous view of that characteristic of the Creator we are now contemplating than by reflecting upon the various orders of being He has marshalled forth, each adorned with the graces peculiar to its kind ; the insect tribe arrayed in the gorgeous hues of their ephemeral existence ; the finned tenants of the ocean or running stream disporting their coats of silver or gold or spotted sable in the watery element ; the feathered fowls of the air exhibiting every variety of unimagined forms, and with plumage lavishly painted and decorated, some hovering over our sea-lashed coasts, to give picturesqueness to the storm, others haunting the inland, that they may give a spirit-like vitality and a spirit-like harmony to the woods : add to these the creatures of another species that walk the earth, in the diversity of other shapes and the singularity of other graces, haunting every possible region, looking down upon us from the Alpine precipices in the glory of fearless independence, or darting into the forest thickets with the interestingness of timidity, or stalking in savage ferocity, yet in forms and striped colours of terrible beauty, through the wilderness that is filled with sublimity by their outcries; while, last of all, we ascend to the human pair. Nor need we look farther than to the spectacle of woman leaning in the softness of her charms upon the arm of man, in order to perceive that beauty, and not strength alone, is the law of the creation and the characteristic of the Creator.

2.—PROVIDENCE.

Here we pass into a new province, where we are called to contemplate not the way in which the works or creatures of God are made, but the way in which they are upheld, preserved, and governed. In this department it will appear upon reflection that there is ample scope both for the display of power in accomplishing these ends, and for a regard to the beautiful or the tasteful in the mode of execution. Let us take up a few of the marvellous things that needed to be compassed in this manifold scheme of Providence, showing how they have been achieved æsthetically.

First, then, it was necessary that God should *provide means of sustenance for the vast multitude of creatures He had ushered into existence.* When a large army is upon the field there is no more difficult duty devolving upon the government of a country than the duty connected with the commissariat department. How often has it baffled their power to make the provisions forthcoming, and baffled their energy or ingenuity to get them conveyed to the army, stationed it may be at some very remote quarter of the globe? Every contrivance is resorted to in order to speed forward the necessary supplies; nicety in the mode of transfer is not much studied; the æsthetics of the dealing is not once aimed at; and even as to the accomplishment of the essential object, though many wise men have been devising the means, and a nation has been drawn upon for the resources, many blunders are possibly committed; the provision does not arrive at the moment required, or the vessels conveying it sink in the storm, or it meets with obstacles in the far-off harbour, and there is the cry of starvation and disappointment in the camp. Need we say that the problem lying for solution before the Divine Being was one of infinitely greater momentousness and difficulty than any ordinary commissariat question? The nutriment itself was to be fabricated, a world was to be fed, a world of innumerable creatures through continually successive generations. The difficulty is met and effectually overcome by the Divine provisions that meet our eyes in the natural world. There is found to be no necessity whatever for any direct interposition of the Creator in this matter; but what demands at present our observation is the circumstance that it is managed without any infringement whatever of the comeliness of nature, but, on the contrary, so as to throw an additional charm around it. For the grass that grows in the fields, the innumerable herbs and fruit-bearing trees that spring up on the surface of our globe, are at once the radical nutriment of the creatures and the ornament of the landscape. Had the earth been destitute of this verdure and this variegated foliage, it would have been a bleak, uninteresting waste; and thus while God makes provision for the essential wants of His creatures, He seems only to be casting a graceful mantle over the nakedness of creation. The fields waving in harvest with golden grain, that rustles as it bends before the autumnal breeze, is an object for poetical description as well as market speculation; and it is plain that the Creator, in meeting the gross emergency of starvation, has studied to gratify the taste of the most exquisite sentimentalist.

When the whole vegetable produce of one year is consumed, how was this to be renewed? The craving appetite of a world of creatures, never satisfied, was to insist every returning year for its usual gratification, and it was necessary that the supplies of nature should be as inexhaustible as the appetite was insatiable. Here again the emergency was æsthetically met. The earth's vegetable products contain not only the material for present consumption, but the seed of a future vegetation. They comprehend within themselves the mysterious means of their own perpetuation, being furnished (and this without any violation of their vegetable elegances) with that which, being deposited in the soil, will die, that it may produce the marvellous spectacle of an ever-recurring harvest. It is true, that in order to the earth being prepared to bring the seed gradually to maturity, there was a necessity for great and deep arrangements of the Almighty; but it is equally true that these are such (we refer to the economy of the *seasons*) as to envelop all nature with the charm of a constantly-recurring variety. These seasons have been the theme of the poet in all ages, and have been the favourite subject of illustration in the painter's landscape; nor do we feel as if we were witnessing a process essential to the earth, but rather as if we were regaled by the spectacle of a wonderful diorama, as we pass from the glow and verdure of spring to the etherial splendours of summer, or, again, from the motley red and yellow of autumnal vegetation, to the stern, naked sublimities of winter.

But there were other problems needing to be solved, in connection with the providential government of human society, besides this elementary one of its sustentation. We shall merely touch upon them to show how they also have received an æsthetical solution.

How was an adequate *occupation to be found for the widely-extended members of the human family?* If, on the one hand, it was necessary that Divine provision should be made for their primary wants, on the other, it must have been to the last degree dangerous that so vast a population should have been left in a condition where subsistence could be procured independently of exertion. There is much beauty in the arrangement whereby God, in the natural world, has made labour indispensable in order to obtaining a due harvest of the fruits of the earth, limiting the display of His power, that there might be room for the exercise of the creature's own energy. The provisions of nature are such as not to supersede the processes of agriculture. So exactly has Omnipotence ceased to interfere at the necessary point, that the mouths of society are satisfied only when its hands are sufficiently occupied. There is the same beauty in the analogous arrangement whereby, while He has provided the *materials* that are necessary for our raiment, our edifices, our thousand articles for use and comfort, He has not superseded the necessity for trades and manufactures. If anything could excite our admiration more than this economising of His omnipotence, it is to observe how exactly He has hit the just limits; so that, let society become as extended as it may, or pass into its most artificial state, the mass of men must work for their livelihood; while, upon the supposition of this law being followed, not a single individual fails to obtain a ration of the earth's available nutriment.

How was society to be sufficiently cemented together? The mere interest begotten of a mutual dependence upon each other for subsistence was not seen to be a cement strong enough to bind the social fabric. The affections of humanity needed to contribute to its security. God laid the foundation of *the family.* By this means all society resolves itself into an infinite number of circles, the members of which are attached to each other by ties unspeakably more powerful than the tie of self-interest. Instead of being an aggregate of isolated units, it is now an assemblage of smaller societies, whereby the whole community is cemented through the affections; and thus there comes up over the dry bones of a mere political order the flesh and blood of relational humanity. Not only is social order hereby secured, but individual happiness is preserved, which must have perished in the confusion of a promiscuous society. In every nation there are thus thousands of domestic bowers reared by love, entwined with the roses of affection, where labour finds its refreshment, and order its best seminary, and childhood its primary protection. The effects so obtained are surely æsthetically arrived at! You ask how the infant, who comes in utter helplessness into the world, is to be preserved? Who shall care for it? Where shall it find nutriment? Look to that young mother, and you see the little head of the creature hanging upon her bosom, triumphing in his provision, half hid in the soft tresses of womanhood. Those breasts! at once the seat of sentiment and the source of nourishment! You inquire—How shall old age be protected? Look to that young son, and you see the aged mother, who once fondled him upon her bosom, now leaning upon his arm. Her tresses are now grey, but *his* arm is now strong, and maternal tenderness is repaid by filial veneration. Well, you can understand how relationship should thus be formed and cemented among those who have lived under the same domestic roof. But you ask—How can the foundation of a *new family* be laid? For here two are to be brought together as world's companions who were not linked together from infancy. How shall the Creator draw those together, who were once apart, into a relationship that requires them to leave father and mother, and cleave to one another for ever? Look, we would say, then, once more, to those two young lovers, who hasten from the walks of society into the solitudes of nature. The whole earth seems to be annihilated to them, who, philosophy would have said, never could have been brought together! Such are the æsthetical arrangements by which the world goes forward.

Another problem, and we have done with this part of our subject. *How was society to be restrained?* Let us consider the fierce passions that agitate the heart of man, with the opposition of interests that maintains in society, and what was to be looked for but universal anarchy? All are not humanised in the family. How was property to be protected—life itself? Human legislation would not have been a sufficient safeguard. It is neither sufficiently universal in its existence, nor sufficiently powerful in its sanctions, nor sufficiently at hand in all emergencies, to constitute the primary protection of humanity. Where then was this to be found? In conscience. What an effectual check! and, æsthetically, how admirable! We are arrested without the serjeant-at-law; condemned without witnesses called from afar; sentenced without the formality of a tribunal. Can anything be more mysterious than this influence exerted upon us from on high, whereby the great agitated sea of humanity is controlled without hands; and, even in the roar of its outgoing passions, when it seems to threaten universal inundation, suddenly returns from a boundary which it cannot overpass. Compared with this " band " of the Lord, by which the governors as well as the governed are restrained, what a cumbersome provision is the printed statute-book, the paid constabulary, the jail, and the penal settlement? But we would not be understood to despise political order. The powers that be are ordained of God. This is only another provision of His infinite wisdom. And now survey the beauty and majesty of the body politic. What a fair spectacle our social institutions; the venerableness of the Legislature, the awfulness of the Bench, the significant unity of the Crown! This is the scheme by which God carries forward the providential government of the world. But, finally, as nations advance, the finer arts, poetry, painting, sculpture, eloquence, are developed. True to His style, the Almighty has thus studied not only the security and vigour, but the decoration of society. In the earlier stages of their history the nations exhibit the rude strength that argues a growing vitality. It remains that they should effloresce into civilisation; and when they have reached this point, but not till then, when they have added refinement to solid attainment and exquisite taste to rough energy—when, in short, the æsthetical has been arrived at, then the Ancient of days takes them up as a flower, looks at them for a moment with complacency, and cuts them down in the evening time.

3.—REDEMPTION.

Having seen that beauty characterises God's other works, it would throw suspicion upon the Divine origin of redemption if it failed to reflect this characteristic. It is not enough to demonstrate that the ends contemplated in redemption have been attained in the exercise of consummate power. We must meet with such displays of the Divine operation as awaken the sense of beauty. We must see the accomplishment coming forth æsthetically from a hand that plays with the impracticable, and communicates colour and charms of proportion even to "the terrible things we looked not for." Well, let us take up some points here.

The Introduction of Redemption.—Nothing is introduced by God in an abrupt or common way ; ordinarily, so as to strike the admiring eye with interest. Thus, ere we have man, there is the beautiful spectacle of infancy, the open brow, the long flowing ringlets, the simple unsuspecting smile ; the season of unrestraint and of chartered liberty; following this —early youth—the young man riding out in the recklessness of early days, attended by guardians and tutors ; appearances enough of strength, yet of slender growth, and proportions unfilled up, needing restraints withal—last of all, manhood. We would not wish to miss this history of development. There is a certain beauty in the sovereign order of this preparation. So also is day introduced to our view gradually, and with precursors adding much that is attractive in the exhibition. Evening precedes it, to show what God can do in irradiating the darkness by lesser luminaries than the sun. What is wanting in kind is compensated by multitude, for here we have a host of luminaries shedding a pure, heavenly, but ineffectual light all round ; and the wan shield of night's queen comes forth, sending a shadowy radiance over mountain and valley. Then we have the morning-star twilight— at last the sun's disc appears above the horizon, and we have ere long the full splendour of day.

This is the æsthetics of creation. In redemption we look for somewhat of the same, and we are not disappointed.

The first rudimental prognostics of it after the Fall how beautiful—the first promise, as it turned "its silver lining to the night"—the easy simplicity that reigned under the patriarchal dispensation, the Church's unrestrained childhood! Under the Old Testament Christ is not yet introduced, but what a strange stellar splendour of types and figures of Him illustrating the darkness of the Fall! Moses, the ruler of this night-dispensation, shines with the dim splendour of a reflected mediatorship. Would there not have been something wanting if this forerunning economy had not made its appearance? Could anything have compensated for the loss of this starred night which preceded the rise of the gospel day? That long line of great and distinguished prophets who ran before, who does not feel the majesty of the procession? They pass before us in the long ages, each of them bearing his flaming torch; each of them arrayed in different garments; all looking forward; all crying with one voice of a coming Saviour. It seems as if this secular procession and preparation would never end—as if the Saviour would never make His appearance. The Deluge-revolution comes, but He is not there. Sinai's fires burn to heaven, but He is not there. This is but the law that is added to the promise until He come. A new commonwealth is erected, whose subjects must for ages observe its symbolic institutions till He come who is to fulfil them all.

Meanwhile the proud nations are stumbling in their vain experimental search after the knowledge of God and a way of salvation, that the folly of human science may be demonstrated ere God's wisdom for salvation be manifested.

And now at last the Morning Star appears, " the burning and the shining light." And behold, above the earth at last, the Sun of Righteousness that taketh away the sin of the world ! What a magnificent preparation for redemption is here !

The Redemption itself.—The primary difficulty to be overcome in achieving the salvation of any of our fallen family was a judicial or forensic difficulty. The parties to be saved were violators of the law, and He who was to save them was the Administrator of that law—the infinitely holy and just Judge of the universe. Supposing God, in the power of His understanding, which is infinite, to have devised a way for our deliverance, we are prepared to expect that the means would be excessively complicate ; or, rather, that society would be convulsed to its centre ere justice could receive its expiation, and the storm of outpoured wrath pass away before a consummated reconciliation.

In these circumstances a spectacle meets our eye. We see a mother with a child in her arms. That child is clinging to her breast. I have already observed that this is an object æsthetically to be admired, as containing a solution of the problem in Providence—How shall the infant lord of the creation be fed and cared for ? But we must look to it again. And here it contains the solution of expiation. That Child lying upon the bosom of the Virgin is the Saviour of the world. In that infant smiling in the maternal arms is comprehended all that is necessary to harmonise mercy with justice, to save the honour of the tribunal, and rescue the victims from the bar, and bring in everlasting redemption for the elect. How wonderful ! And the expiation is already commenced. This condescension of the eternal Son of God to infancy—this His lying in unrecognised divinity upon the bosom of a humble woman—has already gone a far way towards making the atonement. And is there anything ghastly here ?

For let it be observed that, upon the supposition of its being the purpose of God to save an innumerable company of sinners by pouring out the vials of His wrath upon one devoted head, it might have been imagined that the sufferings of this Surety would form a spectacle too awful and terrible to conform with the ordinary observations, or to be borne with the ordinary composures of humanity. It did not appear how humanity could survive the sight of such scenes as must be enacted in this vindication of justice, or survey the sacrificial ghastliness of its Victim. Who could outlive the spectacle of the sufferings of the damned, and endure to see the visages or hear the outcries of these scathed victims of eternal vengeance? And who then might hope to endure the awful exhibition that was to be made of Divine wrath fully exhausted upon a single Surety? God was able to make the arrangements. Owing to the infinite majesty of our Surety, He was able to make the atonement by sufferings which exhibited nothing that was physically hideous or revolting. We say nothing of the pangs of His soul, for these were invisible to mortal eye; but owing to the dignity of His person, He was able to make out the reality of an atonement without its visible horrors. He needed but to represent the spectacle of a somewhat more than ordinarily distressed humanity. There is nothing uncomely to be seen in the manger of Bethlehem. It is only an interesting representation of distressed or incommoded infancy. Gethsemane is a scene of suffering; but there is nothing to revolt us in that moonlit garden, in that Form thrown prostrate upon the ground in bloody sweat, in that angel standing over Him to strengthen Him. Shall we extend the remark to Calvary? We shall only say that in the decease that brought in redemption to the world there was nothing to shock the eye of humanity; and if the countenance of the Saviour in His crisis-agonies assumed expressions too awful for man to behold, these were hidden in the sublime shadow of the preternatural eclipse; and if His suffering at last vented itself in outcries too awful for man to hear, these were drowned in the roll of the earthquake that accompanied the sacrifice.

To what else than this æsthetics of redemption does the apostle refer when he says, "And as it is appointed unto men once to die, but after death the judgment, so Christ was once offered to bear the sins of many, and unto them that look for him shall he appear the second time without sin unto salvation"? He adverts to the beauty of the arrangement whereby the eternal Son of God was able to make the atonement by just living such a life as ours, and dying such a death as our own ; so that a work of all others the most stupendous and anomalous was effected without breaking up the uniformities of the world. Owing to His majesty He could accomplish redemption by simply passing through the ordinary stages and phases of this humanity of ours.

If the divinity of Christ averted the ghastliness of expiation, the expiation, on the other hand, by making an obscuration necessary, averted the unendurable glory that must otherwise have emanated from the divinity. For here was another problem in redemption. How was such a stupendous fact as the appearance of the Son of God upon our earth to be made consistent with the proprieties of this ordinary system of things ? Could our earth bear the entrance of such a Visitant ? Could its inhabitants endure such an approximation of the Deity ? It is all very well that we should have a sun in the firmament over our heads so long as it remains at its present incalculable distance. There it irradiates and cheers us. But nothing could be conceived more disastrous to the human family than that it should draw near to us in the enormity of its disc. And such seemed the consequence to be apprehended from the manifestation of God's eternal Son. How, above all, was it possible that He should live for more than thirty years in our world ? Might human society bear this long sojourning of such a Visitant? and might the land He dwelt and walked upon bear the pressure of the pilgrimage of nations which would doubtless be congregated around Him? In consequence of the very work, however, which Jesus came to accomplish, it was necessary that there should be a complete obscuration of His divine glory, and thus instead of a staggering portent He presented the appearance of nothing more than a common man passing over the stage of life, and departing in an ordinary dissolution. We cannot but marvel at the æsthetical manner in which redemption was thus accomplished. "He was in the world, and the world was made by him, and the world knew him not." Not only did God discover a way by which His eternal Son could be manifested on our earth without producing the disastrous effects of an unendurable prodigy, but the scheme of redemption was such that, in its essential prosecution, it so fell out that His Son was necessarily divested of the splendours of Deity just in His progress through our world—there was at this point an eclipse, so that nothing appeared but his humanity; and He was received up into heaven at that very point of time when, emerging from His obscuration, He became a spectacle fit only "to be seen of angels." There is no movement parallel to this in beauty and sublimity in all the wonders of the astronomical universe.

The singular fact here adverted to, that the humiliation necessary in the Son of God in order to His making the atonement, accomplished the indirect and secondary purpose of His appearing in the only way according to which He could have appeared in our world at all consistently with the proprieties or æsthetics of this life, might seem enough of itself to prove the divinity of the scheme of redemption generally received amongst us. Whoever amongst men invented this scheme must have been very wise indeed; for what have they found out? They have discovered a way by which a Divine Person might be incarnate in our world, and live more than thirty years in it, without disturbing the social system, as it presently goes forward. They have found more. They have discovered that the obscuration necessary for expiatory purposes exactly gives us the result required — the result, namely, of what may be called an æsthetical earthly life in a Divine Person incarnate.

It was not only the ghastliness of expiation that needed to be averted. Although the vindication of justice by God the Father, in subjecting His Son to death, was in itself a glorious act, the transaction required (if it were to be divested of a revolting character) to be managed æsthetically, or with a certain regard to appearances. It is well known that the infidel has endeavoured to raise a prejudice, if not to establish an argument against the scheme of redemption generally received amongst us, by dwelling upon what he considers the monstrous position in which it represents the Father and the Son—the one being no other than the executioner of the other, and the cross the gibbet. Let us consider for a moment the adjustments of Infinite Wisdom for averting what must otherwise have assumed an offensive aspect. Although it was necessary that God the Father should be vindicator of the law, and that He should deal as an offended Judge with the Surety, nothing prevented Him from employing an intermediate agency for the infliction of it. It may be very true, and we grant it to the objectors, that the crucifixion took place by appointment of God the Father; but it is equally true, and they must grant it, and cannot fail to feel it, that it was not God who with His own hands erected the cross. What might otherwise have been somewhat abhorrent to the sensitive imagination of infidelity is thus (greatly to its relief, shall we say, or to its confusion?) taken away by the veil of an interposed agency. But this is not all. The magistrate employs such an agency to put the sentence of the law into execution. But God withdrew Himself still farther than this from any visible connection with His Son's death. He employed an intervening wicked agency. It was by such an agency that His Son's death was brought about. It was by men acting under the influence of enmity to God, and in express contrariness to His commandment—although secretly executing His purpose—it was by the hands of ungodliness and sneering infidelity itself. Thus so far are we from being revolted by the spectacle of God the Father executing judgment upon His own Son, that we are filled with indignation against His enemies who iniquitously compassed this execution; and the crucifixion, instead of appearing in the light of a monstrosity of Divine justice, meets the eye as a monstrosity of man's unrighteousness.

Another point more in the æsthetics of the redemption itself. God's plan in the original covenant He made with the human family was to deal with us all federally in Adam, so that, if he stood and obeyed, eternal life was to be ours by one man. Now when that man fell who had been constituted the federal head of the race, universal ruin seemed to be as irreparable as it was certain. Occasion of triumph to the highest was given to the great adversary of God, for it seemed as if this representative scheme had turned out to be nothing else than a step whereby, the whole human family being reduced to one neck, he could summarily cut it off and destroy it. How any second contrivance could be made to retrieve matters, was inconceivable. Yet God achieved it by one simple arrangement, and this an arrangement exactly analogous to the first. As He said, " Let there be light," and the darkness of creation chaos was dispelled, so in this case He said, " Let there be another man," and the whole consequences of the Fall were rolled back. We cannot suppose anything more humiliating to the arch-adversary than this, that when he was triumphing in the overthrow of the human family by one man, the Almighty should wrest the whole victory out of his hands by the immediate substitution of another man, who had all the conditions in His wonderful mediatory person for averting the consequences of the Fall. In his famous passage in the fifth chapter of the Epistle to the Romans, where Paul adverts to the analogy between the method of our Fall and the method of our deliverance from it, we cannot doubt that he has in his eye the æsthetics of the arrangement, and is calling upon us to notice how in redemption we have an evidence of that singular beauty of operation that is the Almighty's characteristic style.

The Application of Redemption.—The contrivance adopted by God for disciplining the redeemed, and spiritually fitting them for entering upon the inheritance of heaven, is one the beauty of which cannot fail to strike every attentive observer. We have sometimes thought that it admits of being illustrated by the device He employed for disciplining the Jews for Canaan. How that was to be accomplished was a problem no created wisdom could have solved. God solved it at once in what may be called an æsthetical manner. All that is necessary is that they be made to pass through that wilderness which already geographically lay between Egypt and Canaan. So large a multitude, plunged into the desert, will at once be cast helpless upon Him. The wilderness will itself prove, and humble, and try them, and His power will be glorified at the same time. The wisdom which thus finds means immediately before it, without needing to go to a distance, works æsthetically. The sensation of admiration is produced; we involuntarily exclaim, "How beautiful! this is the doing of the Lord."

So in the matter now before us, when the question was how the redeemed were to be prepared and made meet for heaven, God's solution was that they should just pass through this world, turned as it has been into a wilderness by the Fall. No need of any new instrumentality being provided. The consequences of the Fall—afflictions in all their various forms, and death—will be themselves the very best means for their trial and preparation. It so happens, and cannot be denied, that the same conditions of the world which are the penal result of the Fall, which in themselves prove to the unsaved the awful preliminaries and preparations of eternal ruin, admit of becoming gracious and salutary conditions to those who, being interested in God's reconciliation and in gospel hopes, look upon them in an entirely different light, and are carried triumphantly through them, and find them contributive in many ways to their spiritual welfare. Now, can we sufficiently admire the operation of God by which the consequences of the Fall become the machinery of redemption?

To any understanding but the understanding that is infinite, it might have appeared that if the human family was to consist of two sections, the one of which was to be saved and the other left to perish, they would require to be divided by a physical wall of separation, in order to their being placed under entirely different outward conditions. But from the remarks now made it appears that the same essential conditions become answerable enough for the purpose of salvation as prelude and prepare the eternal doom of the reprobate. Accordingly, the redeemed are left intermingled with others in the most promiscuous way—in the same families as well as in the same tribes and nations—and yet their sanctification is perfectly accomplished by the same means, which, alongside of them, issue in nothing but induracy and ruin.

And here that reference has been made to the fact of there being an election of some to everlasting life, while others are passed by—we might advert to the æsthetical solution found by God for the great problem—How was this sovereign redemption to be carried out without such an enmity and jealousy being excited in the minds of the reprobate as would lead to the extermination of the elect? Even as it is, we know that there is an enmity existing between the two seeds. But it has bounds. It evaporates in temporary persecutions; it exhausts itself in Domitian, or Waldensian, or Malaganese periods. And how has God succeeded in thus moderating its effects? This has been accomplished by the arrangement well known to have been adopted, that while redemption was limited in its objects as to purpose, it is administered outwardly to the world in the shape of a universal invitation and offer. Had the call or offer been limited, the consequences must have been fatal. As it is, the mouths of such as really after all belong to the reprobate are shut against complaint. Generally speaking, they go on under the impression that they are saved as well as we; and though this delusion be fatal to themselves, it is so far the safety of others. If you add to this that the jealousy of the reprobate is prevented and quieted down by the identity of outward condition in which, as already stated, God's elect are placed along with them, you perceive the whole admirable contrivance whereby God's purpose, sovereign as it is, is accomplished without any unnecessary division, or fatal and exterminating struggle in society.

The Display of the Divine Perfections in Redemption.—This is a point in the æsthetics of redemption which has been often adverted to. The cross affords the only solution of the problem how God can be infinitely just, and yet the justifier of the ungodly. The solution is such as to be æsthetical. The Gordian knot is not cut by the sword of God's prerogative arbitrarily exercised, but loosed by His wisdom. The solution carries irresistible evidence of being the true one, and evidence as irresistible of being one which created intelligence never could have devised. On the cross there is such a meeting of Divine attributes without collision; such a mutual embracing of each other in a transaction where they seemed certain to clash; such an increased illustration of them all in the accomplishment of an end where it seemed impossible that they should not be tarnished; and such new displays altogether of the Divine perfections; that, as we may say light never was discovered till Newton divided the ray, so may we say that God was unknown to us till His glory was refracted upon the cross. What a true painter has God proved Himself to be in saving us! He has set the chief manifestation of

His glory upon the dark background of the Fall. He has set the highest display of His wisdom over against the foolishness of the Cross. He has given His highest act of love to man, the foil of being at the same time the foulest deed of man's depravity.

The Attestations of Redemption.—Redemption was to be brought in by the eternal Son of God being born of a woman, made flesh, made under the law, made sin, suffering and dying. It was necessary, of course, that when this Redeemer appeared in the flesh He should be sufficiently attested to be a Divine Person. But how this could be done was a problem which would have baffled the understanding of all God's creatures to solve. Coming into the world, as He must do in such a case, a child even as other children, and passing through the various stages of human growth, what prodigious works must be done by Him; what prodigious manifestations of glory, one way or another, must take place, ere He could be sufficiently evidenced to be God as well as man. Could His contemporaries endure these? and, more than all, how could they be supposed to subject so glorious a one to the sufferings and death which yet were indispensable?

This was the difficulty. Here is the æsthetics of its solution. His divinity was not to be attested so much by a display of His divine glory when He appeared. Indeed, He was to appear in a very humbled state. It was to be attested by His fulfilling in the outward conditions under which He appeared the predictions of preceding ages. Once let Him be found to fulfil these conditions, and immediately He has the benefit of the whole supernatural that had been spread over the antecedent centuries; for whatever was extraordinay or miraculous there was all connected one way or another with the Messiah who was to appear. Now this kind of attestation, while in itself it was the most satisfactory of all, was not of a kind fitted to startle or overwhelm the carnal mind of His contemporaries, who, instead of recognising in His "visage, so marred more than other men," the link that connected Him with the whole super-natural of the Old Testament, were offended by it. Meanwhile, in hiding their faces from Him, and afterwards crucifying Him, they were only attesting His Messiahship.

While our Lord Jesus Christ, by fulfilling prophecy in the outward conditions under which He appeared, served Himself heir to all the stupendous signs and wonders wrought by the prophets who foretold His coming, it is noticeable that His own miracles were of a much humbler and less imposing character to the eye than those of a former economy; and this only stumbled the Jews, while yet they afforded in reality the most satisfactory attestations of all, as illustrative of His gracious and redemptive mission.

I might have referred here to the miracles of the Bible in general as bearing the characteristic impress of the Deity.

The province of the miraculous and the extraordinary did not seem to be one where our love of the tasteful or the beautiful could very well be gratified. All our ideas of the lovely and attractive are associated with the ordinary con-ditions of earthly phenomena; and must they not be put to flight, and give way to mere amazement and consternation upon the reversal of nature's laws? In such a department, if our trembling reason be convinced, it seems too much to ask that our imagination should be delighted.

We may judge how difficult it is to observe the laws of beauty in the miraculous by the grotesqueness of the miracles which superstition has suggested or imposture fabricated. They present us with an abundant display of power of a certain kind, but they recommend themselves as little to our taste as they do to our convictions. There may be something graceful about the legends or fables of a super-stitious antiquity, but they revolt our reason, and are in-debted much to the embellishments of the narrator.

Such, however, is the nature of the miraculous, as it meets us in the Bible; so sparingly is it introduced, and with such regard always to strong necessities existing for its appearance ; so skilfully is it arranged in the hands of Him who is able to accommodate even the supernatural to humanity, and throw over it a beauty of its own kind, that the most picturesque passages in Scripture are those that record these stupendous phenomena. The extraordinary interpositions we read of under the Old Testament, as well as the New, come in so seasonably to meet the necessities of a suffering Church, or to humble the pride of outrageous oppression, or to relieve anguished humanity, that, instead of impressing us as a monstrous excrescence upon the face of common providence, they seem rather to remove its sovereign and trying inequalities—to present us for the moment with a perfect providence, which is less mysterious than the other whose uniformity is broken up.

Space will not admit of condescending upon instances. It is enough to say that the painter has always found the most striking subjects for displaying his art in the extraordinary scenes of our Saviour's life. God has remained true to His style ; and we have this remarkable issue as regards the miracles of Christianity, that while all candid persons are convinced by the greatness of them, their beauty is acknowledged even by the infidel.

The Record of Redemption.—To come now to the written Record, or the Scriptures, in any argument maintained with infidelity, the question must turn very much upon the character of the Bible, as a composition. Does it bear the characteristic of God's style ? What of its æsthetics ?

The whole matter of the revelation contained in it might have been there, while at the same time no regard might have been paid to the graces of manner, the beauties or sublimities of writing. Upon that supposition the Bible would have rested its claim to superiority upon the weightiness of its contents, its supernatural discoveries, its perfect morality, its fulfilled prophecies. Nor in claiming superiority upon this ground, in the total absence of æsthetical excellence, would it have placed itself upon a very peculiar footing of acceptance with the public. For the fact is we do not generally expect that works communicating the deepest discoveries should unite elegance of manner with greatness of matter. We do not quarrel with the works of Sir Isaac Newton because they do not sparkle with beauty : they solve the mystery of the stars, if, in composition, they do not reflect their lustre. We pardon the metaphysician of America the plainness of his style. Excellences of different kinds are not expected to be combined. We go for the sublime to Milton, and for the profound to Newton ; we go for beauty to Shakespeare, and for demonstration to Edwards.

Beauty characterises the Bible. Truths are not announced there in their nakedness ; nor are its high mysteries before us in an ungainly abstractness, but invested with the charms of statement and illustration. The histories are always graphic — a series of Divine paintings. The men whose lives it records form a gallery of magnificent portraits. The argumentative parts are not dry or tedious ; there is the beautiful transition, the lively interrogation, the exclamation, the antithesis, the unexpected appeal, the thrilling climax. The religious instruction is conveyed in striking parables and fresh illustrations, that indelibly impress the memory. Respect is paid to beauty in the prophetical revelations ; and, as if it were not enough to benefit us with the prophecy, we have the sublime abruptness of the prophet — all the eloquence of humanity under the frenzy of the Divine vision. There is a sublime beauty, too, in the very symbols of prophecy—as in the Apocalypse of John—so that those who are utterly incapable of understanding their exact reference are yet entranced by the splendour of the imagery ; just as the man who is ignorant of astronomy is impressed notwithstanding by the loveliness of the constellations.

But much more than this must be predicable of the Bible as a composition, ere we can say that its beauty is such as to attest it to have come from God. We must be able to show that its beauties are superhuman, and altogether analogous to those that meet us in creation work.

This we are prepared to do. Look to any of those objects that are lovely in nature—the flowers, for example—and we at once perceive the difference between them and any production of man, however admirable. There is no comparison to be instituted between the finest manufactures and the textures of vegetation—between the finest colourings of the painter and the essential hues of nature. With regard to the former, there is a comparative coarseness about them in their utmost perfection. We perceive the presence of artifice with the naked eye; and if we apply the microscope, we detect the shortcoming. The same may be said of all human authors, as compared with the Bible. We account Milton and Shakespeare masters in their art. But we may all recognise the artifice that is in their compositions. It is concealed, but only within certain limits. When we apply the microscope of a rigid criticism (such a criticism as was never intended, I admit, to be applied to the productions of human genius) we soon see an end of their perfection. But no man has ever detected artifice in the beauties of the Bible. He might as well expect to discover a certain grossness in the textures of vegetation or the loveliness of the new-blown rose. In other words, the grace or charm is of that perfectly essential and unartificial description that distinguishes nature itself.

We remarked already that in the department of creation we cannot separate the beautiful from the useful. The earth is attractive by its verdure, but the grass that adorns it is the food of the creatures that live upon its surface. It is variegated by the blue and winding streams, but these are the sources of its irrigation. Thus there is never an effort after the attainment of beauty, for its own sake: we could not divest nature of its charms without destroying the essential system of things before us. And this is true of the

Bible. In the most masterly productions of human genius, we find that the beauty of them is a species of embellishment. But in the Bible there is not a single figure, or illustration, or expression, in which the lynx eye of infidelity will discover the infirmity of decoration. The beauty is perfectly inwoven with, and inseparable from, the truth or the consolation of the Scriptures. What thrills the amateur of graceful expression as being exquisitely beautiful is appealed to by the controversial theologian as having in every word an important bearing upon some point of faith, or is clung to by the dying saint as fraught with comfort to his soul.

Finally, many of the subjects that are exhibited to us in the Bible arrayed in a species of radiant beauty are of such a stupendous nature that man has never even attempted to pourtray them. When, from surveying the earth, we turn to the skies, and perceive that *they* are garnished and adorned, we feel at once that this must have been done by the Spirit of the Lord, because the region in which this decoration presents itself is beyond the access of the creature. The pen of inspiration has treated of some subjects handled by common writers, and invested them with Divine attractions; but occasionally it describes to us "things which eye hath not seen, nor ear heard, neither hath it entered into the heart of man to conceive." The supernatural truths of the Bible come to us clothed in a certain mysterious beauty. All Divine and heavenly things body themselves forth in a simple, majestic form in the record of the Spirit. The description of the creation is such as could only have been given us by the Creator; the account we have of the generation of Jesus Christ could have been given us by none but Him who sent Him into the world.

We leave it with the reader to say whether the inquiry we have prosecuted do not make out that there is the æsthetical analogy to God's other works which was to be looked for in the work of Redemption. Does not the supernatural manifestation which God has made of Himself in the Church bear the essential characteristic of that other manifestation He has made of Himself in the natural world ? Great things have been done, and there is a marvellous beauty in the way in which they have been accomplished. " New heavens and a new earth have been created," and we encounter the same immensity of conception and inimitable tastefulness in execution. Indeed, compared with this strange work of Jehovah, His former works are not to be remembered nor brought into mind, and we may say, " Strength and beauty are in his sanctuary."

VII.

A WORD TO GEORGE ELIOT AND GEORGE MACDONALD.

THE present state of our lighter literature is such as to excite alarm in the minds of all who jealously watch over the principles of the community. We do not refer at present to the flagitious or immoral tendency of our poetry or our novels. In our higher literature there is less of this than prevailed formerly. "Don Juan" would not be tolerated. The taste for Giaours and Corsairs is obsolete. We must all rejoice that this unclean spirit is gone out of the land, and that we have a band of poets and novelists who, instead of allying vice in their heroes with the highest and most brilliant endowments, seek rather to exalt virtue when associated with the humblest external circumstances. We do not inquire into the causes which have led to this desirable reform. For reasons to be immediately mentioned, it cannot be traced to the power directly exerted by evangelical religion upon our literary writers, who, as a rule, are remarkably exempt from its influence. Indirectly, however, it may be connected with evangelical religion; for as the community has unquestionably been affected by the revival of it, they must in so far accommodate themselves to the constituency for which they write, and must themselves, besides, be so far influenced by the secondary effects of this revival. When the saving power of the gospel has begun to show itself to any extent in the community, we may be sure that even the sections of it which are hostile to evangelical doctrine will be stirred up to unusual ardour in behalf of such religious tenets as they profess, and in advocating morality upon natural principles.   The genuine earnestness which has come down upon the evangelical portion of the community will be confronted with a spurious earnestness in that portion of it which is hostile to evangelism.   There is reason moreover to apprehend that when Christianity in its evangelical form is likely to triumph, its great adversary may avail himself of men of genius and literary endowment to start some new scheme of Christianity, more allied to natural religion, and prosecuted with all the ardour of enthusiasm.   If he get them to be patrons of heresy, he cares not though they should be no longer panderers to immorality.

This is the curse of our modern literature.   Sir Walter Scott and others wrote idly enough, but one could not find fault with their orthodoxy.   Byron was profligate, but he did not become a vendor of heresy.   He had his practical doubts of the truth of the Bible, but never anointed himself to be the apostle of new doctrines; and, if we may believe Madame Guicciolini, he retained secret convictions of the truth of Calvinism, though from his own profligate career he could only forebode the worst to himself from the truth of predestination.   It is otherwise with our present writers. Many of our poets and novelists are teaching an erroneous theology with all the earnestness of missionaries.   If such a crusade be on foot it would be well to remember that heresy is a worse and more insidious evil than licentiousness, and that it cannot assume a more treacherous form than when conveyed in productions which are beyond the ordinary tribunals of theological criticism, and which are recommended to the minds of the young by the irresistible attractions of fancy and genius.   If the charge we bring against the writers in question be true, we are justified in interfering, it being they who have begun to deal in theology, and not we who are presuming to traffic with romance.   If the time has come when poetasters and tale-writers sport the white neckcloth, why should clergymen hesitate to make appearance in ties of green, or of still livelier colours ?

Before proceeding to prove the libel we have brought forward, it may be necessary to touch upon a great change of a general kind which has come over the bards and novelists of our country. Formerly their aim was mainly the humbler one of seeking to please. Content to exercise the æsthetical faculty with which they were gifted, they caught and transferred to their page the beautiful, the terrible, and the sublime in nature, or they reflected whatever is attractive and striking in humanity. They presented us with fairer or darker forms of character than meet us in every-day life, thrown into situations considerably above the average of those actually occurrent, with backgrounds of landscape lovelier than strike the eye of actual observation. They did not profess to aim at being moralists or preachers. They knew that there were others upon whom these more serious functions devolved; and although they did not altogether eschew the useful, or the inculcation of the moral lesson, they aimed chiefly at producing pleasure. Lighter literature assumed the character of a relaxation. We took our theology from the pulpit or from the productions of our divines. We took our morality from a similar source, or from the essays of the moralist. But when at our after-dinner hour we had thrown ourselves down upon the sofa, or poised our legs upon the fireplace, we expected little else from the novel or the poem than an airy recreation. A revolution has taken place. The poets of this age, instead of leading us into the flowery fields of pleasure, are ambitious to aspire to the office of religious teachers. If they do not actually give us long unmeasured lines of proverbs, they indulge in spiritual utterances (chiefly of the melancholy kind), or in something between sentimental and theological speculation. This is so far good in its own way—certainly better than invitations by the bard to drink of his Falernian wine, or to join with him in admiration of the tresses of his mistress. We have nevertheless a secret persuasion that there is a place and a time for everything under the sun; and we think that, upon the whole, it would be a healthier symptom of the age if those who tuned their harps would relax their brows somewhat, and consider that their peculiar office is to delight and entertain the world rather than to preach or to prophesy. They should consider that in the main their productions occupy the same place in the world of mind as flowers do in the world of nature, which sufficiently answer the end of their creation when they throw an indescribable charm over the face of things. It were desirable to have a more palpable wall of separation reared between the province of the poet, which is æsthetical, and the province of the moralist and the theologian. The peculiarity of the age is that the preaching is becoming sentimental and the poetry theological. We have the more reason to complain, as the moral or religious strains of the bard are not of the healthiest description. In many instances they are the doleful exclamations of one who is seeking light for his troubled soul, and who seems unable to find it, though the sun of a gracious revelation is shining with meridian splendour above every head, and, it is to be presumed, above his own also. We have no patience for our part with such sceptical rhapsodies, whether they come from Tennyson himself or the host of his imitators who in various periodicals throughout the land pour forth their mawkish, melancholy, and drivelling hexameters.

Turning to our novelists, there is another change of a very marked kind that has come over the style of their productions. We were wont to be introduced by them to the more aristocratic circles of society, and found ourselves moving among princes and princesses, peers and marchionesses, gentlemen and ladies, at the least. Whatever is most romantic and picturesque in nature was added to all that is imposing in rank and luxury ; the heroine was remarkable for personal charms, and the heroes were distinguished for personal valour. The modern novelist disdains having recourse to such adventitious sources of interest. He boldly transfers his readers to the smoky alleys and miserable tenements of our large cities, or to the cottages of the country poor. His principal characters derive their attraction from the moral qualities they possess, and which inhere in some feminine form destitute of any visible attraction, or some rough artisan of ungainly exterior. This, we acknowledge, is a change to the better. Not that we disown to a lurking partiality even yet for the novelist who, like the immortal Sir Walter Scott, avails himself of all that is most charming in the landscape and all that is imposing in polished society. Still we are delighted to follow virtue to its obscurest abode, and are prepared, we humbly trust, to hail its higher emanations in the least attractive of either sex.

But we begin to perceive an attempt on the part of some of our novelists to exaggerate the moral qualities that are supposed by them to underlie our fallen nature, while they aim, on the other hand, to disparage evangelical religion. We have first a systematic effort made to caricature Calvinism. Its ministers are introduced as preaching only fire and brimstone. If any of the characters that figure in their narrative be of that persuasion, they are either cheating tradesmen, or savage schoolmasters, or hysterical old women. The effects produced by Calvinistic teaching are represented as being the worst. Meanwhile we have placed over against such odious and partial pictures the hero and approved characters of the piece, who are distinguished by a certain sublime love or moral principle. Whence they have derived it does not appear, but we are left to infer that it is some underlying excellence in fallen humanity. At any rate, we are carefully informed that it came not from any Calvinistic, that is, evangelical source. In short, their professed aim manifestly is to subvert the religion taught in our Confessions of Faith and Catechisms. To show that these remarks are not groundless, we shall substantiate them in this article by some illustrations.

We shall begin with " Felix Holt, the Radical," by the authoress of " Adam Bede." The hero of the piece, Felix himself, is described as being, so far as personal appearance is concerned, " a shaggy-headed, large-eyed, strong-limbed young man, without waistcoat or cravat; while by trade he is a watchmaker, and by birth the son of a quack doctor." These are certainly not the surroundings of a hero of our novels of the olden times. But, as already hinted, we have no quarrel with them. We would be the last persons on earth to deny any man's title to nobility from his wanting a waistcoat, or to judge of a man's nobility by the waistcoat he had. Although we never happened to know a watch-maker who possessed qualities entitling him to the admira-tion of the whole community, we repudiate the idea that there is necessarily anything in the business itself that bars one's way to eminence; and though one's father may have gulled the public by puffing off quack medicines, he may, for aught we know upon the mysterious subject of generation, turn out to be a hero. With a rough exterior, Felix Holt is represented as possessing an inflexible moral rectitude and very noble sentiments. That these did not proceed from an evangelical source is plain enough. The authoress is careful to inform us that he had joined no Church. " He saw distinctly, as he said himself, that he could do something better." He did not always go to chapel, and he was not in the habit of reading " Howe's Temple." In thus dissociating any excellence he pos-sessed from such a disreputable source as evangelism or any ordinary evangelical ministration, our authoress has dealt wisely according to her generation as a novelist. It gratifies the pride of the human heart to contemplate a morality which is not the offspring of grace, but our own manufacture. We would recommend this device to every writer of novels who wishes to be popular. He must pander to the pride of life; nor does it signify much whether he do this by introducing a valorous knight-errant or a watch-maker with moral sentiments which are indigenous. But, as he hopes for success, let not the man whose morality is to produce admiration be a reader of " Howe's Temple," or a joined member of any of our Churches. This by the way. Felix Holt has an opportunity of exercising his powers as a moral reformer upon Esther, the heroine of the novel, who was in every respect his opposite, affecting the fine lady, proud of her small feet, and her long neck, and her plaited curls—sentimental, moreover, in her tastes, and a devoted admirer of Lord Byron. Supposed to be the daughter of the Rev. Rufus Lyon, minister of the Independent Chapel, Malthouse Yard, in the market-town of Treby Magna, she spent the days of her early vanity under his roof, and we are informed of his unfortunate failure to regenerate her, and the cause of it. " Her father's desire for her conversion had never moved her. She saw that he adored her all the while, and he never checked her unregenerate acts as if they degraded her on earth, but only mourned over them as unfitting her for heaven. Unfitness for heaven (spoken of as Jerusalem and glory), the prayers of a good little father, whose thoughts and motives seemed to her like the life of Dr. Doddridge, which she was content to leave unread, did not attack her self-respect and self-satisfaction." Be it observed that the Rev. Rufus Lyon is admitted to be a worthy man—a worthy little man—notwithstanding his evangelical sentiments. Felix, who was neither a minister nor a member of the Church, nor a reader of Doddridge or " Howe's Temple," accomplishes the meritorious work by another and a more excellent way. Rough as a bear, and faithful as John the Baptist (without any of his doctrinal nonsense), from his very first interview with Esther he challenges her for her vanity, unveils to her the frivolity of her life, satirises her fine manners and her fine sensibilities, and seeks to impress her with the truth that life is a solemn thing—either a blessing or a curse to many—and to be spent with a due consideration of the myriads of men and women oppressed by wrong and misery, or tainted with pollution.

In this he certainly does the young lady a good service, showing himself to be an excellent moral instructor; and he sets a good example of a new method withal of courtship, which in this case proved to be successful, and which we would recommend to all young men, whether they may belong to trade or to the liberal professions. But our authoress, not satisfied with claiming thus much for Felix Holt, represents him as having by this process accomplished the conversion of Esther! Take the following as rather a good illustration of the sentimental view of the new birth which is fast gaining ground with some of our theological novelists. The saving change of heart (shall we call it?) that begins to take place with Esther is thus described as it showed itself to the gratified eyes of the Rev. Rufus Lyon.

"Let me lift your porridge from before the fire, and stay with you, father. You think I'm so naughty that I don't like doing anything for you," said Esther, rather sadly, to him. "Child, what has happened? You have become the image of your mother to-night," said the minister, in a loud whisper. The tears came and relieved him. "She was very good to you?" asked Esther, softly. "Yes, dear, She did not reject my affection. She thought not scorn of my love." "Father, I have not been good to you, but I will be—I will be," said Esther, laying her head in his bosom. When Esther was lying down that night she felt as if the little incidents between herself and her father in this society had made it an epoch. Very slight words and deeds may have a sacramental efficacy, if we can cast our self-love behind us in order to say and do them. And it has been well observed through many ages that the beginning of compunction is the beginning of a new life."

Upon another occasion of a like kind the minister cannot conceal his joy. "Surely the work of grace is begun in her; surely here is a heart that the Lord has touched." Now, without commenting upon the nature of this notable conversion, it is plain that we are called upon, from the narrative, to believe that it had no connection with the atoning blood of Jesus, or the regeneration of the Holy Spirit, but was accomplished solely by good moral exhortations from Felix Holt ; nay, as the minister of the Independent chapel had administered the gospel remedies, and is represented as having failed, there is an offensive insult thrown upon the evangelical system. As if to aggravate the insult, we are told that the minister had an old servant, Lyddy, who read " Alleine's Alarm " in the kitchen, and who is described as " crying over her want of assurance, instead of brushing the clothes and putting out the clean cravat ; always saying that her righteousness is filthy rags, and really I don't think that is a very strong expression for it—I am sure it is dusty clothes and furniture."

We shall not insist further upon this novel, the merits of which as a whole, and as a literary composition, it will not be once supposed that we undertake to discuss. It bears unquestionable impress of the strong masculine sense and original genius of the authoress of Adam Bede ; and though a large portion of the work strikes us as being heavily written, the conclusion sufficiently shows the singular power she possesses of commanding our moral sympathies. What we have to do with is the religious tendency of the novel. It contains an attempt to undermine evangelical religion by the unjustifiable process of caricature, and to substitute in its place a mere moral sentimentalism.

Belonging to the same school is George Macdonald, a writer whose talents have raised him to a very considerable reputation. As a novelist, he cannot indeed be reckoned as sustaining high rank. Wanting in the creative or inventive faculty, he seems incapable of fabricating a plot which, in its gradual development, may absorb the interest, and finally thrill the heart of the reader ; but what is wanting as a whole is so far compensated by the parts. His works abound in descriptions of nature radiant with a certain spiritual beauty, and in descriptions of life-scenes most graphic and original. We have conversations, those of them especially in the Scotch language, which for humour and strength of expression will bear comparison with those of Professor Wilson and Sir Walter Scott. The fault that sadly mars all is a constant aiming after philosophy. He cannot accept of anything in nature or human life, as ordinary persons are willing to accept them, but must find some deeper lesson behind all—something which is a mystery; and yet this miserable affectation of his, and hunting after something profound, is evidently considered by him to be what he constantly harps about—the " childlike."

But it is with the theology of George Macdonald that we have to do—the great design of all his works being to disseminate his religious opinions, which are most unsound and dangerous. His intense dislike of evangelical doctrine, as we understand it in Scotland, leaves us no reason to wonder that he should say of our Shorter Catechism : " For my part, I wish the spiritual engineers who constructed the Shorter Catechism had, after laying the grandest foundation stone that truth could afford them, glorified God by going no farther. Certainly many a man would have enjoyed Him sooner, if it had not been for their work."

In calling attention to his novels, I might just confine myself, by way of specimen, to two of the best known of them—" Alec Forbes " and " David Elginbrod."

To begin with " Alec Forbes," one of his most popular stories, the heroine, Annie Anderson, a Scotch orphan in humble life, possesses, of course, no personal attractions. On the other hand, as our readers who have any knowledge of this class of novel-writers might anticipate, she is proved to possess a quiet, profound, moral nature of her own—an underlying righteousness—which is, in the issue, to command our unlimited admiration. The great object of the writer is to show, by a series of scenes of his own invention, that Annie Anderson is nothing bettered by any contact she comes into with evangelism or Calvinism; or, more properly speaking, to expose the injury she experienced from those who were its fanatical ministers, or the contemptible disciples of that system of religion.

Annie Anderson, when a child, found herself in the hands of a savage schoolmaster, *Murdoch*, or, as the scholars called him, *Murder* Malison. His savage disposition is represented as growing out of his Calvinistic tenets; for every sin, as the catechism teaches, " deserves God's wrath and curse both in this life and that which is to come," and the master was only a co-worker with God in every penalty he inflicted on his pupils. Our author ingeniously goes on to observe that all the peculiarities of the Calvinistic creed may be traced in our Scotch pedagogues of the older type, acting as they did, for example : first, *of their mere good pleasure ;* next, *conformably to the doctrine of election*, having their favourites among the boys ; and finally, *for their own glory*, skelping a few unfortunate, pitiful, and cowed victims.

Soon after this, as her evil fate would have it, Annie Anderson pays a visit to the meeting-house of Mr. Cowie, an Independent minister, who chooses for his text : " The wicked shall be turned into hell, and all the nations that forget God." His sermon is described as consisting of vague half-monstrous embodiments of truth (our author's definition of Calvinism), and as filling the mind of the girl with alarm and horror. Not that Mr. Cowie is denied to be a sincere man. But, " I wonder," says our author, " if we ever will be able to understand the worship of our childhood, that revering upward look, which must have been founded in reality, however much after-experience may have shown the supposed grounds of reverence to be untenable." From these words, though cautiously expressed, it is plain that there is an underlying piety of nature's growth which he considers to be overlooked in the Independent chapel. Accordingly he sympathises with the spirit of the parish minister more, upon whom Annie makes a call for consolation, and whom she finds sitting comfortably over his wine.

As to those who forget God being cast into hell, he bids her consider whether, because she sometimes forgets her own father, he would deal heavily with her on that account. Our author has his fault, indeed, to find with this clergyman, but it is characteristically expressed, and so as to show that he approves of his illustration. He represents him, indeed, as brought to his right mind by little Annie's visit. "And now the heart of the old man, touched by the motion of the child's heart, yearning after her Father in heaven, and yet scarcely believing that he could be so good as her father on earth, began to stir uneasily within him ; and he went down on his knees, and hid his face in his hands." Our readers will agree with us that this parish minister is well called by the writer one of " God's babies."

The hero of the story, Alec Forbes of Howglen, is introduced to us as a boy somewhat older than the orphan, who champions her from the cruelty of Murdoch Malison and the persecutions of the scholars, and establishes himself from the first in her affections. He is above her in station, however, and removing afterwards as a medical student to a northern university, seems soon to forget her amidst the gaieties of his career. He there falls in with a very singular companion, who lodges in the garret of his landlady: an eccentric genius, who acted as librarian of the college, and was as accomplished a scholar as he was a confirmed devotee of the bottle. Ensconced among his books in the upper story, this deformed figure of a philosopher drew many a visit from Alec Forbes, both fascinating him by his wit, and assisting him in his studies—ay, and until the tumblers of steaming toddy had obfuscated his faculties, when he gave him an instant and peremptory dismissal. Mr. Cupples is as good an illustration as could be desired of one who, through dissipation, has become a wreck and gone to seed; and who, when drunk, presents his boon companions with a brilliancy of talent only to be compared to the spectacle which a ship exhibits when the spirit-room has taken fire and gone up in a sudden conflagration at sea. Not the least affecting feature in his intercourse with the medical student was the solemn advices he gave him to abstain from ardent spirits. These were ere long seen to have been necessary, for Alec, owing to a series of mortifying adventures, bade adieu to morality, and abandoned himself to the profligacies of the city. There were now two drunkards in the same lodgings. But at this juncture a singular scene took place, which issued suddenly in the salvation of them both. Our novelist considers this doubtless as the most instructive part of his book, and as discovering certain latent principles in our nature, from which he augurs more good than from the doctrines of the gospel; but he must forgive us if we cannot read it without some feeling of the ludicrous. In short, on one occasion, when seated together in the garret, Mr. Cupples made a proposal which, considering his habits, was magnanimous to a degree. He swore to renounce his pota-tions if his young friend would do the same. Instantly the covenant was made, and "bang went the bottle into the court-yard." "Thank God!" said Mr. Cupples, as the clash reached his ears. "Both their hearts," adds our author, "were touched by one good and strong spirit—essential life and humanity. That spirit was love, which, at the long last, will expel whatsoever opposeth itself." It is very noticeable that he attaches more virtue to this love that lies in our humanity than to all the truths in our Confession of Faith. In another part of the work we learn that Murdoch or Murder Malison, who owed all his savage propensities to the Westminster document, was reformed and made a new creature by a like process. A poor scholar of his is lamed for life by a kick he gives him in one of his Calvinistic furors. After a long absence in consequence he appears in the schoolroom again, pale, haggard, mild, and forgiving. Murdoch is struck to the heart. A deep affection springs up between them; and this singular pedagogue, who had become a devil by the Shorter Catechism, becomes a saint under the influence of pity and remorse!

We read more wonderful things yet of Mr. Cupples. Alec Forbes, shortly after the scenes we have detailed, being taken with a dangerous sickness, returns to Howglen, to be watched over there by his mother and by Annie Anderson. One night the latter, in her lone vigils over the invalid, overhears a subdued voice singing outside :—

> 1 waited for the Lord my God,
>   And patiently did bear ;
> At length to me He did incline
>   My voice and cry to hear.
> He took me from a fearful pit,
>   And from the miry clay ;
> And on a rock He set my feet,
>   Establishing my way.

This was the reformed librarian, who had first broken his bottle, and was now singing psalms. Our readers shall have the rationale of it, so far as the reformation had yet gone. " A playful humanity radiated from him, the result of that powerfullest of all restoratives—*giving* of what one has to him that has not. Indeed, his reformation had begun with this. St. Paul taught a thief to labour that he might have to give. Love taught Mr. Cupples to deny himself, that he might rescue his friend, and presently he had found his feet touching the rock. If he had not yet learned to look straight to heaven, his eyes wandered not unfrequently towards that spiritual horizon upon which things earthly and heavenly meet and embrace." Thus there is no fear of Mr. Cupples, who, having begun his own reformation, will no doubt finish it.

The conversion of Alec Forbes himself is given as follows. "One lovely morning, when the green corn lay soaking in the yellow sunlight, and the sky rose above the earth, deep and pure and tender, like the thought of God about it, Alec became suddenly aware that life was good and the world beautiful. . . . He was blessed ; so easily can God make a man happy. The past had dropped from him like a wild but weary and sordid dream. He was re-born, a new child, a new bright world with a glowing summer to revel in. . . . He would be a good child henceforth, for one bunch of sun-rays was enough to be happy upon." We are told that Annie, who at this time entered, gazed for a moment, fled to her own room, and burst into adoring tears. "For she had seen the face of God, and that face was love—love like the human, only deeper, deeper, tenderer, lovelier, stronger. He has been wi' me a' the time, my God. He gied me my father; . . . and He has been wi' me I kenna how lang; and He is wi' me noo; and I hae seen His face again; and I'll try sair to be a gude bairn. Eh, me! It's jist wonderfu'! And God's jist naething but God Himsel'."

We have given but a cursory sketch of this novel, but, judging by the sample, what are we to think of it? I say nothing of the caricatures of Calvinism with which it abounds, for one might have charitably inferred that these were suggested by unfortunate specimens of its discipleship which George Macdonald had met with, though he must have haunted peculiar places to meet with them, and have had narrow opportunities of observation in his life not to have been able to correct the impression produced by them. But the fact is that our fault is not so much with what he condemns as with what he approves. He advocates a religion which ignores the existence of any awful controversy occasioned by sin, and is thus not more antagonistic to the whole teachings of the Bible than it is to the judgments of God manifest in this death-reigning world into which he sends forth these sentimental and flimsy novels of his; flimsy we call them, only because they profess to be religious. In attaching importance, besides, to such impulsive acts of benevolence as he ascribes to Mr. Cupples, or to such natural piety as he describes in Annie Anderson, he shows that he has not yet searched out the recesses of our plausible fallen humanity; this, again, because he has not been humble enough to take in his hand the only torch which illuminates them as with fire.

" David Elginbrod," by the same author, is a novel distinguished by powers of imagination equally great, and theological perversities quite as inexcusable.   We are introduced
to characters nearly identical, for in all his tales we meet
with the reproduction of the same theological contrasts.
Margaret Elginbrod, daughter of David Elginbrod, the
steward and head gardener to the Laird of Tirriegraffit, is a
second Annie Anderson, with the addition of a higher poetical
refinement, making her more interesting, but less natural if
one considers her station in life, and quite confounding to the
laird's tutor in his first interview with her.   Seeing him with
his eyes directed to the top of the beech trees in the forest
where they meet, she asks, " What were you seeing up
there ? " — a poser certainly to the accomplished precep-
tor, who, however, very manfully and, as we humbly think,
very properly confesses to being engaged in admiring the
contrast between the light green leaves and the shadows.
This comes far short of satisfying Margaret's Wordsworthian
genius. " I aye expect to see something in this fir wood."
Tutor : " What kind of a thing ? " Margaret : " That's jist
what I dinna ken.   The whole place aye seems fu' o' a presence ; an' it's a hantle mair to me nor the kirk, and the
sermon foreby ; an', for the singing, the soun' i' the fir taps is
far mair solemn and sweet at the same time, an' muckle
mair like praising God, than a' the psalms thegither."   A
kind of mawkish sentimentality goes a great way with our
author, who seems perfectly in earnest when he brings this
candidly expressed preference of Margaret's under our eye
as an example of enlightened and enlarged religious experience.   But David Elginbrod himself is the most prominent
figure in this novel, upon which the power of the artist has
been chiefly put forth.   " His carriage was full of dignity and
a certain rustic refinement ; his voice was wonderfully gentle,
but deep, and slowest when most impassioned.   He seemed
to have come of some gigantic antediluvian breed ; there was
something of the Titan slumbering about him.   He would have

been a stern man, but for an unusual amount of reverence that seemed to overflood his sternness and change it into strong love." The prayer he is represented as offering up, when first introduced to our notice, may best perhaps convey an idea to us of this robust and somewhat eccentric saint. " An' noo, for a' our wrang-doings, an' ill meanings, for a' our sins, and trespasses o' many sorts, dinna forget them, O God, till Thou pits them a' right ; an' syne exerceese Thy michty power e'en ower Thine ainsel', an' clean forget them a'thegither ; cast them ahin' Thy back, whaur e'en Thine ain een shall ne'er see them again, that we may walk bold and upright before Thee for evermore, an' see the face o' Him wha was as muckle God in doin' Thy biddin', as gin He had been ordering a' things Himsel'. For His sake, Amen." This is certainly rather a peremptory style of instructing the Almighty as to the best way of proceeding with his sins, and shows that according to David's theology there was small need of the blood, or for anything more than an exercise of magnanimity, or, as he somewhat irreverently expresses it, a royal act of self-control. He shows a spice of the same spirit as inspired his ancestor who wrote his own epitaph —an epitaph which pithily expresses indeed much of the theology of George Macdonald :—

> Here lie I, Martin Elginbrod,
> Hae mercy on my soul, O God ;
> As I wad do were I Lord God,
> And ye were Martin Elginbrod.

David is represented as not satisfied with the preaching of our Scots divines upon the subject of justification.

" This is just my opinion of it in sma'—*that* man, and *that* man only is justified, who pits himself into the Lord's hands to be sanctified. Noo; an' that 'll no be dune by pittin' a robe o' righteousness upon him afore he's gotten a clean skin beneath. As gin a father couldna bide to see the puir scabbit skin o' his ain wee bit bairnie; ay, or o' his prodigal son either, but had to hap it a' up afore he could let it come near him. . . . . There's a notion in't (that is, in the way Scots ministers speak of justification) o' hidin' sin frae God Himsel'. They speak so that the puir bairn canna see the Father Himsel', stannin' wi' His airms streekit oot as wide as the heavens, to tak' the worn crater, and the mair sinner the mair welcome hame to His ain heart. Gin a body would leave a' that, an' jist get folk persuaded to speak a word or two to God 'lane, the loss would be unco' sma'."

This representation of the preaching of Scots ministers is unfair, for as to any atoning righteousness of Christ interposed in the matter of our justification, they all speak of it as having been graciously provided by the Father Himself, who, seeing the sinner lying in his pollution and guilt, not only washes away the former (which exhausts George Macdonald's idea of benevolence), but covers the other. But passing from these matters, we would observe upon David Elginbrod, as the one character of the novel most powerfully drawn, that unquestionably no nobler subject can engage the artist's pencil than one of the sturdy and unsophisticated specimens of religion to be found among our Scottish peasantry; but that they have hitherto been found only in connection with Calvinism (witness the Covenanters, with their breed of genuine descendants); and that this attempt of George Macdonald's to graft his lax heresies upon the grand stock of character which such men suggested to him is both unfair and produces a ludicrous effect. David Elginbrod, with his strong basis of religious character on the one hand, and his effeminate, silly sentimentalisms on the other, about the Father " stannin' wi' His airms streekit out as wide as the heavens," to receive the sinner without the need of any interposed Mediator (for that is the upshot of it), is a phenomenon as yet unknown in our hamlets—such heresies being found floating (if at all) only in the minds of a few of the most feeble and feckless men of the generation.

Another man who is held up to us in this novel as a paragon of Christian excellence is one Falconer, who, among other acts of kindness shown to the tutor of Turrie-graffit in his difficulties, having paid his railway-ticket, commends himself to our author as a veritable follower of Him who was "a hiding-place from the wind and a covert from the tempest." "Of Him," that is, the Son of man, says our author, " Falconer had already learned this truth in the inward parts, and had found in the process of learning it that this was the true nature which God had made His from the first—no new thing superinduced upon it. He had but to clear away the rubbish of worldliness, cleaving more or less to the best nature for a time, and so to find himself." The sagacious reader will not be astonished to hear that this Christian gentleman who had "found himself "—in the shape of a nature good enough from the beginning, after lifting off a trifle of rubbish that lay above it—professed theological views of a very peculiar kind. With these he is represented as indoctrinating Hugh Sutherland, the tutor, and, in our judgment, does him more damage thereby than all his rail-way-ticket was worth in the way of advantage. He suggests the idea of hell being a place of reformation. He denies the existence of it as a place of eternal punishment, and in the following dream gives a glowing description of the excellent clergyman whose ministrations he honoured with his attend-ance, and who championed the same views.

" I saw a crowd of priests and laymen speeding, hurrying, darting away, upon a steep crumbling height. Mitres, hoods, and hats rolled behind them to the bottom. Beneath, and right in the course of the fire (that was advancing), stands one man upon a little rock which goes down to the centre of the great world, and faces the approaching flames. He stands bareheaded, his eyes bright with faith in God, and his mighty mouth that utters the truth fixed in holy defiance. His denial comes from no fear or weak dislike to that which is painful. On neither side will he tell lies for peace. He is ready to be lost for his fellow-men. In the name of God, he rebukes the flames of hell. The fugitives pause on the

top, call him lying prophet, and shout evil, opprobrious
names at the man, who counts not his own life dear to him,
who has forgotten his own soul in his sacred devotion to
men.   Be sure that, come what may of the rest, that man
is safe, for he is delivered already from the only devil that
can make hell a torture—the devil of selfishness. . . . He
trusts God so absolutely that he leaves his salvation to Him,
utterly, fearlessly ; and, forgetting it as being no concern of
his, sets himself to the work that God has given him to do,
even as the Lord before him, counting that alone worthy of
his care.   He will not have it that his Father in heaven is
not perfect.   He believes certainly that God loves—yea, is
love—and therefore that hell itself must be subservient to
that love, and but an embodiment of it ; that the grand work
of justice is to make way for a love which will give to every
man that which is right, and ten times more, even if it
should be by means of awful suffering—a suffering which
the love of the Father will not shun, either for Himself or
His children, but will eagerly meet for their sakes, that He
may give them all that is in His heart."

With regard to the sentiments contained in this quotation,
and which the author has of late still more plainly and
openly avowed, we can scarcely trust ourselves to cha-
racterise them, because we are unwilling to come down
heavily upon one whose very way of expressing himself
shows the morbid sentimentality that has led him to adopt
them.   But we are not the less bound to brand them
with condemnation.   A very general belief seems to prevail
amongst the admirers of George Macdonald t h at he has
simply been stumbled by the offensive way in which certain
Calvinists state the doctrine of everlasting punishments.
But such passages as the above must convince them that
he denies the doctrine itself, and that his quarrel is therefore with all the Evangelical Churches at home and abroad.
We are not surprised that they should have fallen into
this charitable mistake, but we do confess to a feeling

of surprise that this writer himself, otherwise characterised by manliness and ingenuousness, should have fostered this delusion ; for all his criticisms upon Calvinist preachers and Calvinistic disciples proceed upon it, and the edge of them would at once have been taken away if he had allowed his readers to suppose that he was condemning the doctrine itself of eternal punishment. In the quotation we have just made, he not only denies that there is a place of everlasting punishment, but this clergyman in the dream is represented as a hero because he denies it. His sublime vocation is not to warn men to escape the flames of hell (which has usually been considered the vocation of Christian ministers), but, according to his own strange language, " to rebuke the flames of hell," in the sense of stoutly preaching that there is no such place. With a certain offensiveness of language, which George Macdonald considers, perhaps, that we are bound to receive from an intense man, he represents him as not altogether without a secret doubt in his own mind that, after all, he may be wrong in making the denial ; but as willing to be lost, if that were necessary, in so good a cause, even as against the Almighty. " On neither side will he tell lies for peace. He is ready to be lost for his fellow-men. Be sure that, come what may of the rest, that man is safe, for he is delivered already from the only devil that can make hell a torture—the devil of selfishness." Our author seems to think that there is no other devil than selfishness ; but he may rest satisfied that there are many devils — unwillingness to receive God's testimony being one. But we have no inclination to follow him in this particular style of writing, which is surely as unedifying as it is contrary to good taste.

In condemning the class of novels spoken of in this essay, we wish it to be understood, first of all, that we dislike the sentimental, and silly, and childish representations given us of conversion and kindred subjects. Religious novels form a very questionable sort of production at best; but, in the case before us, it is not merely that sacred matters are brought into grotesque connection with things of a lighter character, they are themselves dwarfed down into insignificance and contempt. We are aware of the defence likely to be made by the authors in question. They will retort that the error lies on our part, who would represent conversion as being some mysterious, supernatural change, lying outside the range of common experience; and in general more as a thing of gloom or transcendentalism than as something joyful, and pervading the lowliest acts of this life. Now it is true that our religion, if genuine, will go down to the commonest and most trivial of our actions, affecting the very words we speak in the house, and the tempers we show in our domestic moments; but we are never to forget that there are graver and more important relations in which we stand to God, to eternity, to the Divine law, and to the Divine law as broken—we are never to forget that man, notwithstanding his connection with the littles and commonplaces of this life, has also a solemn connection with objects infinitely higher; and, keeping these things in view, we shall find that there enters something more serious into experimental religion than we meet with in their sentimental and ridiculous descriptions of it. There is a deceptive appearance of great profoundness in the importance they attach to a religion showing itself in the department of the childish and the small—a religion such as finds God in "the sough of fir-trees," and makes us "a hiding-place from the tempest" to a brother who is unable to pay his railway fare. It is something of the same delusion in theology as Wordsworth fell into in poetry, nor are we altogether without a certain conviction that we are to trace to that poet, in some measure, the tendency that has appeared in our modern bards and novelists to substitute the shallows of natural religion for the glorious mysteries and depths of evangelical theology.

But the extracts we have given prove besides that there

is an insidious strain of heresy pervading our lighter literature.   None will consider that it is to be viewed without
alarm because this is the department in which it appears?
None, surely, will think to allay our apprehension by reminding us that men do not go to novels for their theology? We profess not to belong to the number of those
who think that if truth have possession of the pulpit, heresy
may sport itself in the drawing-room. We take our sons
and daughters to church with us to hear the clergyman who
powerfully warns them to flee from the wrath to come; but
if they bring with them from the circulating library the
volumes that both deny the doctrine they have heard and
throw contempt upon the preacher of it, this last ministration will at least have two powerful allies in the genius of the
novelist and the depravity of their own hearts. Grant that
the more solid reading of the generation is sound, what
signifies this if the lighter literature be heretical? What
though the main courses of the repast be unobjectionable,
if there be poison in the confectioneries? If the writers I
refer to wish to introduce religion into their novels, they are
of course at liberty to do so; but if they mean to bring in a
new religion, the graveness of the task, not to say common
honesty, would suggest that they should attempt it by some
elaborate work of demonstration. A novel is not a fair way
of propagating new religious views. What is first demonstrated may be afterwards painted. But there is nothing,
of course, more easy than to set off any religious views by a
novel, where the characters, being the pure invention of the
writer, can be made so to speak and so to act as to present
those views to advantage, and to make their opposites
ridiculous.

We may be reminded that the author last mentioned has
published his sentiments in a more didactic form in his
small volume entitled "Unspoken Discourses." That work
we accept as an open and manly avowal of his religious
tenets; but none who have read it will assert that it contains

the vestige of a systematic attempt to support them by argument. The volume is stamped with the literary characteristics of the author—a Carlylian intensity, a burning earnestness, a singular beauty and strength and originality of style ; but while these are powerful for enforcement and illustration, they cannot supply the only thing we waited for with anxiety : we mean, of course, demonstration. In his discourse, for example, upon the text, " Our God is a consuming fire," we have his peculiar views broadly and boldly stated—that there is no such thing as a penal dealing of God with sinners, and no such thing as everlasting punishments. He grants that the love of God is inexorable, and leads Him to punish sin with great severity in this life and in that which is to come ; but he maintains that this punishment is sanctifying and intended to sanctify, and he maintains that it is carried on in the next world only for a certain period. He holds, therefore, by a purgatory, and is, in this sense, as bad as the Papists ; but he denies a hell, and is, in this sense, worse than the heathen. These are strange doctrines to be openly avowed in Scotland ; but our fault is with the still stranger fact that this author does not consider it to be necessary to support them by argument from reason or Scripture, but merely to enforce and embellish them, and to establish them by an appeal to the passions or feelings. As instances of this, take the following short quotations from his volume :—

P. 49 : " But at length, O God ! wilt Thou not cast death and hell into the lake of fire, even into Thine own consuming Self ? Death shall then die everlastingly.

> And hell itself shall pass away,
> And leave her dolorous mourners to the peering day.

Then indeed wilt Thou be all in all. For then our poor brothers and sisters, every one, O God ! we trust in Thee, the Consuming Fire, shall have been burnt clean and brought home. For if their moans, myriads of ages away, would turn heaven for us into hell, shall a man be more merciful than God? Shall, of all His glories, His mercy alone not be infinite?"

To the same effect, take p. 229: "Will God look calmly, and have His children look calmly too, upon the ascending torments of our strong brothers, our beautiful sisters! O brother, believe it not. O Christ, the redeemed would cry, where art Thou, our strong Jesus? Come, our grand Brother. See the suffering brothers down below! see the tormented sisters! Come, Lord of life! Monarch of suffering! Redeem them. For us, we will go down into the burning, and see whether we cannot at least carry through the burning flames a drop of water to cool their tongues."

We have no intention of characterising these passages—not even the last sentence of them, which sounds strangely alongside of our Lord's teaching in the well-known parable. There is no accounting for taste, and George Macdonald is entitled to adopt his own standard. However, there is only one way of reasoning, and we cannot allow even him to proceed as if there were another. To reason with the heart instead of the head is always dangerous, but never more so than upon a subject like this. Did it never strike him that such a rhetorical appeal as this of his might have been made just as well against the idea of the whole human family being swept away in their successive generations by bodily death into one huge tomb? It might have been said: "We correct sin very gently, with the frown upon our brow, or with the birch in our hand; and shall God be less merciful than we, and look calmly upon our strong brothers and beautiful sisters going down in all manner of deaths through all their successive generations to one sepulchre?" This is undeniably God's procedure notwithstanding. Does this dispensation of all faces changed to clay, of the winding-sheet, of universal mortality descending through the ages, tally with George Macdonald's theory? It will not do for him to allege that it tallies sufficiently with what he holds of the severity of the Almighty's processes of sanctification. The question is whether the standard he applies, and by which he thinks to explode the doctrine of everlasting punishments, is not found to be egregiously fallacious when applied to the case we have just referred to ? He, no doubt, accepts in his creed of a certain inexorableness in God's dealing, because undeniable facts in the world before us have forced him to do so; but, supposing the death-dispensation to which I have referred to have been subjected beforehand to his credence, the question is whether he would ever have consented to believe in it had he proceeded to judge of it by this fantastic and sentimental criterion of his own? What follows? If left to ourselves we never would have anticipated the heat of such an anger as has gone forth upon the body; and the destruction of the soul may be something also which infinitely surpasses all our anticipations of it.

The author of these Discourses, which were never spoken, and which, for his sake, we sincerely regret were ever written, brings forward no arguments from the Bible to support his tenets. But, more than this, he denies that the Bible is the standard of our faith. This he does in a discourse entitled " The Higher Faith," by which he means a faith higher than that which is bounded by God's written Record.

P. 52 : " Sad indeed would the whole matter be, if the Bible had told us everything God meant us to believe. . . . The Bible nowhere lays claim to be regarded as *the* word, *the* way, *the* truth. The Bible leads us to Jesus, the inexhaustible, the ever-unfolding revelation of God. . . . If we were once filled with the mind of Christ, we should know that the Bible had done its work, was fulfilled, and had for us passed away. Till we have known Him, let us hold the Bible dear, as the moon of our darkness by which we travel towards the east."

This is intelligible enough. According to the view here

propounded, the Bible is only an elementary revelation intended to lead us to Christ. When we come to Christ we are to expect to have many things revealed to us which are not contained there. He considers such of us as limit our faith to the Bible as having what he calls the Lower Faith. He has himself attained to an eminence, and he seems to know it. "I am quoting your own Bible," he says, with an air of self-complacency in one place, when condescending to quote a text from it in support of his views! Meanwhile, observe how conveniently this theory of revelation shields his heresies. When he denies the doctrine of everlasting punishments, for example, and we tell him that it is plainly taught in the Bible, "Which Bible," he asks, "do you mean? Is it merely the Bible received by all Christendom, or is it George Macdonald's Bible?"

So much for his views upon the rule of faith. We trust in charity that no reader expects us to enter into a discussion upon that subject. When we enter upon such a discussion it will be in connection with some production that has the face of argument. As for these discourses, with all their intense, indeed agonizing sentimentality and beauty of diction, they are too slender performances to be heavily dealt with. They will be great favourites with girls who have left or are leaving the boarding-school, and with young men whose beards are in the downy state. We would not have referred to them were it not that their publication has left the community now in no doubt of the sentiments entertained by their author, and we might otherwise have been branded as uncharitable, had we asserted them to be contained in his novels.

We know what will be said by some—that we have been too severe — that we have confined ourselves almost altogether to the condemnatory. Our answer is that when an author has been well nigh universally and unconditionally praised, one writer may surely be allowed to qualify the admiration by calling attention to his errors. If every periodical in the land had come out against his erroneous leanings — if he had been severely handled in the public prints—chivalry would have dictated the necessity of coming forward to the help of a persecuted writer; but when scarcely one publication has whispered of anything wrong—when at one time we see him lionized, and at another sitting in the same chariot with the editors of our recognised evangelical periodicals—we think that there is far more necessity for faithful exposure than for general adulation.

We are by no means insensible to the imposing moral qualities of this author, as these are reflected in his writings, but unfortunately they are always accompanied by some perversity which brings him into collision with the teachings of the Bible, and arrests and countermands our admiration. In his choice of his heroes and heroines, how completely does he show himself above the weakness of being guided by regard to adventitious qualities. With him a poor man is as great as a rich man—a plain-looking woman and a beauty is all one : rank is nothing. But, on the other hand, we find in the issue that these heroes and heroines are sickly specimens of sentimental religion, which he has got up in order to outshine and supplant the blood-washed and regenerate ones whom our Bible commends to our acceptance. How delightful to hear him talk about the childlike. But we are shocked to find that those whom he denominates " God's babies " are the concentration of pride, inasmuch as they reject the peculiar doctrines of Christianity, though these are revealed to us by the Almighty Himself. How glowing— how burning appears to be his benevolence ; but we find ere long that it is not the benevolence which leads him to rescue the perishing from the flames of hell, but something under the influence of which he must needs go down to hell itself in order to save those whose destruction God has declared to be sealed. We protest that none can admire more than we do the descriptions he gives us of nature—quite his own—all sparkling with the dews of sentiment ; but when he hoists his tight rope of daring theological speculation, and proceeds to mount it, that he may show how nimbly he can walk over it, our admiration is at an end ; and when we see him stretch it above a gulf infinitely more fearful than that into which the Niagara Falls descend, and cross and recross it, balancing himself with Denison Maurice's pole, we not only condemn him, but cannot hold the community which goes out to see him, guiltless.

Enough, however, and more than enough of this author ; for it would have scarcely been necessary to sound the trumpet of alarm had he stood alone, in our day, in broaching these sentiments. It is well known that the whole air is infected with the same heresies; and our poets and novelists, being a susceptible generation, are only the first to catch every wind of doctrine that blows, whether of truth or error. What then ? Shall we despond ? He who raised up of old the men that went forth irresistible from the threshing-floor—men that had in their hair the strength of armies—is able to raise up for us in the realms of literature men of another stamp than those who possess the ear of the generation—for who are they ? Sentimental sceptics for the most part—worshippers of earnestness for its own sake—fire-worshippers, and nothing else. We have enough of them in all conscience ; men who dream that they have a mission from heaven to "ring in the Christ that is to come." God help them ! We are satisfied enough with Him whom the angels rang in 2000 years ago, and who has been sufficiently well known in Scotland, and in England too, long ere they were born.

VIII.

ROBERTSON OF BRIGHTON.

"IT is pleasant to many minds to leave the tame, un-romantic shores of common belief, and to start on a voyage of discovery over the boundless ocean of intellectual speculation. But there is danger also in this enterprise. The dreary land of universal scepticism; the chaos of no faith, and the black regions of despair are somewhere out in those seas, and many have ventured there who never returned. I know some who started with the canvas well in the breeze; proudly they passed over the bar, and looked back patronisingly upon the shores of common belief. They sailed; the winds arose; the hurricanes blew; the thunders roared; the lightnings played; they ended in chaos and eternal night.   Luther said, 'Better not flutter too high, but somewhat near Calvary and the cross.'"—Rev. THOS. JONES, on opening the Congregational Union of England and Wales.

The sentences prefixed to this essay are instructive, and show that the man who uttered them knew the words necessary to be addressed, whether to Congregational Unions or to General Assemblies of Presbyterian Churches at the present time. The senior ministers occupying the benches at such annual gatherings may be secure in their orthodoxy. Anchored in the truth, they feel, in fact, only too secure, and can scarcely suppose that the younger brethren who sit around them should be moved away from it. They forget that the evangelical doctrines, forming the things of the Spirit of God, are as unintelligible to human reason as any science is to those who are ignorant of its terminology. They forget that, having been educated themselves in an evangelical creed, they have come to receive as unquestionably true what to the understanding is foolishness, and that the Spirit of grace (if the blessed fact be indeed so) has enlightened them to see its wisdom. Without at all meaning to question the piety of the younger clergy, it is to be remembered that the Spirit of God does not necessarily take possession of each succeeding race ; that if He depart for any interval of time, the doctrines become of course foolishness again, and that there is infinite danger of a recurrence to heresy. We think that the Rev. Thomas Jones has sounded the right note of warning.

But what we need, after all, is not so much a general warning of this nature, as faithfulness in challenging the individual errorist when he appears. Not that a charge of unfaithfulness in this respect can be brought against the courts of our Churches. It is noticeable of those Churches which have any courts at all, or any pretensions to discipline, that no sooner has the youngest minister shown the heretical tendency than he is met by something of the prospect, more or less distant, of a libel. This is well. It is a salutary check upon the overweening vanity and the superficial speculativeness that would otherwise increase to more ungodliness. But the press is to be blamed; nor is it the secular press merely, or so much. There is scarcely a review or magazine of a theological character that speaks out very decisively or flatly against a heretical publication. So many strange opinions are abroad, not upon small points, but points of eternal importance ; infidelity and loose opinions are so rampant, that it is plain a battle of the hottest description is very near at hand. In these circumstances the worst is that the battle-spirit is lost among us. We have become excessively liberal, and disposed to allow questionable doctrines to pass without censure. This for forty years back. Since that time the tide has been running fast

towards nothing but the gratification of our benevolent
sentiments; while error and infidelity, taking advantage of
this invincible good nature, disport themselves on every side.
The man we most need is the man who died at the period I
have referred to — the greatest champion of truth in our
century, and yet for whom (a very significant fact) no
monument of national gratitude has been erected, nor has
even his biography been written! *

These preliminary remarks may appear to our readers to
forebode a very truculent handling of the Brighton incumbent
whose name is placed as the title to this essay. We solemnly
abjure all intentions of the kind. Indeed, no man has
appeared in the present day whose personal qualities are
likelier to save him from hostile criticism than he who is
now to be the subject of our consideration. It is not much
to say that he was amiable. He inherited a certain nobleness of character, and his talents were so much allied with
the intensest sensitiveness of the imagination, that we cannot
conceive of any writer, however bent he might be upon condemnation, failing to extend to him the utmost latitude of
forbearance. We confess to loving him from the commencement. His was a veritable boyhood. A soldier's son,
delighting from the first in the boom of the cannon, one
thinks he sees the glow of countenance and the triumphant
stride with which the little fellow accompanied his father's
gamekeeper in the moonlight expeditions near to Leith.
When he grew up, it is impossible not to sympathise
with the struggle he underwent in renouncing the military
profession, that he might devote himself to the ministry.
Two opinions may be entertained as to the wisdom of the
decision he formed. Passionately attached to the other
profession, a passion that awoke in after years at the very
sight of the red coat, there was no reason why he should
have abandoned it because of the temptations to be found in
the army. Temptations are to be found in every profession,

* The Rev. Dr. Andrew Thomson, formerly of St. George's, Edinburgh.

and we shall have occasion to see that he fell under those he met with in the ministry. No more foolish advice is often given than by pious friends. " Do as your father likes, and pray to God to direct him aright," was the sage counsel given to young Robertson by one of these. The consequence was that having prayed God to direct his father, and thus surrendered the benefit of his own judgment, he came to the resolution of giving up the commission he had in his pocket. What kind of a minister one may make who is born to be an officer of artillery none can tell ; but pious parents would do well to consider that their children glorify God most by pursuing the profession they decidedly incline to. However, there can be only one opinion as to the gentleness and self-sacrificing denial exercised by the young soldier in yielding to the entreaties of his father and friends, and we advert to this as another reason why none of us can fail to love him. The personal interest felt in him increases with the dash of religious melancholy in his character, and becomes painfully intense in connection with the isolation in which his peculiar opinions placed him, the anguish of his last illness, and his premature departure from the world.

If it be true, as we fear can be indisputably established, that he made shipwreck of the evangelical faith, his amiableness and personal accomplishments, while entitling him to the utmost gentleness of treatment, render him all the more dangerous an example to young men, and especially to young clergymen. Hence the necessity of our treatment of him, on the other hand, being characterised by decision and faithfulness. His sermons have obtained a very large sale in this country. We cannot, for our part, believe that this is chiefly owing to the genius or eloquence distinguishing them. Being for the most part notes of sermons, they are necessarily unfinished productions, nor have they much more to recommend them, in a literary point of view, than a certain freshness, and precision of language, and imaginative beauty. He never soars upon the wing through any considerable space—a falcon flight at best, betokening a keen, quick eye, and a nervous rapidity in darting to short distances. To what, then, are we to trace their popularity? Destitute as his discourses are of the gospel, they want altogether the essential interest of sermons; and, again, were they merely philosophical essays, physiological or metaphysical disquisitions, they must have been insipid. The secret of their popularity is, that while they want the interest of the gospel, they are imbued with the earnestness of a man who seeks to introduce another gospel, of what kind we shall attempt to show afterwards; but they have thus captivated the restless and sceptical turn of not a few minds in this age. The more necessary is it to expose the dangerous and most pernicious tendency of the tenets contained in his discourses, and to trace, by way of warning to others, the process by which this writer was seduced into the adoption of them.

In the earlier part of his career, as is well known, he was evangelical and Calvinistic in his creed. Brought up in those tenets, he retained them, much to his honour, during his curriculum at Oxford, where he was exposed to the danger of infection from the Tractarians, who had begun to broach their peculiar doctrines. Though not insensible to the devoutness characterising some of them, he resisted this first temptation to diverge from the evangelical faith. Nothing could be better than the spirit of the following prayer, drawn up by him at this time :—

" The enemy has come in like a flood. We look for Thy presence. Do Thou lift up a standard against him. O Lord! here in Oxford we believe that he is poisoning the streams, which are to water Thy Church, at their source. Pardon us if we err. O lead us into all truth! But, O our God, if we are not mistaken, if the light which is in us be darkness, how great is that darkness! Lighten our darkness in this university with the pure and the glorious light of the gospel o Christ! Help, Lord, for the faithful have failed from among the children of men. My Father, I am like a child, blown about by every wind of doctrine. How long shall I walk as a vain shadow, and disquiet myself in vain? Let not my inconsistent conduct be a pretext for blasphemy against Thy saints, and persisting in heresy. Hear me, my Lord, and remember!"

A prayer this which breathes, if not a very robust, at least a very gentle and beautiful spirit.

During his first short ministry of a year at Winchester he had undergone no change in his religious views. His labours there were apparently much blessed. Martin and Brainerd were his models, and by his own confession not a few were savingly brought to Christ. At this period we hear no complaints from him, such as were afterwards heard, that he could not make himself understood by the people; nor do we read of any who were startled by his doctrine, and subjected him to irritating conversations in the study. He was then preaching that gospel which the poorest perfectly understand, and which the sheep of Christ instinctively know and follow. Happy had it been for him if, contented to pursue this course, he had shunned the more ambitious paths of profitless speculation! His biographer, Stopford Brooke, who has no sympathy with this stage of his religious history, tells us that at Winchester he was decidedly behind every way; "that having been trained in a very restricted school of thought and religion, he could not emerge from it without first going down into its depths; that his letters at this time are not worth reading; that his thoughts were not marked by any individuality; and that his sermons did not exhibit much power, being overloaded with analogies of doctrine and conventionalities of university theology." We have no interest leading us specially to deny that Mr. Robertson's genius and natural faculties were undeveloped during the one year he was evangelical at Winchester, but the attempt here made to connect the two things together is simply ridiculous. Several causes of a more obvious kind than his Calvinistic education may account for a man's

genius and his peculiar gifts not showing themselves immediately. He may be of tardy development. He may constitutionally be of a self-diffident turn, which was largely
true of the subject of this essay, and thus be slow in discerning his own powers. But we demur altogether to the
idea that a man must renounce his evangelism if he would
write good letters, and go down into the depths of German
mysticism ere he can be original. Who ever showed a
more decisive originality than Thomas Chalmers, following
a track of fancy and thought entirely his own, without precedent, and baffling imitation, while after all he was a disciple
of that "very restricted school of thought and of religion,"
which Stopford Brooke considered fatal to lively corre-
spondence and intellectual independence? It is plain that
Robertson of Brighton was from the beginning possessed not
only of talent, but passion and imagination. In him sensitiveness and strong sentimentality existed from his earliest
years. Take, for example, his romantic idealization of
womanhood :—

"The beings that floated before me, robed in vestures
more delicate than mine, were beings of another order. The
thought of one of them becoming mine was not rapture, but
pain. At seven years old woman was a sacred dream, of
which I would not talk. Marriage was a degradation. I
remember being quite angry on hearing it said of a lovely
Swede, the loveliest being I ever saw, that she was likely to
get married in England. She gave me her hair, lines, books,
and I worshipped her only as I should have done a living
rainbow, with no farther feeling. Yet I was then eighteen,
and she was to me for years nothing more than a calm,
clear, untroubled fiord of beauty, glassing heaven, deep, deep
below, so deep that I never dreamed of an attempt to reach
the heaven. So I lived. I may truly say that my heart was
like the Rhone as it leaves the lake of Geneva."

None can doubt that the young incumbent of Winchester
had the elements in him of genius. Meanwhile there was

ample scope for the exercise of it in the path he was prosecuting; and all the freshness, and even more than the
originality of thinking and fancy now apparent in the
sermons of the Brighton preacher might have been forthcoming in connection with a sound theology. Let us grant for
a moment that the unhappy revolution in his religious sentiments contributed to the generation of intenser feelings; that
his transition from the old gospel to a new gospel of Germanic
origin, by the very agitation and agony of mind it cost
him, evoked a genius that might have been otherwise latent.
Shall we not say that this was a species of illegitimate
force—no more to be prized than the melancholy intensity
of passion inspired in Byron, for example, when he broke
loose from the laws by which he ought to have been restrained, and manufactured a kind of genius out of his own
wretchedness? We are to distinguish between the flash-brilliancy of the meteor and the round purity of the star that
keeps its place; between the strange fire that burns in too
bold a censer and the fire taken from the appointed altar.
When a horse, however spirited, has bolted the course, it is
out of the race.

Upon his removal to Cheltenham, Mr. Robertson underwent that singular revolution in his whole religious views
which will form the subject of our consideration in this essay.

Let us examine the account we have of it from the pen of
his biographer, who looks upon it with unmingled satisfaction. He tells us that now " he began to hew out his
own path to his convictions." This, of course, means that
his previous convictions had been reached by paths marked
out for him by others. He had come to be convinced of
the various evangelical doctrines, not by independent
inquiry, but through the blind and prejudiced following of
systematic divines in whom he had been educated. The
best refutation of this is to be found in the following fact
recorded of him when at Oxford by Stopford Brooke himself.

" The necessity of an accurate and critical knowledge of the Bible became more clear to him from this contact with various forms of religious thought (*Tractarians, &c.*). It was his habit when dressing in the morning to commit to memory daily a certain number of verses of the New Testament. In this way, before leaving the university, he had gone twice over the English version, and once and a half through the Greek. With his eminent power of arrangement he mentally combined and recombined all the prominent texts under fixed heads of subjects. He said long after to a friend, that, owing to this practice, no sooner was any Christian doctrine or duty mentioned in conversation, or suggested to him by what he was writing, than all the passages bearing upon the point seemed to array themselves in order before him."

Such was the method adopted by him at first, and which marked the formation of his evangelical views. If by "hewing out his own path to his convictions," it be meant that, instead of studying and following out the Word of God, he now began to make his own reason his guide, that of course was a plan which, whether begun at Cheltenham or anywhere else, would land him eventually in infidelity. If the phrase mean, on the other hand, that he now for the first time became an independent and untrammelled inquirer into the Word of God, it is surely an extraordinary circumstance that at Oxford he should have diligently and for himself compared Scripture with Scripture, which is the plain and approved method of independent inquiry. If, indeed, we had been told that at Cheltenham he took up the Bible a second time, and gave it a more diligent and thorough perusal, we might have felt that his change of views was entitled to be considered as a change to the better. But so far from this, his biographer refers us to the following unsatisfactory and suspicious circumstances, which accompanied the revolution in his mind.

First we are told that he had been studying Thomas

Carlyle, and was sensibly influenced by his writings. "His continual reading of Carlyle marks the state of intellectual ferment in which he now lived. 'I have gained good and energy from that book,' he says, speaking of 'Chartism; or, the Past and Present.'" Brooke denotes the state of his mind—justly, I suppose—"intellectual fermentation." He adds: "German metaphysics took up some of his time, and usefully." It was now also that he came across a friend "well acquainted with the sudden outbreak in this century of theological and philosophical excitement in Germany. The conversations were frequent and interesting, and it was partly at least due to this friendship that Mr. Robertson escaped from the trammels which had confined his intellect and spirit."

We who entertain views of things somewhat different from those of Stopford Brooke, can well understand the danger to which Mr. Robertson was exposed by coming into contact with the insidious rationalism of Goethe and his British disciples. Though possessed of a sufficiently keen and subtile intellect, he was not in all respects the best qualified for resistance on this side, being more distinguished by refinement than by robustness of understanding. Various points of his life might be referred to in proof that with all the boldness of physique that marked him, he was self-diffident, and apt to be swayed by the influence of others. Sensitive to a fault, he had allowed himself at this time to be chafed by what he considered the intolerable dogmatism and illiberality of certain of the evangelical party in their treatment of the Tractarians. While he disapproved of the views of the Tractarians, he considered these evangelicals as inferior to them in piety. "They tell lies in the name of God," he said; "others tell them in the name of the devil; that is all the difference." This excessive irritation under the bad spirit, or faults of those who are sound in the faith, is apt to be a stumbling-block; and, if it becomes so, this is generally a first symptom of heresy, for there must be

something infirm about one's doctrinal belief if it be affected ,
by the tempers or conduct of men, one way or another.
Whatever truth there may be in these remarks, certain it is
that the contact into which Mr. Robertson was now brought
with German speculation shook his belief not only in the
evangelical doctrines, but for a time in the very foundations
of the Christian religion. According to Stopford Brooke, the
first part of this result is, of course, considered as a point of
congratulation, while he reckons that the dread struggle he
had with infidelity was nothing more than the strong reaction
to be expected from the extreme views he had at first taken
up. They who agree with us in thinking that the evangelical
doctrines are interwoven with the whole framework of
Christianity will perfectly understand how the writings and
speculations in question should have subverted his faith in
both together. Having once parted with the great fundamental principle of all safe religious inquiry, that God's
testimony in the Scriptures is to be implicitly accepted, and
not our own fallible judgment, we need not wonder that he
threatened to make shipwreck of revelation altogether. The
same spirit which makes us stumble at the mysteries,
dogmas, or contents of revelation, leads us to stumble at
the miracles which attest the revelation. The hard in
doctrine, and the hard in the sign and seal, is equally offensive to those who have given themselves up to their own
reason, or (which is the same thing) to their own heart as
the test of what is to be accepted.

The anguish of mind which Mr. Robertson underwent at
this stage of his experience was great. None can doubt the
sincerity with which he had held his previous views, intensity of conviction being one of his personal characteristics ;
and when he was tempted to abandon them, it could not be
with the same indifference as many others would have done.
A letter has been preserved, and is given us in Stopford
Brooke's work, from which it appears that the individual
already referred to, who had instilled the poison of scepti-

cism into his mind, and hindered this young minister in his course hitherto well run, had begun, when too late, to dread the tempest he had awakened in the soul of his friend; and the terms in which Mr. Robertson, in his reply, proudly denies that he was indebted to him for his new ideas will scarcely weigh much with the reader. " Set your mind at rest upon one point. Whatever mental trials I may experience, you are not responsible for any. A man must have been profoundly and incredibly ignorant of literature, if these things had presented themselves to him in a few conversations in a new light," &c.

The method adopted by him when reduced to this state of spiritual paroxysm and confusion was one much to be regretted, and to the last degree ill judged. Having travelled to Germany with the view, as we must suppose, of finding the remedy for his scepticism in the country whence he had contracted the disease, he plunged into the depths of its wild metaphysical speculations. His cure for the present distemper was to pursue metaphysics at Heidelberg! "I have found minds here," he writes, "that understand mine, if they cannot help me; and, in the conviction that a treasure lies near me in German literature, I am digging away night and day at the superincumbent earth, in order hereafter to get into it." If we may believe Stopford Brooke, he ultimately succeeded. It was now that he built up what he calls a new temple upon the ruins of evangelism. I shall ere long inquire what praise this structure was entitled to. The same author, observing upon the benefit he derived from his continental travels, says: " In the silence and solitude of the mountains of the Tyrol, his soul, left to explore its own recesses, and to feel its nothingness in the presence of the Infinite, had fixed its foundations deep and strong." It is not much after all that can be brought up out of the recesses of the soul of any one of us; and after studying the system which he excogitated for himself in the Tyrol mountains, we prefer the other which Calvin was content to derive from God's Word upon ⋅ the lake of Geneva.

Before passing from this stage in his religious history, we may quote the following passage from an address he afterwards delivered to the Institute of Working Men in Brighton. We quote it not merely as an instance of the higher strains of eloquence he sometimes reached, but as affording a painful picture of the struggle with scepticism into which he fell at this time, for none can doubt that he refeis to his own experience.

" It is an awful moment when the soul begins to find that the props upon which it has blindly rested so long are many of them rotten, and begins to suspect them all; when it begins to feel the nothingness of many of the traditionary opinions which have been received with implicit confidence, and in that horrible insecurity begins also to doubt whether there be anything to believe at all. It is an awful hour— let him who has passed through it say how awful—when the life has lost its meaning, and seems shrivelled into a span —when the grave seems to be the end of all—human goodness nothing but a name, and the sky above the universe a dead expanse, black with the void from which God Himself has disappeared. In that fearful loneliness of spirit, when those who should have been his friends and counsellors only frown upon his misgivings, and profanely bid him stifle doubts which, for aught he knows, may arise from the fountain of truth itself—to extinguish as a glare from hell that which, for aught he knows, may be light from heaven—and everything seems wrapped in hideous uncertainty, I know but one way in which a man can come forth from his agony scathless : it is by holding fast to those things which are certain still—the grand, simple landmarks of morality. In the darkest hour through which a human soul can pass, whatever else is doubtful, this at least is certain. If there be no God, and no future state, yet even then it is better to be generous than selfish, better to be chaste than to be licentious, better to be true than to be false, better to be brave than to be a coward. Blessed beyond all earthly blessedness is the man who, in the tempestuous darkness of the soul, has dared to hold fast to these venerable landmarks. Thrice blessed is he who, when all is drear and cheerless within and without—when his teachers terrify him and his friends shrink from him—has obstinately clung to moral good. Thrice blessed, because his night shall pass into bright clear day."

Upon this quotation we would remark that there are two cases altogether distinct and never to be confounded, in which men may give way to doubt, and be thrown into a state of painful agitation. The one is when they have been educated in views which are erroneous and contrary to the Word of God, and a partial illumination of the truth begins to lead them to call these views in question. They have found upon a closer examination into the Scriptures that the props on which they had blindly rested so long are rotten, and they begin to feel " the nothingness of the traditionary opinions which had been received with implicit confidence." This produces a painful experience, accompanied with no small alarm at the felt necessity of abandoning views long associated with Heaven's approval, and of approaching to the adoption of others which, though true, had been long looked upon, perhaps, as damnable heresy. With regard to parties who are in this case, every sympathy is due to them, not only in the anguish they undergo, but in the temptation they are exposed to through bigoted teachers and friends, who would have them stifle these noble misgivings of theirs, which have arisen from love of the truth, and to extinguish " as a glare from hell what is really a light from heaven." But while there is this struggle which the man brought up in error experiences on his way to the truth, there is another undergone by the man who has been educated in the truth, and has allowed himself to be shaken by rationalistic or infidel speculations and suggestions. The doctrines in which

he was brought up are true, but through this insidious influence he is led to think that they are " rotten." In reality,
they are the doctrines of inspiration, but he has been seduced
into the idea that they are mere "traditionary opinions,"
which have somehow got mixed up with the Record. This
is a scepticism of quite another kind than the other. There
may be all the agony undergone by the man who is the
subject of it, as was experienced by the other man, but he
is not entitled to the same sympathy from us. The one is
the agony of the hero, and the other is the agony of the
heretic. The one is the struggle a man undergoes in his
noble passage from error to truth ; the other is the ominous
and ignominious struggle which a man has in passing, as
he yields to the insidious influence of rationalism, from the
truth to error. The one is the struggle of him who has cast
off human traditions, being enlightened by the Word of God ;
the other is the struggle of him who has given ear to the
lying spirit of human wisdom, and is nothing else than the
penalty he suffers for having abandoned the eternal moorings
of his soul. The one was the agony that preceded the
Reformation of the sixteenth century, the other is the agony
that now accompanies the infidelity of the nineteenth. What
one desiderates in the quotation is a distinction that would
enable us to know which of the two kinds of agonized scepticism it is which Mr. Robertson refers to. If, as is probable,
he drew the picture from his own case, we must suppose it
is to the last he alludes. But there is something more we
would wish to say in qualification of the passage we have
quoted. We allude to the invidious way in which the essential principles of morality are placed over against positive
revelation, and what may be called the dogma of religion,
when it is hinted that suggestions which rise up in the mind
against the latter may be light from heaven, while it is taken
for granted that the essential principles of morality are to
be received as certain. The state of mind supposed by Mr.
Robertson throughout the passage we have quoted is of

course that of a man who has unhappily been shaken in his faith as to all the verities of religion, including even the existence of God; and with regard to doubts of this kind that agitate his mind, Mr. Robertson resents the interference of those teachers or friends who would call upon him to stifle these doubts, thus representing the dogmatical department of religion (unlike the practical) as being the province of a legitimate scepticism. If the doubts referred to bear upon truths established, whether by the written Word of God or the volume of creation, did he mean to assert that such doubts are to be held sacred? We grant that the moralities of the Decalogue, or what we are to practise, being graven upon our very constitution, have a peculiar certainty attaching to them; but the dogma of religion, or what we are to believe, is set before us with an evidence which, in its own kind, is perfectly sufficient, so that to doubt what ought to be believed is as much a sin as to doubt what ought to be practised. Mr. Robertson, in short, gives countenance to the idea that scepticism in the dogma of religion is to be respected, and that, in point of fact, the whole region of the dogma is fair field for the wildest speculation, while the great principles of right and wrong in the natural man are the only indubitable thing. Finally, we see well enough how, in the case supposed by Mr. Robertson, the man who has been unhinged in his whole religious belief should still retain his moral sentiments, and we perfectly agree with him that he should continue to act upon them; but we wholly deny what he seems to assert, that this is likely to right him in his religious course again. He says, " Thrice blessed is he, because his night shall pass into clear, bright day!" And, again, "I know but this one way in which a man may come forth from his agony scathless." In other words, the hope Mr. Robertson had of a man coming out of that scepticism which has unhinged his faith, is that he holds fast by this at least, "that it is better to be generous than selfish, better to be chaste than licentious, better to be true than to be false,

better to be brave than to be a coward." Was ever such a
monstrous proposition heard of? To show the fallacy of it,
let us suppose that a man has in his possession ten acres of
land (for the commandments being ten, let us keep to the
number). An immensely wealthy benefactor dies, and leaves
him by written testament an estate worth some millions
sterling. This testament is unquestionably valid and legal.
But a friend, full of conceit and ignorance, deceives the man
into the belief that this testament which had filled him with
joy is not trustworthy, and he is thrown into just anguish of
mind on this account, first as to one part of the evidence in
favour of it, then as to another, until at last he is now in a
state of entire scepticism with regard to this last will of his
altogether. His best and most sensible friends tell him that
he should look upon these doubts as to the legality of the
testament as being nothing but a miserable delusion ; but he
will not listen to their advice, and his agony of mind continues. However, if we may believe Mr. Robertson, there
is one thing he is still sure of, and " thrice blessed is he if
he hold by it," and that is, that he has the ten acres of land
at any rate in actual possession ; nay, let him hold fast by
this certainty, and he will come forth from the other agony
of the testament scathless, and " night," as regards the other
point, " shall pass into clear, bright day ! " How this might
chance, or what blessed tendency there would be in his
retaining the croft to reassure him of the estate, we leave it
with the reader to judge. But there lies at the bottom of all
this suggestion of Mr. Robertson the essential fallacy of
those who in our day would place revealed religion in a
certain invidious opposition to natural religion as regards
certainty.

The great anguish of soul which Mr. Robertson underwent
is represented both by his biographer and by himself as
having passed over, and given way to a solid satisfaction,
derived from the new gospel which he had arrived at. We
shall only observe that it does not seem to have been so

solid and perfect after all, judging from incidental expressions. " He had returned to Brighton," says his biographer, " convinced that he had got clear views of truth. In the Tyrol, in 1847, he had despaired ; now, though he was weary of life, he could say, ' I know the right, and even in darkness will steer right on.'" His privilege now, it would appear, was "to steer on in the darkness;" for it is abundantly evident, from various expressions of his own, that he had now lost all certainty in the dogma at least, and steered rather by trust in the supposed infallibility of his own moral sentiments. Hence we find him saying, in the language of Tennyson, who had unfortunately become a theological authority with him, " I am but an infant crying in the dark, and with no language but a cry; nevertheless, I am not afraid of the dark." In his Winchester days he had walked in the light ; now it was in the darkness, only he was not afraid of it ! Perhaps not. We labour under the impression, most of us, enjoying as we do under the Christian dispensation the blazing noontide of revelation, that we are the children of the day ; but Mr. Robertson had now become one of the many children crying in darkness who abound in these times, and with whom we have no sympathy, since the darkness they complain of arises from their having refused God's revelation.

But it is high time that we should now proceed to consider what was the amount of change which Mr. Robertson underwent in his religious views. We are persuaded that it was far greater than many of his admirers are at all aware of, or than any of his evangelical apologists have suspected. Some think that it was merely the Calvinistic tenets he abjured, and that even these he rather received in a qualified form than rejected. A close examination of his views will constrain us to acknowledge that he not only departed from evangelical truth, but was largely unhinged upon much more fundamental points.

One thing is evident, that his faith in miracles, as being

in this nineteenth century available evidence for the truth of Christianity, was shaken. He now accepted of Christianity, not as attested by miracle, but upon a new and rationalistic basis.

In his three Advent sermons, where he shows the bearing of the gospel, as first preached, upon the Greeks, Romans, and Barbarians, he takes notice of the Barbarians as those who laid stress upon the miracle, or the marvellous (instanced by the Barbarians of Melita, when they would have worshipped Paul), and he insists upon it as one characteristic of the gospel that it came to depreciate the miracle and the sign. This leads him to notice the maxim of the French sceptic, "that the worship of the supernatural must legitimately end in atheism as science progresses." How does he meet the sceptic? Does he first object to the wording of the libel here brought against the disciple of Christianity, that he "worships" the supernatural? No. Again, supposing the libel amended and properly stated—that the disciple of Christianity *believes* in the supernatural, so that the maxim now runs that "faith in the supernatural must legitimately end in atheism as science progresses," does Mr. Robertson deny the truth of the conclusion by boldly and flatly maintaining that the progress of science never can affect the miracles of Christianity? that it is a downright absurdity to suppose it should, since science can only discover the laws that hold in the natural world, while the miracles of Christ were a temporary and staring suspension of these laws? Does he stand up in the pulpit of Brighton as the advocate of the miracles upon which Christianity rests against this vile calumny? No; he does no such thing. He meets the sceptic's calumny by the following sentences, which are a virtual acknowledgment of its truth—a virtual giving up of the argument from miracles altogether, and an allegation to the effect that the true claim of Christianity upon our acceptance is its tallying with the testimony of our own hearts and of nature that God is love.

" Yes, all science removes the cause of causes farther and farther back from human ken, so that the baffled intellect is compelled to confess at last that we cannot find it. But the world by wisdom knew not God. There is a power in the soul—quite separate from the intellect, which sweeps away and recognises the marvellous—by which God is felt. Faith stands serenely, far above the reach of the atheism of science. It does not rest on the wonderful, but on the eternal wisdom and goodness of God. The revelation of the Son was to proclaim a Father, not a mystery. No science can sweep away the everlasting love which the heart feels, and which the intellect does not pretend to judge or recognise ; and he is safe from the inevitable decay which attends the mere barbarian worship who has felt that, as faith is the strongest power in the mind of man, so is love the divinest principle in the bosom of God ; in other words, who adores God known in Christ, rather than trembles before the unknown —whose homage is yielded to Divine character rather than Divine power."

Let us dissect this passage for a moment. "All science removes the cause of causes farther and farther back from human ken, so that the baffled intellect is compelled to confess we cannot find it." He means of course that, as science advances, what was thought to be the cause of causes—that is, God Himself immediately working—is found to be only a natural law in operation. Now that may be true as regards many things which were thought by the superstitious to be God Himself immediately working, and when they find, for example, that there is a natural cause for an eclipse or for the appearance of the comet, we may say that science by its progress has proved that what they thought to be a miracle was no miracle ; or, as Mr. Robertson expresses it, that the cause of causes is removed farther back, and that natural law still holds. But the question is whether, as science advances, it is to make as decisive havoc of the miracles of Christianity as of the ridiculous signs accepted by superstition ?

It is plain enough that Mr. Robertson placed the one class and the other in the same category, and came to consider that miracles cannot now be rested in by us as a satisfactory evidence for the truth of Christianity. The extract I have given shows us upon what evidence he was now prepared to receive it.

"The revelation of the Son," he says, "was to proclaim a Father, not a mystery. No science can sweep away the everlasting love which the heart feels. And he is safe, &c., who adores God known in Christ, rather than trembles before the unknown—whose homage is yielded to Divine character rather than Divine power."

He had come to hold, along with the whole school of rationalists, that Christianity is not a "mystery" in the sense that we Calvinists or Evangelicals hold, but a proclamation of what natural religion itself, according to them, teaches, even God's everlasting love, benignity, and goodness. There is no need, then, of miracles to induce us to receive what we are prepared already by our own hearts to recognise and welcome. When Christ comes to be received, it is not as if He were "the unknown," a mystery, in whom we will not believe until we see miracles wrought. We adore "God known in Christ." That is, we recognise God at once to be in Christ, from His being the same God we have known in the world around us.

Now we would observe that this process of proof is only applicable to such a Christianity as Mr. Robertson and his school have arbitrarily fabricated out of their own imagination. It is not applicable to Christianity as set forth in those Scriptures which all Christendom have received upon indisputable testimony as containing the actual record of it. According to the Scriptures, Christ came not only to reveal the everlasting love of God, but also His everlasting justice. In His doctrine the wrath of God is revealed against all ungodliness and unrighteousness, and the mysterious plan is proclaimed whereby God's justice and holiness are harmonized with His mercy in our salvation. Will such a Christianity as this be at once received as true by men, from its tallying with their own feelings and ideas, or otherwise than upon a direct testimony of God, duly authenticated? So far is Mr. Robertson from thinking so, that he himself rejects it—miracles and testimony notwithstanding.

Nay, the very ground upon which he rejects it is, that it does not tally with " what our heart feels "—with the law written upon our natures.

This suggests the remark that he differs from us not merely as to what constitutes the evidence of Christianity, but as to what Christianity is.

What is Christianity, and how shall we know what it is ?

If the word mean anything, it means the religion that was taught by Christ; and what that was can only be ascertained, of course, by historical evidence. What right has Mr. Robertson to take for granted that Christ must necessarily have taught nothing but what tallies with the feelings of our heart, and the views of fallen man, or even that He did not teach doctrine entirely subversive of the law of nature? He may have taught anything. Mr. Robertson proceeds to take up the arbitrary position that Christianity must coincide essentially with the findings and feelings of man; he next wrests and mutilates the Scriptures in the way we shall afterwards show, to bring out of them a Christianity answering to this description; and then he triumphs in the consideration that he has now a Christianity that can be proved without miracles! One thing is certain, that he is not entitled to palm off a religion which he has thus manufactured out of his own nature upon Christ. Another thing is that the same process by which he has thus made Christianity provable without miracles, has made it contemptible, and not worth receiving. The doctrines in which the whole glory and consolation of the gospel lie are its supernatural doctrines, which are foolishness to the natural man. What we needed as sinners was a communication made to us from heaven, assuring us of pardon, and informing us of the way in which it could be bestowed by Him who is the offended Judge of the universe. How could this be authenticated to us without miracles? Finally, it could be shown to be impossible for Mr. Robertson to establish, by his proposed process of proof, that ever such a historical personage as the Son of God in our nature existed. He seems to hold, with Robert Browning, that what of God's love (learned from the natural world) we see in Christ is enough without miracles to prove Christ to be of God, and that He has come in the flesh. But we have shown at some length, in the essay upon that illustrious poet and shallow theologian, that it is utterly impossible to prove the historical existence of Christ otherwise than by historical evidence. Another point upon which the faith of Mr. Robertson sustained essential damage was the inspiration of the Scriptures; for while he still retained his belief in their inspiration, he seems to have adopted very loose views upon the whole subject.

" The prophetic power," he writes, " in which, I suppose, is chiefly exhibited that which we mean by inspiration, depends almost entirely on moral greatness. The prophet discerned large principles, true for all time — principles social, political, ecclesiastical, and principles of life—chiefly by largeness of heart, and sympathy of spirit with God's Spirit. That is my conception of inspiration. ' My judgment is just, because I seek not mine own will, but the will of him that sent me.' "

Most readers will agree with us that, if the only claim the writers of Scripture have to be considered as inspired is that, in the sense here described, they were, as to spirit and character, in unison with God, there are many other writings besides theirs which have a title to be received into the canon. We need not say that his text in support of this view of inspiration is insufficient for the purpose. When our Lord said to the Jews, " My judgment is just, because I

seek not my own will, but the will of the Father which hath
sent me," Mr. Robertson considers Him as claiming His
judgment or deliverances upon Divine things to be just and
worthy of confidence because of a feature in His own personal character, which, wherever it prevails, is a ground for
confidence, viz., that His will was in unison with God's
will —that in short He was upright and holy; from which
he maintains that this is all which is necessary to ground
the claim of the inspired writers to our confidence; we
would reply : (1) Supposing this to be the meaning of the
text, our Lord had in the words going immediately before
them, " I can of my own self do nothing, as I hear, I
judge," set forth another and a higher ground upon which
He claimed His judgment to be just, this being that, whatever He said or did or judged, was a thing first of all
communicated to Him from the Father as to be done or
said.   Now, in his definition of what constitutes inspiration,
what right had Mr. Robertson to omit the first part of the
verse, which shows that, before a man's deliverances or
judgments are to be received as authoritative by the Church,
he must be able to say and to show that they have been
communicated to him by God ?   He omits this part of the
verse, which contains the major assertion, and he brings in
the minor assertion in the verse, as if it were the whole.
(2) Besides, he should have quoted the words which immediately follow : " If I bear witness of myself, my witness is
not true.   I have another that beareth witness of me."   He
then proceeds to show how the Father bore witness of Him.
" I have greater witness than that of John : for the works
which the Father hath given me to finish, the same works
that I do bear witness of me that the Father hath sent
me."   Now, by these works it were in vain for Mr. Robertson to allege that Christ's works of charity and righteousness
are meant, for these could never be the *Father's* witnessing
of Him.   They must mean the miracles which the Father
empowered Him to work.   Thus we learn that a prophet is

no prophet, though he should be as holy as the angels, ,
unless he be authenticated. (3) The words of Christ which
Mr. Robertson quotes have not the meaning he attaches to
them. When He says, "My judgment is just, because I
seek not my own will, but the will of the Father which hath
sent me," He does not mean merely that He claimed
submission to His judgment on the ground that He was
personally holy,—one who merged His own will in that of
the Father in the ordinary sense predicable of all saints;
for may not one who is holy be fallible after all in his
judgment? and might not His opponents have claimed to
have the same point of character which He is supposed thus
to assert? He means, then, that His judgment was just,
because He did not seek, or affect to carry out His own will
at all; but, as a servant, carried out the will of the Father,
which had been first communicated to Him.

Again, when he grants the inspiration of the Scriptures,
Mr. Robertson accompanies this with a qualification : *"That
as God communicated facts in the natural world to the penmen
as they are accepted in the popular mind, not correctly in science,
so His revelation concerning truths of the soul and its relation
to God was communicated in popular and incorrect, not, however,
false language."* "It is the Word of God," he says in one
place, "and it is the word of man : as the former, perfect;
as the latter, imperfect. God the Spirit, as the Sanctifier,
does not produce perfection of character; and as an Inspirer,
He does not produce absolute perfection of human knowledge." Aiming a blow at us who take the higher view of
inspiration which he has thus discarded, he calls us biblio-
latrists, saying, "To be candid, I look upon bibliolatry as
pernicious; dangerous to true views of God and of His revelation, and the cause of much bitter Protestant popery, or
claiming to infallibility of interpretation, which nearly every
party puts forth. I believe bibliclatry to be as superstitious
as false, and almost as dangerous as Romanism."

In the above quotations we have, *first,* a condition attached to the acceptance of the inspiration of the Scriptures, which reduces it to a very low figure in point of value. It appears that " God's revelation in truths concerning the soul is communicated in popular and incorrect language ;" and why should it not, he argues, since it " communicates facts in the natural world " in this way? Now I beg leave to say that there is a great difference in the two cases. Did Mr. Robertson believe that, if the Bible had been intended to teach science, it would have accommodated itself to popular errors regarding facts in the natural world, and would not, on the contrary, have distinctly disabused the minds of its readers of such misconceptions? Meanwhile it is clear enough, I should think, that God *did* design in the Bible to teach " the truths of the soul and its relation to God ;" and therefore the way in which He makes them known will be that in which He would have spoken of the earth in its relation to the sun, and facts of the natural world generally, *in a strictly scientific revelation.* With infinite simplicity, our speculative friend considers, on the contrary, that because God, in a Book *not designed for science at all*, speaks of facts in the natural world according to common parlance, and incorrectly as it were, therefore, in a Book designed for spiritual and theological truths, He will speak of them in popular and incorrect style ! Do our readers admire this logic ? Once grant that in the Scriptures we have doctrines stated " incorrectly," because in accommodation to the views or ideas of man, and how are we to ascertain in what instances this is done, and how far the inaccuracy goes, for that supposes us to know what the correct doctrine is? If we know this ourselves, where was the necessity of this revelation at all, which turns out to be more inaccurate than we are ourselves? Indeed, it is plain that Mr. Robertson, according to this theory of his, maintains that he and others of his kindred have a theology more accurate than the Bible, for it contains, as would appear, a scheme of doctrine inaccurately stated, ay, " in truths of the soul and its relation to God;" whereas he, it must be supposed, has another which is more correct!

Let us next consider the charge of bibliolatry which he brings against us who hold the Word to be a perfect record throughout, containing nothing incorrect, nor of man, and to be received in the letter of it as an infallible rule. He considers this as virtually claiming infallibility of interpretation, and showing a superstition as pernicious as that of the Church of Rome. Now it is absurd upon the face of it to say that we thus worship the Bible, or make an idol of it. Does Mr. Robertson mean to say that God could not, if He had so wished, have given us a Bible in which He did not accommodate Himself to popular language and conceptions at all, but which delivered the doctrines in the perfect form? and if God had done so, did he believe that for us to receive the Bible in that form would have been an act of idolatry and superstition? In what sense do we claim infallibility of interpretation, according to our view of inspiration? We maintain that the whole doctrines contained in Scripture are to be received as unmixed, perfect truth, and infallible, because a deliverance from God. We discard the idea of Bible statements being possibly, after all, inaccurate, through accommodation to man's imperfect views of things. We repudiate the uncertainty which Mr. Robertson thus throws over the Record, but it is the infallibility of the Record we claim for, and not infallibility of interpretation. When we, on our side, insist upon taking the doctrinal statements of the Bible as they stand, and upon their being received, not as inaccurate accommodations to human opinions, but infallible deliverances of God, Mr. Robertson cries out that this is popery; the true reason being that the doctrines, when thus taken up and received, condemn all his rationalistic notions and German absurdities. As for the Church of Rome, when she claimed for popes and councils a power of infallible interpretation, the effect was to bring in a new rule of faith, by giving an authority equal to the Bible to the vain dicta of these popes and councils, or whatever they might choose to deliver, thus opening the way for a flood of superstitions. Is it objected that we maintain the doctrines contained in our Westminster Confession, for example, not to be the fallible opinions of man, but the infallible truths of God? and what difference then is there between the councils of Rome and the assembly that sat at Westminster? The answer is that there are, at any rate, two essential differences. First, the Westminster Assembly gives texts, quoted and compared, for all the doctrines it sets forth, and claims the doctrines it lays down to be infallible upon the ground of the texts produced. The councils of Rome claim for the doctrines they issue to be received as infallible upon the ground of their own authoritative declaration. Secondly, the Westminster Assembly willingly grants that it may have erred in interpreting God's Word; and we who receive its confession are quite willing to this day to be enlightened by any who shall come forward and show us, out of God's Word, that the doctrines set forth by it are erroneous. At the same time, while there are these two essential differences between us and the Romanists, we maintain consistently enough (and here is the ground of Mr. Robertson's wrath with us) that so far are the doctrines contained in our Protestant and Calvinistic confessions from being the fallible opinions of man, that we have renounced all dependence upon these, and hold by the doctrines of our confession as being the infallible doctrines of God upon the ground of texts produced. We are ready to go to issue with all and sundry as to the doctrines in them being nothing else than God's own Word. Nor can any, it would appear, stand before us. What is the proof? The proof is that none others are prepared to meet us upon the Record, or few indeed. As to the Church of Rome, it flies to the dicta of popes and councils, converted into a new rule of faith. As to Mr. Robertson, when he claims a power to say of any doctrine contained in Scripture that it is a mere accommodation of

God's Spirit to the incorrect and imperfect views of man, he too brings in a new rule of faith, which is just as dangerous . as that of the Church of Rome, and calculated to bring in, if not a flood of superstition, a flood of infidelity. As for us, we claim nothing but the right of God's Word to rule us all, if I understand it.

When Mr. Robertson has adopted the perilous position that the doctrines contained in the Bible are not always stated with absolute accuracy, but sometimes accommodated to vulgar conceptions, it becomes an important question to know what is his criterion by which to know what is accurate in the Bible, and what not. His peculiar position once taken up, of course he cannot prove certain passages of Scripture to be inaccurate by referring to other passages of Scripture where the same doctrine is more accurately stated, for both are of equal canonical authority. He was thus forced to set up a new test of truth. By examination of his writings it will be found that the test he adopted was the innate moral sense of humanity. Not that he reckoned this as absolutely trustworthy since the Fall; but he received it as trustworthy enough in all those who have been instructed by the example of Christ's life and character, and who have imbibed that character. The qualification does not very much signify, it still leaves the deliverance of the humanity within us to be the test and standard of appeal; so that, when any doctrinal statements of Scripture seem to contradict this deliverance, they are to be rejected, as being incorrectly stated, or stated in accommodation to vulgar conceptions. He thus came to hold that his innate sentiments, leavened somewhat, — and it does not much matter how,—were the infallible interpreters of Scripture. The Vatican is in ourselves, not at Rome; that is all the difference. And if there is to be popery, surely the pleasantest kind of it, after all, is to sit down in the infallible chair oneself! It was by this new standard that Mr. Robertson rejected all the evangelical doctrines which we hold, and which he once held himself. That we have given a correct statement of his views may be seen by reading his sermon on *Absolution*, upon the text, " Son, be of good cheer : thy sins are forgiven thee." I might quote one passage from his sermon on " The Dispensation of the Spirit," to show that he considers us as not called to walk now by the authoritative rule of the Word, but by this law within ourselves, quickened in us by the Holy Spirit.

" In the Dispensation of the Son, God manifested Himself to humanity through man. The eternal Word spoke through the inspired and gifted of the human race to those that were uninspired and ungifted. This was the Dispensation of the prophets—its climax was the advent of the Redeemer; it was completed when perfect Humanity manifested God to man. The characteristic of this Dispensation was that God revealed Himself by an authoritative voice speaking from without, and the highest manifestation of God whereof man was capable was a Divine humanity. The age in which we at present live is the Dispensation of the Spirit, in which God has communicated Himself by the highest revelation— no more as an Authentic Voice from without, but as a Law within, as a Spirit mingling with a spirit. 'Then shall the Son also himself be subject unto him that put all things under him, that God may be all in all.' ' Henceforth we know no man after the flesh. Yea, though we have known Christ after the flesh, yet now henceforth know we him no more.' The outward humanity is to disappear, that the inward be complete."

It must sufficiently appear from the preceding observations that Mr. Robertson departed not only from the evangelical doctrines, but from the Word of God as the rule of faith.

Let us next inquire what was the doctrinal creed he adopted, now that he had left the authority of the Divine Record, and taken his own moral, or, if you will, Christian, sentiments as his guide.

We find him repudiating doctrines altogether. " I have

almost done," he says in one place, "with dogmatic divinity."
In his sermon upon the " Scepticism of Pilate," he smiles at
the idea of the definite answer which we who are Evangelicals
would probably have returned to Pilate's famous question,
" What is truth?"   He intimates that no dogmatic certainty is to be reached, but that all are to go out to sea to
find out truth as they best may under the guidance of three
things which Mr. Robertson kindly suggests—he does not
say by what authority—"*Independence*," "*Humbleness*," and
"*Action*."   He counts it a mistake to say that we must first
believe in certain doctrines, and then act from them : his
way is first to act, that is, to act out the plain moralities
(such as be just, tender, humble, &c.), and then we shall not
fail to arrive at the doctrines !   When Christ is said to have
come to "witness for the truth," he tells us that this had no
reference to any doctrines He was to declare.   It meant that
He would "exemplify the reality of what God is, and reflect
all the teachings of the universe which ought to be reflected."
He suggests that we should do the same, and "instead of
witnessing for dogmas, which can only engender heat and
controversy, seek to exemplify and reflect whatever we find
God to be, and whatever harmonizes with the spirit and
laws of the universe, which we may do with all the calmness
of men of science, who witness to facts."

It never seems to strike him that, in thus asserting that our
Lord Jesus Christ came into the world only to exemplify the
reality of what God is, and not to declare any doctrines
whatever, he is himself laying down a dogma, which we are
to swallow, besides, upon his own authority.   We are to
receive it as a dogma from his lips that there are no dogmas.
Was ever such a preposterous doctrine as this propounded—
that there are no doctrines at all to be witnessed for ?   How
are we to " exemplify in our life the reality of what God is,"
without believing any doctrines ?   I must at any rate believe,
in the first place, that God is.   That is a dogma which the
atheist controverts.   Am I to cease witnessing for it, lest I

shall get into a controversial heat? I must believe in the doctrine, besides, that there is only one God, and thus witness, it is to be presumed, with or without heat, against polytheists; unless Mr. Robertson holds it to be enough that a heathen exemplifies the reality of what Jupiter was, and Venus and Bacchus. And how am I to exemplify the reality of what God is, unless I have been taught in so many doctrines what He is? for Mr. Robertson holds one doctrine upon that subject and I hold another. He holds that the view I as a Calvinist have " of the reality of what God is," as to His character, is monstrous. Am I then to exemplify the monstrous reality of what God is according to my doctrine? If not, then there must be a controversy after all with regard to our respective doctrines!

Accordingly Mr. Robertson himself soon proceeded to form dogmas enough, though it was after his own fashion. "I have almost done," he says, "with divinity—with dogmatic divinity—except to lovingly endeavour to make out the truth that lies under this or that poor dogma, miserably overlaid, as marble fonts are with whitewash." So his quarrel, after all, was not with dogmas, but with "poor dogmas," by which no one who reads his discourses can doubt that he means the doctrines usually called evangelical. These, besides, he does not deny to have an underlying verity in them; and his mission was to remove the evangelical or Calvinistic " whitewash " from the " marble fonts."

From this the apologists of Mr. Robertson may argue that he was not, after all, so far astray in theology; for does he not grant that there was a truth underlying each of the dogmas of Calvinism? The answer to this is that we shall find upon examination that what he calls the underlying truth can be proved from Scripture to be an error of his own invention. If the truth he found underlying our dogmas were something which we Calvinists receive as truth, while he merely objected to a certain exaggeration of statement we had thrown over it, then his difference with us would

not have been vital. But it turns out that the underlying truth is some rationalistic error of his own. It is not,
then, as to the " whitewash " he differs from us, but as to
" the marble fonts." Secondly, if he were prepared to join
issue with us upon the Scriptures as to what was " whitewash " and what was " marble font ;" as to what was
" dogma " and what was " poor dogma ;" then the difference
between him and us would not have been so essential. But
we have seen that he had departed from our rule of faith.

I shall now show what were the dogmas he substituted
instead of those received among us.

We hold that the nature of man has become radically and
wholly corrupt since the Fall. He came to alter his views
upon this point, and to maintain very much the same views
with Maurice, granting a certain moral disorder to prevail
in our nature, but considering that there is an underlying
righteousness in our fallen humanity. When the Apostle
Paul speaks of the " spirit " as distinguished from the
" flesh," we understand him to refer to the new nature
wrought in us by the Holy Spirit ; but he understands by it
something better and higher in our fallen nature. Thus in
his sermon upon the Trinity :—" That which the apostle
calls ' the spirit ' is that life in man which, in his natural
state, is in such an embryo condition that it can scarcely be
said to exist at all—that which is called into power and
vitality by regeneration." Here regeneration is described to
be, not, as Paul asserts, " the quickening of them who are
dead in trespasses and sins," but the calling into power a
life which is already within us in our natural state. To be
sure, he says that the life within us naturally is in an
" embryo condition." But if embryo mean anything, it
means something already generated. Our Lord said, " That
which is born of the flesh is flesh ; that which is born of the
Spirit is spirit." Mr. Robertson corrects Him, and says,
" That which is born of the flesh is flesh, with the spirit in
embryo within it ; that which is born of the Spirit is this

embryo developed." Is there no difference there? And when we ask him by what authority he utters this statement, it is by the authority he received at Brighton to remove " whitewash " from the " marble font."

It is upon the subject of guilt that Mr. Robertson goes farthest astray.

The heathen who enjoyed no other light than that of nature were fully enough aware that sin, as a violation of the Divine law, was calculated to draw down the positive punishments of Heaven. Even they were enlightened enough to know that this punishment is something to be distinguished from the remorse and self-upbraiding which follow upon the commission of sin. Even they considered that the punishment of sin would be emphatically in the next world, inferring this very logically, for one thing, from the inequality of retribution measured out to sin in this world.

So blinded did Mr. Robertson become by German rationalism, as to maintain that there is no punishment of sin other than the self-accusation which follows the commission of the wrong thing. He repudiates the idea of any penalty, strictly considered, being incurred by sin through the violation of God's law, and holds that any suffering which follows from sin follows from it merely by a natural law. As fire burns, so sin, by this self-accusation, makes the transgressor wretched. In his sermon upon the " Two Sowings," he denies that there is any inequality in the present government of the world, since the true retribution of sin is really suffered by the wicked in the misery of their remorse and conscious wrongdoing, while the righteous are abundantly recompensed by their happy reflections. The present state of things, according to him, is perfect enough, if you only disabuse your mind of the idea of God being under any obligation by justice either to follow up righteousness with positive reward, or to follow up wickedness by any positive punishment. Hell, if we would believe him, is only the same natural law carried out. Thus, in his sermon upon " The Pharisees and Sadducees at John's Baptism," he says, " It is the hell of having done wrong— the hell of having had a spirit from God, pure, with high aspirations, and to be conscious of having dulled its delicacy and degraded its desires—the hell of having quenched a light brighter than the sun's—of having done to another an injury that through time and eternity never can be undone— infinite, maddening remorse—the hell of knowing that every chance of excellence and every opportunity of good has been lost for ever."   It is all this, in short ; but there is no positive punishment inflicted upon men there by God.   In prosecu- tion of the same theory, when he comes to speak of our cleansing by the blood of Jesus Christ, he will not allow of its including deliverance from any penal wrath.   It consists in a kind of Lethe, whereby we cease to have that wretchedness of reflection which (as he had shown already) constitutes the only consequence of our sins by a natural law.   Thus, in the same sermon, speaking of baptism, the sign and seal of this cleansing, he says.: " It is impossible to see that significant act in which the convert went down into the water, travel- worn and soiled with dust, disappeared for one moment, and then emerged pure and fresh, without feeling that the sign but answered to and interpreted a strong craving of the human heart.   It is the desire to wash away that which is past and evil.   We would fain go to another country and begin life afresh.   We look upon the grave almost with complacency, from the fancy that we shall lie down to sleep, and wake fresh and new.   It was this same longing that expressed itself in heathenism by the famous river of forget- fulness, of which the dead must drink before they can enter into rest."   Thus the boon we receive by cleansing with the blood of Christ is not the removal of condemnation and punishment, but an obliteration of our past sins from our ' remembrance, so that we can make a comfortable new start again.

The great object Mr. Robertson had in view, doubtless, in

adopting this theory upon the subject of guilt, was to get rid of what he considered as a doctrine highly injurious to the character of God, that, strictly as a Judge, He consigns the wicked to everlasting punishment in hell. By this theory he thought that he accounted for the eternal misery of the wicked by a natural law, and washed God's hands of it. That his theory flatly contradicts Scripture could be shown in a moment; but as he would have refused to be judged by that rule, let us see how it can abide the test of reason and common sense.

Does it, I would ask, relieve God after all of what he and his friends consider to be an odious imputation, even the bringing of eternal misery upon the wicked? He tells us that it comes upon them by a natural law. But who established that natural law at the beginning? It was God who gave them that moral constitution at first, whereby their commission of sin issues as would appear in a hell of everlasting misery, whether of fire, or of self-condemnation, or remorse, does not signify. They have themselves only, no doubt, to blame for violating a law of nature. But so have the wicked, according to our theory, themselves only to blame for violating a law which was fenced with an eternal penalty. Meanwhile it is plain that God, if He be answerable for annexing the eternal positive punishment to the violation of the moral law, is as truly answerable, according to their system, for giving them from the first a moral constitution of such a kind as He knew would issue, upon their sinning, in everlasting misery. If He was justified in bringing them under a natural law, the violation of which would issue in an eternal hell of self-torture, He was as much justified in bringing them under an authoritative law, the violation of which should issue in a hell of positive punishment. I say nothing here of another inconsistency in Mr. Robertson's theory. He grants that the wicked, when they die, are fixed down into a hopeless eternity of self-remorse. But why "fixed down"? It must be by a judicial sentence. Surely there is no natural law whereby a man who has passed into eternity should get into a hopelessness of state which did not exist here. Thus he lands himself in this result—that the eternity of their misery is after all a judicial dispensation.

He considers that by this theory of natural law he banishes the undesirable idea of a physical misery in hell. But is it not undeniable that when a man commits sin or vice here he entails upon himself, even by natural law, not only self-condemnation, but physical agony? The drunkard has his self-condemnation, but he has also the *delirium tremens.* The gluttonous, high-living man has his sense of self-degradation, but he has the gout in addition. The whole illustration of sin's consequences in this world is to the effect that they consist in a great deal more than self-condemnation; and the rationalistic divine, being a philosopher, is bound to hold by analogy here—especially if he believe, as Mr. Robertson did, in the resurrection of the body—that there will be physical misery in hell as well as mental.

But the main objection of the theory is that it contradicts the whole phenomena of conscience and the common sense of mankind. When we are tempted to commit sin, the conscience does not merely say, "Thou *oughtest* not to do this thing; if thou doest it, thou wilt be seized with a feeling of condemnation." It says, "Thou *shalt* not do this thing, and if thou doest it, then God, against whom thou hast sinned, will punish thee." In short, the testimony of the natural conscience is to the effect that there is an authoritative law of God under which we lie, and which we break when we sin, thus drawing down His wrath. Hence the universal feeling after sin committed is not only self-condemnation, but fear—a fearful looking for of judgment and fiery indignation from the Lord.

Finally, that the Divine government of the world would be impossible upon such principles as Mr. Robertson propounds, might be made palpable by just supposing for a moment that a government so based should be attempted amongst men. If it be the case that the misery inwardly felt by a man who steals, or defames character, or commits murder, is his sufficient punishment, and that he who, through him, has lost his property, reputation, or existence, being an upright, good man, is, upon the whole, the happiest of the two ; if there would be no inequality in the Divine government that allowed this state of things to take its course, leaving natural law to be its own avenger and its own rewarder, why not adopt this system in governments of our own ? Why build prisons and erect the gallows to be a terror to evil-doers, and not rather wash our hands of all concern in the cruelty of such a procedure, and leave to the operation of natural law both the thieves and murderers, who will be sufficiently punished in their own remorse, and our friends the advocates of this theory, who will be suffi-ciently rewarded by the consciousness of not having deserved to be robbed, and the noble satisfaction of having been innocently murdered ? No human government could stand a year and a day upon such a foundation. There must be authority backed up by punishment. Let none say that we have done injustice to Mr. Robertson and his friends in comparing them to those who would do so mad a thing as dispense with criminal punishments in the state. They do an infinitely wilder thing, and more fatal to all human safety, in proclaiming to the wicked that there is no positive, judi-cial punishment awaiting them hereafter — that for aught they know there will be as good an outward condition for the wicked in eternity as they have here—that physically it will, upon the whole, be as well with them in hell as it is with the righteous in heaven.

Our readers are of course prepared to hear that, as there was no positive punishment entailed upon us through sin— no wrath or curse of God—according to Mr. Robertson's theory, so there was no necessity for an atonement. He accordingly discarded this doctrine, which it was Paul's glory to proclaim, and had been once his own privilege to preach. "Let no man say," he writes in his sermon upon "Caiaphas's View of Vicarious Sacrifice," "that Christ bore the wrath of God. Let no man say that God was angry with His Son. We are sometimes told of a mysterious anguish which Christ endured, the consequence of Divine wrath, the sufferings of a heart laden with the conscience of the world's transgressions, which He was bearing as if they were His own sins. The Redeemer's conscience was not bewildered to feel *that* His own which was not His own. He suffered no wrath of God. Twice came the voice from heaven, 'This is my beloved Son, in whom I am well pleased.' Even to the last never did the consciousness of purity and the Father's love forsake Him. 'Father, into thy hands I commit my spirit.'"

When he denies the doctrine of Christ's heart having been "laden with the conscience of the world's transgressions," and of "the consciousness of purity having ever forsaken Christ," he seems to insinuate that we who are of evangelical sentiments hold the monstrous tenet that He was viewed by the Father, and viewed Himself, as having actually committed our sins, so that He was, in a sense, Himself impure, and in His conscience condemned Himself of these sins. It might almost seem incredible that one who was for a time evangelical himself, and must have known our views upon the Suretiship, should have persisted in taking up this old and hackneyed misconception. Yet that he did so is evident from what he writes elsewhere. "To say that He bore my sins in this sense, that He was haunted by an evil conscience and its horrors for this lie of mine, or that criminal word, is to make a statement false and unmeaning." It may be all very well for Mr. Robertson, who considered that remorse for sin committed was the only punishment of it, to argue that, if Christ bore our sins, it must have been this remorse which He endured; but he ought to have remembered that we consider all sin as deserving a positive punishment, and that it was our legal liabilities to this punishment that we hold to have been transferred to Christ. In the passage quoted, his argument to disprove that Christ suffered the wrath of God, is, that God the Father upon more than one occasion expressed directly from heaven His continued complacency in Him. Meanwhile he was perfectly aware, if Bible quotations are to be received as evidence, that we could quote twenty times as many passages directly proving that the wrath of God was lying upon Christ notwithstanding; and did he think that one idea could reconcile these apparently opposite passages? Did it escape him that both things might be true—that our Lord might be the subject of a judicial and wrathful dealing from the Father, whereby the atonement was made; while, having been appointed by the Father Himself to endure this wrath and make this atonement for us (His servant, in short, to carry the atonement out by this awful suffering), He might be the object of the Father's complacency?

Since Mr. Robertson denied the sins of others vicariously borne to be the cause of Christ's sufferings, he would find, so one would think, some difficulty in accounting for these sufferings. But he finds the whole explanation of them in a natural law. A wonderful charm there is for a rationalist *in natural law.* He has proved already that the eternal sufferings of the lost are sufficiently accounted for by a law of this kind, without supposing any Judge. Now he undertakes to prove that the sufferings of Christ are sufficiently accounted for by a natural law, without supposing either sin on His own part or sin imputed. His argument is, in short, that if a man put himself in contact with the wheels of any piece of machinery, he is torn in pieces; and if Christ, in order to exemplify love or character, came into such a world as this, it behoved Him, by a necessary law, to be a sufferer. "Christ came into collision with the world's evil, and He bore the enmity of that daring. He approached the whirling wheel, and was torn in pieces. The sacrifice of Christ comes to be looked upon in the light of a sagacious or ingenious contrivance — a mere scheme. Now remember what law is. Law is the being of God. God cannot alter the laws. If you resist a law in its eternal march the universe crushes you."

Now no man in his sane senses has ever denied that Christ would of course suffer if He came into such a world as this. The mystery which Mr. Robertson had to explain was, why He should have been sent into the world for the very purpose of suffering and dying. It is not that having come in contact with the wheel He should have been torn in pieces, but it is that He should have been put upon the wheel in order to be torn in pieces; in other words, "that it should have pleased the Lord to bruise him." So far are the Scriptures from speaking of the sufferings of Christ as being indirectly unavoidable if He should come into the world in discharge of His office, that it speaks of Him as having been directly missioned to these sufferings. So far were His sufferings from being the effect of His coming into the world, that the endurance of them was the end for which He was sent into the world. The Brighton philosopher mistook the effect for the end — that was all! He came into the world, according to Mr. Robertson, to exemplify love and holy character; and as for any sufferings He endured, they are all explained by the natural law, whereby, if He came into a world of suffering, He must needs suffer. But unfortunately the whole tenour of Scripture runs the other way, and teaches us that He was sent into the world to be suspended upon the cross for sin, while the exemplification of love and holy character was a mere indirect consequence of the other. It is merely that he put the cart before the horse—nothing more, so far as I can see.

In order to prove the doctrine of a vicarious atonement, we are in the habit of quoting those passages of Scripture where Christ is said to have " suffered for our sins." Such language, according to Mr. Robertson, means nothing more than that He suffered for, or from, sins the same in kind as we commit; our sins being essentially the same as those which characterised the scribes and Pharisees who put Him to death. To prove that the language might be adopted in such a sense, he refers to the declaration of Christ that the Jews, in crucifying Him and putting to death His followers, would be guilty of the blood of all the prophets slain by their fathers, which could only be true in the sense that the same sins characterised them as had characterised their fathers in putting the previous prophets to death. This illustration of his, I would remark, is of itself sufficient to refute what he seeks to establish by it. Could any one, speaking of the Jews who lived in the days of our Lord, have said that Abel and Barachias and the old martyr prophets "suffered for their sins," and this because they suffered from sins the same in kind which characterised the Jews in the days of our Lord? And if any one should have said, speaking of the same parties, that Abel and Barachias "suffered for their sins, the just for the unjust," it would have been a bit more incomprehensible still. If he had said that Abel and Barachias "were wounded for their transgressions and bruised for their iniquities," could we have understood him to mean that they were wounded and made martyrs by sins the same in kind as characterised the Jews of the day of our Lord? but if he added that "the chastisement of their peace was upon them," would he mean next that they were chastised by a peace of the same kind as characterised these Jews? If, when Christ is said to have "suffered for our sins, "this means that our sins virtually caused His sufferings, since the same wicked spirit actuates us which influenced the scribes and Pharisees, one can see how this suggests a humbling and self-abasing reflection to us; but how does it happen that such expressions, as employed in Scripture, are considered as announcing a truth to us fraught with triumphant joy? This of course they do, if our Calvinistic exegesis be the correct one; provided, in other words, they mean that He suffered for our sins as a Surety. According to the other exegesis, on the contrary, they convey a fact which rather aggravates our moral guilt by suggesting the most alarming view that can be taken of them, that they are sins essentially of the same kind which actuated the Jews to crucify the Lord of glory; and, although we can see how they might be produced to move repentance in our souls, it is impossible that they should be produced to inspire comfort. If Christ was " delivered for our offences," only in the sense of being the victim of such offences as we commit, does any man see how " he should rise again for our justification"?

Having already exhausted the reader by this examination of Mr. Robertson's religious opinions, we shall not indulge in any lengthened remarks upon the instruction and warning conveyed to us by his ministerial career. In an evil hour he allowed himself to be seduced from the only infallible rule of faith, which is the Bible, accepted absolutely in the letter of it, and to be guided by the deliverances of the natural con-science, granting, no doubt, the necessity of the teachings of Christ's life and ministry, and even the necessity in part of the assistance of the Spirit (though rather of the universal spirit that pervades the universe than what we call the Spirit of Christ), but still allowing the innate sentiments of humanity, thus assisted, to be the standard, and superior to the Bible, which, when it contradicts them, is to be under-stood as speaking inaccurately or in mere accommodation to vulgar conceptions. It was thus that he slipped away from the eternal anchorage! His was upon the whole as melan-choly a case as has come before us in these times. Although there are many others of more brilliant genius than he who have made shipwreck upon this rock, and indeed it is the grand point of danger lying in our modern course, it was most of all affecting to see this vessel, of such a buoyant build, and which "rode the waters like a thing of life," bound to all appearance fearlessly to the best of harbours, suddenly arrested by the felon winds

Which blow from off this beaked promontory,

and, after a dire and ineffectual struggle with them, driven right upon the danger, and broken asunder. If he had belonged to a Presbyterian Church, where provision is made for averting such a catastrophe by the authority and weight of the Church being brought to bear upon the minds of those who begin to err from the faith, and by brotherly and fatherly conferences, he might have been arrested and rescued. As it was, there was nothing but the frown of a displeased rector, neutralised by the license of a sympathising bishop; or at the best, or the worst, there were anonymous letters from dissatisfied members of his congregation, and distressing visits to his study by orthodox ladies who came to exonerate their consciences. A greater mistake never existed than to think that a regulated dealing and discipline, in such cases, of the Church is persecution : it is the ordeal through which the individual who has differed, whether rightly or wrongly, from the mass of his fellows, ought certainly to pass. If, being in the right, he is condemned, he comes forth, with an excommunication that will do him no harm, to be the sealed reformer of the nation; but if, as is immensely more probable, he is in the wrong, he finds his doctrine look excessively untenable when subjected to the judicial scrutiny of a thousand eyes, instead of one pair of them, and these partial. Unhappily deprived of the benefit of this salutary ordeal, our young friend pursued his rationalistic speculations, looking upon the opposition he encountered as the seal of his fidelity; wondering that he was unintelligible—a species of Carlyle in the pulpit (can anything be worse ?); imagining that the sufferings he brought upon himself from various quarters by denying the atonement proved his conformity to Him who went forward to the cross to make it ! What then? I think that his Winchester ministry will stand. Nay, I hope and believe that

the vital godliness and the zeal which he derived from his
first scriptural and evangelical creed wrought much that was
accepted in him at Brighton, though the doctrinal super-
structure he reared there was wood, hay, and stubble —
nothing else. The tree that had flourished at Winchester
cast its leaves, " but its substance was in it."

UNWIN BROTHERS, THE GRESHAM PRESS, CHILWORTH AND LONDON.